The President put his folder down on the table and leaned forward, his hands clasped. "If this were anybody else telling me this, gentlemen, I'd think they were pulling a goddamn joke on me. A strange white light of unknown origins is sending out energy beams and giving people, what . . . superpowers?"

"It's not a joke, sir." Forrestal said. "I know it sounds incredulous, but it's really happening. These people have manifested extraordinary abilities—Enhancements."

"And what exactly do you want to do with 'these people'?" Truman demanded. "Are they US citizens?"

"Most of them," Forrestal said. "Right now, we're keeping them contained, studying them. And expending a lot of energy keeping them off Hoover's radar."

"Good. Make sure that son of a bitch doesn't get his claws anywhere near 'em," Truman said. "But what do we do with them after all that?"

"We want to use them, sir," Hillenkoetter said. "Their enhanced abilities, Mr. President . . . well, they're nothing short of extraordinary. If we can harness their power, we may have something on our hands on the level of another Manhattan Project."

Truman's eyes narrowed. "You want to turn these people into . . . weapons?"

Hillenkoetter shook his head. "No, sir. Assets. They're patriotic Americans, or at least most of them are. If we can work with them, they may be able to help us. If we're really going to have a cold war, then we're going to need a different kind of soldier."

Praise for MJ-12: Inception

"A smart look at a Cold War in many ways even colder and scarier and deadlier than the one we barely survived."
—*New York Times* bestselling author Harry Turtledove

"A heady blend of super-spies and superpowers, *MJ-12: Inception* is Cold War-era science fiction done right. A taut thriller, and skillfully evocative."
—*New York Times* bestselling author Chris Roberson

"*X-Men* meets *Mission: Impossible*. Martinez takes a concept as simple as 'Super spies that are actually super' and comes away with a hit. Filled with compelling, well-rounded characters, *MJ-12* is my new favorite spy series."
—Michael R. Underwood, author of *Geekomancy* and the Genrenauts series

"The Cold War becomes even more chilling as super-powered Americans are trained to become super-spies in Martinez's new alternate-history thriller. It's morally complex, intense, and so steeped in the 1940s, you can smell the cigarette smoke."
—Beth Cato, author of *Breath of Earth* and *The Clockwork Dagger*

"*MJ-12: Inception* is a thriller that blends the best elements of Cold War-era spy stories, supernatural fantasy, and splashy pulp comics."
—*B&N Sci-Fi & Fantasy Blog*

"*MJ-12: Inception* is Michael J. Martinez doing what he does best: taking a selection of great genres and mashing them up into something fresh and exciting, and quite unlike anything you've read before . . . . Or to put it another way, it's like the *X-Files* and *Heroes* went back in time, dressed up in dinner jackets, lit a fuse, and jumped through a window to the theme from *Mission: Impossible.* Absolutely loved it."

—*Fantasy Faction*

"Martinez made a point to recognize the sacrifices made by those in the intelligence community to protect their nation. . . . the characters were all well-developed, their powers were imaginative, the twists weren't obvious and Martinez did a good job capturing the setting. . . . *MJ-12: Inception* was an enjoyable twist on the superhero genre and I look forward to seeing what happens next."

—*Amazing Stories*

"With *MJ-12: Inception*, Martinez weaves an intense tale of patriotism, Cold War politics, the US spy network, and the nuances of human relationships which I simply couldn't put down."

—*The Qwillery*

"Martinez has me hooked, and I'm anxiously awaiting the next book in the trilogy; I imagine more Variants, more subterfuge, and more world-ending risks are to be revealed. It's good stuff."

—*GeekDad*

"*MJ-12: Inception* is both a complete stand alone adventure and a thrilling introduction to a richly reimagined Cold War spy-fi series. I eagerly await Michael J. Martinez's next novel featuring the Majestic 12."

—*Mutt Café*

Books by Michael J. Martinez

The Daedalus Series
The Daedalus Incident
The Enceladus Crisis
The Venusian Gambit
The Gravity of the Affair (novella)

MAJESTIC-12
MJ-12: Inception
MJ-12: Shadows (coming soon)

MJ-12:
Inception

Michael J. Martinez

Night Shade Books
New York

A hardcover edition of *MJ-12: Inception* was published in 2016 by Night Shade Books.

First mass market edition published 2017.

Night Shade books may be purchased in bulk at special discounts for sales promotion, corporate gifts, fund-raising, or educational purposes. Special editions can also be created to specifications. For details, contact the Special Sales Department, Night Shade Books, 307 West 36th Street, 11th Floor, New York, NY 10018 or info@skyhorsepublishing.com.

Night Shade Books™ is a trademark of Skyhorse Publishing, Inc.®, a Delaware corporation.

Visit our website at www.nightshadebooks.com.

10 9 8 7 6 5 4 3 2 1

Library of Congress Cataloging-in-Publication Data

Names: Martinez, Michael J., author.
Title: Mj-12: inception : a majestic-12 thriller / Michael J Martinez.
Other titles: Majestic-12 thriller
Description: New York : Night Shade Books, [2016]
Identifiers: LCCN 2016018313| ISBN 9781597808774 (hardback) | ISBN 9781597808873 (ebook)
Subjects: LCSH: Paranormal fiction. | BISAC: FICTION / Fantasy / Historical. | FICTION / Fantasy / Paranormal. | FICTION / Espionage. | GSAFD: Suspense fiction.
Classification: LCC PS3613.A78647 M55 2016 | DDC 813/.6--dc23
LC record available at https://lccn.loc.gov/2016018313

Mass Market ISBN: 978-1-59780-899-6
Hardback ISBN: 978-1-59780-877-4
Ebook ISBN: 978-1-59780-887-3

Cover design by Lesley Worrell

Printed in Canada

Dedicated to all those who have served faithfully and honorably in our nation's intelligence services. We may never know your names, but we are safer for your efforts.

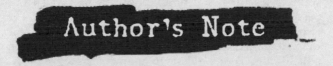

MJ-12: Inception is about the early days of the Central Intelligence Agency and its efforts in the Cold War. Even then, striking the balance between the dual missions of gathering intelligence and covert action was difficult, and ensuring that our intelligence operations and covert efforts adhere to American values is a battle that rages on today. We know from history that the military and intelligence communities do not have, shall we say, spotless records, and this novel recognizes that reality. With that said, thousands of individuals in the US intelligence community have worked tirelessly, anonymously, and within the law to protect our nation, and I am grateful for their dedication and efforts. I also note that the intelligence community has fallen short of our values time and again, and that is something that needs to be fixed.

This novel is also set during a period in which women and people of color were treated *very* differently from today. The struggles of African Americans, in particular, were immensely difficult in many parts of the country, while the women who stepped up to work so hard in factories and offices during World War II were shunted out of the workforce afterward and denied any further opportunities. This period marked the beginning of an inflection point for civil rights and equality in the United States—and there was considerable pushback. I thought long and hard about how to write about race and gender in *MJ-12: Inception*, and ultimately came to the conclusion that the various attitudes of the day needed to be presented in a straightforward manner. Thus, you're going to read about some characters whose perspectives and opinions seem backward and, at times, positively barbaric. These perspectives belong to the characters—*not* the author. I've also made the effort to place these perspectives alongside those of the people who saw discrimination, and worse, on a daily basis. To me, sidestepping one perspective or the other—or just pretending it didn't happen—would be an affront to the memory of the women and people of color who suffered and struggled during that time.

MJ-12

INCEPTION

1.

August 6, 1945

Cities shouldn't be silent.

Berlin, however, felt nearly dead, figuratively and literally, and the thought sent chills up Frank Lodge's spine as he led his men on night patrol through the US administrative area of the former Nazi capital. There was a strictly enforced curfew, of course, so in the middle of the night, there were no civilians on the streets, which were still clogged with stone and debris from the bombings. The only cars to be seen were the ones half-buried under rubble.

There were no streetlights, either: the Allies—and the Soviets as well—were still struggling to restore even the most basic of public services. Sanitation was a disaster, and the smells from the summer heat lingered well after midnight, especially there near the Landwehr Canal, which had become both a watering hole and an open sewer.

Because of all this, the silence was practically audible in its own way, a distinct lack of sound that seemed to fill Frank's ears with an eerie ring. He struggled subconsciously to find something—anything—that might give off a sign of life in this battered city. Sounds would've given Frank's men something to react to, something to follow, something that would alleviate the creeping dread that accompanied each step through the hollowed-out streets.

He got far more than he'd asked for. The gunshot cracked out from the darkness without warning, and a soldier fell almost before the sound was heard.

Frank instinctively hit the deck, the cobblestones jutting into his ribs as he pulled his pistol and aimed at the darkness across the canal. There was nothing there, just a battered, pockmarked bridge serving as a no-man's-land between where the Americans holed up and the Soviets hunkered down in the ruined heart of occupied Berlin.

To Frank's right, the downed man made a gasping, choking noise. One of his soldiers. Again. And yet, the sound caused his heart to race, cleared his thoughts. Immediacy gave purpose.

"Everyone down! Hold fire!" Frank yelled, even though the squad was already prone and scrambling for cover. Rifles were trained across the canal, ready to respond.

"Are the Reds shooting at us, Lieutenant?" one of his men asked. His voice was a mix of bewilderment and raw panic.

"Shut up," Frank growled. "Keep down." He needed to think. Maybe the shot did come from across the canal, which was Soviet territory. If that were the case, they would need to be extremely careful. No use in starting another war so soon after wrapping up the last one.

Frank crawled over to the downed man. It was Private Tony Abruzzo, one of the newer guys who'd come over in the spring, brought in to replace all the casualties in the Ardennes. *Good kid*, he thought. *Funny, just turned twenty a few weeks back. Shit.*

The medic was already there, practically lying on top of Abruzzo, poking around at the wound in his chest. He listened to the private's breathing, then looked up at Frank with a resigned shake of his head. Frank was far from a doctor, but even he could hear it: shot in the lung, damn thing was collapsing. From the angle, looked like it probably got into his gut, too.

The private didn't have long.

"Hold positions!" Frank ordered. "Doc, give me a hand. Let's get him off the damn street."

Together, the two men quickly moved Abruzzo toward the rubble on the side of the Schöneberger Ufer. The squad hunkered down behind the piles of brick and wood and peered into the darkness across the street and canal. The silence settled back down onto them like a pall, except for Abruzzo's labored final breaths and the efforts of the radioman in the ruined building directly above them, trying for a clear signal in order to report in and, hopefully, get some help.

Frank settled the dying man down with the medic and quietly ducked over to his sergeant, a grizzled vet by the name of Sam Grogan. "Sarge?" he asked, trying to keep his cool as he waited for his orders, even as his mind reeled and the urge grew in his belly that the only sane course of action would be to simply turn tail and get out of there.

"Seems like a one-off," Grogan replied grimly, quietly, as he squinted off in the distance. "Pissed-off German or drunk Russki. Take your pick." He paused. "They're going to want someone to investigate, sir."

Frank frowned. "Yes, they are, Sergeant," he said quietly. "Find me a path across that bridge that doesn't leave our asses exposed."

Grogan nodded, and Frank returned to the medic. Abruzzo was breathing quickly, shallowly, labored. He was going quickly now.

Frank knelt down next to the dying man and took his hand. "Private Abruzzo. This is Lieutenant Lodge. You hear me OK?"

Abruzzo's eyes shifted toward his lieutenant, and that would have to be enough. Frank leaned in.

"Listen, Tony. You're getting out of this shit-hole. Not the best way out, but it's out. I'm gonna see you off, and it's gonna be OK. You hear me, Private? It's gonna be OK."

Abruzzo gave a ghost of a nod and tightened his grip slightly on Frank's hand. And with a rattle in his chest and a small, quick convulsion, he was gone.

"Mark the map for retrieval," Frank said simply as he placed Abruzzo's hand gently on his chest. "If we can't get him later, we'll make sure someone does."

The medic nodded and pulled out his tattered map of the city, already stained with someone else's blood. "Every time, you do that," he said. "You think it helps?"

Frank shrugged as he got up. "Nobody should die alone."

* * *

There was no good way to get across the Landwehr Canal with any kind of real cover. Worse, no one could identify the usual Red checkpoint on the other side of the bridge. The last thing Frank wanted was to cross over into Russian-occupied territory, only to run into a Soviet squad, especially if Grogan was right and they'd been hitting the vodka. The Reds were fanatics about their turf in Berlin; every bridge and street had a well-armed, well-staffed checkpoint. And even if the Russians didn't have enough men to staff every little intersection, this was the Wilhelmstrasse, one of Berlin's biggest thoroughfares. So, where the hell was it?

Grogan ducked over to Frank's position to report. "I got nothing over there, Lieutenant. All dark. Seems like there's some kind of emplacement there, but it's unmanned, far as I can tell. I don't like this one bit."

Frank nodded in grim agreement. "Anything from base?"

"Yeah," the sergeant said, holding up the Handie-Talkie radio. "No friendlies out here. We're trying to reach the Russians now, but it's now official: we've been ordered to investigate."

Frank clenched and unclenched his fists as he stared out across the canal, into the pitch-black night. Orders were orders, and one of his men was dead. Despite all the horrors Frank had experienced in fighting through France and Germany, he couldn't let that stand. Frank didn't care about which country held which city block, but he'd be damned if he was going to let some drunk Russian get away with murder.

Grabbing Grogan by the arm, Frank ducked over to where the rest of his squad was huddled. "All right. Weapons out but not aimed. Form up, stick to the sides, and double-time across. Cover on either side unless we run into the Reds. Then hands up and say '*Privyet*.' Got it?" Frank said. The men nodded. Grogan led the way across, with Frank taking up the rear, keeping an eye out for trouble behind them.

There was none. And there wasn't any at the other side of the bridge, either. Two piles of sandbags on either side of the street marked the checkpoint, but it wasn't manned—damned odd. Beyond that was an intersection, ruined buildings on every corner. There were a handful of guttering lights in the windows, but otherwise total darkness and a deathly silence. The streets were barren; after midnight, the Reds were just as strict about curfew as the Americans, British, and French were. Nobody trusted the Germans.

The squad took cover behind the sandbags, peering off down the dimly lit street, looking to Frank to lead. "I don't like it," Grogan repeated—this time, loud enough for the rest of the squad to hear. "We're in Red territory but they ain't here. Something's wrong."

Several of the men nodded in agreement, and Frank couldn't blame them one bit.

"I don't like it either. But Tony's dead and we've got orders. So, let's go take care of it," Frank said, squaring his jaw. "Same two groups. Stick to the sides of the street; use rubble for cover. We head up Wilhelmstrasse until we either find our shooter or meet up with some Russians. Let's go."

The men moved out, but Grogan waited a moment behind and sidled up to his lieutenant. "You know we're about three or four blocks from the Reich Chancellery," he said quietly, so as not to worry the men. "That place will be crawling with Reds."

Frank nodded; the Russians had been the ones to take the city back in April, and they had held on to the best parts of it since, including all the Nazi government buildings and Hitler's headquarters. Nobody Frank had spoken to really trusted the Soviets. They had been in bed with Hitler before they got screwed over, for starters. Their troops all looked desperate and malnourished, yet mean as hell and drunk

off their asses more often than not. Some of the horror stories from the Soviet occupation zone were tough to think
about—food and property stolen from civilians, women
and girls raped, men killed for no goddamn good reason.
Allies was too good a word for 'em, Frank thought.

"Then I guess we better step lively, Sarge. Let's go."

The men started up Wilhelmstrasse as ordered. Every
murmur and footstep echoed off the silent walls; every bit
of rubble kicked up skittered across the street like an ava-
lanche. Frank gritted his teeth. With each step, he became
more convinced that they were sitting ducks, caught out in
territory that, while not strictly enemy turf, wasn't exactly
friendly, either.

Another block went by at a slow crawl. For a moment,
Frank saw a shadow move across a window three floors
up. He raised his pistol, but by then it was already gone.
He fought back the growing feeling of frustration, the urge
to storm the building, barge in, take prisoners, protect his
men at all costs. But they weren't, strictly speaking, soldiers anymore. They were kind of like cops now. Frank had
heard that the Russians were pretty cruel to the Berliners in
their quarter of the city, and the United States was determined to act better. Frank could only hope that the shadow
at the window was merely a curious onlooker, just as nervous as he was.

It wasn't the window Frank should've worried about.

The first bullet zipped all too close to his head, and the
sound of multiple shots and muzzle flashes filled the street
around them. Frank ducked behind a pile of rubble and
got low, barking a quick "Cover!" to his squad. He risked
a quick glance out into the street and saw two of his men
were dead already, crumpled in the middle of the thor-
oughfare. And the shots were still coming.

"Return fire!" Frank yelled as he readied his pistol.
He eyed the M1 that one of the downed men still had in
his hands and cursed himself for not grabbing a carbine
before joining the patrol. No way this was coming from the

Russians, but where were they? This area was supposed to be pacified.

Shots and flashes turned the dark, silent streets into a cacophony of sound and light. Frank couldn't see or hear much. He fired blindly ahead, hoping they could at least buy themselves enough room to retreat back across the bridge. But they were under constant fire, and it was coming in heavier now.

Radio. Frank looked around for the signal corpsman who kept the radio handy. He spotted him on the other side of the street, slumped lifelessly against a pile of rubble, blood pooling around him. Of the eleven men he'd crossed the bridge with, Frank could only account for five still shooting.

A flash of light from above startled him; he looked up and saw more fire from the second and third floors of the ruined buildings around him.

Ambush. He should've worried about the windows after all.

"Inside!" Frank shouted. "Get inside!" Entering a building with known combatants wasn't the best plan, but it was better than sitting in a shooting gallery. Frank crouched down and rushed toward a door-sized hole in the wall of an old townhouse, grabbing the arm of one of his men as he ran past.

The soldier fell lifelessly over on his side.

Reaching cover, Frank allowed himself a moment to gather his wits. Maybe four or five men left. No sign of Grogan. Limited ammo. And the goddamn radio was out in the open on the street. From the sounds of gunfire he still heard, he figured there had to be at least six snipers still firing. *Six!* And where the hell were all the Russians?

Frank looked around desperately, trying to work the problem and find a solution rather than give in to panic. He was in the ruins of a townhouse. The furniture in what he guessed was the front parlor was half-crushed with rubble and covered in dust, and there was a gaping hole in the ceiling where a nice chandelier had probably once hung. It looked like some-one had punched a hole in a *Better Homes and Gardens* mag-azine. There was movement in other buildings, glimpses of light and shadow he could catch from the ruins of the door-way. But friend or foe? He couldn't say.

Moments passed. Frank was about to edge toward the doorway, prepared to shout for retreat, to have his men stay moving within the gutted ruins for as long as possible, then regroup where they'd left Abruzzo's body.

But before he could take another step forward, he felt cold metal press against the nape of his neck.

"*Guten Abend, Herr Leutnant,*" the voice behind him said.

At the same time, an older man in civilian clothes emerged from the shadows in front of Frank—training a rifle at his chest.

His heart sinking, Frank dropped his pistol and slowly raised his hands. "Evening, boys," he said, tired and defiant all at once.

The man behind him threw a sack over Frank's head, and Frank wondered if he'd ever see light again.

* * *

He might not have had his vision, but Frank still had the rest of his senses, and there were a few crucial things he knew. One: his hands were tied behind his back. Two: he was pretty sure he'd been led underground. And three: wherever they were, it was a long goddamn way back to the bridge, let alone base. Then the sack was ripped off his head.

He found himself in a surprisingly large, window-less room the size of a gymnasium, but with a dirt floor instead of planks. There were Nazi banners hanging on the walls, which looked like smooth stone or concrete. There were torches—actual, for-real burning torches—in sconces on the walls, and the smoke rose toward a small shaft in the ceiling. It was a long way up.

In the center of the room was a large antique table sur-rounded by six Nazis in uniforms of one stripe or another.

There were another dozen people scattered throughout the room, mostly wearing civvies but all armed. One of them shoved Frank to his knees . . . right next to one of his men.

The young man looked right at Frank with desperation in his eyes. It was Petersen; Frank couldn't, for the life of him, remember his first name. He was shaking like a leaf, and his pale, freckled face was streaked with dirt and tears. Blood had dried at the corner of his mouth; the Germans had taken a few swings at the kid on the way down there. The Nazis had a reputation through the war for beating the crap out of enlisted men, though they treated enemy officers better. But Hitler was dead, and this wasn't a sanctioned German military maneuver. This was the last resistance against Allied occupiers, and Frank wondered how long the whole honor-and-glory thing would last.

They were screwed after all.

"Keep your mouth shut and don't do anything stupid," Frank whispered. "We'll be OK."

"Lieutenant, what the h—" the kid choked out, but before he could finish, one of the Nazis behind them whacked the kid with his rifle butt, sending him to the floor again. The guard—a big, burly man with blond hair and cold eyes— pulled Petersen back to his knees and slapped him on the side of the head with his palm. "Quiet," he said in English.

And Frank was kind of grateful, because Petersen swayed a bit but finally stared straight ahead, silenced. One less thing to worry about for now.

And there they stayed, kneeling and under guard, while the Nazis around the table continued to . . . actually, Frank couldn't tell what the hell they were up to. Several of the uniformed bigwigs in the center of the room were checking their wristwatches and pocket watches regularly. One was a *Generalmajor* and another an *Oberst*, with a third wearing the telltale insignia of the SS. Frank knew the Nazi ranks and insignia by heart, they were posted all over the base, in the hopes that patrols might ID and capture a senior officer if they got lucky. Getting captured by one hadn't been given much consideration.

The Germans were waiting on something, Frank figured, and when they weren't looking at their watches, they were looking down at something on the table—a map, maybe?—or fiddling with the knobs on a small radio set tuned to what sounded to Frank like a stream of gibberish. There was another, larger machine against the wall, about the size of a chest of drawers, with panels full of buttons, switches, dials, and lights—a big, bulky thing emitting a low hum. What it was for, Frank couldn't begin to guess; he'd never seen anything like it. But between that gizmo and the radio, it looked a lot like how top brass might stand around waiting for an incoming broadcast. Maybe Frank's patrol had gotten a little too close for comfort? He dismissed that idea out of hand; they were safely on the other side of the canal and wouldn't have been any wiser. And they were shot at first, after all . . .

. . . and lured across the canal to investigate.

Frank's blood ran cold. Maybe the errant shot had been a trap to get them across the bridge. Maybe they were meant to be guinea pigs for whatever strange crap the Nazis were working on.

But again, where were the Russians in all this? Frank's men had only been a couple of blocks from the Reich Chancellery when they were ambushed. There was a goddamn firefight out in the open! Sure, the treaty officially dividing Berlin was only a few days old, but the Soviets had gotten cozy quickly, moving into the few houses left standing and pressing the locals into service—with severe consequences for anyone who pushed back. It was a dangerous place for anyone not a Soviet to be. So, what the hell was the Nazi resistance doing—well, that's what they were, right? Some kind of resistance force, setting up shop right under the Russians' noses?

Maybe they'd taken back this neighborhood, Frank thought. Killed the Russians who were supposed to be at that checkpoint on the canal, scraped together a few blocks they could call home. Then it was guerilla warfare in the streets, no doubt. But why drag the Americans in?

None of it made sense, and Frank knew the Germans didn't even take a shit without a plan in triplicate first. Whatever they were up to, the fact that he and Petersen had been left alive was no accident.

Petersen's trembling grew more pronounced. The air in the massive bunker had an unsettling chill to it, and they were wearing summer-issue fatigues. But Frank knew it wasn't that kind of shiver.

The kid wasn't doing a good job of keeping it together, but he kept his mouth blessedly shut. Whatever the Nazis were doing, Frank wished they'd do it quick. He thought of home, his family in Boston, his fiancée Elizabeth. He tried to put those thoughts out of his head fast—he wanted to be sharp. But throughout all his battles in the waning days of the war, he'd never felt this sense of dread, of impending doom, before. Maybe they'd be tortured for information. Maybe the Germans were hoping for a prisoner swap. Or maybe these crazy fuckers just wanted to make them die in unholy ways.

The sound that erupted from the radio shook Frank to the core. At first, it sounded like a big spike of static and feedback, but it continued . . . and continued . . . and soon Frank knew without a doubt that it was a scream, utterly inhuman, laden with pain and terror. It was the single most unnatural and eerie thing he had ever heard, even during the worst of war.

"What is that?!" Petersen shrieked. "Oh, God, what is that?!"

The Nazis all either rushed toward the machine or circled the table in the center of the room. One of them—a tall, lanky bastard with a thin, cruel face—started furiously scribbling on a piece of paper in front of him. Frank overheard him addressed as "*Herr Doktor*" and figured him for the man in charge. But given what had been discovered at Dachau, Frank had very little regard for any Nazi they called "doctor."

"Lieutenant?!" Petersen cried above the shouts of men and the piercing, otherworldly scream coming from the radio. Before Frank could respond, the private's guard gave him another whack upside the head with his hand. The kid straightened in response, a wet stain spreading around his crotch. For the first time in all his long months at war, in a million awful situations with dozens of scared kids, Frank wondered whether trying to get Petersen home in one piece was going to get them both killed. The shame of the thought wasn't as overwhelming as he wished it had been.

Then Frank went blind.

A huge white light burst forth from the center of the room, turning everything around him into a blizzard of ill-defined movement accompanied only by that infernal screaming still emanating from the radio equipment and the shouts and cries of the Nazis as they reacted—some of them sounding actually joyful.

Frank doubled over in pain, his eyes screwed shut, his heart racing. There was something fundamentally *wrong*, a feeling in his gut that erupted inside him the instant that light exploded into being around him. The screaming through the radio increased in volume and slowly began to . . . separate, somehow: a million different voices filled with pain and fear pouring into Frank's ears.

And then, inexplicably, everything abruptly stopped.

Frank slowly opened his eyes. The Nazis were all standing stock-still, looking upward at a point nearly six feet above the table, in the center of the room.

Frank had no idea what it was, or how on God's green Earth it could even exist.

It was about six feet around, a spherical white light that looked like it was both swirling and hovering motionlessly at the same time. The edges trailed off into the air like mist, and the light was somehow present without actually shining or illuminating the room.

It was utterly unnatural, and staring into it, Frank felt as if he were looking into some immense, unknowable abyss.

The Nazis moved into action. Long metal instruments, roughly soldered together with long cords trailing out the back and across the dirt floor, were directed toward the hovering light. They began shouting readings at each other, their hands fluttering across the controls, while others quickly scribbled down their findings. And in the middle of it all, Herr Doktor was soaking it all in, a broad, wicked smile spreading across his face like a disease.

Petersen choked out a ragged sob. "What is that? Dear God, what is that? What are they doing? What the hell is that?" the private said, over and over, a rosary's worth of desperate prayer.

Before Frank could respond, a pulse of blinding light filled the room and another scream—this one far clearer and horrifyingly nonhuman—ripped through his ears. Everyone in the room turned away; even some of the Germans looked horrified at this. But most of them continued to poke and prod at the light with instruments. Frank could see it was definitely swirling now, like water going down a drain.

A spasm of pain rippled through Frank's head. It was as if something had pushed its way into his skull and was somehow . . . *writhing* . . . inside his brains. He could practically feel ethereal fingers splitting the two halves of his brain apart and shoving something inside, something alive and unnatural that grafted itself to his mind and soul. It was a violation of his very being, his every sense becoming acutely aware and heightened. He pitched forward and fell onto his side, feeling each speck of dirt on his skin, the shouts from his guard echoing in his bones.

He didn't know the exact moment that the pain became bearable enough to regain control of his body. But when Frank unscrewed his eyes, he found the German doctor looking down at him.

"You are not feeling well?" he asked in accented English.

Another wave of pain pushed through Frank's head. "What the hell is going on here?" he finally said through gritted teeth, his own voice sounding like a radio turned all the way up in his head. "Who are you people?"

The doctor grinned, then pivoted away from Frank to bark out more orders in German. A moment later, probes and equipment were all over Frank as he lay on the ground, trying to control his breathing and somehow rein in everything going in his head, attempting to assume some sort of control over the *thing* that now resided inside his skull. When he was able to look up again, the doctor was back, a strange grin on his face.

"It is your lucky day, it seems."

"I doubt it," Frank gasped as he slowly pushed himself back up onto his knees. "What did you do to me?"

"I can honestly say I do not know yet," the doctor said. "But we will find out, yes?"

Frank felt strong enough now to give the German a disgusted look. "You seriously think I'm going to help you, '*Herr Doktor*'?"

The doctor shrugged. "No, of course not. But you'll help your soldier, yes?"

He then switched to German and barked something to Petersen's guard. The man nodded and, without any warning, raised his rifle and pulled the trigger.

Frank didn't even have time to shout. Petersen's chest erupted in a bloody mess. The look on the poor kid's face was one of mild surprise, as if he'd been told the soda counter was out of Coca-Cola. Then he fell face-first onto the ground as Frank managed to scramble to his feet—no mean feat with his hands still bound.

"What the hell am I supposed to do now?" Frank screamed. "You killed him!"

The doctor nodded in Petersen's direction. "Save him if you can. Take revenge if you cannot."

Frank didn't move for several seconds, uncomprehending, even as one of the other Germans freed his hands. Were they mistaking him for a medic? Was their English not as good as it seemed? "W—What?" he finally stammered.

"Go! Save him! He has moments left!" the doctor shouted.

That got Frank moving. He dashed over to Petersen's side. "Kid? Kid! Can you hear me? Can you . . ."

Frank grabbed Petersen's shoulders and started rolling him over—and as he did, he felt the thing in his mind start to writhe excitedly, causing him to gasp and wince in pain.

"*Mike Petersen. Duluth.*" Frank wasn't sure where those words came from, and wasn't even sure if he had spoken them himself, aloud, or if someone was giving him directions.

The energy drained from him, and Frank collapsed on top of the dead man, then rolled onto his back. The Nazi doctor knelt down and leaned over him. "What is it? What is happening to you?" he demanded.

"*Basketball player. Daisy, oh Daisy, she's going to be so sad.*"

The Nazi kept talking, but Frank couldn't hear. There was too much else going on, and he pressed his hands to his head as if to keep his own thoughts from leaking out—or to keep other thoughts from coming in.

"*Mom and Pop and little Jimmy, too, they'll be devastated. Letters every week, back and forth from Minnesota.*"

The Nazi looked up suddenly, fear on his face. Next to him, one of the armed civilians fell to the ground. In the back of Frank's mind, the sound of gunshots registered.

"*That house, that was a great house over on Lake Avenue, but the family moved years ago.*"

People were running now. Frank rolled onto his stomach and tried to crawl away, but the images and sounds kept flowing uncontrollably through his brain. All he could figure out was that there were more people in the room now. And there was shooting.

"*Such drawing ability! A great future in art, or maybe architecture.*"

Frank looked up and saw another soldier, pale and seemingly malnourished. He had a red star on his uniform.

Frank tried to get up but only managed to roll onto his side as images and words flowed through his mind in a torrent. His body trembled violently, and he could no longer hold back the vomit.

The last thing he remembered before falling into blessed unconsciousness was an emaciated Russian boy in uniform, looking at him as if he were a ghost.

2.

October 8, 1945

D anny Wallace had never really known how silence could be "deafening." The idea seemed not just contradictory but ludicrous. Yet on this day, as the young US Navy lieutenant walked down the streets of downtown Hiroshima in the light of the morning sun, he understood completely.

There were no sounds. No cars, no trolleys, no people. No birds, no movement. A testament to the devastating power of the atom bomb and a quiet, yet angry, protest against it.

He was still at least a mile from the center of the blast that had torn through the city three months prior, and yet the destruction was so complete, the land so *cleansed*. The idea that people had died right where he was now walking seemed incomprehensible.

But seventy thousand people had, many of them instantaneously. They were the lucky ones. Danny had heard painfully detailed stories of horrific burns and victims that lingered for days, weeks, before dying. There were still wounded on the outskirts of town, in makeshift hospitals and in family homes, still not yet dead—either stubbornly clinging to life or, perhaps more cruelly, waiting for an end to the excruciating pain.

The streets were bare, for the most part. There was debris, lots of it, and a number of burned-out trolleys and cars on each block. But the road's outline was easily followed amid the destruction. In fact, Danny looked up to the sound of sweeping from an old woman tending to her section of the street, brushing it clear. There was no house behind her, just a pile of charred wood and stones.

It was all the same, everywhere around him. Where there were once buildings two, three, even four stories high, now it was just rubble: burned wood, broken brick, and fine ash, most of it in piles no more than a few feet high. In the far distance, reinforced concrete structures stood gutted and burned out like ghostly skeletons against the sky, a sky so blue it almost seemed to mock the fate of the city below. Most had structural damage from the sheer kinetic force of the A-bomb. It didn't matter that they were still standing; they could never be used again.

Someone on a bicycle dashed by—upon what errand, Danny couldn't begin to imagine. A couple knelt in the street and prayed before a piece of blasted ruin, a stick of lit incense wedged between crushed masonry. Danny hadn't the faintest what the Japanese did for religion, but he knew mourning when he saw it. He had to keep it together, he told himself. He had a job to do.

"This is good," the man next to him said.

Danny wheeled about and wiped a stray tear from his eye. "What could be good about this?"

Dr. Kaoru Shima put a gentle hand on Danny's shoulder. "I mean it is good that you see this, Lieutenant Wallace. It is good that you cry a little for us. I never supported this war against the Chinese, against the Americans, but this type of destruction is something that I never imagined would happen on Earth."

Danny tried to think of something to say but could only nod. Shima ran a hospital in Hiroshima. He had been out of town the day the bomb fell. He'd lost everything and yet was set on rebuilding his facility and, in doing so, focusing on the care that those far less fortunate than him desperately needed.

There were a lot of unfortunates in Hiroshima.

It had only been a few days since the Navy had landed at the city's main port to take over administration. Japan's top experts had already proclaimed Hiroshima safe, and

Danny had reviewed their data and found the science sound. But that wasn't why Danny was there. Captain Roscoe Hillenkoetter, head of intelligence for the US Pacific Fleet, had personally approved this particular mission, and Danny had had to sign more than his fair share of confidentiality agreements before being given the green light.

Shima was already well known as a local guide. He'd been one of the first to greet the Americans at the docks, though he had made no effort to conceal that it was strictly in the hopes of getting medical supplies to his suffering people as quickly as possible. Thankfully, those higher up on the chain of command had seen fit to stuff the Navy ships with all kinds of medicine, as well as food and potable water. The Americans had become, if not popular, then certainly less hated in Hiroshima in relatively short order. And Shima had made himself an accessible and friendly local presence.

Now, of course, Danny understood why. *He wants to show me the Hell on Earth we created. And I can't say I blame him.* They were among the very few people walking the streets: the dignified Japanese doctor with jet-black hair and moustache, wearing a suit and tie, looking as if he were just going to the office like any other day; and the young, blond-haired, bespectacled young lieutenant in shipboard khaki, as out of place there as a gun in a nursery.

They walked by a tall, domed building—gutted but still technically standing. "Our prefectural industrial hall," Shima said, noticing Danny's look. "It is—was—a place where we would showcase the best efforts of our domestic goods, where other countries would come and see and buy from us."

Nothing else needed to be said. Danny knew those industries were gone, the workers dead. He wondered how in God's name anybody could rebuild after this. Where could you possibly start? If it were him, if he were a survivor of something like this, he'd leave and go as far away as he could.

As they continued, Danny noticed that the rubble and ruin were slowing piling up—it was now maybe three or four feet deep in places—and less strewn about. They were very close to where the center of the blast had occurred. The bomb had ignited when it was still a thousand feet above the city, and the buildings right below it had suffered a massive thrust of pressure and fire. Everything was crushed, straight down into the ground.

"Here," Shima said, pointing to a half-standing concrete doorway surrounded by rubble. "This is where my clinic was."

Danny opened his mouth to ask how many people had been in the building at the time but decided against it. In all honesty, he didn't want to know. Instead, he let Shima lead him through a trail the doctor picked out amid the ruin, all the while mentally cursing the aim of the US Army Air Corps. They were supposed to target the Aioi Bridge, a half mile away. Instead, the bomb had exploded right over a goddamn hospital.

Like it would have mattered, he realized. The way it happened, the people in the hospital died instantaneously. If the bomb had been on target, they would've had an extra few seconds of agony before it was all over. Danny shook his head at the thought, saddened and awed by the new calculus of war the A-bomb had created.

A handful of people ahead were picking through the wreckage of the hospital, including a woman in a nurse's uniform. Danny watched as she bent over, tugging at something stuck under a chunk of concrete, then pulled out a two-foot-long bone bleached white from the blast. She placed it gently into a sack marked with Japanese characters.

Shima walked through the doorway—and it was just a door frame sticking out of the ground, nothing on either side or above it, a gesture so bizarre that Danny would've laughed under any other circumstances—and pointed toward a partially excavated stairway. "Most of the bones of our people are down there, in the basement, with the rest of the building," Shima said. "We have worked steadily to recover as many as we can. They will go to a shrine dedicated to our lost people."

It was becoming more and more difficult for Danny to keep focused on the assignment in the face of so much loss and suffering. "How deep did you get?"

Shima motioned Danny forward. "Deep enough. That is why you are here, correct, Lieutenant?"

Danny turned and looked at Shima to elaborate, but the doctor merely smiled sadly and waved him on. "Do not touch anything, Lieutenant. I cannot say how strong the walls are."

As Danny turned on his flashlight and headed downward, the doctor following behind him, he wished he had brought a few MPs along to take point. But Hillenkoetter had given strict orders: keep it contained. The less that knew, the better.

"I have not let many people down here," Shima said, as if Danny had been thinking out loud. "I cannot allow more to risk their lives. So it has been myself, my nurse, and a single worker. That is all."

Looking around, the entire basement was choked with rubble, so much so that in many places, Danny couldn't tell where the floor or ceiling started or stopped. It was just a big pile of junk. Concrete, wood, metal, and electrical wiring had all come down in little pieces, and he was burrowed somewhere in the middle of it.

Shima took out his own flashlight and assumed the lead. *Burrowed*, as it turned out, was the right word—the doctor and his people had managed to carve out a tunnel through the rubble no more than four feet high and three wide, held up by a few impromptu supports wedged into the walls.

"Why did you tunnel?" Danny asked. "Why wouldn't you start from the top?"

Shima shrugged. "It is hard to explain. The laborer I hired to help in here insisted on going down to the sub-basement. He said it was important. He recovered many remains, so I did not argue with him. I originally assumed that is why he tunneled."

"What happened to this worker?" Danny asked. "I may need to speak with him."

"He was Korean. I believe he went home after a while. He did not show up one morning. I can't say I blame him. If this is not your home, why would you be here?"

"Maybe he found something."

"It is all as we found it," Shima said. "Do not worry."

Danny ducked a bit lower to get through a particularly tight passage. "Nonetheless, doctor, I'll need the worker's name."

"Of course."

After a few more minutes, during which the tunnel grew tighter and delved deeper, the passage finally opened up into a smallish room somewhere far in the hospital's basements. Danny could just barely make out tiled walls and a concrete floor. He estimated they were at least two or three stories beneath street level, with several tons of rubble above them. And yet there was enough room here for both Danny and Shima to stand and stretch.

And in the center of the room . . . there it was.

Danny exhaled under his breath. *Holy shit*. It was true.

"Dr. Shima," he said, turning to the doctor, clearing his throat. "I'm afraid that under the authority of the Supreme Commander of the Allied Powers, this area is going to be under quarantine from here on out."

To Danny's surprise, Shima merely smiled. "It is a rare thing, Lieutenant Wallace, to have something of value in the midst of this kind of devastation."

"Excuse me?"

"What we have here, I know you wish to study. This is why you came. And because you came alone, Lieutenant, it is safe to assume you are one of the only Americans who know that it is here."

The air had become heavy with tension, and in the same motion, both drew their firearms and stood, less than five feet away, weapons pointed at each other in silence.

"I have no wish to harm you, Lieutenant," Shima finally said.

Danny stared hard at his guide-turned-adversary. "Then you should drop your weapon."

Shima smiled and lowered it to his side. "I just wanted you to know that I could have shot you, but I will not. You seem an honorable young man, and I hope we might treat each other with honor here."

Danny knew better than to mince words—or holster his sidearm. "What do you want?"

"I want your word that your government will rebuild our city."

"You're serious?" Danny asked. Shima's face remained unchanged. "I'm just a junior officer. You realize I don't have that kind of authority, right?"

"No, but those that sent you here—without anyone to protect you—I'm quite sure they do."

Smart guy. "I could just shoot you, Doctor."

Shima shrugged. "You could. But before I die, I could detonate the charges I've placed around these tunnels, burying you and me and keeping your discovery from ever seeing the light of day. How long do you think it would take them to find this room again, if ever? How long to find your body?"

"I can carry your request up the chain. And I'll make sure you're able to treat as many victims here as possible."

Shima nodded. "Where are you from, Lieutenant?"

"St. Louis."

"And if someone bombed your city into dust and ash, would you not do all you could to see it rebuilt?"

Danny finally lowered his weapon. "We should continue this conversation back aboveground, Dr. Shima."

"If you come back in force, I *will* detonate the charges. I want assurances." And with that, Shima turned his flashlight back on and made his way up the tunnel.

Danny made as if he would follow but paused for a moment in that room underground and closed his eyes. He could hear *them* much more clearly here, and louder, too—the whispers clear as day as they tumbled about in his head. He focused, trying to pinpoint from the echoes where their actual locations might be. Wherever it was, it was far.

In time, maybe Danny could find them. And that light—
that vortex of blindingly white light swirling in a sub-
basement of a hospital decimated by history's mightiest
weapon—just might help him do that.

A few minutes later, Danny emerged into the clear, sunny
day and took the Handie-Talkie out of his pack. "Patch me
through to SCAP," he said. "I need Captain Hillenkoetter
ASAP."

TELETYPE

WAR DEPARTMENT
GENERAL STAFF-INTELLIGENCE
TOP SECRET-MAJIC
FROM LTG VANDENBERG USA
TO CAPT HILLENKOETTER USN, CO USS MISSOURI
CC SECNAV FORRESTAL
DATE 14 JAN 46

RECEIVED YOUR REPORT ON HIROSHIMA PHENOMENA AND
INITIAL SCIENTIFIC INQUIRIES INTO WHITE VORTEX AND
VARIANT INDIVIDUALS. ALL FURTHER COMMUNICATIONS ON
THIS TOPIC NOW CLASSIFIED TOP SECRET-MAJIC. MAJIC
COMPARTMENTALIZATION CLEARANCE IS GRANTED TO LT
WALLACE AND THOSE ADDRESSED ON THIS TELETYPE.

AS PER PREVIOUS ORDERS, YOU ARE TO REMAIN IN COMMAND OF
USS MISSOURI. YOU WILL ALSO SERVE AS GROUND COMMANDER
OF ALL EFFORTS SURROUNDING THESE PHENOMENA. LT
WALLACE WILL CONTINUE TO REPORT DIRECTLY TO YOU VIA
ENCRYPTED TELETYPE OR TELEPHONICALLY.

YOUR ORDERS AS PER WHITE VORTEX ARE AS FOLLOWS:

1) DR VANNEVAR BUSH AND TEAM WILL DEPART FOR JAPAN
ASAP TO JOIN LT WALLACE IN STUDY OF PHENOMENA. THE
PRIMARY GOAL OF INQUIRY IS TO DETERMINE WHETHER THE
PHENOMENON IN HIROSHIMA CAN BE MOVED SAFELY TO US
SOVEREIGN TERRITORY.

2) IF PHENOMENON CAN BE MOVED, DESTROYER USS THE SULLIVANS WILL BE RECOMMISSIONED FOR USE IN TRANSPORTING IT. AT YOUR DISCRETION, LT WALLACE MAY ASSUME RANK OF LIEUTENANT COMMANDER AND CO DUTIES ABOARD THE SULLIVANS FOR THE DURATION.

3) ONCE IN US TERRITORY, PHENOMENON WILL BE TRANSPORTED TO SECURE LOCATION. WALLACE WILL CONTINUE TO COORDINATE SCIENTIFIC AND MILITARY EFFORTS.

4) THE BUSH TEAM WILL CONTINUE STUDY TO DETERMINE WHETHER OR HOW THE HIROSHIMA PHENOMENON IS LINKED TO EMERGENCE OF VARIANT INDIVIDUALS BOTH HERE AND ABROAD, AND TO DETERMINE MOTIVE OR INTELLIGENCE BEHIND THE EMERGENCE OF WHITE VORTEX AND-OR VARIANT INDIVIDUALS.

YOUR ORDERS AS TO VARIANT INDIVIDUALS ARE AS FOLLOWS:

1) THE INDIVIDUAL REFERRED TO IN YOUR INITIAL REPORTS AS SUBJECT-1 IS ORDERED TO RETURN TO US TERRITORY NO LATER THAN THREE MONTHS FROM RECEIPT OF THIS TELETYPE UNLESS CIRCUMSTANCES SURROUNDING WHITE VORTEX PHENOMENON DICTATE OTHERWISE.

2) ONCE RETURNED TO US TERRITORY, SUBJECT-1 WILL CONTINUE TO SEARCH FOR VARIANT INDIVIDUALS WITHIN THE UNITED STATES AS PER METHODOLOGY OUTLINED IN YOUR REPORT. SUBJECT-1 WILL ALSO COMPILE FILES OF STANDARD METHODOLOGY, SUCH AS POLICE REPORTS OR NEWS CLIPPINGS, TO CREATE PAPER TRAIL AND ENSURE SECRECY.

3) WHEN VARIANT INDIVIDUALS ARE DISCOVERED, THEY ARE
TO BE DETAINED BY MILITARY OFFICERS. INVOLVEMENT
OF LOCAL POLICE AND/OR FBI IS NOT ADVISED. SECRET
SERVICE OR US MARSHALS MAY BE AVAILABLE AS NEEDED.
THESE VARIANT INDIVIDUALS WILL BE THEN TAKEN TO
NEAREST MILITARY FACILITY TO BEGIN STUDY.

4) VARIANT INDIVIDUALS WHO AGREE TO STUDY, AND
WHOSE ABILITIES ARE DEEMED TO BE USEFUL, WILL REMAIN
IN MILITARY CUSTODY. YOU ARE AUTHORIZED TO BEGIN
SCIENTIFIC STUDY AND INDIVIDUAL TRAINING REGIMEN AS
RECOMMENDED IN YOUR REPORT.

5) AS IT REMAINS POSSIBLE THAT EMERGENCE OF VARIANT
INDIVIDUALS RESULTS FROM JAPANESE OR NAZI WARTIME
ACTIVITIES, INDIVIDUALS WHO RESIST CAPTURE, DO NOT
AGREE TO STUDY, OR ARE DEEMED DANGEROUS TO THE
PUBLIC MAY BE DETAINED INDEFINITELY OR, AT NATIONAL
COMMAND AUTHORTY DISCRETION, EXECUTED AS WARTIME
COLLABORATORS UNDER THE APPLICABLE MILITARY CODES.

6) NATIONAL COMMAND AUTHORITY RESERVES THE RIGHT
TO DETERMINE WHETHER VARIANTS, INDIVIDUALLY OR
COLLECTIVELY, ARE A CLEAR AND PRESENT THREAT TO US
SECURITY AND SOVEREIGNTY. THIS DETERMINATION HAS NOT
YET BEEN MADE, AND WILL BE RESERVED UNTIL FURTHER
DATA AND INTELLIGENCE ARE PROVIDED.

7) IF VARIANT INDIVIDUALS ARE DETERMINED TO BE A
THREAT TO US SECURITY AND SOVEREIGNTY, DETENTION OR

ELIMINATION OF VARIANTS, INDIVIDUALLY OR COLLECTIVELY,
MAY BE ORDERED AS PER ABOVE GUIDANCE. IF DETERMINED TO
BE UNTHREATENING, VARIANT INDIVIDUALS MAY CONTINUE
TRAINING FOR EVENTUAL USE IN INTELLIGENCE OR MILITARY
OPERATIONS.

8) THE IDENTITY OF SUBJECT-1, AS PER YOUR
RECOMMENDATION, REMAINS KNOWN ONLY TO YOU, LT
WALLACE AND LTG VANDENBERG. SHOULD MORE VARIANT
INDIVIDUALS BE FOUND, IDENTITY OF SUBJECT-1 WILL BE
REVEALED TO NATIONAL COMMAND AUTHORITY AS WELL.

ANY FURTHER REPORTS OR INQUIRIES TO WAR DEPARTMENT
ON THIS MATTER MUST BE CONDUCTED TELEPHONICALLY OR
IN PERSON. OPERATIONAL SECURITY REMAINS PARAMOUNT.

(SIGNED) VANDENBERG

D r. Jane Fitzgerald closed the manila folder in front of her in disgust and slid it across the table. "With all due respect, Bob, he's a psychopath. You let him into the program, he'll end up corrupting the whole bunch all over again."

US Army Major Robert Staver gave a weary sigh—sending a former OSS analyst to Nuremberg just to second-guess his every move had to be the Army's sick idea of a practical joke. He picked up the folder and opened it, glancing at the dossier and accompanying pictures of the bespectacled physicist inside. If they said no, it wasn't even worth it to fight their recommendations.

"Kurt Wilhelm Schreiber, worked on the V-2 rocket, naturally," he said as he flipped through the pages. "Well, we've got plenty of those guys already and I suppose we don't *need* another one. He did have a hand on the *Uranprojekt*, the German A-bomb effort, under Walther Gerlach, but we know how to make those ourselves. So . . . uhh . . ." He stopped and leaned in to take a closer look. "Hm . . . what the hell is that?"

Staver held up a photo of Schreiber—tall, widow's peak, thin, very *Nazi-looking*—inspecting a line of cadaverous, emaciated people in some kind of examination room. The German had a Geiger counter in his hand, but there were several pieces of machinery on a table in the foreground that Staver—whose specialty was researching and occasionally stealing new weapons technology—was unexpectedly at a loss to identify.

"That's at Dachau, one of the Nazi concentration camps," she said. "We're told Schreiber was conducting radiation experiments on prisoners there."

Staver's eyebrows inched higher. "Holy hell. Trying to see how much they could take?"

"Not exactly. Our best intelligence indicates that the intended goal of the tests was to genetically alter the subjects. We don't have much in the way of testing results or journals, but what we're being told is that the Nazis were looking to *enhance* a human's physical and mental abilities. They were trying to make them bigger, faster, smarter, not kill them, even if many of the test subjects were treated about as humanely as lab mice might be. The reports haven't been confirmed, but there were also disturbing signs that some of the experiments Schreiber was conducting had their origins in occult literature. Black magic. More evidence, Major, that the man's a nut. Why the hell would we want to pardon and recruit him?"

Staver closed the folder and leaned back in his leather chair, closing his tired eyes a moment. "Well, if there *is* a compelling reason, we will find out soon enough. He's next up."

They sat in silence for a few minutes, shuffling through paperwork and other dossier files in the wood-paneled, book-lined conference room inside Nuremberg's Palace of Justice. Several floors below, Germany's remaining Nazi leaders were on trial for crimes against humanity—and dear God, there were so many goddamn crimes. More than once, Staver had wished out loud that the trials could have been held in Auschwitz or Dachau—let the bastards come face-to-face with what they had done.

And yet he was now advocating that some of these particularly sick bastards were useful enough to the United States to avoid the swift hand of justice. Life was horrible that way sometimes. But he was under orders, and this new Operation PAPERCLIP, he was assured, was incredibly important to the balance of power between the United States and Stalin's Red hordes.

There was a gentle knock on the door, and both Staver and Fitzgerald stood as it opened. A white-helmeted MP led Schreiber in by the arm, while another kept just behind them, his rifle at the ready. It was a formality; Schreiber was far more hollowed and emaciated than he looked in his photo, moving with the speed and gait of a disoriented prisoner. Still, he looked a damn sight better than the poor SOBs in that picture from Dachau, and even if Staver was considering sparing him the death penalty, he sure as shit wasn't going to give him an inch more than that.

Schreiber was guided to an armchair and seated by the MP, who then shackled each arm to the thick wooden armrests and tested their security before leaving. The Nazi scientist gave the MP a surprised, bemused look at this treatment.

"Something wrong, Dr. Schreiber?" Fitzgerald asked as the door closed.

"Not at all, *Fräulein*. This will be a most interesting meeting between you and I, I am sure," Schreiber responded in excellent, lightly accented English.

"What makes you say that?" Staver said.

Schreiber shrugged as best he could under the circumstances. "I am not under guard, perhaps for the first time since I was traded by the Russians to the Americans six months ago. So, I wonder why you traded for me, all this time. And I think right now I will find out."

"We just wanted a complete set, that's all," Fitzgerald said with obvious satisfaction. "You assholes are like baseball cards. You'll look better hanging side by side." But Staver caught the look she'd flashed his way immediately after, and he was thinking the exact same thing: *What trade?*

"What do you think will happen here, Dr. Schreiber?" Staver asked.

"If you have done your research, then you will have understood my value to you, and I will agree to help you."

"And why would you want to help us?" Fitzgerald asked. She'd lost count how many times she'd asked that over the last few months.

"Obviously because I do not want to die," Schreiber answered calmly. "I am not so married to Nazi ideology or German nationalism that I would not wish to save my own life. So, I will help you, and you will let me live."

Staver had no choice but to smile at that. "Well, that's the first goddamn honest answer we've gotten to that question so far," he said. "There's just a small problem, Doc. We already got V-2 scientists. We got nuclear scientists—and by the way, ours are better. And we got plenty of people willing to rat out, in detail, every fucked-up thing you bastards did in those concentration camps. So, what exactly do you think you can give us that we don't already have?"

This, too, was a carefully posed question, one they asked at every single one of these meetings. It had all started to follow a familiar pattern. Some would break down and plead. Others would go stoic and silent. A few—and those were the real paydays—would open the floodgates and give up the farm right there and then, all for the possibility that they might live to see another day.

Yet once again, Schreiber surprised them.

"You mean you do not know?"

"Know what, exactly?" Fitzgerald asked.

Schreiber smiled and sat back in his chair. He made to cross his arms against his chest, forgetting his shackles, but his restricted movement only seemed to amuse him more as he let his arms rest on the armrests again. "And here I was worried that this, too, was an area in which you were well ahead of us. But you are merely children! You are children with new toys who are incapable of understanding what they do."

Staver frowned. "You're talking about the A-bomb. That's where your research came in, right?"

At this, the Nazi actually laughed. "Oh, you Americans truly are lost. But you are young, both of you. You are a . . . major, yes? A mid-level officer. And you, *Fräulein*, I would assume you are from the intelligence agencies, yes? A spy? So, maybe you do not know what your superiors know. But as I said, I wish to live very much, so I will help you. Write this down."

Schreiber waited, patiently, until Staver rolled his eyes and picked up his pen.

Over the course of the next few minutes, the Nazi gave up . . . very little, actually, in terms of actual volume. There were a few places and dates. A handful of names. Times. And a sparse handful of details so insane and convoluted that Staver had to ask the German to repeat them slowly so he could get it down in the right order.

"Is that it?" Fitzgerald asked when he was finished. "This is crazy. You expect us to believe any of this? What are we supposed to do with this fairy tale?"

"Call Washington, of course. Call your superiors, and ask to speak to *their* superiors. I humbly suggest, for I am the prisoner here, that you go as high up the chain of your command as you can, because only at the top will they know of this. And they will also know what to do with me."

Staver looked at the single page of notes he'd taken. "It's not enough. We'll need a hell of a lot more than this if you think we're going to risk running this up the flagpole for you, pal."

"This is a 'nice try,' as you say, but I think I am done talking for now, because you are obviously not the ones who will decide my fate," Schreiber said. "So, we are finished."

Schreiber then sat back in his chair, muscles relaxed, and closed his eyes. The two Americans traded looks. Then Staver summoned the MP, who dutifully removed the prisoner from the room. Schreiber would return to the prison on the grounds of the Palace of Justice and sit tight with the rest of his Nazi compatriots as they awaited the world's judgment.

"Well . . . that was interesting," Fitzgerald said when the door was closed behind them and the two were alone again.

"You were right, Jane. Psychopath, definitely."

She shrugged. "I think he was intentionally fucking with us, mocking us. One last spit in the face before we hang him."

Staver looked down at his handwriting. "I think he's just crazy. But in any case, it's a clear rejection. We'll take your recommendation on this one and cross him off the list." He slumped back in his chair again. "I'm gonna grab some lunch, see if I can get a call in to my kids before they go to school. What do you say?"

Fitzgerald stood and stretched. "Sounds good. I'll be back at two."

They put their files in their briefcases and walked out of the room, heading off in different directions. But as soon as they were out of sight of one another, both broke into a dead run. Staver headed for the military tribunal's communications center and demanded a secure line to the War Department. Fitzgerald went down into the basement, into an unlabeled room next to a maintenance closet, where her own secure line ran to a nondescript building in Foggy Bottom, an unremarkable DC neighborhood, where the people who answered were decidedly descript and remarkable.

April 21, 1946

The sun shone brightly over manicured lawns and white adobe-style houses and buildings, giving the entire campus a sense of resort-like tranquility. Pathways laid out in concrete and tarmac crisscrossed the grounds. People in white coats and smocks were everywhere, giving the uniformed military officers genial smiles—and wide berths.

"Nice place, this," said the Marine captain with ANDERSON on his name badge. "Get a couple girls, some drinks . . . could be a swell place to spend a few weeks." He walked with the precision of a disciplined military man across the grounds, his eyes scanning for danger the entire time and his prodigious muscles unconsciously flexing.

Next to him, Lieutenant Commander Danny Wallace smirked and shook his head. "Trust me, Andy, you don't want to be here if you don't have to." Danny knew Anderson from their time together in the Pacific, and had pestered Hillenkoetter—still his superior despite the captain's new command—for some help. If all went well, Danny had plans for Anderson. If only the latter man could start getting a little more comfortable with . . . unusual situations.

A moment later, they watched as several white-coated attendants, all of them big, hulking men, rushed inside one of the low-slung buildings, where screaming could be heard. Not long after, they dragged a man out—one attendant per kicking, thrashing limb—and set him down just outside the building's entrance, where they struggled to get him into a straitjacket. Someone forgot to secure the man's head, though, and with an unexpected twist, the patient managed to sink his teeth into the forearm closest to him, prompting a cry of anger—and a meaty right hook to the screaming man's face.

It was much easier to get him into the straitjacket after that.

"Gentlemen, I'm sorry you had to witness that," came a voice from behind the two officers. They turned to find a bespectacled, bearded man, burly and bow-tied, smiling the weary smile of an overworked doctor. "Agnews State Hospital practices a positive approach to therapy whenever possible, but of course sometimes the health and safety of the hospital's other patients, as well as our staff, must take priority, and we have a handful of patients who simply don't respond well to anything we do."

Danny nodded grimly and extended his hand, which the other fellow took and shook with seeming gratitude. "I'm Lieutenant Commander Dan Wallace. This is Captain Andrew Anderson. I don't know if my message was passed along, but I called yesterday inquiring after one of your patients here."

"Of course, Commander. I'm Dr. Stanley Abrams, director here at the hospital. I'm so glad you came. We would of course be glad to assist the military in any way we can. If you'll follow me?"

Danny and Anderson followed Abrams through the hospital campus as he gave them what felt to Danny like a typical VIP visitor speech. The mental hospital—*insane asylum* was, apparently, no longer a term in use—was the finest serving the San Francisco and San Jose areas. They used traditional "talk therapy," as Abrams put it, but were also experiencing a lot of promising success with hydrotherapy and, more recently, modern "electro-shock" treatment.

If someone strapped me down and shocked me, I'd tell them anything they'd want to hear to make it stop, Danny thought. *No matter how crazy I am.*

"Excuse me, Doc, but maybe we can get on to the part about why we're here?" Anderson eventually interrupted.

The doctor smiled obsequiously. "Of course, Captain. Let me just check my folder here." Abrams shuffled through the papers he carried as they walked, and finally pulled out the right one. "Ah, here we are! Margaret Ann Dubinsky, age twenty-seven, hailing from the Chicago area. Moved here when she was eighteen, before the war. Became an elementary school teacher."

"You have a lot of elementary school teachers here?" Danny asked.

"No, no, it's actually quite unusual," Abrams said. "Saddest thing, actually. She was teaching up in Mill Valley, receiving very high marks, I'm told. There was an incident during a meeting with the parents of one of her students. She had asked for the meeting to discuss the possibility that the child's low marks might have been due to a learning disability."

"A what?" Anderson interjected.

Abrams shot the Marine a look. "A mental issue that keeps someone from understanding the information presented to them in an academic setting, Captain. A minor mental issue, but one we're now recognizing among students who might have simply been considered 'slow.' At any rate, she explained the matter to the parents, who were reportedly dismissive of the whole matter. They believed their boy was simply being lazy. Miss Dubinsky disagreed strenuously, and the meeting became confrontational. Then the father suddenly became violent. He attacked Miss Dubinsky as well as his child and stormed out of the meeting. From there, he acquired a knife from the cafeteria and took several school employees hostage in the main offices. He killed a janitor and a secretary before the police shot him dead."

"Jesus Christ . . ." Anderson muttered. "Was she seriously hurt?"

"She was knocked out before the father got the knife," Abrams replied. "A slight stroke of good luck, if you care to look at it that way. But Miss Dubinsky isn't a patient at Agnews because of any physical condition, as I'm sure you're aware. Following the attack, she became withdrawn and introverted. She apparently blames *herself* for the incident and began experiencing severe depression. Her condition deteriorated to the point where she eventually quit her job. I'm told she'd been living for two months on the streets of San Francisco, avoiding contact with all friends and family. The police picked her up on a loitering charge and soon determined that she would be best served if they brought her here."

"So, she went crazy after the shooting," Anderson said, shaking his head. "Understandable."

Abrams wheeled on Anderson, literally getting in front of him as he walked so that they both came to a halt. "Captain, please understand. We practice serious medicine at Agnews and do *not* use that terminology here," he said with what could be best described as polite urgency. "Nor do we use 'insane' or 'nuts' or anything else like that. We strive to maintain a positive environment. These people are patients, and they are being treated for an illness. I cannot have you using that kind of language around Miss Dubinsky or any other patient!"

Danny moved between the two men and held his hands up in mock surrender. "Our apologies, Doctor. We understand. I'm sure all the captain meant is that it would've been tough for anybody to go through that."

Abrams nodded curtly before turning and resuming his way at a quick pace, leaving the two officers rushing to keep up. "Most days, the patient is nearly catatonic. She bathes and dresses, she eats, she sleeps. The rest of the time, she seems to be just staring off into space. She'll answer our questions, depending on the day, but won't really engage in conversation beyond a few words. She avoids any gatherings of the patients, even though interaction with the other residents here at Agnews is something we actively encourage for anyone staying with us."

Danny thought about this a moment. "I bet it doesn't go well when she attends, does it."

Abrams shot him a look before answering. "This is a mental hospital, Commander, and yes, there are risks of incidents when even the most docile patients are placed together. For example, the man you saw just now has progressed significantly since he first arrived. But just like us, our patients have bad days now and then. Their bad days are simply far more pronounced."

"Have you seen progress in Miss Dubinsky?" Danny asked.

"Progress is measured differently with each patient, Commander," Abrams began. "It's simply unreasonable to expect just because one of our patients shows—"

"She's been here twelve weeks and there hasn't been a single indication that her condition is improving, has there, Doctor?" Danny pressed.

Abrams sighed. "We've tried many different therapies to bring her out of her fugue, from hydro to electric-shock to experimental drug treatments. I admit, we haven't had much success," Abrams said as he came to a stop before a secure wooden door in one of the smaller buildings. "These are the residences. Each patient has a small room of his or her own. Maggie isn't a danger to herself, so it will look familiar to you. Shall we?"

Danny nodded, and Abrams rapped on the door. "Maggie! It's Dr. Abrams. You have some guests here to see you. May we come in?"

There was no response, and Abrams produced the keys to the room. "It's unlikely we would have received a reply. Let's go in."

A few jingling keys and several deadbolts later, the three men entered the sunny room. And to Danny's surprise, Abrams was right—it looked more like a hotel room than an asylum or mental hospital or whatever they were calling it these days. There were a nicely made bed and pillow, along with matching dresser, desk, and chair. There were a small closet and a little bathroom, and the décor was California cheery, with lots of peach and mauve colors. A floral throw rug covered most of the tiled floor.

The woman inside, though, was far less welcoming.

Margaret Ann Dubinsky, in Danny's estimation, was on the plain side of pretty, with a broad, sort of flat face and blue eyes. That was probably unfair, though, given what she'd been through. She kept her blond hair straight and parted right down the middle, with very little effort put into it. No makeup, either, and whereas she might've qualified for "curvy" once, she was looking kind of wan and pale. Her cheeks were a little hollow, her eyes a little unfocused and tired. Her clothes were standard-issue white pajamas, though the closet seemed to be stocked with other, more colorful and ladylike options. She was sitting cross-legged on the bed, no shoes.

She didn't acknowledge her visitors whatsoever, just continued staring off into space while the radio at her bedside played some ballad or another.

"Creepy as hell," Anderson muttered, earning a whack on the arm from Danny and a glare from Abrams, who entered the room slowly and made his way to the girl's bedside.

"Maggie, these gentlemen came from the naval base up in Alameda to see you," Abrams said slowly and clearly. "Can you say hello to them?"

Maggie's head turned slowly in their direction, acknowledging their presence for the first time. Danny's eyes met hers, and he was shocked to find just how detached her gaze was. It was as though the girl saw right into his goddamn soul and found nothing there to remark upon.

"You can go ahead and ask questions if you like," Abrams said after a moment of silence. "Perhaps the new stimulus will be useful to her."

Danny and Anderson exchanged glances. Given that Danny outranked the Marine, and it was his idea to come out there in the first place, there was no question who would be providing the stimulus. Anderson extended his hand in the patient's direction, as if to say, "She's all yours, Commander," and retreated to the other side of the small room with Abrams. Danny took a quick breath and pulled up a chair next to the bed.

"Hello, Miss Dubinsky," he began, speaking quietly and leaning forward with his elbows on his knees. "My name's Dan Wallace. I'm with the Navy. Your case came to our attention through, uh, various channels we . . . keep a watch on."

Danny paused. Maggie simply continued staring forward, unmoving. Her breathing was so measured, she could've used it as a metronome. Danny had never really tried to talk to someone this unresponsive before.

"So, Miss Dubinsky," he continued, "I'd like to talk to you about what happened up in Mill Valley. You know, with that student's father. It seemed really . . . out of character. Can you perhaps tell me a bit about what happened?"

Still nothing. The woman's face was utterly blank, her eyes lacking any spark at all. There were photographs with more life in them than this woman, Danny thought as he leaned in closer to her. Time for plan B.

"I have a theory about what happened. I'd like to tell you about it," Danny whispered. "You see, people don't just up and go mad like that. OK, sure, a few do. But I read that father's file. He was a stand-up guy, real pillar of the community: banker, Methodist, Mason. They say he was a rock. Never so much as spanked the kids."

Maggie blinked a few times. Her breathing hitched momentarily.

Danny couldn't help but smile slightly, feeling as though he was getting somewhere, and an idea began to form in his head. "So, what makes a man angry as all that? Sure, nobody likes it when a teacher tells them they're all wrong as parents, but I don't think you did that. And I took a look at the paperwork you prepared for little Johnny there, about how he might've needed extra help because of . . . what's that word? Dyslexia? Some sort of reading thing. Never heard of it, but figure you're up on that sort of thing."

Danny heard Abrams clear his throat a bit. "I'm not sure, Lieutenant Wallace, how this is supposed to help Maggie," the doctor said, somehow sounding both apologetic and defensive in the same friendly-sounding breath.

"Not sure she needs help, Dr. Abrams. Do you, Maggie?" Danny replied, not taking his eyes off her as she began to shift slightly on the bed. "Your student there, Johnny, he just couldn't read very well. You knew he wasn't being lazy or anything—the boy couldn't help it. But maybe the parents didn't see it that way. Maybe they just ignored you, or maybe they thought you were trying to tell them their boy was sick, somehow, or crazy. Either way, they weren't going to do anything. So, what happened then? What made that father go off like that?"

A single tear trailed down Maggie's face. Her hands clenched. Her breathing grew quicker. And she screwed her eyes shut tight.

"I don't know what happened, and you do, Maggie," Danny said. "You can't hide here forever. If you can tell me what happened, maybe I can help you. Maybe together we can . . . oh . . . oh, God."

Danny stopped and clutched at his chest. His muscles suddenly felt like they were constricting, pulling taut, and there was a brief moment when he thought he was having a heart attack. His heart raced and his head swam and panic began to take hold. But there was something more, too—an emptiness inside him, blossoming from deep inside him, as if anything meaningful in his life was somehow wrenched away. Everything around him struck him as immensely sad, from the vase of flowers on the table that would wither and die in days, to his own once-strong hands now trembling before him like leaves. And this woman, Maggie, was the saddest thing of all, her eyes now full of tears that broke his heart over and over again with each drop.

Eyes that were now intensely focused on Danny. And not just full of life again . . . full of sadness. Longing. Fear.

There was a gasping sob behind him, and Danny turned to see Anderson doubled over, his arms wrapped around himself defensively, weeping. Next to him, Dr. Abrams had one hand on the wall, another over his eyes, and his cheeks were wet with tears as well.

Danny slowly turned back to Maggie. "This is what you wanted," she said quietly, tears running down her cheeks. "This is what happened. Is that what you came to see?"

Danny choked off a sob. "Oh, God, I'm so sorry. Yes, this is exactly what I came to see," he cried. "This is exactly what I wondered if you . . . you could do. *You're* doing this. And, oh God, this is how you feel about what happened, isn't it?"

Maggie's gaze was cold, even as more tears escaped her eyes. "This is *exactly* how I feel. Each and every goddamn day. Morning, noon, and night. That boy, that father, those other people—they're dead because of me."

Danny tried to stand but could only stagger backward. He knew, somewhere inside himself, that what he was feeling wasn't real. It was . . . manufactured. And with that came the sense of being separated from his body—that there was the real Danny, now more aware of his surroundings, and then there was the force that was puppeting him around, making him feel so incredibly, hopelessly bereft. He tried to focus past the sadness but simply wasn't strong enough yet to wrest control back from his own emotions. His chair got away from him and he fell on his ass onto the tiled floor. "Maggie, oh, Maggie . . . I'm sorry. So very, very sorry," he said through clenched teeth. "But I have to ask you now . . . please, I beg you, can you . . . can you rein this in? Can you please stop this?"

She looked at him and slowly shook her head, quickly wiping a tear from her face. "You think I can turn this on and off like a light switch? You think I enjoy what's happening right now?"

Danny got onto his knees and put his arms on the bed next to her, as if he were praying for some kind of divine intervention. His mind flashed from thoughts of his mother, his father, and the horror of war and everything that ever made him miserable to the promise that this intensely sad woman had within her. "Maggie, what if we can find out a way to help you? What if . . . what if we can teach you to control it?" he sobbed.

And then, suddenly, the vise on Danny's heart loosened. It didn't go away, but it definitely stopped squeezing so goddamn hard. He still felt sad, foreboding, lonely . . . but there was something else there. Just a thin sliver of hope, enough to begin staving off the darkness a little bit.

Maggie looked at him intently. "How do you plan to do that, sailor boy?" she asked, menace in her voice. "You didn't even know for sure until now what I could do. How are you gonna pull that off?"

Danny straightened up as best he could from his kneeling position before her, his self-control coming back in tiny bits and pieces that he desperately tried to reassemble. "I . . . I don't know. But I can at least give you some hope. I . . . I think I just did. Maybe that's something right there."

Maggie stared hard, but something in her eyes relented just a tiny bit, and Danny felt like he could finally take a breath without holding back a sob. But she wasn't done with him. "I know what I can do. This goddamn curse I have, I know what it can do to people. People *died* because of me. And you . . . you're from the Navy. And the Marine over there. What do you even know about any of this?"

Danny felt a new stirring inside him . . . anger. He could see where arguing with her could escalate quickly. Even as his sadness waned and his temper rose, he clamped down on everything and focused on his answer. "Right now, Maggie, I can't tell you. I don't know exactly what it is, because I don't know the extent of it yet. But right now, we're the only ones who believe you. The only ones who even have a *chance* of helping you. Please. Come with us."

Maggie regarded him for several long seconds, during which Danny's mind cycled through every emotion in the book. Anger . . . fear . . . and hope. How much of that was hers and how much was genuinely his, he couldn't say.

"Fine," she said finally. "Let's go."

TOP SECRET / MAJIC
EYES ONLY
NATIONAL SECURITY INFORMATION

```
**************
* TOP SECRET *
**************
```

CENTRAL INTELLIGENCE GROUP MEMORANDUM

DATE: October 12, 1946
CLASSIFICATION: TOP SECRET
TO: RADM Roscoe Hillenkoetter (USN)
FROM: Detlev Bronk
CC: LCDR Daniel Wallace (USN)
RE: Subject 7-A

Gentlemen,

Under your standing orders, I traveled to Mobile, Ala., to meet with Ellis J. Longstreet, age 34, former owner of Longstreet Automotive Sales and Service. Mr. Longstreet, known to us as Subject-7, was found in a conference room at the county courthouse, where he was the defendant in five different lawsuits relating to the automobiles his business had sold and serviced over the past ten months.

Mr. Longstreet was handling his own defense in these matters because he could no longer pay his attorney—and said attorney, according to Mr. Longstreet, believed his cases were unwinnable. Having identified myself only as an interested party, Mr. Longstreet nonetheless showed me the evidence against him through written reports, photographs and scientific testing. He struck me as very eager—perhaps desperate—for any kind of assistance.

Mr. Longstreet confirmed to me what our intelligence reports had gathered: the nature of the lawsuits against him all concerned certain parts within automobiles sold

or serviced by Mr. Longstreet's establishment that had
proven defective, though none appeared to be the result
of shoddy craftsmanship. Parts of each vehicle—large
or small, no matter—were found to be made of something
completely different than the material they originated
as prior to arriving at Longstreet Automotive. A few
examples are listed below:

- A piston made of coal that exploded within an engine

- An axle made of wood that snapped within a half-mile
  of the dealership

- A rear fender, perfectly shaped, made of the thin-
  nest tin foil

No fewer than thirty parts were found to be defective
in a similar manner, though not all of the instances
resulted in suits; many were caught in time. Of the parts
that remained recognizable after the automobile acci-
dents resulting from their use, they were found to be a
perfect facsimile of the required part in every way—except material composition.

Mr. Longstreet admitted to personally servicing each
of the vehicles in question, as well as the individual
parts, but was unable to provide any logical explanation
for these discrepancies. His only defense in the matter,
which he has stated repeatedly, is that he is the subject
of an elaborate prank by two former Negro employees
whom he had recently fired—claims, I will add, I find
specious based on the evidence at hand. Mr. Longstreet's

personal cultural biases, and his agitation over the day's
proceedings in court.

Following confirmation of the intelligence we received, I
identified myself appropriately and told Mr. Longstreet
our belief that he had undergone a recent Permutation,
and that this alteration was directly responsible for the
material composition manipulations in question. Following
a period of belligerent indignation, which covered both
his dire financial situation as well as his strong belief
that the Negro race is responsible for both his own personal tribulations as well as much of society's general
woes, Mr. Longstreet agreed to join our effort.

Note that I have requisitioned a considerable sum in
order to settle the claims against Mr. Longstreet with
all due haste, along with legal counsel to oversee said
settlements. Mr. Longstreet readily signed the agreement
to undergo United States government training and treatment for an unspecified period of time, and was greatly
relieved to know that he would draw a government salary
of similar compensation to what he insisted he made running a profitable auto repair business.

Of further note: Mr. Longstreet is likely to be among
our more difficult subjects. His Enhancement is among the
more remarkable we have seen to date, but his aggressive
personality and strong discriminatory cultural beliefs
may make him, at best, a frustrating candidate for this

program, and from my brief time in Mobile it was clear
that Mr. Longstreet has developed an unsavory, possibly
untrustworthy, reputation among many in the area. In
particular, I recommend that contact between him and
Subject-3 or Subject-11, should the latter be success-

fully recruited, be minimized as much as possible.

(SIGNED) Detlev Bronk

Roscoe,

You and your people have done a good job identifying these
folks, and your initial training ideas sound fine—grabbing
the Camp X playbook from OSS is a fine idea. But you've
been lucky to intercept these Variants—is that the term
we're using now?—before they've gone public. What happens when someone slips past you? We absolutely have to
brief HST on this, and soon. We need to decide whether
we're going to use these people, and how. Otherwise, we
need to figure out how best to contain or eliminate them.

—J.F.

5.

December 10, 1946

Calvin Hooks dumped bucket after bucket of lampblack into the vat of scalding rubber and chemicals in front of him, careful to avoid the giant metal paddles and blades continuously stirring the mixture. It was impossible to work with the powdery pigment, made from soot, without it getting all over his body, coloring his black skin even blacker and making his overalls look like they'd been hung in the chimney. He'd recently developed a nagging cough—a small miracle that he'd lasted six years at the factory without one—and had finally brought a bandana to work to tie around his nose and mouth, which he found was uncomfortable and cumbersome to work with, but at least his spit had turned a lighter shade. An hour into his shift, the red bandana was already as gray as the short curly hair upon Cal's head.

Every single employee at the Firestone Tire factory in Memphis knew that lampblack duty was reserved for two types of workers: newcomers who didn't know any better than to demand being transferred to a different station, and Negroes.

Cal always got the very worst jobs. And by far the worst companionship on the line.

"Hey, nigger!" called Rudy, whose job was to ensure the proper amount of raw, chemically produced rubber went into the vat. "That there's a pretty bandana you got yourself there. Gonna go rob the corner store on your lunch break? Wouldn't surprise me none."

Cal had his back turned to everyone, but he heard the chuckles behind him. Third shift mixers—the workers who oversaw the "recipe" for proper tire treads—were not a kind bunch, God help them. Cal dreamed one day of making second shift but knew it was only a fantasy. The bosses came by the plant during first or second shift, and Cal had been told in no uncertain terms that they wouldn't take kindly to seeing a Negro on the line. Even one on lamp-black duty.

"I just insulted you!" the young man shouted. "Ain't you gonna do something about it?"

Cal grimaced as he dumped another bucket of soot into the mixer, feeling waves of heat lash his face. Cal was a good six inches taller than Rudy and probably had fifty pounds on him. Years of hard labor—sharecropping since he was a boy, then the factory when the war broke out—had made him strong. There were times when Cal's emotions got the better of him, and even though he was a good Christian, God-fearing man, he'd often imagined walking up to Rudy and laying him out. It would be quick and easy.

But just as fast, he'd be out of a job, beaten to a pulp by every white man in the building, and sent to jail. He thought of his wife, Sally, and his boy, Winston. Cal took extra shifts and overtime to save money so that Winston might one day go to school at Howard or Grambling. His grades were good. They just needed the money. So, Cal kept his head down, minded his own business, and went home after work every shift to remind his son he had to work twice as hard at everything he did, because for a black man, only twice as good would be just as good as a white man.

"I'm gonna pray for you," Cal shouted back as he tossed aside the bucket and reached for another. "This Sunday, I'm gonna pray for you."

He would, too. But Jesus knew full well that it wasn't easy to spare Christian charity for these boys. Not easy at all. He would wrestle with it in his mind as he knelt, and he would have to ask for forgiveness, there in the church, for the evil thoughts of revenge that plagued him. Only then, with his soul laid bare, could Cal find it within himself to pray for men like Rudy.

"Awfully kind of you, boy," Rudy shouted gleefully, his mop of blond hair lightly sprinkled with soot. "Just for that, I'm gonna add more rubber in here and see if we can't get out of here early tonight!"

Cal looked up, alarmed, as he saw Rudy open up the feeder, clumps of raw rubber now flying into the vat. He was accustomed to the occasional prank—hiding the empty lampblack buckets or kicking over full ones and leaving them for Cal to clean up. But adding so much rubber into the vat so quickly was dangerous and mighty stupid, even for an ass like Rudy.

"What the hell you doing, boy?" Cal shouted angrily. "You're gonna cause an overflow!"

Rudy stormed up to Cal, hands clenched at his sides. "What did you call me, nigger?"

"Damn it, look!" Cal shouted, pointing to the feeder. "If you don't shut down the feeder and let me even this out, this whole floor'll be covered in boiling rubber!"

By now, all of the workers in the vicinity of the lampblack vat had stopped working and turned to watch. "Ain't my fault you can't keep up, you lazy, stupid old shit," he sneered, inches from Cal's face.

Christian charity would have to wait.

Cal put a meaty hand on Rudy's shoulder and shoved him aside easily—the boy was really a scarecrow under his overalls—and muscled past two of the others, rushing for the feeder. He shut it down just in time—the superheated chemical stew was just inches from the lip of the vat. And with that, the line alarms went off and the Firestone Tire line slowed to a halt.

"Did you see him lay a hand on me?" Rudy shouted at the white workers around them. "Did you see that nigger put his grimy paws on me like that?"

There were nods of assent and murmurings among the others, and Cal found himself hoping that with the line stopped, the foreman would show up fast to investigate.

Even the furious harangue he was in for was far better than burning alive.

But the boss was nowhere in sight, and Rudy was headed for him quickly, five of his friends right on his tail, likely with a mind to do some harm. Cal adjusted his stance and took a breath—it wouldn't be the first beating he'd dealt with on the line.

The beating never came, though.

His fist raised, Rudy charged toward Cal—and slipped. He turned and twisted, waving his arms like a windmill to keep upright, but there was nothing to grasp.

Except the edge of the vat. And even then, Rudy misjudged it. His boot caught a hose snaked across the ground and he lurched forward uncontrollably, his momentum unstoppable as he slammed into the side of the vat and over the lip, his right arm plunging into the rubber up to the elbow.

Rudy's blood-curdling scream echoed off the walls of the vast factory. He yanked his arm back immediately but the damage had already been done: it was covered in a thick coating of black, superheated pitch, steaming on the outside—and cooking his arm beneath.

The second scream was even worse than the first.

"Oh, Lord! Oh, no! Oh, Lord!" Cal shouted as he lunged for Rudy and caught him as he staggered backward and fell, his arm still held out in front of his saucer-wide eyes. Drops of rubber fell onto Cal's coverall, and the fabric sizzled as the thick liquid quickly ate through it.

"Get the first aid kit!" he yelled at the others, all standing around, staring in shock at what had transpired in the last few seconds. Jesus, but they were young and stupid. "GO GET HELP!" Cal finally bellowed.

They ran off.

"Now, you listen here, Rudy; you stay with me and you stay focused on me, all right?" Cal said, looking down. Rudy shuddered as he drew in deep breaths, sweat pouring down his face. "We're gonna get you help, all right?"

Rudy turned to Cal, looking up at him, his face white as a ghost. "It hurts. Oh, God, it hurts so bad. My arm. Oh, God."

The boy's eyes started to glaze over, and Cal knew that wasn't a good sign. "Come on, now, Rudy. Stay with me here. We're going to get you help."

Cal set the injured man down on the factory floor gently. The boss would be there soon and would be able to help Rudy more than he'd ever be able to. The only thing left to do was wait.

Cal put his hand on the boy's shoulder and prayed.

"Dear God, please let this damn fool live," Cal breathed. "I don't care what he did; I don't care what they gonna do to me here. Just don't let him die. Please, God, don't let him die."

Cal closed his eyes . . . and something was suddenly different. He felt something rise up within his chest, a warmth pulsing in time with his heartbeat. It moved out into his arm, down into his hand . . . and finally into Rudy, the man who called Cal "stupid" and "lazy" and "nigger" over and over, night after night.

Cal grew dizzy and started to feel weak. He took his hand off the boy's shoulder and tried to steady himself, but couldn't find his balance anymore. He collapsed onto the factory floor next to Rudy as his world went dark as lampblack.

* * *

He was in a cell when he awoke.

Cal knew it before he even opened his eyes. The clanging metal, the shouts that echoed from off in the far distance . . . it was all too familiar. Once upon a time, he was a hotheaded kid who got in scrapes almost every day—this was his first time back in quite a while, but he knew he'd never forget that feeling.

Cal's heart sank as he opened his eyes and slowly sat up, swinging his tired, aching legs to the floor, remembering everything that had happened. Those damn white boys probably blamed Cal for the accident. Maybe even said he pushed Rudy toward the vat. Hell, that mob probably claimed they stopped Cal before he threw Rudy into the vat altogether, or . . .

Why the hell were his legs aching so much? And his arms? Cal stretched and found his body tired . . . so damn tired. There had been a time the last year when Cal pulled extra shifts and worked for ten nights straight, then went to church that Sunday morning—and he *still* didn't feel as tired then as he did now.

It didn't matter now—Cal had much bigger problems. There were a few black lawyers in Memphis, but Cal knew he couldn't get any of them to put in the time and effort for a case like this. Not that any jury would spare an honest word in court for a Negro, anyway. At best, he'd probably spend a few months in prison. He'd certainly already lost his job—when he got out, he'd have no choice but to put his head down and look for another one.

Cal ran a tired hand across his face and up over his head and . . . what the hell? He stopped over the top of his head and rubbed a bit.

That bald spot hadn't been there when he'd woke up earlier that afternoon, before his shift. Maybe some of the rubber had splattered when Rudy pulled his arm out . . . but wouldn't his scalp be burned? Didn't feel like it; there was a smooth patch of skin where there was hair yesterday. Or was it yesterday? When did he collapse? What time was it now?

Dear Jesus, what the hell was going on?

By reflex, Cal looked about for a mirror or any kind of reflection, but there was nothing in his cell—just a decrepit sink and toilet in the corner. At least, he thought ruefully, he warranted his own private room. Also on the bright side, he was still wearing the clothes he wore to work under his overalls. No black and white stripes . . . yet.

An hour or two passed, more questions piling up in his head without any real answers, before a guard appeared at the door to his cell. The patch on the man's uniform had the state of Tennessee on it, which only made Cal feel worse—it had to be serious if he was in a state prison. Maybe that damn fool Rudy up and died. So, why was he still in civilian clothes?

"Let's go, Hooks," the guard said. "You got visitors."

Wordlessly, Cal stood—and Lord, it took effort just to walk!—and followed the guard out into the corridor. No other cells were occupied on the entire block, which seemed odd, and there was only a single guard, armed with just a billy club. Cal struggled to keep pace as he followed him down the empty corridor, marveling at the fatigue that dogged every step.

After what seemed like an eternity of walking that left Cal practically wheezing for breath, the guard opened up the door to a conference room and ushered him in. Waiting there were two men—one middle-aged and in a business suit, and, incongruously, another, much younger, with glasses and wearing a military uniform—both of whom were white, as Cal expected. The hat on the table had an anchor on it. The table they were seated at had a pitcher of water on it, some glasses, and a stack of folders with papers inside them.

"Mr. Hooks, please, have a seat," the businessman said, with a smile that Cal wasn't at all expecting. "How are you feeling? Can we get you anything?"

No white man had ever been this polite to him—of that Cal was certain. He didn't know what to make of it, or how he should respond. "I feel . . . fine, I guess. Tired, matter of fact." His eyes settled on the pitcher of water, and the two men across the table followed his gaze.

"Here you go, Mr. Hooks," the Navy man said, pouring a glass and passing it across the table—another unheard-of kindness. "My name is Lieutenant Dan Wallace, and this is Dr. Detlev Bronk. I imagine you're wondering what you're doing here."

Cal took the water with a soft "Thank you" and downed it all in one go. "Sorry, didn't realize how thirsty I was. And yeah, I do have a few questions, if that's all right. How's that boy doing?"

Bronk smiled. "He'll be just fine."

Cal slumped in relief. "Thank Jesus. He lived. I guess he lost the arm?"

The two men traded a look before taking seats across from Cal. "Let's step this back a bit, Mr. Hooks," Bronk said. "When I say fine, I mean that Rudy is perfectly fine. His arm is fine. He's probably getting ready for his next shift at the plant right now."

It took several moments for Cal to get his head around that statement. Finally, he put his elbows on the table and leaned forward. "You mean to tell me . . . now, I saw what I saw. That boy had his arm in a vat of hot rubber up to the elbow. I smelled the meat cooking clean off his bones! Now, Lieutenant Wallace—"

"Please, call me Danny."

"Okay . . . Danny. How the hell do you expect me to believe that he's perfectly fine?"

Danny smiled. "You really don't know, Mr. Hooks? Can you tell us the last thing you remember?"

Cal frowned and looked down at the tabletop to think. "I saw the boy pull his arm out and heard him scream. I rushed over to help him and caught him before he hit the floor. I told the others to go get help. And then . . . then I prayed over him. I got dizzy. And that's it."

"That was two days ago, Mr. Hooks," Bronk said. "And it seems that your prayers were answered."

Cal opened his mouth to argue but caught himself. Was it a miracle? Did Jesus hear his prayer? It seemed sacrilegious to cast doubt so quickly. But did miracles even *happen* anymore?

"And there's something else, Mr. Hooks. *You* were taken to the hospital, not Rudolph Leary," Danny said. "The company sent you to the state hospital, and once the doctors there found you were otherwise healthy, they brought you here at our request."

"Actually, we requested you be kept comfortable, but the state of Tennessee has some curious thinking on that point," Bronk added.

Cal's eyes narrowed and he shook his head. "Hold on just one second, now, please. You said 'otherwise healthy'? What do you mean by that?"

The two men traded another look. "I'm sorry . . . you've only been awake a little while, and I've just realized that

prison cells don't have mirrors." Danny fished around in
his briefcase and pulled out a small grooming kit, where he
fished out a hand mirror. "Take a deep breath, Mr. Hooks,
and stay calm," he added, handing it over to Cal.

There was something deep down in Cal that already
knew, somehow, what he'd see. There, before him, was a
man easily fifteen years older, in his sixties, with a head of
thinning white curly hair and a virtual maze of lines and
furrows across his once-handsome face. His eyes were
sunken a bit more in his head. His cheeks drooped.

"Lord have mercy, I'm an old man," he whispered.

The lieutenant gently took his mirror back. "Well, technically, you're only two days older, but yes, we believe your
body's aging has rapidly accelerated since Rudy Leary was
healed. Now, theoretically, this is only a temporary side
effect, but your Enhancement is a new one, and unfortunately, this will have to be a game of 'wait and see.' We
asked the authorities to monitor you closely but . . . well,
as we discussed, they're less than cooperative and, frankly,
more than a bit skeptical when we told them your real age."

Cal snorted. "They don't care about an old Negro."

"Maybe not, but we most definitely do," Bronk said.
"I know this all must seem bizarre to you right now, but
you've been the recipient of an extraordinary gift, and we'd
like to work with you to figure out how to use it properly."

There was another long pause as Cal digested this. "There
are others like me," he said finally. "Otherwise, you wouldn't
be here. You wouldn't even know what to look for."

Danny smiled. "That's right, Mr. Hooks. You've undergone what we're calling a Permutation, and you're not the
only one. The United States government is interested in
helping you and the others we've found get a handle on it."

Cal leaned back in his chair, exhaling, and ran a hand over
his now-wrinkled face. "I got a wife and a son. I'm the man
of the house. I got to work. I'm saving so my boy can go to
college. I ain't got time for this, frankly. Appreciate it, though,
but family's the most important thing. And I figure Firestone
done let me go, so I gotta find another job now, too."

"Mr. Hooks, we understand completely, and we sympathize," Bronk said. "We spoke with your wife and son this morning to reassure them you were in good health and would be well taken care of. They're worried sick, of course. I'll be sure to let you telephone when we're done here. But think for a moment: What happens if you can't control this ability? What happens if another incident occurs? What if you grow even older? What if it kills you? Mr. Hooks, trust me when I say that accepting our offer is the best thing right now for you and your family."

Danny nodded in agreement. "And if you accept, you'll be a government employee with a fine salary, several times more than you made at Firestone. We can even have the checks sent directly to your house."

Cal eyed the two men warily. "If I agree, I get the feeling I'm gonna have to leave Memphis, leave my family behind."

Both men nodded somberly. "Studying these Enhancements takes resources we just don't have in Memphis," Bronk said. "You would, of course, be entitled to paid leave once you showed you could control your Enhancement to a more acceptable degree. But now, Mr. Hooks, you're a danger to yourself... and to those around you."

Cal thought about it some more, then slowly began to nod. Sure, he'd be gone, but hell ... he worked all night and slept all day, anyway. And taking their offer would mean Winston would go to college like he wanted.

"I'm gonna make that telephone call, and if it's all right with you, I'd like to see all this in writing before I agree to it. That all right with you gentlemen?" Cal asked.

"Absolutely. Whatever you need," Danny said. "We want to help you. You have a rare talent."

Cal smiled a bit at that but shook his head humbly. "I don't know. I just think Jesus heard me. About time, too."

6.

September 17, 1947—Nine Months Later

Lt. Cmdr. Danny Wallace walked across Pennsylvania Avenue at a rapid clip, struggling to keep up with the two men in front of him while juggling their briefcases and paperwork as well as his own. Typical military, to have the guy giving the briefing haul all the stuff for the guys who would take the credit.

Ahead of him, Admiral Roscoe Hillenkoetter chatted amiably with James Forrestal, the United States' very first secretary of defense—apparently, *secretary of war* was too, well, warlike. Hillenkoetter, Danny's old boss from Pac-Fleet intelligence, was now the director of the Central Intelligence Group, successor to the now-defunct Office of Strategic Services and, rumor had it, the foundation of an even larger intelligence agency currently in development.

Danny presented his identification at the White House guard post—Forrestal and Hillenkoetter were senior enough to be waved through on sight—then once again increased his pace to catch back up with his superiors, who hadn't bothered to wait. The two were making small talk as they strolled across the sun-dappled lawn on the way to the West Wing—when suddenly Forrestal stopped and turned to Danny.

"Commander, you rehearsed this like I told you, yes?"

Danny nodded vigorously. "Yes, Mr. Secretary, I'm quite prepared. Notes are all arranged."

Hillenkoetter, dressed in a civilian suit that seemed to hang off his frame, smiled and put his hand on Danny's shoulder. "You're gonna do fine, Wallace. Just think of him as a regular guy. Actually, he's probably the most normal man we've had in there since Lincoln. Easy as pie."

Danny nodded and thanked his former CO, then turned to Forrestal, expecting to hear something similar. But he merely grimaced and kept up his purposeful pace across the lawn. Word at the War Department—er, *Defense* Department— was that Forrestal was as high-strung as they came, and seemed to believe that both budgets and Communists were running high surpluses these days. Not often you see a hawk want to cut military spending, but there you go.

Then again, tensions brewing with the Soviets were shaping up to become anything *but* a normal war. Folks around the office had started calling it a "cold war," which made a lot of sense to Danny. It was better than a "hot" one, he supposed, especially for countries that want atomic bombs at their disposal—and even more destructive weapons in the works.

There was another security checkpoint, but eventually the three men were ushered into the White House's West Wing and walked down a fine, well-appointed hallway, at the end of which was a woman at a desk. She nodded, rose, and opened the door, and ushered the men into . . . an oval office. *The* Oval Office. It was a plaster-walled room with a fine carpet underfoot, some well-appointed couches, and various paintings. There was a model of a jet-engine airplane on a credenza near the bookshelf, and a large portrait of the late President Franklin D. Roosevelt, looking over the room with a gentle smile and a keen eye.

And there, behind a huge, dark wooden desk, was a slight, balding man in spectacles, his feet up, reading a file folder. His suit jacket was tossed over one of the sofas and his bow tie was undone, but Danny could tell his clothes were first-rate. He looked, for all the world, like a successful haberdasher inspecting his latest order.

Of course, Harry S. Truman was arguably the most successful haberdasher in history.

"Ah, there you are, boys!" the President of the United States said as he stood. "Come in! Come in! Rose, let's get some coffee in here for Jim and Roscoe. And . . ." The President stopped and walked over to a shell-shocked Danny. "Harry Truman. You are?"

Danny managed to put down the briefcases and papers on a low coffee table before saluting smartly, then taking the President's hand. "Lieutenant Commander Daniel Wallace, Mr. President. It's an honor, sir."

Truman smirked. "Let's see how you feel about that honor after we're done," he said slyly, motioning Danny to the center of the room. "Roscoe here, in particular, has been saying this is gonna be a barn-burner."

Danny glanced over at Hillenkoetter, who looked amused. Forrestal, meanwhile, stiffened visibly. Danny knew both men understood the gravity of the situation— they just had diametrically opposite opinions on how to deal with it. And that difference, Danny considered as he nervously organized his papers for the countless time, maybe wasn't a bad juxtaposition for a president to have among his top advisors.

Danny handed out three file folders to his audience, each with identical photos and reports. Forrestal and Hillenkoetter had already seen them, of course, but they'd likely want to follow along and answer questions as needed. A young Navy valet came in with a silver tray of coffee and cups, placed it on the table, and left, closing the door behind him with a secure click.

Danny really wanted the coffee, but nobody else went for it, and he certainly wasn't going to be the first. So, he just stared at it sadly for a moment before launching into his report.

"Mr. President, I'm obligated to remind you, as well as Secretary Forrestal and Director Hillenkoetter, that the contents of this briefing, and the papers I've just given you, should not be shared beyond the confines of this room," he began.

Truman's eyebrows rose. "Hell, son, I know *that*. You're in the Oval Office. Get on with it."

His heart racing faster, Danny nodded. "Of course, Mr. President. We wanted to update you on our running inquiry into the anomalous phenomenon in the ruins of Hiroshima, which we first discovered in October 1945. We continue to believe it was a byproduct of the atomic bombing of that city. We continue to receive information indicating a similar phenomenon occurred in Berlin at the same time as the bombing—August 1945—and while these reports are unsubstantiated at the moment, there's enough of them to make us believe that it may be possible that Soviet-occupied East Germany, and thus the Soviet Union, may be developing their own project along similar lines."

"A strange white light is wreaking havoc on the intelligence agencies of the preeminent world powers, and everyone's worried that another country is going to beat them to the punch," Truman said, chuckling grimly. "We figure out exactly what it is yet?"

Hillenkoetter cleared his throat. "Short answer: no, Mr. President. Long answer . . . well, that involves a lot of science and physics and no shortage of new ideas and experiments."

Truman nodded. "But we got it out of Japan?"

"Yes, sir," Danny said. "It took us quite a while, but we figured out a way to transport the phenomenon out of Hiroshima using a system of magnetic and electrical fields."

"And where is it now?" Truman asked, peering over the top of his glasses.

Forrestal answered. "Nevada. There's an old Army Air Corps auxiliary station called Indian Springs. It's near a dried-out lakebed called Groom Lake, about a hundred miles away from pretty much anything. We've been keeping it there on an ad hoc basis, but at this point, we figured we might as well create something more permanent there."

Truman reviewed the map Danny placed in his folder. "Who's in charge of the nearest military installation?"

"We're considering Bob Montague, Mr. President," Hillenkoetter said. "He's nowhere nearby—he's just been put in command of Sandia out by Albuquerque—but we've worked with him on sensitive information before. Plus, he's got the aircraft we'd need to travel to and from the base. I don't see us driving out there a lot. Better to fly, anyway."

"You trust him, Jim?" Truman asked Forrestal.

"I do, Mr. President."

Truman shuffled through his papers. "So, we have an old Army Air Corps base in Nevada under the presumed command of a two-star in Albuquerque," the President said, somewhat amused. "Approved. Now, I know you didn't need my permission for that. So, why are you really here?"

Danny cleared his throat. "The light phenomenon releases minute amounts of energy. Fairly consistently, actually, even though it's in small bursts. Between October 1945 and July of this year, we've recorded at least thirty-two such occurrences. We're able to track them directionally when they do occur, and found up to a dozen aimed at various points around the forty-eight states, as well as other locations in Europe and South America."

"I don't suppose you could be any vaguer, could you?" the President scoffed. "Should I be worried? What kind of energy are we talking about here, Commander?"

"Well, like I said, it's directional, for sure. San Francisco, Memphis, Mobile. We're looking at an unusual mix of non-ionized radiation over an incredibly br—"

Truman held up his hand and cut in. "Now, just wait one minute! 'Radiation'? *A-bomb* radiation?"

"No, Mr. President," Hillenkoetter interjected. "Non-ionized, which means it's not harmful. It's the same kind of radiation that comes from the sun, or radio waves—just really tightly focused. I can get Vannevar Bush in here to brief you up on that if you like, sir."

Truman shook his head, waving them on. "I shouldn't have to tell you how strained our relations are with the Russians. You mention 'radiation' around here and I have a right to be concerned."

"Of course, sir," Danny said. "Moving on, we believe we know what's happened to that directed energy. As you can see in your folder, we believe that energy has actually targeted . . . individuals, throughout the United States. And elsewhere. In fact, we've tracked down and recruited several of them for scientific testing."

Frowning, Truman began to flip quickly through his folder. Danny began to talk, but Truman held up his hand once more to stop him. Hillenkoetter had warned Danny about this—Truman didn't like being talked at when he could just as easily read for himself. He finally arrived at the right section, and his brow furrowed in concentration.

Several long minutes later, the President put his folder down on the table and leaned forward, his hands clasped. "If this were anybody else telling me this, gentlemen, I'd think they were pulling a goddamn joke on me. A strange white light of unknown origins is sending out energy beams and giving people, what . . . superpowers?"

"It's not a joke, sir." Forrestal said. "I know it sounds incredulous, but it's really happening. These people have manifested extraordinary abilities—Enhancements."

"And what exactly do you want to do with 'these people'?" Truman demanded. "Are they US citizens?"

"Most of them," Forrestal said. "Right now, we're keeping them contained, studying them. And expending a lot of energy keeping them off Hoover's radar."

"Good. Make sure that son of a bitch doesn't get his claws anywhere near 'em," Truman said. "But what do we do with them after all that?"

"We want to use them, sir," Hillenkoetter said. "Their enhanced abilities, Mr. President . . . well, they're nothing short of extraordinary. If we can harness their power, we may have something on our hands on the level of another Manhattan Project."

Truman's eyes narrowed. "You want to turn these people into . . . weapons?"

Hillenkoetter shook his head. "No, sir. Assets. They're patriotic Americans, or at least most of them are. If we can work with them, they may be able to help us. If we're really going to have a cold war, then we're going to need a different kind of soldier."

Truman turned to Forrestal. "This doesn't sound like your kind of idea, Jim."

"It's not, Mr. President," the defense secretary replied, leaning back into the plush sofa. "Honestly, the Enhancements these people possess . . . I won't deny that some of them are incredibly powerful. But that's the point. There's been virtually no testing done. We don't even really know what we're dealing with, and very few of these people have a real handle on their capabilities. They are walking liabilities and, under the wrong circumstances, could be profoundly dangerous."

"So, why do I get the feeling you're still in favor of this program?" Truman asked.

Forrestal grimaced. "On the one hand, our national security, I believe, is threatened by the very existence of people like this. Today's cooperative civilian could become tomorrow's criminal—or worse—with powers like these. In fact, you should know, Mr. President, that we have contingency plans in place for every individual we've collected, so that if something goes wrong, we'll be able to—"

Truman held out a forceful hand. "I don't want to know. I assume you'll be able to handle whatever comes up. Move on, Jim."

Forrestal cleared his throat. "Of course, Mr. President. Suffice it to say, I don't fully trust these individuals, and I doubt I ever well. But our intelligence—*good* intelligence from the CIG—indicates that the Reds have their hands on another light . . . thing. Phenomenon. Whatever Wallace here is calling it. As for any individuals affected, we've intercepted some interesting messages between the East Germans and Lavrentiy Beria, Stalin's security chief. Could be unrelated. Or . . ." Forrestal shrugged.

". . . or Stalin may have a line on this like we do," Truman finished. "He's already trying to recreate the A-bomb. What will he do if he gets his hands on people who've been affected like ours have?" Truman closed his eyes momentarily, lost in deep thought. Then he looked over at Danny. "You're the one studying this on the ground, Commander. You know this better than anyone."

"It's still early, Mr. President, but we've been working with them to better control their abilities, with varying degrees of success. Each one of the Variants—that's what we're calling them informally, sir—each one thinks about his or her ability differently. One woman believes she's cursed, another man thinks he has psychic powers, and a third attributes his Enhancement to divine intervention—"

"Are they dangerous?" the President interrupted.

"The more we work with them, the less dangerous they become, sir," Danny said. "The more control over these Enhancements they learn, the less likely it is that their abilities are accidentally triggered at the wrong time."

Truman nodded. "So, we work with them and help them. And then, if they're inclined to cooperate further?"

"We study them," Danny said. "It's important to determine how this happened to them and whether it's preventable, or even reproducible. And if they're willing—they *are* American citizens, after all—we can deploy them as assets."

Forrestal leaned forward. "While this idea has my *conditional* recommendation, based on the cooperation of those involved and a thorough assessment of their conditions, I want to state something very plainly, Mr. President: I strongly recommend that these individuals be detained for the foreseeable future. We simply do not know where this energy has come from, why it has affected these particular individuals, how it will affect them, and whether there is any kind of ulterior agenda behind it all."

This prompted a short bark of a laugh out of Truman, which seemed to surprise everyone else in the room. "Whose agenda, Jim? God's? The devil? Aliens? Stalin?"

Forrestal persisted. "We simply don't know, so I would prefer to assume there *is* one, until such time as we can determine otherwise."

Truman shook his head in slight disbelief. "Well, Jim, that's why I have you here. Now, meantime, I want this thing kept incredibly secret. I shouldn't have to tell you what might happen if the general public, not to mention the Reds, got a whiff of what we were up to."

Hillenkoetter's eyebrows went up. "It's already a top secret operation, Mr. President. Less than fifty people are involved."

"Right, but what we're talking about here is of astronomical . . . I mean, just the . . . plus, I see here you want to recruit one of the PAPERCLIP men, too. Not only are we harboring s-perhumans out in the middle of nowhere in Nevada, but you want to throw a disgraced Nazi into the mix. God help us all if people start poking around that Groom Lake base."

Something suddenly occurred to Danny, and against his better judgment, he cleared his throat and spoke up. "You know, sir, we had that surveillance balloon crash out in Roswell, New Mexico. Caused a bit of a local stink. Someone reported that the Army Air Field there found an alien spacecraft. We were having a good laugh over it, actually, in the office."

"Commander Wallace—" Forrestal began.

"Let the man speak, Jim," Truman said. "What are you suggesting, Commander?"

"Well, sir, it's just that this thing is already unbelievable as is. So, if we bury a little-green-men story at the bottom of all the secrecy, to put it completely over the top, maybe folks will dismiss it out of hand. There might be a few yahoos who'll even take this alien business seriously, and that'll lead them *away* from the Variants. It sounds ridiculous, but it could be enough to provide a legitimate distraction from our actual operations."

Truman was stone-faced for a moment, and Danny realized he'd spoken out of turn and just put forth to the President of the United States a preposterous, potentially career-ending idea.

But then the President began to smile, and he looked over at Hillenkoetter, whose practiced calm was briefly broken with an amused grin, and then to Forrestal, who seemed to be suffering through a migraine. "I like it. What do you say?"

"We can make that happen, Mr. President," Hillenkoetter said.

Truman rose, prompting everyone else to their feet. "Good. I'm going to need to read this over a few more times. I'll be back to you in a few days with a final decision on all this. Thank you, gentlemen."

Pleasantries were exchanged, and Forrestal lingered in the Oval Office to go over other matters, leaving Hillenkoetter to lead Danny outside.

"Christ, Danny . . . *aliens*?"

Danny smiled and relaxed for the first time all day. "Well, if the secretary's right, sir, maybe the little green men really *are* behind it all."

That earned him a laugh from his boss. "All right. How many more to go?"

"Just one more that I know of," Danny said.

October 18, 1947

Brennivín was a beautiful, horrible thing.

Passed off to tourists as a kind of homemade liqueur with birch and licorice flavors, it was marketed as something that little Viking grandparents would have in little glasses before an early bedtime under the Northern Lights.

But among themselves, local Icelanders called it the "Black Death," which was very typical of their dark but good-natured humor. Brennivín went down with all the grace and subtlety of strong vodka.

The fisherman at the bar on Laugavegur Street was already several shots deep by 6 p.m.—although that wasn't particularly noteworthy given that the sun was already down. In the few short months he'd been working on the Reykjavik waterfront, he'd become a regular, and one that his fellow patrons had grown to tolerate. He wasn't from around there, and never would be; Iceland was a small country, and either you were from Iceland, or you'd always be from somewhere else.

It didn't hurt, though, that he had a biting wit, and an eagerness to smooth over ruffled feathers with alcohol. After the Black Death, it just didn't seem all that important, and so the outsider grew to suit many of the locals just fine. They were fishermen and dockworkers, laborers and tradesmen, all hard workers who drank just as hard and smelled vaguely of salt and crud at the end of the day anyway.

A-8

TOP SECRET
EYES ONLY
THE WHITE HOUSE
WASHINGTON

September 24, 1947.

MEMORANDUM FOR THE SECRETARY OF DEFENSE

Dear Secretary Forrestal:

As per our recent conversation on this matter, you are hereby authorized to proceed with all due speed and caution upon your undertaking. Hereafter this matter shall be referred to only as Operation Majestic Twelve.

It continues to be my feeling that any future considerations relative to the ultimate disposition of this matter should rest solely with the Office of the President following appropriate discussions with yourself, Dr. Bush and the Director of Central Intelligence.

Harry Truman

TOP SECRET
EYES ONLY

The fisherman knew where he stood, and he'd worked hard to earn the locals' respect, even if it was a rather begrudging one. So, he was irritated this particular evening when two military men entered the bar. It wasn't the first time the British and Americans had ventured into local establishments like this one, but most saw the woolen-clad fishermen—and the distinct lack of women—and turned right around, or stayed for a single drink if they were feeling particularly polite or brave. It didn't feel like these two were going to do either.

The fishermen slowly lowered his eyes, fixed on the brennivín in front of him. He desperately wanted a beer, but Iceland was a curious and antiquated place; prohibition laws forbade it. Leave it to the descendants of Vikings to outlaw beer but wholeheartedly embrace the stronger stuff.

"Excuse me," came a voice from behind.

The fisherman didn't look up. "*Láttu mig í friði*," he replied, hoping they'd take the hint or at least be confused by the language. None of the Allied troops really bothered to learn Icelandic, anyway.

He could hear the chatter behind him. "You sure about this, Commander?" the stern voice said.

"Yes, sir," a younger man replied. "It's him, all right."

Aw, hell. The fisherman turned around and looked at the two, trying not to register surprise when he noticed the older, lanky fellow had two stars on his collar. "*Ég veit ekki hver þú ert. Þú ert rangur maður. Leyfðu mér að drekka í friði.*"

The younger man—a Navy guy, glasses, nebbish-looking—smiled. "Your Icelandic almost fooled me." He held up a file folder with, presumably, the fisherman's photo in it. "The beard ages you, Lieutenant."

"Fuckin' hell," Frank Lodge grumbled, grabbing his shot glass and downing another Black Death. "I'm discharged fair and square, guys. Medical discharge, in fact. Section 8. So, I don't know what you're looking for or why you think I have it. But you're barking up the wrong tree."

The two-star wasn't having it. "I'm Major General Bob Montague, and this is Commander Dan Wallace. And you know damn well you never really leave the Army, son."

Frank shrugged. "And here I thought the Army left *me*. Got more shock therapy in mind, General? Or did that English shrink come up with something worse? I ain't your guinea pig anymore, fellas."

"You were right all along, Lieutenant," the young guy said. "We didn't understand back then, but we do now. What you reported in Berlin in 1945 . . . all of it was right. We've learned a lot since then."

In a violent, sweeping motion that made the local barflies gasp, Frank rose and grabbed Danny by his pea coat lapels. "Yeah? You believe me now? What about then, when I was fucking crazy and trying to figure out just what the hell I saw? I suppose I'm expected to just forgive and forget? Let bygones be bygones, huh?"

"We can help you, Frank," Danny said, trying to look the angry man directly in the eye—and not do anything to attract any more attention than they already had.

It was several more seconds before Frank finally released him and slumped back into his seat. "Don't need your help," he muttered before turning to the bartender. "*Annan drykk.*"

"Come on, Wallace," Montague said, putting his hand on Danny's shoulder. "I told you this was a waste of time."

Danny took a long, hard look at Frank, and Frank looked right back. Then he shrugged and turned back toward the exit, taking a few steps toward the door. *That was easy*, Frank thought, and had nearly turned back to the bar when Danny stopped in his tracks.

"There *is* just one thing I'd like to know before we leave. Where did you learn Icelandic, Frank?" Danny asked. "Your file says you have no foreign language skills, and yet this is one of the rarest languages in Europe. Sounds like you speak it well."

"Just enough to get drunk," Frank said, giving the kid a sidelong glance. The little prick was on to something. "What's it to you?"

Danny opened the folder. "Over the past two years, you've lived in Ireland, France, Portugal, and now Iceland," he said. "Each time, you've taken on jobs that require working with—and communicating with—the local population. Fine, the Irish speak English OK, but French? Portuguese?"

"Guess I'm a quick study," Frank said, frowning through another swig of brennivín.

"Specialized jobs, too. Takes a lot of know-how to be a good fishing hand," Danny said. "Trust me, I hated basic seamanship at the Academy. But before this, you did construction in France and worked a railroad in Portugal. How does a Harvard man like yourself just happen to have all those trade skills under your belt?"

Frank slammed down the glass. "Why don't you cut the shit and just tell me why you're here, so I can tell you again, a little less polite this time: fuck off, and let me get back to my drinking, all right?"

Montague straightened up taller, looking as if he was restraining himself from punching Frank in the nose. "We're here, *Lieutenant*, to offer you a clean record and a job. I can have that Section 8 changed to an honorable discharge or even a full reinstatement. And you can help us out with a project we have going stateside."

Frank actually laughed at this. "You think an honorable discharge is going to change my mind? I got everything I need right here. Good job, good drink, enough goddamn fermented shark meat to last a lifetime. Why go with you?"

Montague glanced at Danny, who nodded back. "Because we think we know what you're capable of, Mr. Lodge."

"Yeah? What's that?" Frank snorted.

Danny took a deep breath. "When someone dies, you can absorb things from their lives as they . . . depart this world. It happened with that soldier next to you in Berlin—"

"That soldier's name was Mike Petersen," Frank interrupted, suddenly getting very serious. "Mike. Petersen."

"Right," Danny said slowly. "Mike Petersen. His memories, his life experiences, his learned skills, they all transferred to you. This is also how you've picked up all these languages, different trades, isn't it?"

Frank sat silent.

"It's hard on you," Danny ventured.

"It's damn hard," Frank said under his breath.

Danny nodded. "Hard to control, too?"

Frank slumped further on his stool. "I can't even walk by a hospital anymore without getting hit by it, having someone's life flash before my eyes. Sometimes, I can't even focus it. And I can't shut it off."

"We can help," Danny offered. "We're working with others."

For the first time in two years, something clicked inside Frank. "Others?"

"Others. Like you, Frank."

" . . . Berlin. It was Berlin."

Danny opened his mouth to reply but caught a stern look from Montague. "We can talk about all that later. There's . . . well, now, all you need to know is that we can help you. And in return, you can help us out too."

Frank thought hard, the alcohol swimming around in his head, making everything just a little fuzzy around the edges. It'd been a tough couple years . . . so many lives, lost and borrowed. Too many voices in his head to listen to each and every goddamn day. No matter where Frank would run, he couldn't escape them. Not even freezing his balls off in the middle-of-nowhere Iceland. And God, he hated the taste of brennivín.

"Fine. You help me with this, clear my record, and if it's not too shitty a job, I'll help you," Frank spat. "So, what happens now?"

Montague nodded. "Get your things. We're leaving." The general tossed a few *krónur* on the bar and, turning on his heel, strode out of the building, leaving Frank to put on his coat while Danny watched uneasily.

"I said I'm going with you, kid. What more do you want?"

"When it happens, you know . . . does the person dying have to be . . . killed?"

Frank looked at the Navy man with an odd smile. "You're wondering if we're going to have to rub out people so I can practice?"

Danny shrugged. "Surprisingly, it's not the strangest question I've asked over the past couple years."

"I'll bet," Frank said. "And no . . . any old death will do. The violent, sudden ones, though . . . they're tougher, harder to control. But I think I get more out of them."

Danny held out his hand toward the door. "We'll start slow."

"Great," Frank muttered as he ventured out into the brisk, dark Reykjavik afternoon.

PERSONNEL ASSESSMENT

AGENCY: Central Intelligence Agency
PROJECT: Majestic—12
CLASSIFICATION: TOP SECRET—MAJIC EYES ONLY
SPONSOR(S): DCI ADM Roscoe Hillenkoetter USN
ASSESSOR(S): Detlev Bronk, LCDR Daniel Wallace USN
SUBJECT PERSONNEL: 1LT Francis Cabot Lodge, USA
DATE: 29 Nov 1947

Subject—12 (Frank Lodge) has been collected as per project directives, which are as follows:

(1) Collect information on potential rogue Variants, and bring them in for further examination.

(2) Assess Variant, including a thorough, recorded demonstration of subject's enhanced capabilities and limits.

Subject—12 claims to possess the ability to telepathically glean information from the minds of people in the moments before death. This ability to absorb a dying person's memories, which would include facts and information known previously only to the dying subject, also extends to broad knowledge and skill sets such as learned languages, trade skills, and weapons training. Each utilization of Subject—12's Enhancement will be referred to as a Transfer.

In order to prove and quantify Subject—12's abilities, we sought to make the following determinations:

* TOP SECRET *
* * * * * * * * * * * * * *

- The exact moments during a person's death in which
  a Transfer is possible, e.g. the amount of time in
  which Subject-12 has access to information within
  the minds of the deceased.

  The type and nature of the information that may be
  available to Subject-12 during a Transfer.

- Subject-12's ability to control the flow of information available to him during a Transfer, and whether
  a Transfer can be controlled to filter only select
  facts, skills, and/or broad knowledge.

- How long new information is retained by Subject-12
  following the end of the Transfer.

- Any ill effects suffered by Subject-12 in the process
  of a Transfer.

- Whether the circumstances of death—violent, disease,
  old age—have any effect on a Transfer.

EXPERIMENTAL PRAXIS

Subject-12 was sent to Bethesda Naval Hospital in
Bethesda, Maryland, assuming the position of nursing
assistant in the terminal ward for two weeks, from 4
Nov to 18 Nov. Our team worked in an office immediately
adjacent to the ward. The staff were given instructions
to notify Subject-12 and the assessors as to the health
of the patients in their ward on a regular basis, and
to alert them immediately should a patient begin dying.

Subject-12 was present at the deaths of five patients over
the two-week period, individuals ranging from a 19-year-
old Marine Corps private to a 71-year-old former U.S.
Senator. (Biographical information regarding the deceased
may be found in the relevant Appendix to this report.)

In each of the five cases (hereafter named Episodes 1-5),
Subject-12 was able to reach the bedside of the dying
patient in the necessary time needed to proceed with our
evaluations.

Episode 1 was used as a baseline to determine the basic
parameters of Subject-12's Enhancement. We recorded the
beginning and end times of the Transfer, as well as the
amount and type of information Subject-12 could receive
without an active focus. We did not ask Subject-12 to focus
or in any way seek to affect the outcome of the Transfer.

In Episodes 2-5, Subject-12 was asked to focus on four
specific areas during the Transfer: (1) distinct facts or
memories; (2) a particular technical skill; (3) a language;
and (4) a field of study. Other factors—time of death,
length of Enhancement, depth of knowledge gleaned—will
continue to be measured.

EXPERIMENTAL RESULTS

In each of the five Episodes, the Transfer began when the
patient's heart stopped, and continued for a period of

TOP SECRET / MAJIC
EYES ONLY
....
* TOP SECRET *
....

004

two to five minutes following death. There appeared to be some correlation between the age of the deceased and the length of time the Transfer could be active; older patients resulted in longer Transfers with more acquired information.

Without any attempt to control his Enhancement (Episode 1), Subject-12 acquired haphazardly categorized information of varying use. Detailed images and information regarding Greek Orthodox funerals, the location of a safety-deposit box with tattered photos within it, and, according to Subject-12, a newfound skill at billiards, a game with which he claimed to be previously unfamiliar, were all recorded.

When Subject-12 was asked to focus by simple concentration, the results improved considerably and were easier to verify. In Episodes 2-5, Subject-12 acquired the following:

-   The ability to service and repair motor vehicles, verified through an afternoon at a nearby mechanic's garage.

-   A broad and deep knowledge of military history and tactics, roughly equivalent to a master's degree, verified through oral and written testing of the type given at West Point.

....
* TOP SECRET *
....
EYES ONLY TOP SECRET / MAJIC   T52-EXEMPT (E)
EYES ONLY

004

....
* TOP SECRET *
....

- The names and last known addresses of three of
  the deceased's mistresses (which would undoubtedly
  be considered closely guarded personal information),
  verified by personal interviews with the subjects in
  question. (Details from the interviews are available
  in a separate Appendix.)

- Fluency in Russian, verified in conversation with three
  separate native Russian speakers in the Washington
  area, all of whom concurred that Subject–12 spoke
  with an accent closely identified with the Leningrad
  region.

Of the five subjects who died, only one suffered what
could be considered a violent death (automobile accident), while the others lingered from disease or old age.
There does not appear to be any discernible effect on
the quality of the Transfer, no matter the cause of
death.

It is worth noting that some of the above information was supplied by Subject–12 himself and could not
be independently verified—the beginning and duration
of the Transfers, for example. However, the knowledge
Subject–12 demonstrated after each Episode was prodigious, and our team is in agreement that the benefits
of each Transfer manifested themselves too suddenly and
well developed to have been falsified or learned earlier
in Subject–12's life.

Thus far (11 days after the end of our testing), all the
knowledge Subject-12 acquired during the Transfers our
team oversaw has been retained. An ongoing testing regime
will be developed to determine whether there is any
long-term degradation.

SIDE EFFECTS

Unlike other Subjects within the MAJESTIC-12 program,
Subject-12 suffers few significant side effects from the
use of his manifested abilities. The following are conditions that, while considered by our team to be of lesser
importance, should continue to be monitored.

Subject-12 claims that each Transfer exposes him to
the emotional lives of the deceased as they pass away.
Strong feelings of emotion (Subject-12 described vari-
ations of intense fear and regret as well as love and
contentment during our observations) are common during
a Transfer, and violent or sudden deaths carry far more
intensity of emotion. Subject-12 appeared psychologically
affected after each Enhancement, and was reduced to
tears after Episodes 2, 3, and 5. It is difficult to say
whether Subject-12 will experience such intense reac-
tions as he conducts an increasing number of Transfers.
He has experimented with both exercise and sleep regimes
as a coping mechanism, but our recommendation is that
Subject-12 be submitted for specialized psychiatric care.

Secondly, when using the skills gleaned from a Transfer,
Subject—12 claims that he is instructed by the deceased
individual who had the knowledge prior to death. In the
case of the afternoon at the mechanic's shop, Subject—12
said that the deceased "talked him through" the recon-
struction of a vehicle engine; it was akin, he said, to
having someone talk quietly in his ear while observing
his activity from right behind him. Oddly, this does not
occur with regard to language skills; Subject—12 simply
knows how to speak a given language once it is acquired
during a Transfer.

Finally, Subject—12 claims to have heard "whispers" during
the Transfers in Episodes 4 and 5. Subject—12 described
what he heard as similar to "people in a crowded theater
whispering to each other during a bad film." Subject—12
was confident that what he heard was not part of the
life experiences of the deceased in question. "Somewhere
else, beyond" is the extent to which Subject—12 could
speculate as to where he was receiving these additional
stimuli. At this time, we are taking the claim seriously
and will monitor for it in future Transfers, though it
may simply be a side effect of the Transfer process or a
sign of mental fatigue suffered by Subject—12.

CONCLUSION AND RECOMMENDATIONS

Subject—12's skill sets, languages, and knowledge have
all been greatly enhanced by the Transfers he has so
far conducted. He now speaks English, French, Icelandic,
Portuguese, Greek, and Russian. He has learned several
trades, and is likely qualified to teach military theory

to the Corps of Cadets at West Point (as the deceased in Episode 4 had done a few years prior to his death).

Unlike other Variants, the immediate, tactical application of Subject—12's Enhancement would fall within a narrow range. However, his usefulness to the MAJESTIC—12 program may be extraordinary regardless. If the parameters of his Enhancement remain constant, he may become an agent of immense capability and flexibility. The skills and knowledge necessary for any task or assignment could be transferred within his mind in the space of minutes, so long as a suitable individual—similarly skilled, and near death—can be found.

We also remain concerned as to whether there is an upper limit to the amount of memory, skill, and knowledge Subject—12 may carry with him at any particular time. The next phase of our experimentation plan is to determine whether Subject—12 may somehow forget the information gleaned after it is no longer deemed useful—we plan on starting with the Icelandic language, which is only spoken by a bare handful of people and has not been used by Subject—12 since leaving the country. We also plan to develop a variety of memory—enhancing techniques, and are looking into the benefits of meditation and other unconventional practices as well. We now plan to limit Subject—12's Transfers to once every two weeks.

We recommend that near—death individuals with the following skills, talents, and expertise be found and, if possible, transported to Groom Lake under appropriate cover:

* TOP SECRET *
****

- Military abilities, such as advanced marksmanship, handheld weapons combat, advanced unarmed combat, munitions, advanced driving, and aircraft piloting.

- Soviet—sphere languages, as well as Spanish and Arabic.

- Academic knowledge, to include chemistry and medicine, among others.

- Physical abilities of an athletic nature, such as gymnastics and track—and—field.

It is difficult to know how well knowledge of hand—to—hand combat and athletics will transfer to Subject—12 during a death episode. In a worst—case scenario, Subject—12 could receive the know—how but would still need to train extensively to bring his body into shape. It is possible, however, that he may also receive the "muscle memory" and reflexes developed by those with advanced physical skills. Regardless, while Subject—12 appears to be fit from over two years of physical labor, we also recommend he undergo a full, advanced physical training course while at Groom Lake, in addition to his Enhancement testing regime.

ADDENDUM

There is one more potential ability Subject—12's Enhancement may allow him, though it is, at this point, highly theoretical and extraordinarily difficult to test for without losing significantly important assets. This hypothetical ability should be considered highly sensitive information, and should be discussed only in person with the highest levels of MAJESTIC-12 security clearance.

8.

January 12, 1948

The roar of propellers made conversation pointless, even though Maggie really felt like talking to someone. So, she was left looking out the tiny window in the second-rate cargo aircraft she'd been herded onto that morning. She'd gotten notice of her departure only a moment before she actually had to leave, and her few personal effects had been unceremoniously shoved into an olive-drab duffel bag. She'd never really had a chance to unpack them, anyway.

As she looked out over the desert mountains and parched valleys, she wondered—not for the first time—whether she would've been better off back at Agnews. At least in the looney bin she'd been left alone most of the time, and hadn't been transferred around the country every other month. Plus, the plants there smelled nice. The plane, by contrast, smelled of sweat and grease—as did most of the places they took her to.

Since leaving the hospital with Danny, she'd been poked and prodded, tested and retested. She'd undergone countless physical and psychological evaluations and been subjected to mental exercises concocted by military psych guys completely out of their depth. She asked to do something physical to help pass the time, and ended up getting into pretty fit shape. She even completed the basic training course given to Army draftees—solo, of course, because there was no way they were going to let her train with the boys.

Not that they'd bother her once she was done with them.

In fact, she'd dealt with a whole lot of men over the past year and a half. She'd made them cry. She'd made them scared—so scared, several of them pissed their pants and shit themselves. She'd enraged others to the point of animalistic frenzy, and had made more men fall in love with her in a month than all the boys there ever were in her neighborhood growing up. There was one guy she could've sworn she'd even made . . . well, he left the room in a hurry after she let the lust slough off him. At the time, she'd thought it was hilarious. Looking back, it just made her a little sad, and a little scared, too.

Then there was the guy who had a heart attack during an experiment intentionally designed to provoke fear. Thank God he lived, because it had taken all her newfound discipline not to blast anger and sadness and rage on everybody in that goddamn room for putting her through that.

The person in charge of her evaluation turned out not to be Danny but someone named Detlev Bronk—what a name that guy had. Middle-aged, graying scarecrow of a man—not what she'd expected from a government spy. He was the one who had come up with the whole plan to help get her curse under control. She was skeptical at first—how can you control a curse, really? If God or the devil decides to mess with you, what can a bureaucrat in a bad suit do to make it all better, even if he was some kind of pioneer in biophysics?

It turned out that Detlev's big plan was practice. Over and over and over; several times a week, in fact. Sometimes, the people they brought in were volunteers, and sometimes they didn't even know they were part of an experiment—not exactly a surprise she'd wish on anyone, but it was the Army, and she learned pretty quickly that they could do to their soldiers whatever they wanted. So, they would travel from base to base around the country, never staying for more than a few weeks or a month of testing before packing up their things again and heading on to the next one. She'd been to eight different bases since leaving California, enough that eventually they began returning to some of the places they'd first visited to experiment on the same test subjects a second time—she guessed they wanted to see the effect of repeat mind-fucks.

But they were all the same, first-timers or not. She let herself loose, and they folded like a bad hand. There were a few who managed to keep it together, like Danny. Maggie liked the little bookworm, and he came to visit and check on her regularly. There was a sense of compassion about him that her other handlers didn't have. She'd thought about using her Enhancement—that's what he kept calling it, but no matter what silly name the government wanted to give it, she would always think of it as her curse—to get Danny to tell her more about what was going on. But she liked him too much for that. Besides, she'd begun to develop her own rules about how she chose to use her ability, because the US government sure as hell wasn't going to cry foul about ethics. She was a tool for them, and she knew it. She just didn't know exactly *how* they were planning to use her—which was another scary, lonesome thought that would sometimes plague her in the middle of the night.

And even if she felt inclined to get Danny to talk, she knew there would be consequences. When she met with Bronk—or any other people for training or therapy—she was under "remote observation." Most rooms had microphones, and one even had a massive camera that Bronk said was for television (it was the first time she'd ever seen a television camera before). Either way, Maggie was always monitored, twenty-four hours a day, seven days a week. If she tried to use her Enhancement on the guards, or on Bronk, they'd know about it fast—and she had no idea what would happen to her, other than it'd probably be bad. Everything she did, every place she went . . . secrecy and paranoia were right there with her. Sometimes she felt like a prized pupil, but other times she felt like a guinea pig or, worse, some kind of threat.

It made sense, of course, since she guessed she was pretty unique, but . . . it was tiring. All of it. Constantly observed and monitored, keeping her ability reined in when she got depressed or angry or lonely or just hot for company. It was like she couldn't have *any* emotions of her own, because of how dangerous it could be for the people around her.

She did get a nice present for Christmas, though. Over the holidays, they flew her all the way out to an island—probably in the Caribbean, but they never gave her specifics—and set her up in the best little cabana by the beach, stocked with great food, a radio, plenty of books. And they left her there for four days, completely by herself. It was so freeing to just have a good cry, to laugh, to let her guard down and take a walk without being monitored or feeling like she might hurt someone.

Yet at the same time, being completely free on the island only made her "normal" routine—if you could call it that—feel like some kind of captivity by comparison. She was a guest and a prisoner at the same time, and while she was never mistreated, she wasn't free to deviate from the schedules set before her. When she was on the island, she thought about swimming for it, but she figured she'd drown before she reached another island. So, after vacation was up, it was back to work—back to therapy and testing and practice and lots of discipline training. All the while, in the back of her mind, she hoped they'd let her go back there again for a little taste of freedom.

But that wouldn't be anytime soon. Maggie had been at some base in New Mexico for a few weeks. Now she was on a ratty cargo plane heading west—and she wasn't alone. For one, there were two armed guards, both sitting as far away as possible, just out of the demonstrated range of her ability. Of course, she could get up, take two strides, and make them go fetal before they could reach for their guns, but . . . best to let them have their sense of security.

They were still close enough for Maggie to "feel" their emotions, though—a surprising but not unwelcome development as she honed control over her Enhancement. And what was more, when she focused on it, her range was even greater. She could feel the boredom of the pilot, for example, if she concentrated on it, the nervousness of the copilot—probably aiming to please his senior officer—and the weary vigilance of the guards.

And there were others on the plane, much closer to her—her fellow passengers. One was an old black man, dressed in simple clothes, who had kind eyes and two lifetimes' worth of struggle written on his face. He'd been helped aboard by a couple of military policemen who were surprisingly gentle with him, and he sat now with his back against the bulkhead, eyes closed, resting. He seemed content, surprisingly. That was the last thing she expected.

Across from the black man was someone Maggie took to be his polar opposite: a smartly dressed blond young man who fidgeted with his seatbelt straps and paused to glare disdainfully at the black man from time to time. He was all nerves, masked poorly by an insouciant grin and given away by a clenched jaw and bouncing leg. Then again, maybe he just had to go to the bathroom. But his green eyes held none of the serenity of the old man; they shifted and darted, suspiciously taking in everyone on the plane. When they fell on Maggie, she could practically feel him give her the once-over, and the grin that followed sent a shiver up her spine. She was sorely tempted to give him a dose of fear or sadness, but she knew she'd get in serious trouble for that. Too bad.

Finally, there was the man who sat near the back and gazed out the window, a hollow look on his face. He was maybe around thirty, and pretty strong by the look of him. He moved gracefully but purposefully, the kind of movement she'd seen in farmhands and laborers who did their jobs well. His brown hair was cut short, his jaw had a couple days of stubble, and he wore a ratty woolen sweater, dungarees, and work boots. He was smart, though; Maggie could tell. Like the younger, shifty guy, he checked out everyone on the plane when he boarded, but in a dispassionate, analytical way, as if he were calmly gauging each person's strengths and weaknesses to determine if they were a threat. She recognized the look well, because she'd done the same when she boarded. This one was guarded, pure and simple. There were no other emotions with him at the moment—merely alert and ready.

The plane began its descent with little warning, just a dip and a turn that Maggie barely noticed. She looked out her window and saw a massive dried lake bed the color of chalk nestled in one of the gray-brown valleys below. She stuck her face as close as she could get to the glass, looking for any indication of a nearby town or city, but the guards were up now, moving toward them cautiously.

"We need to ask you folks to put these on," the one wearing sergeant's stripes said. He held out pieces of black cloth. Blindfolds. "Security reasons."

Gingerly, the young well-dressed man took one, followed by the old man; the former, Maggie could tell, got a whole lot more nervous, while the old man almost seemed amused. Finally, the big, competent guy took one with a grimace, and while he didn't show it, she could tell he got a case of the nerves too. If Maggie was being honest with herself, the whole thing made her uneasy. Of all the places she'd visited around the country, all the flights she'd taken, blindfolds were an unwelcome first. What could possibly be such a secret?

But nonetheless, she took it and tied it over her eyes. They were shaped like sleep masks, like the kind Maggie's mother used to have, padded and dark. They made it impossible to see, and without her sight, the pitching and bobbing were amplified as the plane made its approach. Maggie took a deep breath and focused her energy on figuring out how close they were to landing. She reached out with her ability, tracing the threads of emotion toward the cockpit, where she felt the pilot perking up and the copilot calming down. Maybe training was overcoming nerves? Or maybe he was just better at landing than taking off. Hard to say.

Then the nose of the plane started to rise, and the gears rumbled as the landing gear was lowered. A dip, a screech, and a pitch forward . . . and they were on the ground. That was all Maggie knew, though she was pretty certain they were near the dried lake bed they saw, because they hadn't gone far enough to land anywhere else amid those mountains.

After a few minutes of rolling down the runway, the door on the side of the plane opened, and she heard boots on metal flooring. "Lady and gentlemen, each of you will be getting a hand. Please keep the blindfolds on until you're told otherwise," said a new voice, a young man who sounded very accustomed to being in charge. "This is for your own safety. Now everybody up! Sooner we move, sooner you get to see again."

Maggie would've bet a dollar he was a Marine officer—but then, she realized, that was purely because of his emotional attitude and nothing concrete. But then, perhaps this ability of hers was concrete enough? Or was she jumping to conclusions? Some days, it was just really hard to tell what was popping into her head from her ability, and what was just an overactive imagination, fueled by equal parts anxiety and boredom.

Maggie stood and waited with her head down. She tried to pinpoint where everyone was on the plane. She could feel the young, shifty man's tension, the old black man's resignation, the big guy's hair-trigger alertness. The cockpit crew and the guards escorting her fellow passengers were mostly bored or otherwise neutral, though there seemed to be a bit of idle curiosity among one or two of them. Made sense, given that none of the passengers would ever be mistaken for regular military. The man she pegged as a Marine, though—he was the one who grabbed her bag and took her arm gently to lead her forward, and he suddenly swung from confident to nervous, almost unreasonably so. He must have known what she was doing there, what she *was*—it was the only possible explanation. *He's scared of me.*

Jumping to conclusions again, she thought. *Not smart.*

They made their way slowly through the plane and down the steps to the ground. There was tarmac underneath her boots—standard Army issue, far more practical than the shoes they originally tried to foist on her—and she was soon guided to a waiting jeep and gently placed in a seat by the still-nervous soldier. The emotional threads belonging to the old man—fatigue, curiosity, bemusement, worry—snaked toward her in gentle, pastel hues from the seat next to her. Her guide took the wheel, and she also felt another person in the jeep as they pulled away—probably a grunt, his emotions steady and generally nonplussed.

Soon, there was warm wind in her hair as the jeep sped off in what felt like a straight line—they had to be doing at least forty miles an hour, and it seemed their final destination was some ways off, as it took about three minutes by her reckoning before the vehicle came to a halt. They were well away from the runway—probably well away from the usual assortment of hangars and outbuildings she'd seen at other air bases.

"You can take those off now," the officer in charge said. She did so and recognized him as the man she'd first met along with Danny at the mental hospital so very long ago. Anderson, his name was, dredged up from memories she wanted to forget from her time there. No wonder he was put out—he probably remembered her *very* well. On the bright side, her hunch was right, and she quietly enjoyed the little victory.

They were at a small cluster of buildings at the end of a very long road—far enough from the landing strip that she could barely make out anything from where they'd come from. The buildings here, though, were pure government prefab, corrugated metal and wood framing and canvas, and they looked pretty new, given the general lack of dirt and dust on them. There was a wood-framed watchtower in the middle of it all, with a couple of soldiers looking at them closely—weapons at the ready, though not aimed.

The layers of barbed wire fence surrounding the little encampment were, she had to admit, less than promising.

Maggie jumped out of the jeep and moved around to the other side to help the old-timer, who already had tried to get out of the car without his escort. He seemed strong enough but still had that uncertainty of movement that came with old age. But he soon stood and took in his surroundings before looking at her with a smile. "Thank you, miss."

"Welcome, Pops." She had to wonder: if this guy was a Variant of some kind, it had better be a pretty impressive ability, because otherwise he wasn't going to be very useful to the government people. Then it struck her, as she took his arm, that maybe she *should* be more nervous than she was. But she wasn't. *Definitely too much time cooped up*, she considered.

The two other passengers from the plane, having arrived in another jeep, were already walking toward one of the smaller buildings, surrounded by a couple of suits and a half-dozen soldiers. Maggie and the old man followed, only to find Danny Wallace waiting for them.

"Good to see you, Maggie," the young officer said with a smile, offering his hand. "Good flight?"

"Depends on where I've landed," she said quietly, keeping her hands to herself and eying him warily. "Where are we?"

Danny turned his extended arm toward the old-timer instead. "Middle of nowhere, Nevada," he replied. "You'll learn more inside. Now, Mr. Hooks, let's take it easy here. How're you feeling?"

The old man smiled and shook hands. "I'm all right, Mr. Wallace. Can't complain. Been building up my strength since our last little test. Feeling better today. But I'll let you nice folks wait on me just the same."

Danny nodded toward the door. "Right inside, then. We'll get started when you're all comfortable."

Maggie held the door for the old man as he shuffled in, then followed as they were ushered into a large room full of chairs and tables—she'd been to enough army bases now to recognize a mess hall when she saw one—that had been turned into an impromptu conference room. The two others from the plane were already sitting there, folders in front of them; the rugged fellow was already leafing

PERSONNEL ASSESSMENT

AGENCY: Central Intelligence Agency
PROJECT: Majestic—12
CLASSIFICATION: TOP SECRET—MAJIC EYES ONLY
SPONSOR(S): DCI ADM Roscoe Hillenkoetter USN
ASSESSOR(S): Detlev Bronk, LCDR Daniel Wallace USN
SUBJECT PERSONNEL: 1LT Francis Cabot Lodge, USA
DATE: 29 Nov 1947

Subject—12 (Frank Lodge) has been collected as per project directives, which are as follows:

(1) Collect information on potential rogue Variants, and bring them in for further examination.

(2) Assess Variant, including a thorough, recorded demonstration of subject's enhanced capabilities and limits.

Subject—12 claims to possess the ability to telepathically glean information from the minds of people in the moments before death. This ability to absorb a dying person's memories, which would include facts and information known previously only to the dying subject, also extends to broad knowledge and skill sets such as learned languages, trade skills, and weapons training. Each utilization of Subject—12's Enhancement will be referred to as a Transfer.

In order to prove and quantify Subject—12's abilities, we sought to make the following determinations:

to the Corps of Cadets at West Point (as the deceased in
Episode 4 had done a few years prior to his death).

Unlike other Variants, the immediate, tactical application
of Subject-12's Enhancement would fall within a narrow
range. However, his usefulness to the MAJESTIC-12 program may be extraordinary regardless. If the parameters
of his Enhancement remain constant, he may become an
agent of immense capability and flexibility. The skills and
knowledge necessary for any task or assignment could be
transferred within his mind in the space of minutes, so
long as a suitable individual—similarly skilled, and near
death—can be found.

We also remain concerned as to whether there is an
upper limit to the amount of memory, skill, and knowledge
Subject-12 may carry with him at any particular time.
The next phase of our experimentation plan is to determine whether Subject-12 may somehow forget the information gleaned after it is no longer deemed useful—we plan
on starting with the Icelandic language, which is only
spoken by a bare handful of people and has not been used
by Subject-12 since leaving the country. We also plan to
develop a variety of memory-enhancing techniques, and
are looking into the benefits of meditation and other
unconventional practices as well. We now plan to limit
Subject-12's Transfers to once every two weeks.

We recommend that near-death individuals with the following skills, talents, and expertise be found and, if
possible, transported to Groom Lake under appropriate
cover:

• TOP SECRET •
TOP SECRET / MAJIC
EYES ONLY
EYES ONLY

T52-EXEMPT (E)

002

* TOP SECRET *
****

- Military abilities, such as advanced marksmanship,
  handheld weapons combat, advanced unarmed combat,
  munitions, advanced driving, and aircraft piloting.

- Soviet-sphere languages, as well as Spanish and
  Arabic.

- Academic knowledge, to include chemistry and medicine, among others.

- Physical abilities of an athletic nature, such as
  gymnastics and track-and-field.

It is difficult to know how well knowledge of hand-to-
hand combat and athletics will transfer to Subject-12
during a death episode. In a worst-case scenario,
Subject-12 could receive the know-how but would still
need to train extensively to bring his body into shape.
It is possible, however, that he may also receive the
"muscle memory" and reflexes developed by those with
advanced physical skills. Regardless, while Subject-12
appears to be fit from over two years of physical labor,
we also recommend he undergo a full, advanced physical
training course while at Groom Lake, in addition to his
Enhancement testing regime.

ADDENDUM

There is one more potential ability Subject-12's
Enhancement may allow him, though it is, at this point,

TOP SECRET / MAJIC

A-4

004

EYES ONLY
. . . .
* TOP SECRET *
. . . .

highly theoretical and extraordinarily difficult to test for without losing significantly important assets. This hypothetical ability should be considered highly sensitive information, and should be discussed only in person with the highest levels of MAJESTIC-12 security clearance.

. . . .
* TOP SECRET *
. . . .
EYES ONLY TOP SECRET / MAJIC   T52-EXEMPT (E)
EYES ONLY

004

through the pages, while the young, shifty one was smiling and shaking hands with the four others inside.

"OK, if we can take our seats here, we'll get going," Danny said, walking toward the front of the room. "General? You want to start us off, sir?"

A man with two stars on his army uniform stood up and nodded at Danny. "Thank you, Commander. Welcome, everyone. My name's General Bob Montague. I hope your trip went well. I know you've all been poked and prodded and tested for quite a while—a year or more in some cases—and your country appreciates your time and cooperation.

"We're moving on to the next phase of our study," the general continued. "You may recognize a couple of the gentlemen at this table. This is Dr. Detlev Bronk," he said, motioning to a silver-haired man in a sharp suit and glasses, who gave them all a smile, "and of course you all know Commander Wallace here."

Maggie looked over at Bronk and gave him a thin smile that he returned in kind, though she could practically see the strands of tension and discipline emanating from him. Such a serious guy. The idea of making him giddy enough to skip and dance briefly crossed her mind, and she had the feeling that it would've been the very first time he'd done either.

Bronk rose from the table with a folder in hand. "You may have already gathered by now that those around you are fellow Variants. Starting more than two years ago, you've each somehow acquired an unusual ability of some kind, an Enhancement—and yes, each one of you has a *different* ability. For the past year, we've been measuring the extent of your abilities and the control you have over them. That was phase one of our study. Phase two is much more experimental. We're putting the four of you together to see how your abilities interact with one another's. Through this, we're hoping that we'll learn more about what you can do and more about the source of these Enhancements."

"You mean you don't know?" the rugged man said. "All this time, you still haven't figured it out?"

Bronk frowned. "Never said that, Mr. Lodge. At the moment, any information about the source of Variants and Enhancement has to remain classified, though, yes, studying you in action will certainly add to our understanding. We're also hoping to step up the training you've received so that you can better use your abilities on behalf of your country."

At this, the younger man smirked and laughed. "All well and good," he said with a genteel Southern accent. "But what if, after all this time, we decide we have our abilities well in hand and don't want to play anymore? I got a wife and kids, Dr. Bronk. I sure would like to go see 'em."

"And we will make arrangements for that, Mr. Longstreet," Bronk replied tersely. "As for your voluntary participation, I need not remind you of the expense and effort the United States government has already invested in each of you. The men who graduate from West Point or Annapolis are required to spend four years in the military, at minimum, as recompense for their education. The agreement you all signed stipulated a similar length of service, commensurate with the time and study you've received. In your case, you would be free to leave in approximately sixteen months—and, I should add, you would be given no further training in the application of your Enhancement. Plus, you would have to compensate the United States government for the assistance we've rendered you thus far. Are we clear, sir?"

The man named Longstreet frowned and slumped back in his chair, silent.

Bronk smiled slightly at this, then addressed all of them once more. "You are all, of course, United States citizens, with all of the rights *and* responsibilities that come with that privilege. You have abilities, yes, but we've seen how dangerous they can be. We must approve each of you, individually, before you are allowed to leave this facility, and will only do so once the training regimen we've given you has satisfied us that you have enough control so as to not harm the people around you. And yes, you've all signed agreements to serve your country after your training and evaluation is complete, and we are paying you generously in the interim. Your country is trying to help you, and we expect you to do the same for your country. Any other questions before we get started on the briefing?"

The old black man raised his hand, earning him a scowl from the Southerner. "Yes, sir, if I may. First, I want to thank you again for allowing me regular calls with my wife and son, and for the salary you've given me. My boy's been accepted to Grambling, and I'm mighty grateful to you that we can afford to send him."

"Congratulations, Mr. Hooks!" Bronk said, favoring him with a genuine smile. "That's fine news indeed. Now, what's your question?"

To Maggie's surprise, she could feel waves of disgust and anger peeling off of that Longstreet man, despite his placid demeanor. She'd read about attitudes in the South, but feeling it so . . . viscerally . . . was a horrible thing and would only be worse if it had been directed at her.

The black man, however, continued. "Can you tell us exactly where we are?"

The question hung in the room for several moments before Montague answered. "Your exact location is highly classified. In fact, only about two hundred people know this installation exists, and only thirty-five know the extent of what we're doing here, including everyone in this room. All you need to know is that we're at a former US Army Air Force Auxiliary facility. The Atomic Energy Commission mapped this area out last year, and we're using their designation for it in our official communications.

"You're at a place called Area 51, the operational base for a project called MAJESTIC-12. And if you ever say either of those things out loud to anybody not in this room," Montague said simply, "you'll be arrested for treason and shot.

"Now let's get started."

Maggie looked around as everyone else opened up the folders on the tables in front of them. Lodge, Longstreet,

Hooks . . . they were just like her. Variants. Different, but still very much everyday people in their concerns and desires. Love of family, worry about money, wanting to know what the heck had happened to them. All perfectly normal.

Except that it wasn't. And despite what Bronk had said, there wasn't going to be a normal, she felt. Ever again.

With a sigh, she opened the folder in front of her and began reading a letter from Harry S. Truman.

9.

January 23, 1948

Life without booze was surprisingly OK.

Frank Lodge hoofed it through the last stretch of his five-mile run at a steady pace, leaving his compatriots in the dust—literally, as the whole Indian Springs complex was covered in a fine film of khaki-colored sand. Well, at least the parts he was allowed to see.

After their initial MAJESTIC-12 briefing, the four "Variants"—what an anemic name that was!—settled into their new digs. Everyone had their own small quarters separate both from each other and from the rest of the base. That large mess hall area was used for meetings and meals, which they shared with about twenty-five other base personnel, including their personal physical trainer, a Marine captain named Anderson with piercing blue eyes, a blond buzz cut that could serve as a carpenter's level, and a voice that could shake mountains. There was also a cook named Smitty and a sorry-ass Air Force grunt who basically did all the shit jobs and whose name nobody bothered to learn.

The rest were Air Force military police, guarding the little complex as if it were a prison. Hell, maybe it was.

Frank fit in pretty well, of course, given that he was the only Variant with any extensive wartime experience. But that also meant he continued to build his situational awareness each and every day, getting the lay of the land, looking for patterns, and evaluating everyone he came in contact with. And whatever he missed, deceased general Sam Davis's voice would kick in to add pertinent information.

Their little encampment at Area 51, set at least a couple miles from the landing strip and, presumably, the main base, was comfortable, but there was no mistaking it—it was a prison. There were two guards on a mobile patrol around the small cluster of buildings, which were surrounded by a barbed wire perimeter fence eight feet high. There was a watchtower on top of the guards' barracks, with solid sightlines over the entire base, always staffed by at least one MP. At night, the fence was pretty well lit with a series of lamps atop high posts. There was a single gate into the complex, with a third guard posted by it 24/7. That meant there were four MPs on duty at any one time, with at least twelve others ready to go at a moment's notice.

It had only been a few weeks, but at least a quarter of the guards had already rotated out, their replacements ushered in by jeep from elsewhere at Area 51. Every day, a small group of white-coated civilians and mid-level military officers would come to observe or assist in training—both physical and otherwise.

The first order of business was to whip the Variants into shape physically. There was a lot of running, a lot of push-ups and jumping jacks, even some dumbbells (the weights, not the MPs) in a small, makeshift gymnasium. Anderson seemed to go at Ellis the hardest, as he was the youngest and seemingly the least accustomed to physical exertion, protests about his college football days notwithstanding. Anderson didn't cut Maggie a lot of slack, either, but Frank had to admit, the girl was keeping up well with the boys. As for the old man, Cal, they were taking it pretty easy on him—understandably, since his Enhancement wasn't too kind to his physical well-being. Yet even though he could have used his long recovery as an excuse to get out of training exercises, Cal still insisted on working as hard as he could. When Frank asked him about it, he just smiled and said, "Twice as good, just as good."

Aside from the physical exercise, the Variants underwent daily individual testing specifically related to their unique Enhancement, usually with some sort of pencil-necked science guy and an officer. Danny Wallace rotated through regularly, keeping tabs on things—Frank had him pegged as the one who designed the Enhancement testing and training, though he really didn't know what had qualified him to do that, because who the hell would even have insights into this kind of thing? The more time he spent around him, the more it felt like the Navy guy was really playing it by ear, though it was pretty obvious the kid was smart.

Anderson was not only in charge of the physical training but had promised a thorough course in covert action and spycraft. On their first full day at Area 51, he'd gathered them in the mess hall for an introduction—he was former OSS, had worked with the Reds in Greece and the Balkans during the war—and a warning.

"This isn't going to be like anything you've done before," he said, staring coldly at each of them in turn. "Not even you, Lodge, with your experience. You're going to make split decisions, lie your ass off, and kill people who may not deserve it. You're going to make tough calls, and worse, you're going to have to live with them. Now let's get started."

And then suddenly, a guy in civvies burst into the room, followed by two MPs. The civilian raised a gun, and Frank immediately hit the deck, grabbing Maggie's arm and pulling her down with him. The guy traded a few shots with the MPs across the mess hall, then dashed out the back, the soldiers in hot pursuit.

When Frank looked up to see Anderson unsuccessfully trying to stifle a smile, he knew he'd been had.

"Everybody come get a pencil and paper," Anderson ordered. "You are to write down every detail you can think of about what just happened, from the descriptions of the individuals to their individual actions. You have twenty minutes."

As it happened, Ellis Longstreet recalled the most, followed by Cal; to Frank's embarrassment, he'd done the worst, but consoled himself by noting he'd been the only one with the foresight to hit the deck when the bullets flew. Turns out it was an old OSS training exercise used at Camp X, the Canadian outpost used by the Americans, English, and Canadians to train their spies.

With the focus on physical education and Enhancement testing, they hadn't gotten back to spycraft again, but Frank had to admit that he was looking forward to it—if nothing else, it could help him figure out the rest of Area 51's secrets.

The Camp X exercise provided a kind of instant bond between the Variants; Frank had seen it during the war, how new soldiers would quickly and suddenly bond after their first firefight. From the first night's how-do-you-dos over Army-standard grub, it hadn't taken them more than a week to begin sharing everything else about themselves. They were, after all, Variants—different from everyone else by definition. Two weeks in, they were already talking about their abilities and testing, and to Frank's surprise, nobody seemed to mind—odd, given the secrecy all around them—though they were always under the watchful eyes of at least two MPs during training and meals. Maybe MAJESTIC-12 saw the four as a team already, and wanted them to get along. Maybe it was an oversight on Danny's part. But either way, Frank knew it would be valuable, and encouraged the information sharing, especially about their abilities.

Maggie was working to fine-tune her ability; she remained pretty heavy-handed in manipulating emotions. She described one test where she had been charged with making a test subject—the scientist monitoring her, in fact—slightly nervous. She laughed as she described the man pissing himself—so much for subtlety. Frank laughed too—but he noticed the edge in her eyes and wondered if she was enjoying herself a bit too much.

Ellis's weakness was turning his ability off when he didn't want to use it. Occasionally, he'd pick something up—a salt shaker on the mess table, or a jump rope in training—and it would turn into water or stone. He was making progress, though, and on a few occasions had actually succeeded in making the end result something he actually wanted, like turning a stone into soft clay. Frank knew that would be a handy thing to have going, if Ellis could get a grip on it. *If* was the keyword there—there were still too many spontaneous manifestations to really trust him, and Frank wondered how that would go over in the field. What if Ellis's gun turned to butter in the middle of a firefight?

Cal was a different story. He was on a pretty strict regimen of *not* healing people, but they were busy drawing up plans for him for when he got stronger. To hear Cal tell it, he needed to figure out how to expend just *enough* of his own health to heal someone else without suffering too much damage himself. He had to differentiate between healing a cut and a bullet wound. Not that anybody was shooting anyone at Area 51—the day-one exercise had used blanks. They were also busy codifying Cal's recovery rate, to determine how long it would take for him to get his strength back, depending on how much he healed.

For his own part, Frank's mental training was fine—they had him doing memory games and number puzzles to keep him sharp, which was a perfectly decent way to spend the afternoon. Trying to mine his past experiences was something else entirely. They gathered a lot of information on the folks who died around him and tried to test him on it—who was so-and-so's brother, where did this guy go to school, what color was her favorite dress. Try as he might, he never had answers to those specific questions unless he had specifically focused on it during the . . . transfer, for want of a better word. Transfer of memories. Of lives.

He'd been able to choose what memories and talents to take the last few times before he came to Area 51. But it seemed that he wasn't getting any more information than the specific topics he chose. And when he didn't choose, he just got random stuff. Maybe it was what the deceased wanted to be remembered for, or what was on their mind in their last moments—or even what they wanted to give him. He had no idea, really, how it worked. And he accessed the memories not as his own but as if the deceased who had the memories or talents were there with him, speaking right in his ear, telling him what to do or drawing his attention to a specific matter.

So, when he'd train on his individual talents—engaging in tactical simulations, fixing a car, et cetera—Frank could hear them whispering. *The left flank is vulnerable. That crankshaft is bent. Put pressure on the wound before you do anything else.*

There were now ten people in his head . . . and counting. The scientists were monitoring hospitals in Nevada and Arizona for more potential "test subjects," and they had a small plane standing by to rush him to some poor sap's bedside if the opportunity arose. He'd been excited at the prospect at first, until Anderson told him he'd be blind-folded and earplugged each time he left the base and until they landed or arrived at their destination. Whatever they had going on at the rest of Area 51, Frank definitely wasn't cleared for it.

He'd taken to writing down details of the individuals he transferred, keeping them in a little book. Frank had been able to get some biographical details and would occasionally try to engage them in conversation. That didn't work, though; the voices would only tell him about the skills or memories he'd focused on during the transfer. But Frank thought it was important to try anyway. Just as he once felt responsible for his squad, he now felt a certain duty to the memory of the people he'd sat with as they died.

There were definitely days Frank wished he had a different Enhancement. Most days, in fact. At least the exercise and the memory games helped Frank clear his head and focus on himself rather than the dead.

The others really didn't see their abilities as burdens, from what Frank could tell. Ellis, in particular, loved the thought of being a superhero, which Frank took as evidence that Ellis needed to stay away from the Sunday funnies for a while. Cal saw his as a blessing from God, and it wasn't for Frank to say whether he was right or wrong there. Maggie seemed to be resigned to the whole thing, though she admitted that she didn't see it as a curse the way she used to. She even seemed mildly amused by it occasionally.

Frank had been out of the Army a while, but despite his best, selfish intentions, he caught himself thinking of the others as "his" team. Maybe that was the point, maybe that was exactly what Danny was banking on, but for whatever reason, he had a kind of paternal thing going. It was annoying, frankly, but he figured he'd better at least keep an eye on the others, since he was the only one with any real military experience.

Overall, the Variants were well treated, except if Anderson felt they were slacking in training, of course. Then it was an extra set of push-ups or a lap around the inside perimeter—a mile-long perimeter, conveniently enough. And every now and then, Frank would catch Anderson looking at one of them in a funny way. What did he think of them? What did anyone think of them? Hard to say. He wasn't even sure these days what to think of himself.

Frank's thoughts snapped back to the run as he lapped Cal, who was taking it at a walk. Without brennivín, Beaujolais, or beer, the training was the only mood-altering substance he could manage, but he had to admit, it felt good. He stopped at the finish line and turned to find Maggie less than twenty-five yards away. "Not bad," he said after she finished.

She bent over at the waist and worked to catch her breath. "We better be ready if and when they call us up."

"My gut says that'll be happening sooner rather than later," he said quietly. "My quarters, 1900 hours. Tell Ellis; I'll tell Cal."

Maggie gave him a quizzical look and grinned mischievously. "Sounds like you're plotting an unsanctioned meeting."

Frank shrugged. "They want us to be spies? Let's be spies. Don't everyone show up all at once—stagger it so the guards just think you're going for a walk." He jogged off before she could reply, knowing he already had her.

Sure as shit, everyone showed up starting a few minutes before seven. Frank ushered each of them into his small quarters—a twelve-by-twelve with a bunk, a desk, a chair, and a dresser—and offered them seats. Cal was given the chair for his old bones, leaving Maggie and Ellis to perch on the bed while Frank leaned against the back of the door. The room was lit with an overhead bulb and a little lamp on the table, leaving much of the room bathed in the dusky, slightly ominous light of the sunset coming through the window.

It seemed fitting.

"So we're all briefed up," Frank began. "They want us to be useful to the military, to this new Central Intelligence Agency. It's all top secret; that's what they keep saying. Anybody curious about knowing more?"

Maggie nodded. Ellis looked a little suspicious. But Cal spoke up first. "What's there to know, Mr. Lodge? They're training us, helping us with our Enhancements. Miracles, I say. Anyway, they're training us and taking good care of us. And we get to help our country."

"I told you, Cal, call me Frank."

Cal chuckled and put his hands up, as if to say he gave up. "Southern manners. Been with me so long that they've turned into a hard habit to break."

"Well, you're right; we could be getting treated a lot worse," Frank continued. "But this is a big valley, and when the air's clear and the light's right, I can see a couple other outposts along the lakebed. There's a big one in the center. Seems like there's at least one big building there, maybe a hangar or something. What's in there? What do they have going? And I think there's another smaller base further north and west, but it's hard to tell. I'd love to get some binoculars."

Maggie nodded again. "I can get those," she said. "Maybe get a guard to lend me his."

"How you gonna do that, if I may?" Ellis drawled. "You gonna make the poor boy piss himself again?"

She just smirked. "Believe it or not, I don't need this thing in my head to bat my eyelashes at a guy. I'm probably the only woman in a hundred miles of here."

"Good. Let's keep this short before we get a knock on the door here," Frank said. "Maggie gets some binoculars, hopefully to keep a while. Ellis, I heard you talking about poker with Smitty the other day, yeah?"

"Sure. I've played a little," Ellis said with a shrug. "What of it?"

"Get a game going. I can spot you some money if you need it. I want you to make some friends and see what slips out over cards."

"All right, then. I suppose I can do that. Can't hurt to see if these fine young men have any cash to part with." Ellis grinned.

Frank turned to Cal. "This is voluntary, Cal. I don't want you to do anything you're uncomfortable with."

Cal just smiled. "Well, I admit you got my curiosity up, Mr. Lodge. What you got in mind?"

"Same thing, just with the medics and the folks taking care of you. You're an old man these days, so use some of that grandpa charm and see what they tell you," Frank said. "That goes for all of us, but some of us are more charming than others."

Cal nodded. "I can do that. You know, when they had me in yesterday, Danny told me they got a hospital around here. I figure it's where you're talking about—the main base, I guess? He says when I'm strong enough again, they gonna take me up there for a healing so they can watch me close-up. I'll keep my eyes open when that happens. Let y'all know what I see."

Frank nodded. "Good man." He then turned to the rest of them. "Look, they're paying us well. They're helping us learn about what we can do. But I know there's more to this than they're letting on, and I know you all have had the same thoughts. We still don't know why we have these abilities or where they come from. That's the kind of information I'd like to have, wouldn't you?"

There were general murmurs of agreement, and with that, Frank let them out. Ellis was the last one to leave, and he stopped at the door with an odd look on his face.

"Frank, I gotta say, this is a helluva lot more than I bargained for, all this business. There are days I just want to go home, see my wife and kids, get back to normal, you know?"

Frank nodded, feeling a twinge of sympathy and regret. "I know, Ellis."

"So, what happens if they find out we're spying on them? Or worse, what if all this training is for some nasty business we don't want to get involved in? What happens if we find out exactly what's going on . . . and then wish we hadn't?"

"I don't know."

Ellis looked at Frank a moment longer, then shrugged. "All right. I'm with you, but I don't understand why you're bringing Cal Hooks into this."

"Come again?" Frank asked, though he already sort of knew where this would go.

Ellis gave Frank the pained smile of someone who had explained himself many times over. "Look, where you're from up north, I understand that you may see some things differently than me, and that's fine. But trust me when I tell you, Frank, that boy can't handle something complex as all this. My Negroes, when I had 'em working for me down at my garage, they could barely handle simple instruction. They're children, Frank. Not that bright. Asking him to do this spy stuff, well, it goes against the nature of things."

"Ellis—" Frank began, but was quickly cut off with a wave from Ellis.

"I know, I know. I ain't gonna convince you. You just ain't seen what I have. No experience with it, and that's fine. I'm just trying to help. Cal is too *simple*. Either the MAJESTIC folks will figure that out and send him home, or he'll spill on what you're trying to do here, figuring out what's going on. So, I'm just saying, you'd best keep an eye on him, that's all."

Frank simply shook his head sadly. He'd been at the Battle of the Bulge in Belgium and the Ardennes during the war, and saw the men of the 333rd Field Artillery Battalion remain in position in the face of withering enemy fire to support the 106th Infantry. The battle had been lost that day, but the sacrifice of the 333rd made it possible to eventually take back that position and advance on Germany.

Weeks later, when that little spit of Belgium was reclaimed, Frank saw the bodies of eleven men of the 333rd outside the village of Wereth. They were tortured and massacred by the Nazis. The Wereth 11, like the rest of their battalion, were black, and they died horribly *because* they were black. Frank would never again accept "the nature of things" after seeing that.

"Don't worry, Ellis," he said simply. "I know who to keep an eye on."

10.

January 19, 1948

Maggie stared idly at the man seated across the table from her, a youngish, tweedy fellow with horn-rimmed glasses, slicked-back hair, and a weak chin, wearing a white lab coat. She could sense mild impatience and slight boredom from him as he fidgeted with a pen and leaned back in his chair.

"Commander Wallace," the man said with a Boston accent, "when are we starting this up? I have to get back to check on something I have running."

"We just needed to establish a baseline, Doctor," Danny said. "Wanted to make sure you have a clear head."

Behind Danny, a tall, reedy man in Navy whites—and a couple of stars on his shoulder boards—waited with arms folded, scowling slightly, and a Navy corpsman stood ready next to him with a first aid kit. At the door, one of the MPs stood guard. Maggie favored him with a slight smile, which he returned with all the subtlety an Air Force airman barely out of his teens could muster. Roger—the guard's name was Roger Fitton—was smitten with her, of course. She hadn't even needed her Enhancement to convince him to lend her his binoculars, which now sat locked away in her quarters.

"So, what are we going for today?" Maggie asked Danny.

"Well, it's not strictly an emotion, but I was thinking maybe we'd try *sleepy*," Danny replied. "Let's see if there's some kind of connectivity there between an emotional state and physical exhaustion."

The scientist frowned, not having been briefed on the specifics of today's testing. "What?"

Maggie held out her hand slightly. "Hush, now," she said, focusing her ability to calm the alarms going off in his brain. A moment later, the scientist sat back in his chair again, at ease, and Maggie congratulated herself silently for her control. "Commander, I can calm someone. Like I just did here. But sleep?"

Danny merely shrugged. "It's a reach. See how calm you can get him, for starters."

Scowling slightly, Maggie turned back to the man across the table, who was firmly disinterested in pretty much anything going on at that moment. Normally, she drew upon her own emotional experiences to find the right thread in someone else. She would visualize her own emotional thread and entwine it with the other person's moods, then coax the color she associated with that emotion to overtake the others. In this case, she would use the deep blue of mellow disinterest to slowly overcome the yellow-green of the man's annoyance.

"All right, buddy. Let's make you calm," Maggie said, realizing from the look the two-star gave her that she may have sounded like a pet owner addressing a dog. And there were days it felt like that.

The man behind the table shrugged. "I'm already feeling pretty calm."

Not yet, you're not. Maggie closed her eyes slightly and tried to think of nothing but the serene calm she occasionally felt right before sleep, and fixed that feeling in her mind's eye. She could see it, could practically reach out and cup that feeling in her hands, like a tennis ball of midnight-blue energy that hummed inside her head.

Then, gently—because, hey, this had to be calm—she let that energy snake off toward the man across the table. If the feeling were more extreme, she'd pretty much shove it up his nose. But not today. *Calm.*

She opened her eyes to see her test subject still sitting there, eyes half-lidded, smiling slightly. Maggie breathed in slowly, concentrating on keeping his emotions stable. "I think . . . well, he's really calm. Not sleepy, but . . ." She smiled slightly. "Hey, can you lend me five bucks?" she asked him in a gentle voice.

"Don't have my wallet with me," the man mumbled in reply.

Right. Something else. "You have really nice ears. Can I see 'em?" she asked.

The man's eyebrows twitched slightly, prompting Maggie to caress his emotions once more. "Sure, I guess," he mumbled.

Maggie stood and walked toward the other end of the table. She took one of the man's ears—admittedly, they were kind of large—and tugged slightly. Under her emotional guidance, he had no reaction. She gave it a harder tug, prompting his neck to bend a bit, but the scientist was still too mellow to react with anything other than a very slight wince.

A few moments later, Maggie was actively flicking the man's ears, pinching his nose, and mussing his hair. She reached inside his jacket pocket and produced his wallet, removing the ten dollars inside and placing it back in his coat. All the while, the man was still in his half-lidded, day-dream state.

"Why didn't he give you the five bucks?" the two-star asked.

Maggie shrugged. "It's emotional control, not hypnosis. If he doesn't want to give me the money, I can't actively make him do it when all I'm projecting is calm. Heck, he even lied about having his wallet. If I wanted him to love me, or fear me, then he'd be more *inclined* to give me the money. But I can't *make* him do anything except feel."

Danny waved a hand in front of the scientist's face and watched as the test subject's eyes idly tracked the movement. "He's still awake, but this is pretty good. How much effort is this for you?"

"It varies," she replied. "Peaked a bit when I took his wallet, because that's going against his self-interest. Remember, he didn't want to give me money, but I can tamp down the desire to get it back, to the point where he doesn't care."

Danny looked over to the two-star, who nodded and asked, "What would happen if I punched him?"

"I'm not sure," Maggie replied. "Let's find out."

And with that, she reached out and slapped the scientist hard across the face.

His eyes widened a moment, but Maggie stared down at him intently, and all he did was shift slightly in his chair before settling back down. There were red finger marks on his cheek—she hadn't held back.

"Christ, Maggie," Danny breathed. "We talked about this."

"That sounded like a direct order to me, Dann—I mean, Commander," she replied quietly.

"Airman, I think we're finished here. Can you please escort our friend here back to where he belongs?" Danny ordered. The guard gently brought the man to his feet, and Maggie began to let his emotions slide back to him. A few moments later, by the time the man got to the door, he turned around and fixed Maggie with a stare that was half anger, half bewilderment.

"Where's my ten dollars?" he demanded.

Maggie smiled and handed him the folded bill. "No hard feelings," she said, fixing him with her best embarrassed smile.

The scientist snatched it from her fingers and rubbed his face as he was led out.

"Miss Dubinsky," the two-star asked, "when you're affecting someone's emotions, how do *you* feel?"

Her brow furrowed at this. "I'm not sure I understand the question, Admiral," she replied. He was Navy and had stars, so *admiral* seemed appropriate.

"Well, you're manipulating the emotions of another person—and doing a bang-up job of it, I'd say. But how do you feel when you do that? You're playing with someone's feelings. Like clay."

Maggie thought a moment, then shrugged. She didn't think the admiral really wanted an honest answer, and couldn't think of a good reason to give him one. "I don't know, sir. I'm not sure I feel anything."

* * *

Roscoe Hillenkoetter didn't exactly blend in with the rest of the desert—not with Navy whites and a pair of gleaming stars on his shoulder boards. Had the admiral given advance warning of his visit, Danny Wallace might've advised some shipboard khakis, at the very least. The director of the new Central Intelligence Agency had been technically placed on reserve/detached duty with the Navy to wrangle Washington's intelligence community into something approaching cohesion. But apparently habits die hard.

Like Hillenkoetter, Danny was on detached duty with the CIA—though Secretary Forrestal still seemed to think Danny was under *his* command. And Danny hadn't been in the Navy long enough to care about wearing an uncomfortable officer's uniform out in the full-blown Nevada sun.

"I want to have a chat with your PAPERCLIP man," Hillenkoetter said as they rode in the jeep that would take them from the "asset containment area" to the main base at Area 51.

"Yes, sir," Danny replied, "though there hasn't been a lot of progress yet. He's got some ideas, though."

"That's fine," the director said. After a moment, he asked, "How often does Jim Forrestal call you here?"

"Call? He doesn't call, sir," Danny said, shouting slightly over the wind as they rode. "He sends a cable every few days, asking about something or another."

Hillenkoetter shook his head with a rueful grin. "Fucking son of a bitch, that man. The whole idea of a Central Intelligence Agency is that information is *centralized*. What the hell's his bugaboo?"

They pulled up outside the base office building and parked the jeep.

"Mostly 'Asset Development,' sir," Danny replied as they walked toward the entrance. "Spends a lot of time going over the profiles, speculating over which asset might do what. But it's too early to determine if any of them will be effective in the field. That's my assessment, anyways, sir."

Danny opened the door for the admiral and ushered him in. A couple of Air Force clerks scrambled to their feet to salute; Hillenkoetter's return was barely a wave as Danny led them to his cramped office, ordering one of them to track down the PAPERCLIP man. The admiral replied only when the door was firmly closed.

"Anyone in particular he's on about?"

"Forrestal?" Danny nodded. "Subject-1, as always."

Hillenkoetter frowned deeply. "Of course he is. Gotta find more Variants, right? He's really bent on this covert ops idea. But what we *need* is intel. Any of your assets showing signs of help there? That woman sure seems like she could get some secrets out of people."

Danny ushered his boss to his marginally more comfortable office chair behind the desk, while Danny himself took one of the folding camp chairs across. "They're *all* potentially useful, sir, whether it's ops or intel. Some may be more inclined toward one or the other, but it's all in how you use them. And right now, there's a lot of preparation left to do."

"Right. Marine Corps training regimen, OSS training. We really need to come up with our own curriculum for the CIA. Maybe what you and Anderson got here is a good start, based off that Camp X material. Write that up for me when you have a moment," the admiral said.

"Aye, sir," Danny replied, wondering exactly when he might *get* that moment. "We're also looking at bringing in a specialist to assist with some tradecraft training. Can we clear John Mulholland to give us a hand?"

Hillenkoetter smiled at that. Danny had done his research, and Mulholland was one of the finest stage magicians in the country. He'd given the OSS tips on sleight of hand and misdirection. "Absolutely. Consider it done. Just be sure he doesn't get anywhere near the labs. Anything else I need to know?"

Danny thought a moment. "The assets are honing their Enhancements pretty well. We're finding that most of them come at a cost, though, so we need to keep an eye on that."

"Like that Negro's long recovery period."

"Exactly. Some of them, like Maggie, we haven't identified yet. Still working on it."

"And that's why we can't let Jim Forrestal get his hands on them before we got this all worked out," the director said. "So, what's your SOP when he cables?"

Danny shrugged. "We're not sending MAJESTIC-12 intel over cable, so I tell him to sit tight for the next report. We agreed on weekly updates, which go to him, you, General Montague, Dr. Bush, Dr. Bronk—basically everyone with MAJESTIC-12 clearance except the President."

Hillenkoetter nodded. Danny had wondered why Truman wasn't looped in on the weekly reports from Area 51, but figured the President was a pretty busy fellow to begin with. And a bunch of reports with unanswered questions wouldn't do much to help Hillenkoetter—or Forrestal, for that matter—keep the President happy.

"I'll have a talk with Jim. I don't care how many code words we use, we can't have him asking about this over a cable. He'll have to wait for copies to fly in, just like everyone else," the director said.

Danny breathed a sigh of relief. "Thank you, sir."

"Any luck running down any more signals? Or Variants?"

"Not since the one in Boston, sir. Honestly, I've been busy setting up shop here, but the phenomenon isn't putting out any more pulses, either. When it does, I'll be ready to go," Danny said. "Should I focus more on Variant searches instead?"

Hillenkoetter shook his head. "No, Commander. You keep on this project. With Montague in Albuquerque, you're pretty much *de facto* base commander, and between the lab work and the asset training, you've got enough on your plate. I have a couple analysts looking through the wires and newspapers for anything interesting, but as you said, there hasn't been a signal in months. We'll have to start figuring out how to look overseas, too. But not right now."

"Yes, sir."

"And, Commander . . . when Jim Forrestal asks about Subject-1, you don't tell him a damn thing beyond those reports. You read me?"

"Loud and clear, sir," Danny replied, realizing in that moment just how difficult it was to have two bosses at odds with one another.

They were interrupted by a knock at the door, which Danny rose to get, ushering Dr. Kurt Schreiber into the room. Schreiber had been one of the beneficiaries of Operation PAPERCLIP, the program designed to bring Nazi brains to America to work for the United States, so long as their war records weren't *too* atrocious. It was a rotten deal with the devil, Danny thought.

He couldn't help but grimace at the man. He'd seen Schreiber's file. The Nazi should've been shot. But . . . the doctor knew about nuclear phenomena, and if there was only one man alive with any inkling of what it was—it was Schreiber. And even that was still a lot of guesswork.

"Dr. Schreiber," Hillenkoetter said, waving the white-coated scientist to another chair. "Do you know who I am?"

The German gave a thin smile as he took his seat. "I can only assume from your rank, and the fact that you're here, that you're in charge of Mr. Wallace here, if not more."

"Suffice it to say, Doctor, that you wouldn't be here without my approval, which, I should tell you, was only given reluctantly," Hillenkoetter said. "I've read your reports, and frankly, I don't have a science-to-English dictionary. So, tell me exactly what's going on with this phenomenon. And use small words for me, OK?"

Schreiber nodded in reply. "Very well, Admiral. You know, yes, that the phenomenon has magnetic properties and is emitting a broad spectrum of radiation, mostly of the harmless variety. However, it also has no mass. So, that has us wondering where the radiation and magnetism is coming from, yes?"

The CIA director nodded. "And your theories?"

"We do not know for certain, but it is safe to say that if there is no mass here, yet the radiation is occurring, then it stands to reason that it must be coming from somewhere else. That this phenomenon is less a thing unto itself and more a window or door to another place."

"Where?"

Schreiber shrugged. "We cannot say. If it is a door, I believe it is one-way."

This prompted a frown from Hillenkoetter; Danny knew this tidbit wasn't in the last report he'd seen. "Come again, Doctor?"

"Perhaps, Admiral, a demonstration is in order. Shall we?" Schreiber rose and opened the office door. A moment later, after a bit of consideration, Hillenkoetter walked out, Danny in tow.

The German scientist led them across the complex from the office building to a gigantic metal-sided building, three stories tall and larger than a football field. The MP at the door checked everyone's ID badges assiduously, even though both Danny and Schreiber were known by sight. They took security seriously there.

Once inside, Schreiber led them through a corridor with offices on either side, which eventually opened up into a large room with a bare concrete floor. There were shaded lightbulbs hanging down from the steel-beam rafters and banks of machinery lining the walls. In the center of the room, sandwiched between two large electromagnets, was the phenomenon—now eight feet wide on all sides, still white, still swirling. Just as Danny had first seen it in Hiroshima.

It still disturbed him for some unknown yet profoundly elemental reason.

There were a handful of scientists working at tables about ten feet away from the vortex, and they scattered as Schreiber approached with his guests, a gesture from the German doctor sending them back to their offices. Schreiber was technically not the project lead, but the other scientists who reported to Danny behind Schreiber's back called him a genius and, surprisingly, a decent colleague.

"So, gentlemen, there is a thing here that has no mass but has magnetic properties and is emitting radiation, yes? So, we can assume that the radiation comes from somewhere else and this must be a doorway. Do you follow?" Schreiber asked.

"I suppose," Hillenkoetter said as he stared at the vortex of white light.

Schreiber picked up a tennis ball from a bucket perched on one of the work desks. "But what kind of door? And how does one go through it?" And with that, Schreiber pitched the ball directly toward the center of the light.

It passed through and bounced onto the floor on the other side.

"We have done this many times, with these balls and other objects. We have studied them afterward and found no changes whatsoever as a result of their passage. We have been experimenting on small animals as well. Again, no measurable change," Schreiber said. "Meanwhile, seemingly at random, the phenomenon will emit another pulse of radiation and energy that, we believe, creates another Variant."

"How closely can we track those pulses?" Hillenkoetter asked.

"It is very difficult. The best we can manage is directionally, from the point of emission. We cannot determine how far it goes yet, not without dedicated equipment placed across the country—the world, really. So, it is up to your . . . other assets, I suppose? . . . to find the new Variant."

Danny frowned. Schreiber had been nibbling around the edges of the Variant part of MAJESTIC-12 for some time now, even asking to examine each subject to determine how the energy affected them. Danny didn't even need to refer to Hillenkoetter's standing orders to decline that request.

"What I'm failing to grasp, after all this time, Doctor, is how you knew to create one of these in Berlin in the first place, and how you knew what it would do." Hillenkoetter said, finally tearing his eyes away from the vortex to fix a stern glare at the German. "Never did get an answer I liked there."

To Danny's surprise, Schreiber shrugged and sounded apologetic. "The answers are there, whether you like them or not. My directives came from Hitler himself, and he would not share the *why* of what I did. He simply ordered me to do it. And so, when Hiroshima occurred, we put our plan into motion, as laid out by the Führer himself. What he knew, the foresight he had, died with him—and to be perfectly honest, Admiral, I believe this to be for the best."

"How so?" the CIA director demanded.

"Do you wish to have such a man in command of an army of supermen?" Schreiber asked, wide-eyed and genuine, at least as far as Danny could tell. "I can honestly say, having worked with him personally, I do not. If that means we must work to find the truth here, so be it."

Hillenkoetter's gaze returned to the vortex. "What do you need to take this further?"

When Schreiber told him, the color left the admiral's face.

11.

January 27, 1948

Today was a good day, praise the Lord.

Cal Hooks got up and, for the first time in what seemed like forever, didn't feel every bone and muscle in his tired body protest to high Heaven. That was reason enough to embrace the morning despite the winter chill of the Nevada desert before sunrise.

Plus, today he'd get to call home. The Army folks—Cal well knew they weren't really from the Army, but the Air Force name was still pretty new—had been letting him call home once a week ever since he had signed on. And last summer, he'd been given two whole weeks to return home, though his wife and boy were worried something fierce when they saw the condition he was in. And that was after the Army folks had given him a month to recuperate from any experiments before his vacation.

He got up from his bunk and stretched. Freed from the drudgery of third-shift factory work, Cal found he was a morning person after all. He flipped on a light, noting how sure his hands looked. No trembling at all. And in the mirror, the white hair had been darkening considerably, to the point where there was only a bit more gray than when he had first started down this strange road. All good signs.

He'd come a long way since the incident at the Firestone plant. He was bouncing back better now—faster. Today, he felt maybe ninety percent back to the last time he'd clocked in at the Firestone plant. He could walk briskly and, over the past few days, had been able to participate in some of the exercises the others were doing.

Cal could heal a paper cut without much trouble at all now. He could also focus all his energy into the gravely ill—they told him he had cured a woman with cancer last spring. Hearing that made the three months he was bedridden for afterwards almost entirely tolerable.

Truth be told, though, when he used his power, he never quite bounced back all the way. The doctors had confirmed it, but he had already felt it in his bones. Each time he used his miraculous gift, a tiny little bit of his life was sacrificed.

But that was fine by him. Over the course of the past year, he'd healed dozens—dozens!—of people. The woman with cancer, a boy out in Michigan who'd been in a terrible car crash, soldiers dealing with wounds left over from the war. It was God's work, that much he truly believed. Whatever ills he might suffer, he was helping people, helping his country. His boy was going to college. It was more than a fair trade.

Cal got himself dressed and briefly read from his Bible before heading over to the mess hall for breakfast. He never quite thought of himself as an overly God-fearing man— the way he grew up, it was simply part of what he did and who he was—but there was more than enough swearing and other sorts of . . . behaviors . . . on the base that he felt a little brushing up on the Word was in order. Today, it was Ephesians. Tomorrow, maybe a Gospel passage.

The sun was still hiding behind the mountains as Cal walked down the dusty paths between buildings. He looked off through the chain link fence, toward the bigger base in the distance. Miss Dubinsky had gotten her hands on those binoculars, and sure enough, there was a lot of activity there, just like they thought. Lots of men in lab coats, more Army folks, some offices, and some big electrical generators. Planes buzzed in and out of the base almost daily.

It was a busy place, Area 51. Cal might not have been educated, but a man could see around himself just fine without a college degree. Whatever else was happening there seemed to be very important.

Cal entered the mess hall and nodded genially at those having an early meal. He usually sat with the other Variants, but at breakfast, he typically sat alone: mornings were for thinking, not talking. So, after he got his eggs and bacon, he was surprised when Frank Lodge plopped his tray down across from him and took a seat.

"Morning, Cal."

"Good morning, Frank. What's got you up so early?"

Frank ran a hand across his face and gave a small smile. "They flew me out to Las Vegas overnight. Bad construction accident; one of the workers was in critical and wasn't going to make it. So, they brought me in."

Cal nodded somberly. "You get there in time?"

"Barely. Mexican fella. Came up here to work, maybe bring his family over. Sad, really." Frank stared down into his black coffee.

"Well, you were there for him," Cal said, hoping it might comfort the young man. "I wish I could heal everyone, I truly do, but I know it'd probably kill me inside a week. You, though, you have a gift to preserve the memory of those gone home to God. I think that's a beautiful thing, Frank."

"Yeah, well, I don't know how many more I can do, either," Frank said. "It's not the toll, really. If anything, feels like I'm getting used to it a bit too much, you know? It's like the surgeons would all tell me back during the war—you see so many die, you get numb. No, it's more about feeling . . . full. I feel like I've got so many people in my head, and it's sometimes hard to sort them out. It's scary."

Cal nodded with sympathy, though he really couldn't relate, and he doubted anyone but Frank would ever know exactly what he was going through. He thought about asking him if he wanted to sit a moment and pray, but Frank didn't strike him as a prayerful sort. Besides, he didn't want to push anything on the man. Especially now. "What do the doctors say about it?"

Frank shrugged and took a swig of coffee. "The usual bunch of mental exercises, memory games, meditation, that sort of thing. They're focused more on the skills I can get or the stuff I can learn. 'Operational Asset Accumulation,' they call it. Doesn't sound so bad when you say it like that, huh?"

"Did you get any of that from this boy last night?" Cal asked.

"Well, if the Commies decide to recruit a bunch of villagers up in the mountains in the middle of nowhere, Mexico, I can speak Spanish and Nahuatl now," Frank replied with a little grin. "Other than that, not really."

"So, what are you trying to keep in mind, then?"

"Memories, I guess. Who these people were," Frank said. "It seems like . . . I don't know. It seems important somehow. Don't know why yet, just a feeling in my gut, you know? I know I should just aim for the operational stuff—the languages or the skills. Medicine or science, stuff like that. But I'm telling you, Cal, I can't shake the feeling that keeping the memories of these people is important."

"It's the right thing to do," Cal agreed. "I think it's God's burden for you, for this gift, to be the caretaker of these memories—just like it's my burden to bear the wounds I heal."

Frank raised an eyebrow. "You really do believe this is a miracle, don't you."

Cal gave a broad smile. It wasn't the first time someone had been skeptical of his faith. "Frank, every day you and I wake up is a miracle. Some miracles are just bigger than others."

Just then, another of their number—the boy from Alabama, Ellis Longstreet—sat down at the table with a hello that Cal knew was only meant for one of them.

"Well, figure I better be getting on," Cal said, rising to excuse himself.

Frank gave him an apologetic smile, and Cal shook his head slightly to let him know it was all right. He didn't have any issue with Frank, or with Miss Maggie (he could not, in good conscience, call the young woman just "Maggie"), but he knew that look of Ellis's very well indeed. The Alabaman hadn't spoken a single kind word to Cal since they all arrived, and pointedly excluded him from conversation.

He knew boys like Ellis. They'd never change, and even if one in a hundred might, it wasn't worth the effort. The MAJESTIC people saw Cal's worth, and Frank and Miss Maggie did too. That was more than enough motivation to simply keep his head down and stay away from trouble.

Cal walked back to his quarters, taking stock of the base as it awoke from its slumber. A half-dozen military folk were out running in formation, doing push-ups, that sort of thing. In his prime—well, even a year before—Cal could keep up with them reasonably well. Now his doctors were telling him to take it easy, but he was feeling fine this day and promised himself to do his best in whatever training they had cooked up for him.

"Sir? You're not allowed out of this area."

Cal looked up in surprise to see he'd wandered a bit off track. Before him were two MPs, and beyond that, the gate that led out of the fenced-in area toward that massive building where all the scientists went every day. The "mystery hangar," as Miss Maggie called it.

"Sorry 'bout that," Cal said with a friendly grin. "Mind wandered, feet followed."

One of the two guards gave him a smile back. "No problem, Mr. Hooks."

Cal nodded and turned back toward his cabin to get changed into his Army-issue exercise get-up. Nice boy, that guard. Cal had lived in Tennessee all his life, but he was beginning to think the rest of these United States were a far sight friendlier than the South, especially to an old black man such as himself. Maybe he'd move his family north after retirement. Snowy weather beat disrespect any day.

Thoughts of cold climates and kind folks followed Cal to morning exercises. One of his doctors asked him whether he was up for it, but he said he'd simply do his best. Frank, Ellis, and Miss Maggie were all younger than Cal by at least a couple decades, after all—but he'd still try to keep up.

Another thing Cal found in living with respectful people was that he had a bit of self-pride after all. He just hoped the Lord would help him keep it in check.

"All right, people," Captain Anderson said as the Variants arrived and lined up—sullenly, in the case of Mr. Longstreet and Miss Maggie, Cal noticed. "Today, we got a special treat for you. You're going to go through the official Marine Corps obstacle course, which we had flown in all the way from California for you lucky ducks. And you'll be *real* lucky if one of you makes it through without quitting."

Cal had no illusions about where he stood on that count, though he was heartened by the fact that Anderson hadn't automatically excluded him. As for the others, Ellis looked put out as usual, while Frank simply nodded—Cal's money was on Frank. But Miss Maggie had a little glint in her eye now, and that girl kept up with most everything they threw at her. Couldn't count her out, either.

They were all given combat boots, heavy packs, helmets, and dummy weapons, then marched out of their little fenced-in area, in the growing heat of the desert, toward an elaborate set of obstacles set up about fifty yards off. There was mud and barbed wire, ropes and walls, tires and Lord knows what else. At least a half-dozen Air Force MPs stood on either side, some of them armed—more obstacles, maybe, or just there to yell at them. Military boys did a lot of yelling.

"To make this a little easier on you, we're gonna go in order, based on the aptitude you've shown so far. Lodge, you're on point. Miss Dubinsky, you get to go next. Longstreet, you'll go right after her and see if you can catch up to a girl. And Mr. Hooks, how you feeling?"

"I'm right to give it a try," Cal replied.

"Well, your doctors agree for once, so you'll bring up the rear. But if you feel anything at all, you're under orders to stop at once. Ain't no shame in it."

"Yes, sir," Cal said. "Like I say, I'll give it a try."

Anderson nodded. "All right, then. Lodge, you're up."

Frank nodded and started jogging toward the course. It wasn't long after that the first shots were fired by the soldiers on either side, and Cal watched Frank dive to the ground. From there, he began slogging through the mud on his stomach, barbed wire over his head and soldiers firing guns just a few inches above that.

"Are those real guns?" Ellis asked, eying the course nervously, then looking pointedly at Cal and Maggie.

"Yes, Longstreet, the guns are very real," Anderson said.

"You seriously going to make me do this?" Ellis asked, his eyes drawn to the weapon flashes before flickering back to Cal. Something was on Ellis's mind, Cal could tell. He was more nervous today for some reason, but then, Cal wasn't too keen on the gunfire either.

Anderson walked over with all the menace a Marine officer could muster, which was considerable. "Longstreet, I am thoroughly and completely in charge here. If I tell you it's Easter, you'll goddamn hide eggs until I tell you to stop. Understood?" Ellis grew pale under Anderson's withering gaze until the latter man broke it off and turned to Maggie. "Miss Dubinsky, whenever you're ready."

Maggie gave the Marine a grim nod and jogged off toward the course, hitting the ground where Frank had and crawling forward under a hail of fire. It was obvious that she seemed to find it easier to navigate that first section than Frank—she was smaller, after all.

"Don't worry, Mr. Longstreet," Cal said. "Ain't gonna use real bullets on us. They didn't bring us all the way here to put us in danger like that."

"Didn't ask you your opinion," Ellis said under his breath, just loud enough for Cal to hear, then dashed off toward the course without even waiting for Anderson's signal.

"Your turn, Mr. Hooks," Anderson called out.

Cal took a breath, shook his arms out, and began a slow jog toward the course. Frank was already through the mud and over the first wall, while Maggie was just finishing up the muddy part. Ellis was floundering through a bit—he'd followed the trail Frank and Maggie had forged, and there wasn't much left to push off of.

But there was plenty of fresh mud elsewhere on the course, Cal thought. *Don't have to follow in a straight line, do I?*

Cal heard gunfire off to his left and half-knelt, half-dove for the ground, his knees protesting a little. But once he was down, he found the elbows-and-feet crawl to be pretty intuitive, and since he chose a different path through the mud, he was able to make decent time under the barbed wire.

Once out of the mud, Cal rose to his feet as quick as he could and jogged over to the first wall—a wooden panel about fifteen feet high, with handholds scattered around it. He couldn't see Frank or Maggie anymore, but Ellis was struggling up one side—again, following exactly where the other two went, using the same handholds now covered in slippery mud.

Cal tromped his feet on the ground to shake off the mud and ran his hands over the top of his helmet—probably the only part of him not dirty now. Then he went over to another part of the wall and started climbing.

"Don't go the same way they did," he yelled over at Ellis, who was trying without success to gain a muddy foothold near the top. "Pick the spots that ain't been used yet."

Ellis grunted something Cal couldn't hear in reply, but there was something in Ellis's eye that Cal knew wasn't very friendly. Ellis was sweating profusely, there were rings under his eyes, and he looked like a particularly volatile stew of scared and angry. But in all honesty, there wasn't much Cal could do about that, so he began his ascent with a shrug. *Think what he gonna think, say what he gonna say. No helping it.*

One foothold, then a hand, then another foot, another hand. One at a time. *Just keep on.* Cal's knees and shoulders were barking a bit more, but he really wanted to get over the wall. He saw Ellis finally flop over the other side. *If that soft boy can do it . . .*

Cal reached up for the next handhold—and felt it implode in his right hand. Sharp pain sliced into his palm.

He shouted in surprise and drew his hand back to find pieces of glass sticking out of it. Then the foothold beneath him gave way. Awkwardly, his weight pressed his body against the wall itself—which groaned almost imperceptibly, cracked, and shattered.

Cal fell forward onto a bed of broken glass, large shards cutting deep into his arm, his side, his leg as he hit the ground hard.

The pain was something awful; it felt like being pierced by a million needles. He could feel the blood flowing out of him onto the glass and sand. He squeezed his eyes shut to help him get over the first waves of agony—then opened them to find Ellis standing over him.

"Don't you ever tell me what to do again, you stupid nigger," Ellis whispered, his eyes wide and angry. He then turned toward the soldiers alongside the course and started waving his arms wildly to draw their attention. "Man down! We need a medic quick!"

"You . . . you son of a bitch," Cal groaned quietly. "You did this."

"Oh, my God, I'm so sorry, Mr. Hooks!" Ellis screamed loudly. "I don't know what happened—I couldn't control it. Medic!"

Pain lanced through Cal in bursts, and every time he so much as moved, the glass shards only sank into him deeper. But more than that, there was anger, a mounting, righteous *fury* coursing through his veins, rising as Cal swore under his breath he'd never let any man—black or white or goddamn polka-dotted—do something like this to him again. The pain and the rage bubbled over and before he knew what he was doing, he'd reached out . . .

. . . and grabbed Ellis's ankle.

Ellis looked down in surprise and cried out.

"What are y—"

Suddenly, before Cal's eyes, Ellis's hair turned pure white. His cheeks sagged. His skin grew dry and hung loose off his bones. Lines appeared around his eyes, blossoming across his face into wrinkles.

A sudden burst of sensation rippled through Cal's body, giving him the strength to stand.

He let go of Ellis's ankle and hauled himself to his feet, shaking his injured hand—and watching in amazement as the glass fell away from his wounds—which were *closing*.

Cal then turned to Ellis, who collapsed into his arms just as the soldiers and medics arrived. He looked down at the Southerner and saw he was a man of eighty now, if a day.

And Cal . . . well, Cal hadn't felt this good in thirty years.

Then he remembered the Bible verse he'd read that very morning: *"In your anger do not sin. Do not let the sun go down while you are still angry, and do not give the devil a foothold."*

Cal began to shudder and found himself holding back tears. "Damn you, Mr. Longstreet. You just stay still now."

With that, Cal placed his hand on Ellis's forehead and prayed—prayed like he'd never prayed before in his life.

PERSONNEL ASSESSMENT—ADDENDUM

AGENCY: Central Intelligence Agency
PROJECT: MAJESTIC-12
CLASSIFICATION: TOP SECRET-MAJIC EYES ONLY
SPONSOR(S): DCI ADM Roscoe Hillenkoetter USN
ASSESOR(S): LCDR Daniel Wallace USN
SUBJECT PERSONNEL: Mr. Calvin Hooks
DATE: 2 Feb 1948

On 27 Jan 48, Hooks and subject Ellis Longstreet were
involved in a training incident at Area 51 during the
Marine obstacle course. It was determined that Longstreet's
Enhancement caused one of the climbing walls to turn into
glass while Hooks was climbing. The handholds shattered
under Hooks' grip, and the wall collapsed from under him,
causing him to fall onto several shards and sustain serious
injury.

By his own admission, Hooks blamed Longstreet for intentionally using his Enhancement to injure him, and grabbed
Longstreet's ankle as the latter stood over him.

At this point, it appears Hooks subsumed Longstreet's
life force, which caused Hooks to heal his own injuries
while severely aging Longstreet to the approximate age
of 85. Indeed, Hooks appeared to be in his mid-30s to the
Air Force Military Police on the scene.

Hooks immediately used his previously known Enhancement
ability to heal Longstreet, which happened in a matter of
moments and left Hooks in the worst physical condition

we've ever seen him in. He remains in intensive care here
at Area 51. Longstreet, meanwhile, seems to have suffered
no lingering effect from Hooks' Enhancements.

THESIS AND EXPERIMENTATION MODELS

It is now obvious that Hooks can manipulate life force
not only to heal, but to harm. In retrospect, this possibility should have been considered sooner. We initially
believed he was simply giving his own life force to others
in order to heal them. We know now that it's more complex than that.

We now believe Hooks is both a conduit and a kind of
battery for life energies. Hooks easily took Longstreet's
life force and aged him rapidly, while just as quickly
gaining strength and youth. Hooks then healed Longstreet,
undoing the aging and damage and greatly depleting his
own life energy to do so.

We theorize Hooks can take life-energy in a similar manner as he gives it. It is possible he may seriously injure,
or possibly kill, just as easily as he heals.

There are, of course, significant barriers to proving
this thesis. The first is in getting Hooks to agree to
explore this particular aspect of his Enhancement. When
I first broached the subject the day after the incident,
he burst into tears. Since then, he's been more lev-
el-headed, but still has grave reservations about ever
using his Enhancement in this manner again.

I suggest we begin an experimental model using animal test subjects. There are a number of cattle ranches near Hiko, Nev., about two hours' drive from our operations area. I recommend purchasing cattle from a ranch—or an entire ranch itself, if the owner is willing—so that we may use the herd as test subjects. A veterinarian can be flown in to help with test subject assessments.

Once test subjects are secure, I recommend the following:

—   Determine how much life energy Hooks can hold.

—   Experiment on the levels of harm Hooks can inflict, from minor to fatal, and how quickly and easily they can be reversed.

—   Determine whether Hooks can inflict specific types of harm. Just as he's been able to heal a wide variety of injuries and diseases, determine if he has the same command when withdrawing life energy.

—   Tests to determine whether he may reverse aging in ANY subject, not just in subjects upon whom he's inflicted advanced aging.

Note that all of this is contingent on the availability and effectiveness of animal test subjects. I cannot condone human experimentation unless and until Hooks shows complete command of this newly discovered Enhancement on animal subjects. Even then, we would have Hooks reverse the process almost immediately after causing it.

If we do not have access to animal test subjects, or if
they prove ineffective, I suggest that we shut down this
avenue of experimentation entirely, and forbid Hooks to
use it unless his life is in extreme danger.

In a broader sense, this confirms my supposition that
Enhancements overall must adhere to a certain economy,
in which energies taken or bestowed must be drawn from
elsewhere. How this plays out with an Enhancement like
that of subject Margaret Dubinsky remains to be seen, and
further experimentation is needed in this regard as well.

PERSONNEL RECOMMENDATIONS

Should animal experimentation go well and Hooks demon-
strates the command over his harmful Enhancement as
much as he has his healing ability, I recommend Hooks
be included in MJ-12 operational team planning. As a
healer, a reserve role was deemed best. However, his
ability now gives him far more flexibility in covert operations, up to and including the removal of enemy combatants. Furthermore, if he can indeed store life force
within himself, he may demonstrate the physical aptitudes
necessary for full operational efficiency.

As for the actual incident at hand, it speaks well of
Hooks' character that he had never before attempted to
use his Enhancement to hurt anyone. While he admits to
wishing harm upon Longstreet in the heat of the incident, he claims no foreknowledge of his demonstrated

capabilities. He also immediately worked to reverse the
effect—at the cost of his own health and well-being. He
seems genuinely remorseful, and has spent much of his
time in intensive care with the base chaplain. I recommend no disciplinary action against Hooks at this time.

I also recommend further counseling for Hooks due to
the potential repercussions of this incident. Hooks' view
of his healing Enhancement was that it was a miracle
from God. Absent more information, I believe this to be a
healthy viewpoint for him to possess. However, Hooks must
now integrate this new aspect of his Enhancement into
his belief system, and both psychological and continued
religious counseling likely will be needed.

As for Longstreet, he claims his Enhancement—transforming
the wooden climbing wall into glass—was spontaneous and
accidental. Longstreet's psychological profile and his
observed actions while at Area 51 make clear his disdain
toward Negroes, and Hooks in particular. However, he
also does have a history of spontaneous Enhancement, in
addition to his growing confidence in his abilities, which
I believe to be a side effect that adheres to my economy of energy theory above. (See ADDENDUM—Longstreet,
15 Jan.) Thus, I cannot recommend official disciplinary
action against Longstreet. Unofficially, however, he has
been warned against further incidents involving his fellow
Variants, particularly Hooks. Lodge and Dubinsky were
also seen having words with him shortly after the incident,
and Longstreet seemed suitably chastened thereafter.

12.

February 25, 1948

Barbecue night was starting to become a regular thing around Area 51.

Frank watched with bemusement as Cal Hooks manned the makeshift pit, where brisket and beef ribs smoked under his watchful eye. The first time they had had beef, a few days before, the cooks had simply chopped it into hamburger. Now, to Frank and most everyone else, hamburgers were practically luxurious in the middle of the desert, even stuck between slices of white bread.

But Cal wasn't having any of that. And to Frank and Maggie's surprise, Ellis backed him up. Apparently, if there's one thing a black man and a white man from the South can agree on, it's barbecue, even though they were more accustomed to spare ribs and pulled pork than beef ribs and brisket. No matter—they lobbied Wallace to have one of the guys in the shop cut a steel drum in half and fix a firebox to it—an old jerry can, in fact. Someone then managed to fly in a couple cords of oak from God knows where. Shortly after that, they hauled another dead steer from the lab where they were evaluating Cal's new ability, and barbecue night was born.

Cal ended up doing the cooking after repeated arguments with Smitty, the Air Force cook, over proper barbecuing technique. As a result, the whole damn base fell in love with Cal. Even General Montague, on a rare visit from Albuquerque, went back for seconds—and thirds.

Frank nodded at Danny as he sat across from the Navy man. "You know, Commander, you're a smart guy," Frank said.

Danny had a face stuffed with beef rib, so could only reply with a quizzical look. Frank took pity on him.

"Everyone saw what Cal did to Ellis—not that Ellis didn't have it coming—and I know some of the guys on base were really nervous around him after that. Anderson went positively pale. But you went and let Cal be the barbecue guy. That's a good move. Just saying."

Danny shrugged as he finally swallowed and wiped his face with a napkin. "Well, I'm just glad experimenting on the cattle worked. And we can't let all that beef go to waste. I'm a little surprised Ellis backed up Cal's request. They getting along better?"

Frank frowned. "Ellis is smart. He's a car salesman, right? He knows when he has to step up. But other than the barbecue thing, Ellis hasn't said one word to the man. Mostly just stays clear of him. And the rest of us, too, for that matter."

"I think he joined a poker game with the enlisted men. I suppose that's good to see," Danny said. "You think he's . . . well, you think he's a problem?"

Frank sat still for a few moments, thinking. "Well, he's doing everything we ask him to here, but he's a cagey son of a bitch. Out in the field? I think he'll be OK. It's one thing to mess around in a training exercise; you put us out there in some godforsaken place with only ourselves to lean on, I think he'll fall in line. Again, he's not dumb."

Danny looked over at the mess line again, where Cal was busy serving ribs with a big smile, then turned back to Frank. "You know, we still don't know what we're going to do with you all, not really."

Frank eyed Danny steadily. "Not until you figure out what you got on your hands over at the main base."

Danny's eyes met Frank's for just a split second, and Frank thought Ellis would very much enjoy taking the man's money over cards. "Come again?"

"Doesn't take a genius, Commander," Frank said. "We've been here weeks now. We know you got something big at the main base, and there's a smaller one further to the north and west, around the northwestern side of the lakebed. Given that you aren't spending one hundred per-cent of your time here, what's happening at those other sites has to be at least tangentially related."

"Not bad, Frank," Danny allowed. "And that's all I can say about it."

Frank nodded. "It's all right. Just passing the time while we train up. Obviously, we'll be busy when the time comes. All this secrecy, our paramilitary training, that fun sleight of hand stuff with Mulholland we did last week. This Cold War is replacing actual war, and I'm sure we'll be off fight-ing it at some point."

"You think?" Danny said neutrally.

"I don't think it's an accident that I now know every lan-guage spoken between Berlin and Moscow. When are you going to clue us in on the rest of all this?"

Danny slowly put his rib down and wiped his hands carefully with his napkin before responding. "I don't like keeping you in the dark, Frank. I really don't. But that's not my call. I can ask, but it'll have to go all the way to the top. It'll take a while."

"Who's at the top?"

The two stared each other down for several moments before Maggie interrupted them, plopping down next to Danny. "Either of you seen Ellis? This whole thing was half his idea. Can't find him anywhere."

Frank waved it off. "Probably moping in his bunk, or on the phone with his family. Something where he doesn't have to deal with the rest of us."

"When's the last time you saw him?" Danny asked.

Maggie had to think about that one for a moment. "Just after morning exercises, I think. He said he was going to the machine shop to work on a few things."

Danny frowned and glanced down at his plate; it looked to Frank as if he was trying to remember something. Danny turned and motioned for one of the MPs, who came over immediately. "I need you to find Longstreet. Take a few men. If you can't find him, I need to know ASAP."

Fifteen minutes later, Area 51 went into full lockdown.

* * *

"We don't get lots of Southerners out these parts, especially hitchhikers," the truck driver said as the pickup bounced down the dirt road. "How'd you get out here, son?"

Ellis smiled at the man. "Took a wrong turn, probably a few more after that, then ran out of gas. Just lucky you were heading to Las Vegas, same as me."

Ellis engaged the driver in conversation for the entire two hours it took to get to Las Vegas—he often found it better to be friendly than not, even if you didn't mean it. In retrospect, he probably should've applied that lesson to Cal Hooks—even if it was only to get his hands on decent food—but frankly, he found the entire idea just too distasteful. Those folks in the North and Midwest and California just didn't know the proper order of things. They hadn't seen what the South had become. They didn't know, and trying to correct them was pointless. Sometimes, you just had to draw a line in the sand and stand your ground on the right side of it.

Cal's powers, though, were something else, having experienced it firsthand. To be able to heal or kill was something special, he'd give him that. But Ellis knew his own Enhancement was far more versatile in the right hands. *His* hands, specifically.

The driver dropped him on the very edge of town, ostensibly so he could use the can. Instead, Ellis walked toward town with an eye to the ground, looking for just the right-sized pieces of rock—small, but not too small. Maybe an inch per side, tops. He found six of them and stuffed them in his pockets as the road began to turn into a street, with buildings on either side.

It was dusk by the time Ellis made it to Fremont Street and Las Vegas's burgeoning casino strip—Glitter Gulch, they called it. There were already folks out and about in short-sleeved shirts and linen pants. It reminded him of his summers in Mobile. He'd get there soon enough. First things first.

The sign said PAWN spelled out in garish lightbulbs. Inside, a middle-aged lady sat sweating behind a barred counter. Ellis had no doubt there was a shotgun somewhere behind there with her.

"What'cha got?" the woman said tiredly. Ellis couldn't help but smile at the thought of the poor souls who'd been on the other end of that question through the years, a parade of losses trying for one more stake, or maybe just a bus ticket home.

"I have this, ma'am," Ellis said, pulling a rock from his pocket and squeezing it tightly for a moment before setting it on the counter.

The woman's eyes widened. "Where'd you get that?"

Ellis smiled. "Had some luck in a private game," he said. "Care to get your scale so we can come to a price?"

Ten minutes later, Ellis walked out with a wad of bills in his pocket. He went to the other two pawnshops in town, repeating the trick, then checked himself into the suite at the Hotel Apache, ordering the most expensive items on the room service menu and a bottle of Kentucky bourbon. He thought about calling home but decided it'd be better to show up unexpected, relishing the thought of the look on Sarah's face as he walked in the door. Tomorrow, a plane ticket and home.

Tonight, bourbon and sleep in a real bed.

* * *

The pounding at the door woke him at 3 a.m.

"Do you have any idea what ungodly hour it is?" Ellis shouted as he staggered toward the door. "What do you want?"

"I'm sorry, but there's a problem with your bill, sir," the voice came from the other side of the door.

Ellis peeked through the peephole and saw a young man in a bellhop uniform looking nervous. And so he should be, waking a man in the middle of the night.

"How can there be a problem with my bill when I paid cash?" Ellis grumbled as he unlocked the door. "I even paid the room serv—"

A huge hand knocked Ellis backward into the room. It was attached to an even bigger man wearing a suit and shiny shoes, walking through the door as if he owned it. Two other men, only slightly smaller but just as well dressed, stood in the hallway. The bellhop was nowhere to be found.

"Who the hell are you?" Ellis said. "What the hell is this?"

The man turned on the light, revealing a squared-off face with a big chin and a bigger scowl, topped with slicked-back jet-black hair. "The problem with your bill, Mr. Ellis Longstreet, is the manner in which you paid it," the man said with a distinctly odd accent, like a New Yorker crossed with . . . something else. Something foreign, like in a movie.

Ellis clambered to his feet and did his best to stand his ground, despite the indignity of being in his underwear. "And when is *cash* an issue?" he demanded. "Are you the owner?"

The man ignored the question. "The issue is how you got the cash. Those were three pretty nice nuggets of gold you had there, Mr. Longstreet. I saw them earlier tonight. Really impressive."

Now Ellis was confused. "You own the pawnshops, then? I can assure you, they weren't stolen. I won them, fair and proper, in a private game earlier today."

The man gave Ellis a smile and shook his head. "And there's where you went wrong, Mr. Longstreet. I *run* all the private action in this town. And I got a piece of most of the legal action, too. Nobody's ever seen you before you walked into that pawnshop. So, I'll give you one more chance. Where'd you get the gold?"

"I . . . I found it," Ellis said, his hands fluttering now. "Out in the desert. My car broke down, and I saw it along the side of the road as I hitchhiked. Seemed like Providence was looking out for me after all."

The man in the suit considered this a moment. "All right. Seems like you need to get your car. I think we can help you there. We'll take you to it, and you'll show us where you found these nuggets. We'll even be sure to get you a tow truck. How's that sound?"

Ellis cleared his throat. "Well, it was a very old car. Given what I've found, I'm sure I can simply get a new one and head back home. If you like, I can draw you a map. Didn't see anything else there, but you and your boys can certainly have a look-see."

The man turned to his friends out in the hall and spoke in rapid-fire . . . something. Ellis was never one for languages, but they were slipping in some conversational German and Russian in his training at Area 51. And it sure didn't sound like they were speaking German.

"It really doesn't work that way," the man said, turning back to Ellis and drawing a revolver from his suit jacket. "Get your clothes on. You'll show us where you found it, and then we'll see if we leave you out there dead or alive."

His mind racing, Ellis reached for his pants. He tried to think like Frank or Captain Anderson—like a military man. One armed target in the room. Two targets in the hall, also probably armed. He was certain now that no amount of talking would help him—and had to admit that his alibi was poor indeed. His only asset was . . . his Enhancement.

That could work.

"Have you seen my shoes?" Ellis said. "Where did I put them?" Before the man could answer, Ellis fell to all fours and began looking under the bed.

He heard the large man snap his fingers, and from his new vantage point, saw two other sets of feet enter the room. Then a third. *Four, then. God damn it all to hell.*

"Help Mr. Longstreet here to the car. He can get his shoes later," the man said.

Now or never.

Ellis cleared his mind and focused on the floor, placing his hands upon it. A moment later, the carpet turned to sand.

"What the hell?" the large man muttered. "What bullshit is this?"

That's when Ellis realized the floor itself, his real target, was *under* the carpet. "Aw, hell," he muttered.

The sound of multiple guns cocking echoed in the room, and Ellis heard one of them say something short and brutish. Quickly, Ellis brushed away a spot of sand in front of him, revealing the wooden floor of the room. Another touch, followed by a silent prayer to the Almighty or whoever was listening.

The men shouted. A shot went off, the bullet exploding into the sand just inches from Ellis's right hand. Then they fell.

They all fell, in fact—including Ellis.

Too much! Too much! He tried to stop the Enhancement, but it was too late. He started sliding downward quickly, at the last moment catching his hand on a piece of plumbing once hidden by the wooden floor, now hanging in the empty space between floors.

The four other men landed with loud crashes in the room below, except for the one who had fallen softly on the bed. However, a moment later, Ellis's own bed crashed down on top of the goon, abruptly turning his good luck bad. Ellis's dresser followed, along with a chair and a rickety desk.

Ellis dropped down onto the floor below and immediately made for the door, but one of the men was laid out in front of him, gun raised. "What the fuck was that?" he said through gritted teeth, his leg at a very odd angle from his fall.

"Strangest thing, wasn't it?" Ellis drawled as he used his bare feet to move the edge of the carpet away from the wooden floor. "Never seen that before."

"How you do that?!" the man shouted; his accent was far less Brooklyn, far more Slavic. "You some kind of wizard? Fuck!"

Before Ellis could reply, a wave of concern came over him. Sure, they were trying to kidnap him, maybe even kill him, but he wasn't like them, was he? He wasn't a criminal. He was a citizen just trying to get home. So, maybe he should at least call someone.

But then that would alert the police, and they'd see the sand on the floor . . . Ellis's heart started racing. He looked around and realized just what he'd done, what a massive security breach this was. They'd know to look for him now, the MAJESTIC people. They'd track him down, capture him, throw him in a cell. And what about his wife? His family? What would they do then?

Tears formed in Ellis's eyes as he sank to the floor and sobbed, knowing with complete certainty that life as he knew it, all that he loved and cherished, his wife and family—it was all completely gone. Completely. All due to his selfish, stupid actions.

The other men still conscious and alive were also sobbing when Maggie Dubinsky walked in the room.

"Ellis, you're a genuine idiot, you know that?"

Through his tears, Ellis saw Frank, Danny, and Cal behind her, all looking down at him. "I know . . . I know . . ." Ellis sobbed. "You . . . you're doing this to me, Maggie? Please. Please make it stop. I can't take it."

Danny turned and nodded, prompting Frank to enter the room around Maggie and pull the shattered bed frame off the man on the bed. "He's bleeding out," Frank said. "I can already feel him slipping. No saving him." Grimacing, Cal walked over and held out his hand, then hesitated. Frank put a hand on Cal's shoulder. "I'm starting to access his memories. Believe me, he's not worth saving," Frank said. "Might as well go the other way."

Cal sighed and nodded. "I'll want to know later," he said. "I want to know that this did some good."

"I'll tell you. Go ahead, Cal."

Cal placed his hand on the dying man's head. A moment later, Cal's salt-and-pepper hair grew darker, his arms more sinewy and strong, his eyes brighter. And the shattered man . . . withered. Aged. His hair grew white, his skin sallow.

He stopped breathing less than ten seconds later.

Danny joined them at the dead man's side. "Frank?"

"Got him," Frank said simply. "Doesn't seem like Cal's Enhancement did anything to affect mine." He turned to look at the dead man. "God, he was awful. I don't want him in my head."

Danny nodded. "Try sorting him out. Pushing him away, just like we planned."

Frank closed his eyes, his brow wrinkling. A few moments later, he opened them. "Huh. Might have something there. I didn't get much, just one or two tidbits that stuck. Some thoughts about his wife, and his girlfriend of course, and some stash in the basement of an abandoned building a few blocks down. And . . . something about Russian. A Russian, or the language. Something."

Danny went wide-eyed at this. "Someone in here?"

Frank shrugged. "Don't know. I was pushing him away, not sifting through. Sorry."

"All right, then," Danny said finally. "Maggie, how we doing?"

She'd been busy collecting weaponry from the rest of the crying men on the floor. "All clear. We keeping these guys?"

Ellis saw Danny fixing him with a hard stare, which caused him to sob once more—and he wasn't sure if Maggie was still on him with her damn powers or not. "We have to," Danny frowned. "They might know something. And it's all because Mr. Longstreet here decided to get clever. We'll have to torch the hotel. Maggie, pull the fire alarm and make sure the floors are clear as you head down. Frank and I will start the fire up here and get these guys out. Cal, get Ellis down into the car. No need to be gentle."

Cal reached down and yanked Ellis's arm with surprising strength, easily pulling him to his feet. "Trying to get yourself killed," Cal muttered. "Lord, give me patience with fools and children."

* * *

"Well? What the hell, Ellis?" Frank growled, his voice hushed.

They were back at Area 51 at breakfast the following morning. Ellis had spent the night under strict guard, which meant this was the first opportunity the other Variants had had to speak with him face to face. Maggie and Cal were joking it up with some of the MPs a couple tables down, distracting them.

As planned. Nobody was paying much attention now.

Ellis gave a rueful smile. "I went and looked at the perimeter like you said, Frank, just before dawn, making like I was gonna do some extra laps. But turns out that if you turn the sand to water, it sinks right down in the ground. So, I did it at that spot we found—the blind spot the guards can't see behind the latrines—and rolled out. From there, it was a quick run to the foothills before the sun came up."

Frank looked as though he was ready to haul up and punch Ellis. "Our one goddamn spot to get out, Ellis! You jeopardized that!" he hissed.

"I filled it back up, I swear!" Ellis protested. "I took an extra pillow and blanket from the supply closet, stuffed it in behind me, then changed it to dirt, just like the dirt around it. Tamped it down good and everything. I ain't a fool, Frank. I covered my tracks. I even did a quick lap around the outside of the fence so they couldn't figure out my footprints."

Frank relaxed slightly, but to Ellis's eye, he still looked like a man itching to hit something. "So, it worked. It's a good exit."

"Appears so."

"So, why'd you leave, then?" Frank said, narrowing his eyes. "Of all the goddamn things, you could've thrown a wrench into everything we're trying to do here!"

"Everything *you're* trying to do, compadre," Ellis retorted. "Look, as long as I'm here, I'll help you play spy and figure out what's going on. But I had a chance and I took it. They're keeping us prisoner here, Frank. Ain't no paycheck big enough to hide the fact that I ain't seen my family in months, I tell you. Months. Those phone calls are wearing thin. I worry that my wife's gonna miss me just a little too much and go do something rash. I worry my kid ain't gonna know his daddy. Whatever they got in mind for us, we better start doing it soon."

Ellis stared into the Yankee's eyes until Frank relented with a nod. "All right. We'll move soon. We need to see what's up at the main base. Are you with us?"

Ellis grinned. "Like I say, Frank, while I'm *here*, I'm with you."

CENTRAL INTELLIGENCE AGENCY

INTELLIGENCE REPORT & ANALYSIS

CLASSIFICATION: TOP SECRET—MAJIC EYES ONLY
DATE: 3 Mar 48
TO: MAJESTIC—12

SUBJECT: VARIANTS WITHIN SOVIET SPHERE

BACKGROUND

It has long been suspected that the Soviet Union had knowledge of the purported "Berlin anomaly," which according to previous reports may be similar in size and scope to the Hiroshima anomaly, now since moved to Area 51. There have been reports of heightened Soviet activity at the former Reich Chancellery for years now, the alleged site of the Berlin anomaly. However, given the building's significance in the Nazi regime, and its location within the Soviet administrative zone of the city, a large Soviet presence there is understandable without further speculation.

Meanwhile, accounts of the Berlin anomaly come from only two sources, neither of which are wholly unimpeachable. Thus, Soviet activity at the former Reich Chancellery was, in and of itself, not a cause for further investigation, especially with so many other avenues to consider.

INTELLIGENCE

On 27 Feb 48, Station Chief—Warsaw was approached by
a man who greeted the Chief in Russian, then switched
to English and asked for a private place to converse.
Thinking quickly, Station Chief—Warsaw ushered the man
into his car and took him to a cafe on the very outskirts
of Warsaw, well away from all but commercial inter—city
traffic.

The man identified himself as Colonel Grigory Yushchenko
of the Soviet Ministry of State Security (MGB). He knew
Station Chief—Warsaw's cover name and cover position, as
well as his real name and CIA position, all of which were
offered up as proof of his bona—fides.

Yushchenko then offered knowledge of a secret project
under the auspices of the MGB, one that involved our
"discovery in Berlin" as well as "those affected by it."
When pressed, Yushchenko offered up two more items:
the Bekhterev Research Institute, and the name Leonid
Leonidovich Vasiliev.

Yushchenko refused to release any more information until
such time as it was possible for him to defect to the
United States or Great Britain. Station Chief—Warsaw was
told only that Yushchenko would be in Istanbul soon, and
would expect to be contacted there when appropriate.
Yushchenko then left the cafe and, apparently, made
his own way back to the city, as Station Chief—Warsaw's
attempt to follow was unsuccessful.

FOLLOW-UP INTELLIGENCE

Yushchenko is of Ukrainian descent and has been confirmed as a high-ranking officer within the Soviet MGB,
having been a highly decorated political officer at
Stalingrad during the war. While a political officer—more
akin to an ideological policeman than a soldier—Yushchenko was decorated for valor under fire, and reports
have him leading a squadron after its commanding officer
was killed. He is, by all accounts, an upstanding and
up-and-coming member of the MGB. He has a wife and two
children in the Leningrad area.

The Bekhterev Research Institute is located in Leningrad.
Founded in 1907 by Vladimir Bekhterev, the institute
concerns itself with the study of psychology, psychiatry,
neurological science, and other medical research associated with the brain. It is loosely connected to the
University of Leningrad. Station Chief—Leningrad reports
the entrances are guarded by uniformed personnel wearing MGB insignia.

Leonid Leonidovich Vasiliev is a professor of physiology
at the University of Leningrad, and a former researcher
at Bekhterev. His academic focus is on neurology, and
some of his published work hints at the potential of the
mind to engage in psychical activity. Vasiliev is approximately 55 to 60 years of age, married, with three grown
children.

ANALYSIS

The preceding intelligence points to the likelihood that
the Soviet Union:

- Has knowledge of the Berlin anomaly similar to that
  which was provided by our sources.

- Has begun researching the anomaly, with a possibility
  that it has been moved to somewhere in Soviet territory, possibly even the Bekhterev Institute.

- May have knowledge of Variants, based on
  Yushchenko's statement about "those affected," as
  well as Vasiliev's research.

ACTIONS TAKEN

Station Chief—Leningrad has been ordered to place immediate surveillance on both the Bekhterev Institute and
Vasiliev. Other high-ranking officials seen entering and
leaving the institute may likewise be tracked and identified, time and resources permitting. A thorough examination of the grounds and facilities also has been ordered,
and analysts in Washington are tracking down others who
may have worked there at some point, with a specific
focus on former Russian and Soviet nationals now living
in the West.

•••••••••••••
• TOP SECRET •
•••••••••••••

Station Chief—Moscow has added Yushchenko to his watch list, with the highest priority, and will soon begin twenty-four-hour surveillance.

We are undertaking a rapid effort to develop a full profile on Yushchenko as soon as possible. A similar effort is underway on Vasiliev, and we have reached out to secret-cleared academics to find all the work that members of the Bekhterev Institute have published, past and present.

Station Chief—Warsaw's cover is blown and he has returned safely to the United States. A separate oversight panel will investigate how the loss of cover occurred. Station Chief—Warsaw has been placed in an analysis role in Washington until the investigation is complete. At this point, we do not believe any CIA activity in Poland has been compromised, but we will begin rotating personnel through the country and ensuring that all current projects are secure.

Station Chief—Istanbul has been alerted to the possible presence of Yushchenko, and is prepared to begin constant surveillance if he's seen entering Turkey.

RECOMMENDATIONS

We believe that an international conference may very well provide the backdrop necessary for a successful meeting of this type, and note that American and

Soviet diplomats will be present in Istanbul on 11 May
48 through 14 May 48. The conference is to discuss the
future of the Jewish people in the Holy Land, and both
the United States and Soviet Union are actively culti-
vating the nations in the Middle East region for support.
It is highly likely that the MGB will send several agents
to the conference.

We recommend that the CIA prepare an officer or officers
to meet with Yushchenko in Istanbul. We also recommend
an extraction team be put in place should Yushchenko
wish to defect while there, or if the case officers deem
it necessary to bring him back immediately.

Once a fuller picture of Yushchenko's family ties emerges,
we also recommend creating extraction scenarios for his
closest family members by 10 May 48.

That said, obtaining Yushchenko's full intelligence
regarding the Bekhterev Institute and Leonid Vasiliev is
critical and should be deemed a high national priority.
His safe removal to the United States, and the safety of
his family, are secondary to this goal.

....
• TOP SECRET •
TOP SECRET / MAJIC
EYES ONLY   EYES ONLY

T52-EXEMPT (E)
006

13.

March 7, 1948

Harry Truman stalked the Oval Office slowly with predatory movements, staring at his guests with eyes made cat-like by his eyeglasses.

"Now, you gentlemen tell me why the hell one of these Variants got out and ended up in Las Vegas, of all places, and tell me exactly how the hell this won't happen again!" the President barked.

Hillenkoetter and Forrestal traded a look, a you-go-first-no-you-go glance that Forrestal ultimately lost. "The Air Force is responsible for security at Area 51," the defense secretary said. "We're working to make sure it doesn't happen again. Of course, that means figuring out how it happened in the first place."

Truman finally pounced. "Jim, goddamn it, the man can turn wood into sand! He can turn metal into water! You can't *make* a cage that's going to keep him in line. So, how's that not going to happen again? Tell me!"

"We make it worth Mr. Longstreet's while to stay," Hillenkoetter said simply. "Because you're right, Mr. President—a man like that can't be kept in. Better yet, he can't be kept out of anywhere, either."

Truman threw a sheaf of reports he'd been clutching down on his desk. "Worth his while? This car salesman makes more money than I do already! And I'm the President, last I checked. Though I won't be for long, with a thirty-six percent approval rating. And let me tell you, when word gets out that I approved a stable of supermen out in the desert with magic powers, your next President will probably end up having them shot. Or worse, put them in a position to take over the country. So you see, gentlemen, we need to get this thing well in hand now, before you go sending them anywhere, let alone—where'd you want to send 'em, Hilly?"

"Istanbul, Mr. President," Hillenkoetter replied. "A sensitive mission that could lead to some of the best intelligence we've had since the end of the war."

"A wild goose chase," Truman said with a sigh as he plopped down behind his desk. "How sure are we that won't happen?"

"We're not sure of any of it, Mr. President," Hillenkoetter replied, trying to keep his voice calm and level. "That's all part of the game. Sometimes you get a busted straight. Sometimes you make it."

Truman smiled slightly at that. "I know my cards, Hilly. What's your boy Wallace think about these Variants? Which ones do you want to send?"

"First team. Lodge, Hooks, Dubinsky, and, yes, Longstreet."

"Which leads me back to my first question: How are we going to keep Longstreet in line?"

Forrestal cleared his throat. "Longstreet is now under 24/7 surveillance, Mr. President. He's being guarded night and day. We've put a television camera in his room, and someone is watching at all times. He leaves his cabin for any reason, he'll have a man with a gun waiting for him."

"That's the stick. What's your carrot? More money?" Truman asked.

"He gets to visit his family. We'll set him up with a nice vacation someplace warm, maybe Los Angeles. They can go see Hollywood, hit the beach in Santa Monica, catch a show. And we'll be watching the whole time," Forrestal reiterated.

"Better not be FBI," Truman warned. "Hoover needs to keep his nose out of this."

"Of course not, sir. We're using Secret Service. They won't be told why they're watching, just who and what phone numbers to call and when," Forrestal said. "Mr.

President, I share your concerns, and there may come a point where we have to take more definitive action. But for the moment, I concur with the CIA director here that the MAJESTIC-12 program can deal with the question of this sort of . . . unbridled independence . . . on the part of the assets. For now, at least."

Mollified for the moment, Truman turned back to Hillenkoetter. "How sure are we on this intelligence about, oh, what's his name—Yushchenko?"

Hillenkoetter shrugged. "About as sure as it gets. Again, it's cards, sir. We'll have a presence at the Istanbul conference anyway. Five or six more won't hurt."

"Not four?"

"I want Wallace there as team leader. He's the only one the Variants really trust."

"And *these* four," Truman said, gesturing to the folder on his desk. "Not a mix of this group and any others. Just these four."

"We've compartmentalized MAJESTIC-12 pretty tightly, sir. They don't know of any others besides themselves."

"Even Subject-1?" Truman asked.

At this, Forrestal sat up, while Hillenkoetter scowled. Truman closed his eyes a moment to compose himself before continuing. "Jim, would you mind giving Hilly and I a moment, please?"

Forrestal stiffened. "Mr. President, as secretary of defense, I—"

"—serve at the pleasure of the President and follow orders according to National Command Protocols," Truman finished. "Look, Jim, this is exactly why we have a civilian spy agency rather than a military one. We don't need your people getting gung ho. Now, if you don't mind?"

Rising to his feet, Forrestal gave Truman a nod and made for the door without looking back. Once it was closed, both men sighed deeply.

"Sorry, Hilly," Truman said, leaning back in his chair. "Hard to keep track of who's goddamn cleared for what around here."

"Understandable, Mr. President. You're the one cleared for all of it."

"Subject-1."

Hillenkoetter nodded. "None of the other Variants know about him, but we'll need him there. We need to know if Yushchenko is a Variant or not, for starters. And if he's important to the Reds, they may have assigned one of their own Variants to keep an eye on him. Subject-1 can spot him, too."

Truman smiled. "You have to admit, in retrospect, that was a neat bit of misdirection on my part."

Despite himself, Hillenkoetter smiled back. Pissing off Jim Forrestal made up for a lot of sins. "I just feel for Wallace, Mr. President. He's gonna be fielding a lot of angry phone calls now."

"I'll order Jim to go through Montague instead," Truman said. "That young man has enough on his plate as is."

Truman rose, and Hillenkoetter followed suit. "Are we approved for Istanbul, Mr. President?"

The President shook his head. "Not yet. I want a plan with all the contingencies neatly mapped out, and I want you and Jim to swear up and down you have these people well in hand before I sign anything. If there's another incident like Las Vegas, it's your ass. All right?"

"Understood, Mr. President."

"One more thing," Truman said, eying his CIA director carefully. "That Russian mobster you caught going after Ellis in Vegas."

Hillenkoetter nodded. "Timofeyev. Grigoriy Timofeyev. Brighton Beach guy, came over as a kid after Lenin took over. I have a cop friend in New York who says they have some mob stuff going on there—shakedowns, that sort of thing. Makes sense they'd try to maybe work with the Vegas bunch."

"Or maybe he's a spy," Truman countered. "Makes me nervous we had a Russian so goddamn close to one of our Variants."

"He's not going anywhere," Hillenkoetter said. "We'll keep the pressure on him to talk."

Truman frowned and closed his eyes a moment. "See that he does. Anything else?"

Hillenkoetter cleared his throat. "Just your final sign off on our request to piggyback on the SANDSTONE testing. They're setting off the first one next month out in the Marshalls."

Truman opened his eyes. "Right, that thing. Seems a bit Don Quixote, doesn't it? All those damn experiments on the whatchamacallit—the 'anomaly.' And nothing to show for it. What's the point?"

Hillenkoetter shrugged. "It's stubborn. It does nothing for months, then emits a blast of energy. That's it. Otherwise, it's like it's not even there. We consulted with Einstein on it—without bringing him in, just some theoretical stuff—and he wrote back that we were wrong and physics doesn't work that way. But it's there in the lab, so somehow Einstein's wrong."

"Well, that's wonderful. When the geniuses are wrong, we're all in trouble," Truman said with a weary look on his face. "All right, you're approved for SANDSTONE. Try not to get in their way, OK?"

"Yes, sir. Trust me, nobody wants to get in the way of SANDSTONE."

14.

March 19, 1948

Frank peered through the scope of his Winchester Model 70 bolt-action sniper rifle and saw his target through the crosshairs. It was far—easily a mile and a half away, impossible to hit anything at that range, no matter the size. Gravity would tug the bullet to the ground before it could even get halfway there, to say nothing of accuracy at that range. In practice, Frank once hit a target three hundred fifty yards off. Once.

Good thing he wasn't shooting at anyone today.

The operational security at Area 51 was absolutely top-notch, something for which Frank had a very grudging admiration after weeks of probing analysis. But occasionally, very occasionally, they screwed up ever so slightly, and each time they did, Frank got just a tiny bit smarter. Like when they set up the shooting range so he could aim away from their little base and off toward the vast expanse of Groom Lake's salt flat.

That meant that the major facilities at Area 51 were right in his scope, and the scope was better than the crappy binoculars they got off Roger the Airman.

Frank turned his attention briefly to the target, roughly two hundred fifty yards off and slightly to his right, and squeezed off a round. Even with his utter inattention to the task at hand, he managed to put one in the outer ring of the target.

"Adjust for wind next time. Remember to exhale right before you take your shot." The voice of Gunnery Sergeant William Collins echoed in his head a moment, just one of

the many voices swirling around in there. Thankfully, they only seemed to offer opinions—and yes, it was an awful lot like having a room full of opinionated people in your head—on the subjects that Frank consciously gleaned from them at the moment of their deaths. Having subsumed the skill and knowledge of at least four different military veterans, Frank imagined he'd get an earful if they all chimed in. Collins had been a crack shot, a WWI sniper-turned-instructor who had died down in Phoenix a few weeks before.

"I wasn't really aiming," Frank muttered to himself before turning back to the main base and the "mystery hangar" that all the white coats and brass kept visiting, over and over, every day. During one of Cal's hospital visits, he'd seen just the one entrance to the building, heavily secured by men and procedure. The guards checked IDs and lists every time someone went inside—even if they had just stepped out for a cigarette or lunch. There were patrols all around it. It was very well lit.

"*What about the back? May have some limited sightlines and low light in the back,*" General Sam Davis whispered in Frank's head.

Frank filed that one away, wishing for the umpteenth time that he could simply *use* the expertise he absorbed without getting the voices as well. But it just didn't work that way. At least the voices didn't *demand* attention. It was as if Frank simply remembered those people saying those things to him, even if they never actually had.

Other than the big hangar, there were several other buildings—offices and probably some laboratories, Frank guessed, along with the base hospital, plus the usual assortment of barracks, personal quarters, storage areas, that sort of thing. The labs might be of interest, but if they were really going to try to break in somewhere, the hangar was the obvious goal.

Frank focused on the target again, getting a quick read on the wind speed and remembering to exhale right before he took the shot.

Not quite a bull's-eye, but solidly in the inner ring. If it were a person, they'd be good and dead.

"*Nice one,*" Collins whispered.

"Thanks," Frank muttered, shaking his head slightly.

He then focused his scope on the *other* Area 51 facility, a full three and a half miles away on the northeastern shore of the salt flat. At that distance, he couldn't see much. Buildings, single story probably, no more than a dozen give or take. Guard tower. Fence.

It all looked eerily similar to where he and the other Variants were being kept.

* * *

"I think there's other groups here," Frank said quietly that night as the four of them sat eating in an otherwise sparsely populated mess hall.

"Other groups of what?" Maggie whispered, looking up from an Army manual on camouflage. She was always reading stuff like that—Frank thought she'd make a helluva soldier.

"People like us. Variants."

That got everyone's attention. Cal looked up from his Bible and Ellis stopped staring off out the window. Frank explained what he'd seen through the sniper scope, and how the camp was structured.

"Makes sense," Cal said. "Commander Wallace only comes 'round once a week for a day or two. If there's other groups here, he's probably checking on them, too."

"He's the liaison," Frank agreed. "He's the one in charge of keeping tabs on us, training us, probably reporting up to Montague and whoever else is in on MAJESTIC-12. He's young for his rank, but he's high up enough to command a destroyer. So, he's smart. Science specialist, probably, or maybe a spy."

"What about Anderson?" Ellis asked. The Marine captain had been doubly tough on Ellis since his escape; the fire in Vegas ended up destroying three buildings, not one, and injuring dozens. In fact, he'd been tougher on all of them lately and far less chatty. Maggie said she noticed he was more nervous around them, more suspicious after Ellis's little trick.

"Anderson's just the trainer," Frank said dismissively, then thought better of his tone. "I mean, sure, former OSS, he's good, no doubt. We're learning a lot from him. And he's also helping out on security, too. I heard some of the MPs say he personally took custody of those guys in Vegas Ellis got friendly with. I think he has our back, but sure, we probably pissed him off. All that said, he's not the one working with us on our abilities. We're learning to be covert soldiers from him, but that's it. I bet the other two groups have someone like him training them, too."

"So . . . we're really going to be spies? Like in the novels?" Maggie asked, with just a little too much excitement for Frank's tastes.

"Kind of. Spies are actually people who live in a foreign country and give information to us. We'd be the ones either making contact with them or doing other things that the government doesn't want too many people to know about."

"So, secret agents, then." Maggie said, smiling.

"Let's not get ahead of ourselves here," Cal cautioned gently, sounding much older than his current appearance; Frank had him pegged currently at a very healthy thirty. "I mean, we've only been here a little while. Takes years of training for that sort of thing, right? And besides, not all of us can be secret agents. Why, what do I know about that sort of thing? I'm an old man!"

"You ain't gotta be, boy. You know that. You can be young as you like," Ellis said darkly, prompting a scowl from Cal.

Frank held up his hands. "Obviously, we're being trained as soldiers, and it's likely we're going to go places and do things most other folks couldn't handle. Makes sense. It also makes sense that there's others like us, and that the government would round 'em up. I'm guessing that if they have more than one group of us here, whatever's in the mystery hangar is related to our Enhancements—and maybe, just maybe, we can get some answers."

"Answers to what?" Cal asked. "What exactly do you suppose we're gonna find in there?"

"I don't know. Maybe I'm wrong. But I want to know the full extent of everything that's going on here before I commit to it," Frank said, surprising even himself with the assertion he'd only now just thought of, let alone spoken out loud. And it was true—weeks and weeks of training with little further explanation was not what he had in mind when he'd originally signed up.

"Where's all this coming from now?" Ellis demanded. "I rocked the boat and look what happened. Why you want to do that again?"

"Because of what happened with you. Exactly that," Frank said. "We had to burn down half a city block just because you turned a floor to sand. They're serious about keeping us *very* secret. This whole base is a secret. And I want to know everything about it while I can."

Ellis shrugged. "Well, good luck with that. They'll come down on you hard. Trust me. They'll catch you and come down hard."

"Not if we do this together."

The silence among the four of them was thick like tar, despite the scattered sounds of background conversations and the clinking of plates from elsewhere in the mess hall. Maggie finally spoke. "So, what's the plan?"

Frank smiled at her; he knew she'd be the first aboard. She didn't love the military, after all; she loved the *action*. "Gotta have everyone on board," Frank replied. "Gentlemen?"

Ellis looked down at his tray of food, then shrugged. "What the hell. Now you got me thinkin' about it, I feel as though I ought to know and I don't. I'm in."

"Cal?"

Cal still had the depth and fatigue of wisdom behind his eyes, staring off into space in front of him. "They could retaliate, you know. Pull my boy out of college. Make lives miserable for our families."

Frank nodded. "I thought of that. Thing is, though, you know anybody else who can heal or kill with a touch? Play with emotions? Turn objects into sand or gold or whatever? Even if the other folks in the other groups can do exactly what we do, how many of us could there really be? They need us a *lot* more than we need them, no matter what they say."

Cal thought about this in silence for several long moments. "The one thing I've always worried about here is how what they have in mind for me to do is gonna square with the Word. I ain't never gonna do anything that goes against God. So, if they ask me to be a soldier or secret agent or whatever, I need to know just what that might entail." Cal looked hard at Frank. "I'm with you, but we aren't gonna hurt anybody doing anything. Agreed?"

"Agreed." Frank stood up and pressed his hands together, a slight smile on his face. "And I got it all planned out."

* * *

Pat O'Reilly was a Long Island kid and Kevin Dolan was from Boston's Back Bay. Both had enlisted in the Army at age eighteen in the waning days of the war, and both ended up, years later, walking perimeter patrol at Area 51 in the middle of the night as part of the new Air Force. They spent it talking—and fighting—about baseball. Everyone who'd stepped within a few dozen feet of their patrol knew it, and it was accepted knowledge around the base that if it weren't for their shared Irish heritage and upbringing, they would've come to blows within a week of being posted together.

"How can you even compare DiMaggio to Ted Williams? No contest!" Dolan said as they walked, scanning the darkness beyond the base lights. "That's the dumbest thing I've ever heard. Only thing that doesn't surprise me about it is that it's coming from a New Yorker."

O'Reilly chuckled. "You're just sore because ever since we got the Babe from you guys, you ain't won jack shit."

"This is the year," Dolan vowed. "You'll see. I . . . oh, God. Oh, God, *no*. Oh . . . oh . . ."

Dolan collapsed to the ground in a faint. A moment later, O'Reilly lay there next to him.

"Not bad, Maggie," Frank whispered. "You've been practicing."

The two dashed out to drag the two guards back into the shadows behind the latrines. "The trick is to scare 'em so hard they faint, but not so much that I scare 'em to death," she replied. "Harder than it looks."

Frank checked the two boys' vitals. "Shit. I got one going into shock. Get Cal here."

Maggie dashed off and, a few moments later, returned with Cal and Ellis. "I got him," Cal said, looking down at Dolan's body. "Let's see if I can do something here."

Cal reached out and put his hand on Dolan's forehead. A moment later, the boy's shallow, rapid breathing normalized. In fact, he began to snore, leaving Frank looking up at Cal in confusion.

"Gave him enough to get him stable, then just made him tired enough to fall asleep proper," Cal said, his smile practically the only thing visible in the shadows as he rolled the guard over onto his side; the snoring stopped. "It's hard— Commander Wallace and I been working on it for a little while now. Didn't even tap me too much."

"Well done," Frank said. "All right. We take this from the shadows and approach the hangar from behind. Once we're there, we'll do some spot recon. Ellis, you're up."

With a grin, Ellis put his hand to the ground at the edge of the fence. Slowly, the ground gave way, turning to water and immediately filtering through the dust. He moved his hands left and right, making more water, until there was enough of an opening beneath the fence for someone to roll under and up the other side.

"*They should've fixed the sightline problem*," General Davis muttered in Frank's head. Frank ignored him as he rolled under and out, then stood to help Maggie up. The woman ignored his outstretched hand, though, and practically leapt to her feet.

Everyone handed Ellis a large article of clothing or bedding—a sweater, a spare pillow, a blanket. Ellis shoved them under the hole and then laid his hands on them, turning them back to desert dirt. It wasn't perfect, but it'd do.

"What about footprints?" Cal whispered.

Frank pointed toward a small ridge about four hundred yards off. "We get there, we can travel over rock to cover our tracks. It's been breezy these past few days—let's hope it keeps up tonight. Let's move."

Ellis nodded and took off through the darkened desert in a crouch-run, still exploiting the failed sightline of the guard tower, followed by Maggie and Cal. Frank looked ahead and then behind them to ensure their little trick didn't capture any attention, before sprinting forward to catch up with the group.

A half-hour later, they were approaching the rear of Area 51's main base. To Frank's surprise, nobody had raised an alarm yet, but the two airmen were the only ones on night duty, and it seemed Maggie and Cal's combined Enhancements had put them out of commission for a while. Maybe luck really was on their side.

Frank led them toward the very back of the massive mystery hangar, which was very close to the ridge they had traveled to get there. He dashed across a dangerously well-lit stretch of rock and collapsed into a shadowy pocket between a huge, noisy air conditioning unit and some other machinery sticking out from the side of the building. The smell of ozone filled the dry night air. One by one, the rest of the team joined him. Ellis looked to Frank as he approached; Frank nodded to give him the green light.

Ellis placed his thumb against the metal prefab wall and screwed his eyes shut for a moment. His thumb then sank through the wall as the metal turned to water, leaving a peephole. Ellis peered through a moment, pressed his ear to the opening, then turned to the others.

"Dark," he whispered. "Probably a machine room."

Inadvertently, Ellis's hand dropped to his side and came to rest on the ground—which immediately turned to pure white salt. Frank looked up at him, and the Southerner just shrugged.

"It's never something good like gold or diamonds," Ellis whispered as he brushed some sand over the salt to obscure it.

Frank looked out a moment, ducking his head back around the AC unit to ensure they weren't being followed, then studied the wall carefully before pointing at a shadowed corner. "Make it small. No liquids."

Ellis frowned; he had more control over water than solids, but after a moment's thought, he smiled and placed both hands on the steel wall. It didn't look like anything until he poked a finger into it and began to rip through.

"Paper," he whispered.

Frank and Maggie traded a look and a smirk; Ellis was getting smarter about using his Enhancement. It only took him a minute to quietly rip away the paper wall, leaving a two-foot circular gap in the metal. He stood and dramatically waved his hands toward it like a magician might do to conclude a particularly clever trick; the *Voila!* was left unspoken.

This time, Frank took point, with Maggie close behind. As he crawled through, Frank realized she could react to potential targets far faster than he could. But he still had issues putting a girl up front—even one who regularly kicked Ellis's and Cal's ass in training. He scurried through quickly and allowed Maggie to slide into the building; she did so without so much as a sound, and with a grace that he'd not seen in the woman before.

Frank unhooked a flashlight from his belt—another present Maggie got from Roger the Airman—and clicked it on. Thankfully, the glass was grimy and the bulb dim, so while it was just enough light for him to get his bearings, it wasn't bright enough that they needed to worry about it being seen a mile away. They were indeed in a machine room of some kind—a big one, too. Frank couldn't make out the ceiling in the dim light. As for the machines around him, Frank shuffled through the memories in his head—a machinist from the Navy, a couple of guys in construction, an engineer—and came up with very little. There were vacuum tubes and more air vents, tons of electrical generation and plenty of wiring and pipes, but it was beyond his experience—beyond a lot of people's experience, in fact. There were a number of sort of half-finished comments from the people in his head, but overall, Frank's impression was that there was a collective shrug from his assemblage of memories.

"Where to, boss?" Cal whispered deeply, quietly, like a rumble from the desert floor itself.

Frank held the flashlight aloft so as to cast enough dim light for everyone to see. "Doors. Let's find 'em."

The group fanned out in pairs, Ellis joining Maggie and Cal staying with Frank; putting Ellis and Cal together on anything just seemed damn foolish, no matter how much better they seemed to behave together lately. And while Ellis was many things, he remained surprisingly gentlemanly around Maggie, in that way only Southerners could manage. Of course, the fact that Maggie could reduce a grown man to a babbling puddle in seconds likely wasn't lost on Ellis either.

It took about thirty seconds for the team to find two exits. Ellis created floor-level peepholes near each and quickly reported that one led to a simple janitor's closet. The other led . . . out. There was light on the other side of the door—harsh, fluorescent light—but they could tell nothing beyond that.

Except, of course, that there didn't appear to be any cover to be had. They would be completely exposed.

Frank whispered out the orders, and the team wordlessly took their places. Ellis opened the door for Maggie, who quickly walked out and pressed her back to the wall to the right. She then gave a hand signal back through the empty door—all clear. The rest followed and were soon out in the open.

And it was a very *big* open. With a very big light inside.

Even knowing its general dimensions from the outside, the hangar seemed oddly more cavernous when you were inside it, Frank noticed. Perhaps that was because of the large, swirling white light in the middle of it—hovering in place, about four feet from the ground. It was vaguely spherical, maybe eight feet across, but it was so hard to look at that it was tough to say, really. One got the impression that its dimensions were constantly changing on a nearly imperceptible level.

Frank started walking forward, all pretense of stealth forgotten. He knew that light all too well.

"Frank!" Cal hissed. "What you doing? Dammit, Frank! Get back here!"

But he kept going. He heard Ellis and Maggie whisper-arguing whether he was in his right mind or if he'd been somehow entranced by the vortex. But he knew exactly what he was doing.

And it didn't have a damn thing to do with the light itself but the men standing around it with their recorders and instruments. One man in particular, out of the dozen or so in the sprawling corrugated room, was firmly in his sight, and for the first time in three years, Frank wished for nothing more than a gun in hand.

He could hear the others jogging behind him to keep up, and part of him knew he should've ordered them back—should've gone back into the darkness of the machine room himself to think things through, to plan better, to do more reconnaissance. All his Army training, his training at Groom Lake, was firmly shoved into a very dark, silent corner of his mind.

Hands grasped at his shoulders and arms, but he shook them off. Then someone stepped directly in front of him, causing him to gasp.

"Frank, we need to get you out of here *now!*" Danny whispered, his face a mask of anger.

The others, apparently having paid more attention to their surroundings, had already turned back toward the equipment room, moving as fast as they could without attracting noticed. But Frank wasn't going anywhere. Finally, he broke his stare and looked Danny in the eye.

"You know who that guy is." It wasn't a question.

"I know. I'll explain everything. But let's step outside," Danny said, his eyes softening a moment. "Frank, you can't be here."

"That man is a goddamn Nazi!" Frank hissed. "Why should I listen to you?"

Danny put both hands on Frank's shoulders. "Because I'm not one of them, Frank. I'm one of you."

"What?"

"There's something you need to know. I'm a Variant too."

15.

March 20, 1948

Maggie Dubinsky's biggest secret—and she had a lot of them these days—was that even though she was under strict orders never to use her Enhancement outside of officially sanctioned MJ-12 exercises, she was *always* using it.

Always. Almost constantly for the past two weeks now.

How could she not? For one, she'd gotten pretty good at sensing the emotional state of those around her. Was that part of her Enhancement? Danny didn't seem to think so; he thought she was simply better at reading people now. It was a theory that admittedly carried a little weight; for one, she didn't feel the same kind of . . . *surge* . . . inside her that she did when actually changing emotions.

But she was still scary good at it, and the better she got, the more the line between observation and manipulation blurred. After figuring out what people were feeling, she found herself tweaking them in one direction or another—subtly, oh so very subtly, of course—as her control increased. Around Maggie, a good day got just a little better, and a bad day could always get a little worse. It was nothing, really. It was easy. And they were just . . . people.

Right now, Maggie was doing her best to ensure Frank Lodge didn't have a worse day than he already did, because it was clear to her that he was already on one hell of an edge, pacing the floor of the mess hall like a caged tiger. She knew when someone was about to pop, and it took a fair amount of effort on her part to keep him anywhere close to even-keeled.

"You mean to tell me, *Commander*, that Harry S. Truman himself allowed this sick, sorry bastard into this country? He ought to hang! He's a goddamn Nazi! He had Gestapo and SS guys saluting him under the goddamn Reich Chancellery. *I saw it myself!*"

Danny was also trying to keep it together but in a different way. Maggie could tell he agreed with Frank but couldn't say so. And speaking of secrets, Danny had unleashed a doozy. And yet they hadn't yet bothered to ask him about whatever Enhancement he had, because Frank was still moments away from a murderous rampage.

"Frank, I know. Kurt Schreiber was a top-level guy in the Nazi science department. He personally briefed Hitler on some things, though he says it was the other way around, and that he was just following Hitler's orders," Danny replied. "But you now know what we have in there, and you know firsthand how dangerous it is. Schreiber *knows* this stuff better than anyone else on the planet. Better than *anyone*, Frank. And so we brought him over to help."

Frank looked ready to rip Danny's head clean off. "You don't play forgive and forget with the Nazis!" Frank barked. "I don't care how much they know. Torture him until you get all the information you need and then leave him for dead. In fact, I'll even sit with him as he goes, so we get every scrap of intel out of his sick brain."

"We're better than that, Frank! He spent a full year at Nuremburg!" Danny shot back. "And let me tell you, we weren't exactly kind to him there." Danny stopped, fists clenched at his sides. "We need him. And frankly, that should be enough for you."

Frank continued to pace, while the others sat at one of the tables with cups of bad coffee in front of them. Once Danny had hustled them out of the science building— with that . . . *thing* . . . inside it—he personally drove them back to their little barbed wire playpen, where he dressed down the guards for failing the "exercise" and called for double watches until further notice. It was a smooth move on his part, and Maggie could tell without even using her

Enhancement that Danny was worried—he wanted to spare them any discipline for their little adventure.

After that, only Cal had the wherewithal to think about making coffee. "These kind of talks at two in the morning, you need beer. But we ain't got beer, so we'll do coffee," he said as he puttered around with Smitty's coffee urn. Ellis merely sat, arms folded, staring at Danny intently, as if he could rip into his soul with X-ray vision or something. Maggie could tell Ellis was surprised and angry and very, very curious.

She couldn't take Frank's pacing any more, though. "Frank, please, sit down," she said, trying to push a little more calm his way. Grudgingly, he stopped, shook his head, and plopped down onto a bench. *Good boy.* "Now, Danny, I think you need to start at the beginning. And tell us what your Enhancement is."

Danny smiled wearily and took the seat across from her, away from Frank, and accepted the coffee Cal slid toward him. "Well, those two things are related, Maggie. The beginning, of course, was August 6, 1945. You remember that day?"

"Hiroshima?" she asked.

He nodded. "That's the same day, in fact, that Frank got his ability. He knows this because he stumbled into a shit-show in Berlin and was captured by a cell of underground Nazis who'd somehow anticipated the whole thing."

"How did they know?" Frank demanded. "You're now pals with the same guy who was in charge that day in Berlin. How did they know?"

Danny frowned. "Frank, I'm not sure I even understand it. The Nazis did a lot of really questionable experiments in a lot of areas we would've considered pseudoscience at best, occultism at worst. Schreiber was one of 'em." Danny stopped and closed his eyes a moment, realizing his slip. "Fuck. Don't fucking repeat that name to anybody."

"We won't," Maggie soothed. *Focus.* "Go on."

"So, that vortex you saw in there . . . there was another one in Berlin—Frank knows that because he was there. Schreiber knew something would happen because the

Gestapo still had a few moles in Washington, and he thought the sudden release of energies would create some sort of anomaly. And he was right. It created two."

"Berlin and . . . Hiroshima?" Cal asked.

Danny nodded. "Why there were *two* . . . a fissure in *what* . . . we don't know. The vortices emitted several dozen streams of strange radiation and signaling for several days after. That signaling strength has reduced significantly, but they're still throwing off a string now and then. And that's how people become Variants, by somehow absorbing these streams. Again, why us? We don't know. We're studying it."

"And so, what happened with you?" Maggie asked. "Your power?"

"I was on Guam, serving on Admiral Nimitz's staff. I was doing intel, reporting to Admiral Hillenkoetter—he was a captain at the time, head of Pac-Fleet intel. It was the middle of the day when I felt something . . . happen. And suddenly I could hear all these people. In my head. Everyone else who'd been affected. The Variants."

There was a long silence, broken by a few sips of coffee here and there. "That's how you found us," Ellis said after a while. "You said you were looking at newspapers and court records and whatnot. But you weren't, were you. You already knew who we were and where we were."

"More or less. The range isn't always that great —maybe five hundred miles, tops—and after that initial surge, I discovered I had to concentrate really hard to find someone. So, I still needed to do the research. Think of it like a really good head start. But there'd be times when I'd just go to a new city and I'd home in on someone. That's how I found you, Maggie—I did the paper trail afterward, right before I visited you for the first time," Danny said.

"Who else knows?" Frank asked. "Who knows you're one of us?"

"Hillenkoetter and, well . . . Truman."

Everyone went a little wide-eyed at this, and there was more absorbing silence. "So, it goes up that far," Cal said finally. "The President himself."

"There are less than a dozen people who know about MAJESTIC-12," Danny said. "Truman, Hillenkoetter, Secretary Forrestal, Montague, Dr. Bronk, Gen. Vandenberg, a couple others. That's it. Nobody else in the White House, nobody at Defense or CIA. Nobody in Congress, for damn sure. That's it."

Maggie thought about asking about all the secrecy, but knew the question was dumb before she spoke it. If word got out . . .

"Tell us about the others, the ones at the north end of the base," Frank demanded.

"No."

"Excuse me?"

Danny stared Frank down as best he could. "No. You already figured out there *are* others. You're a smart bunch, real smart. But right now, you don't get all the details. You probably won't ever get all the details. You gotta get used to that, for your own good."

"And what happens when they come for us?" Frank asked, his voice rising as he stood. "What happens when the people with comic-book powers get too scary? Or stop being useful? Then what? How will we even know they're coming for us?"

"That's why only the President and Hilly know about me," Danny replied. "Because if it gets to be that bad, I'll be the one to tell you to bug out. I'm still one of you. I brought you together for the sake of our country, and if that country turns on you, then it turns on me, too."

"And how can we trust you? How do we know you won't just cut yourself a deal? How do we know you haven't already?" Frank shouted, so much so that Maggie reached out again with her ability to calm him—with only partial success.

Danny, however, was surprisingly even-keeled. He was a lot braver than Maggie had given him credit for. "You could all be in jail right now. Or worse. Instead, I got you out of there. And now, you're going to finally go to work."

"Come again?" Cal said.

For the first time all night, Danny smiled at Frank. "You're ready. I had a field test devised for you, a dry run—something covert and objective-based—but you went and did that on your own anyways and managed to get into a very secure facility using only your wits and your Enhancements. So, we'll check that one off as done. Which means you're ready for deployment, so long as I can trust you to stay out of trouble. If you don't, we'll have to hunt you down and lock you away, and nobody wants that."

"Deployment where?" Ellis asked doubtfully.

"Any of you ever been to Turkey?"

* * *

Four hours later, Danny was in bed, wondering whether to skip the morning run and get another hour of sleep, or just forego sleep entirely, thanks to Cal's coffee. The decision was made for him by a rap on the door.

"Yeah?" he called out, groggy and grumpy.

"Sir, Secretary Forrestal wants to talk to you," came a voice from the other side—a young airman detailed as Danny's clerk.

"He's not supposed to call here," Danny muttered as he swung his legs out of bed and sat upright. "Tell him I'll call back in ten."

"Sir," the airman replied hesitantly. "He's here. In your office."

Cal's coffee had nothing on that. Danny practically leapt to his feet. "Ten minutes," he called out as he dashed into the washroom.

Nine minutes and forty-five seconds later—and yes, Danny checked—he walked into his office to find a grumpy-looking Jim Forrestal waiting there alongside a man in Air Force blue with four stars on each shoulder. Even before the man turned to give Danny a handsome smile and extend his hand, he knew it was General Hoyt Vandenberg, vice-chief of the Air Force and Admiral Hillenkoetter's predecessor as Director of Central Intelligence.

"Mr. Secretary, General," Danny said, saluting before shaking Vandenberg's hand. "Good to see you both."

Forrestal fixed Danny with a hard look. "You're not in uniform," he said. The secretary did not offer his hand.

Danny took the seat behind his desk. "I'm on detached reserve, Mr. Secretary. CIA's a civilian agency. Besides, it's Saturday, if I'm not mistaken."

"I always liked to do surprise inspections on a Saturday," Vandenberg said with the charming smile that had landed him on the covers of *Time* and *Life* during the war. "Puts more surprise in it. And the secretary had some concerns here regarding security. Since the Air Force is in charge of your safety here, he asked me to come along."

Danny nodded; Vandenberg was one of the few others cleared for MAJESTIC-12, given his previous post in charge of intelligence. In fact, Vandenberg had been helpful in shepherding the whole idea through Washington and, in fact, probably set up Hillenkoetter as his successor largely because of MJ-12.

"I'm happy to report that, overall, the Air Force MPs have performed well, General," Danny said neutrally.

Forrestal's permanent frown grew deeper. "Skip the sugar coating. Honestly, Commander, I don't know how any of your so-called Variants can even be remotely contained, except for perhaps Lodge. The rest? Their abilities are too flexible, too powerful."

Danny closed his eyes a moment and took a deep breath before speaking. "Mr. Secretary, that's why we're using a combination of security *and* incentive to keep the Variants engaged here. That's why they're paid well and given perks unheard-of in the history of civil service. It's also why we keep snipers on them twenty-four hours a day, because nearly all of them are ineffective outside of a twenty-five-yard range. Tranquilizers at first, then bullets if need be. This all has been detailed in the security planning you and General Vandenberg received when we set up shop here."

"So, how did Mr. Longstreet end up in Vegas?" Vandenberg asked, his smile waning.

"That assessment is ongoing—the head of Air Force security here has taken it up, sir," Danny replied. *Security is your detail, not mine. I have more than enough to do. Sir.*

"And what about last night?" Forrestal interjected. "Seems you had some activity. Dr. Schreiber noticed a ruckus inside the damn containment lab, where our Variants *should not be*."

"Training exercise," Danny replied, hoping he didn't sound like the liar he was. "You and Admiral Hillenkoetter asked for a final assessment before their first assignment. What better way to determine their ability to infiltrate a facility than right here in one of the most secret locations in America?"

"They entered the containment lab! They saw the anomaly!" Forrestal thundered.

Danny's heart was pounding like a drum corps in his chest, but he kept his composure. "They performed far better than anticipated. In fact, I'm going to have words with the security detail today about that. As for what they saw, they caught barely a glimpse and have zero understanding of it. I do not consider this a security breach."

"The security detail wasn't notified about this exercise," Vandenberg pointed out.

"And they won't be notified when it's the real thing. This is, after all, supposed to be the most secure facility in the United States. Sir."

For a moment, Vandenberg seemed ready to raise his voice a notch but apparently thought better of it. "Fair point, Commander."

There was a long, awkward silence, Forrestal staring daggers at Danny and Vandenberg looking at his hands folded in his lap.

"So, what else can I do for you, Mr. Secretary? General?" Danny asked.

"When's your report on the training exercise going to be ready?" the general asked.

"Later today. I need to further debrief the Variants once they've gotten some sleep."

"I want to be there for the debrief," Forrestal demanded.

"Of course, Mr. Secretary. Shall we?"

Forrestal and Vandenberg stood and headed out of the office, with Danny a few paces behind; he needed to grab a couple aspirin from his desk and dry-swallow them before he could continue. Once in the main office area, he saw Forrestal chatting with Andy Anderson, the Marine trainer, who nodded and smiled as he shook the secretary's hand.

And that's why they showed up at the worst possible time, Danny realized.

When the two VIPs walked outside, Danny stalked up to Anderson and shoved him up against the plywood wall of the offices. Or tried to—the shove didn't really move Anderson much.

"What the *hell*, Andy!" he growled, anger overcoming discretion and a fifty-pound weight difference. "You just went over my head?"

Anderson, to his credit, didn't immediately roll Danny into a small, bloody ball of meat. "I work for the Corps and DoD, *Commander*. Not CIA," he hissed.

Danny shoved Anderson again. "What about *them*? You've been training them for weeks now! Forrestal gets his way, they'll be chained up like dogs until we need 'em!"

Anderson finally pushed Danny back, the force of which sent the smaller man into a desk. "And maybe they should be! You've seen what they can do! Honestly, it scares the shit out of me, no matter how goddamn *nice* they are! All four of them slipped the leash last night, and where were you?!"

Danny straightened up. "Training exercise, Captain, and they fucking *won*. Where were *you*, anyway? They slipped right out of the pen and you were, what, sleeping? Jacking off to the girly mags?"

Anderson lashed out, grabbing Danny by his jacket lapels and lifting him high, to the point where he was barely on tiptoes. "Say that again, Navy man, and I'll rip your fucking head off."

Despite an inability to move or resist, Danny stared directly into Anderson's eyes. "Captain, unhand me right now and report to the security chief to be confined to quarters until further notice. You're under arrest for failure to adhere to the chain of command, gross insubordination, and attacking a superior officer. *Dismissed*."

The look on Anderson's face turned from anger to a mix of anguish and fury, but he slowly lowered Danny to the ground, giving him one final shove as the two airmen in the office stood—hopefully to back Danny's play, but he couldn't be sure. They simply stood there, aghast, at the sight of two officers almost duking it out and probably wondering just how much of the exchange they'd be ordered to forget.

"Aye aye, *sir*," Anderson spat before wheeling on his heel and stalking out of the building.

Danny straightened his jacket and nodded toward the airmen.

"You want us to escort him, sir?" one asked.

He stuffed his trembling hands in his pockets and shook his head. "No need, airman. The captain's on his own recognizance. As you were."

With the two airmen watching, Danny walked out of the office and into the desert sunlight that, despite the brightness, did nothing to illuminate his way.

CENTRAL INTELLIGENCE AGENCY

OPERATIONAL MEMO
CLASSIFICATION: TOP SECRET-MAJIC EYES ONLY
TO: LCDR Wallace (USN-TDA)
FROM: DCI Hillenkoetter
CC: SECDEF Forrestal, GEN Vandenberg (USAF)
DATE: 6 Apr 48

You are hereby approved by National Command Authority
to launch Operation OUTREACH on 22 Apr 48, as per the
operational plan submitted 29 Mar 48. You are further authorized to employ MAJESTIC-12 assets Dubinsky,
Hooks, Lodge, Longstreet, and Subject-1 in pursuit of
operational goals, and asset Stevens in pre-operational
support.

As outlined in operational planning, your primary objective will be to make contact with Target INSIGHT and
determine nature and veracity of Target's intel. If possible, according to the scenarios outlined in operational
planning, you may retain and bring Target INSIGHT to
safety, at your discretion.

While in operational theater, you will be under the nom-
inal command of GEN Vandenberg, who will be present in
the capacity of liaising with foreign military. He must be
notified of any objective adjustments taken as part of
the operational plan, and must approve adjustments not
part of the operational plan.

Should MAJESTIC-12 assets be captured or compromised,
all other Operation OUTREACH objectives must be super-
seded by the need to rescue assets or, if necessary,
permanently deny them to the capturing or compromising
parties.

(SIGNED) Hillenkoetter

16.

April 14, 1948

The sun had yet to rise over the placid waters of the Pacific, but Roscoe Hillenkoetter was already up and at 'em, a steaming cup of shipboard coffee in hand as he looked toward the purple-pink eastern sky. It was his favorite time of day at sea, when both water and crew were calmest, and there was more promise in the air than fatigue.

Hillenkoetter took another sip of coffee, which tasted just as horrible as he remembered. Sailors were a dumb, overly romantic bunch—himself included.

His reverie was interrupted by Dr. Schreiber, who had taken over one of the larger holds aboard USS *Mount McKinley*, the amphibious assault ship leading this particular mission. Admiral William Blandy—"Spike" to his friends, including Hillenkoetter—commanded a large flotilla of ships all aiming a stunning array of scientific equipment at a tiny island out in the middle of nowhere.

Even if he weren't the CIA director, he probably could've hitched a ride. His rank and position merely meant he could bring along Schreiber and a couple of his pencilnecks, along with a whole lot of equipment.

"Yes, Doctor," Hillenkoetter said, a touch of morning fatigue in his voice.

"The equipment is ready. The electromagnets are in place. If there is to be an anomaly, we shall capture it," Schreiber said.

"And how certain are you of that?"

Schreiber gave one of his usual shrugs. "I cannot say. This is very different from the last time. The materials are not the same, the location not the same. At worst, I hope that our readings will tell us something more."

Hillenkoetter nodded and checked his watch. "Four minutes. Get in there and get it going. Make sure the cameras and reel-to-reel are working. I'll stay out of your way."

The German—the goddamn Nazi that Jim Forrestal approved for PAPERCLIP, dammit—went back inside without a word, leaving Hillenkoetter on deck by himself once more, looking north. Here, in the middle of the very definition of nowhere, new fronts of new wars were being waged. Impossible weapons, both mechanical and human, would reshape history.

And it was Hillenkoetter's job to ensure both those weapons stayed on the leash men created. If they didn't . . .

"Two minutes," came the voice from the shipboard loud-speaker. "Two minutes."

Hillenkoetter thought about heading inside, up to the bridge, where Spike would be managing the ballet of ships. But that wasn't his place anymore. For now, at least, his place was away from the front line, in the shadows. Watching.

"Thirty seconds."

Hillenkoetter steeled himself, a sudden wave of fear washing over him. It was damned silly, of course, and he chided himself for it. They were ten miles off and upwind. They'd be fine.

"Ten seconds."

It didn't matter. It was terrifying, knowing what would come next.

"Ignition."

A blinding white light erupted off the starboard side of *McKinley*. It quickly reddened and grew—an atomic fire-ball soon surrounded by the massive condensation cloud that gave it the now-classic mushroom shape.

"Jesus," Hillenkoetter breathed. Then a wave of heat hit him, easily a hundred and twenty degrees, if not more, and his coffee cup went over the side of the ship as he squinted and grabbed a railing, eyes still on the growing mushroom cloud that now dominated the sky.

A few seconds later, the rumble of explosion grew, rolling across the water and, ultimately, erupting into Hillenkoetter's ears—a wrenching, furious cacophony that sounded as though God had reached down and torn a hole in the very Earth.

But it wasn't God.

"Detonation successful," came the voice over the loudspeakers.

No shit. The new levitated core was impressive. That much destruction . . . it was beautiful and horrible all at once, and the only thing that made him feel better was knowing that a man like Truman had the key to it. Well . . . and that Hillenkoetter himself doled out the information that would determine whether Truman turned the key or not.

And Hillenkoetter was damned sure that, no matter what, such a weapon would never be used again on real people, so long as he could do anything at all about it.

The heat washed past him, the rumbling subsiding and the light cast by nuclear fission gone mad dimming just in time for the sun to begin peeking over the horizon. Hillenkoetter wished he hadn't dropped his coffee into the goddamn Pacific. But . . . he had better check in first.

The CIA director went inside the ship, took a left, then a right, then went down the ladder toward the hold where the MAJESTIC-12 scientists had set up. He opened the hatch and found Schreiber and his two assistants poring over their machines and clipboards.

There was no bright light in the room, trapped between the two electromagnets. There was nothing out of the ordinary at all.

"Didn't work, I take it?" Hillenkoetter asked.

Schreiber looked up and smiled; Hillenkoetter found that seeing an actual grin on the man's face was unsettling in the extreme. "It did not work, Admiral, but I think we have made progress, yes?" The other two scientists—both

American, thank God—nodded vigorously. "Yes, we have made progress. The readings have been most useful."

"Useful for what?"

Schreiber turned fully toward the CIA director. "We have determined how the radiation signatures of an actual nuclear explosion compare to that of the anomaly we have previously studied. Many of those signatures are the same, but there are differences—and it is in those differences we may find answers."

"And your initial impressions?" Hillenkoetter asked. He'd have to brief the President, after all.

Schreiber paused a moment, as if gauging his words. "It is too soon to say, but I will ask this: What is the difference between this test and the explosion at Hiroshima, at the most basic level?"

Hillenkoetter hated riddles this early, but one answer immediately sprang to mind. "Nobody died here."

Schreiber's creepy smile grew a little wider. "Exactly, Admiral! Nobody died here. And taking into account all of the technical differences between the two bombs, I wonder if we shall find that to be the only notable difference."

Hillenkoetter took a moment to process all that, then simply nodded and left.

Screw another cup of coffee. He was going to pull rank and raid Spike's liquor cabinet.

April 19, 1948

Can someone explain exactly what it means to 'permanently deny' us if we're captured?" Ellis demanded as they reviewed operation planning for what seemed the millionth time. "Maybe I'm not the brightest bulb, but it sure sounds like you're authorized to put us down."

Danny smiled at this, leaning back in his chair. "Well, yes, Ellis, that's exactly what I'm authorized to do. In fact, each of you are authorized to do that to each other, should one of you be compromised or captured and there isn't a reasonable expectation of escape."

Cal really couldn't help but shake his head. Now, he didn't want to hurt anybody, especially the folks he'd spent weeks getting to know, working with, sweating with, living through strange times with. That even included Ellis, the idiot cracker who still didn't quite understand how deep the mud was here. But while Cal swore to the Almighty he'd never harm Ellis again . . . there wasn't enough spiritual fortitude in the entire world for him to resist enjoying the man's discomfort.

He made a mental note to reread that passage from Ephesians again. At the rate he was going, he'd have to write it down and keep it in his pocket just in case.

"Commander Wallace, sir, I admit I got a problem with that," Cal said, wresting his attention away from Ellis. "These are good people here. They're my fellow Americans, my fellow Variants. Some of us have gotten close as kin. And even those of us that ain't, well . . . I don't want to kill anybody. Period."

Danny's smile faded and he nodded gravely at Cal. "And if we all do our jobs, it won't come to that. You've all been reviewing the ops plan daily for the past few weeks now, and you know what we expect you to do if things take a turn. This is last-resort stuff, and it's an expectation that will accompany every assignment you folks carry out. You don't want to kill someone, and I truly respect that, Mr. Hooks—I've been in the military all my life, and I've never killed anyone. I don't want to start, either. So, let's be sure that we're so well trained and well prepared that we exhaust every single avenue before that happens."

Cal nodded, deep in thought. He thought about protesting yet again but remained silent. He knew, just as sure as he knew his own name or his child's face, that he would not take a life—not even with a gun to his head. At least, he hoped not. He knew men came back from the war different from the men they'd left as, even as they went to church and prayed for salvation and the strength to follow His Word.

Cal knew from day one this was going to be hard, but was only now considering just how hard it was going to get.

If nothing else, at least they got to leave Area 51. They were at Fort Dix, in New Jersey, in a for-real room—no government plywood held together with wire. That was something, wasn't it?

"Now, let's bring in Mrs. Stevens and we'll get you equipped," Danny said. "Mrs. Stevens?"

A moment later, a motherly white woman entered the conference room—Cal put her age in the early thirties or so, with blond, coiffed hair and a very prim, proper, floral-print dress. Pearls and low heels. But she cradled a clipboard with a thick sheaf of paper in one hand and carried a large duffel in the other.

"Good morning, everyone," she said in a soothing voice that sounded like one of the women on the radio selling soap or makeup. "I'm Mrs. Stevens, and I'll be your quartermaster for . . ." At this, she looked on her clipboard. "Operation OUTREACH."

Cal traded a look with Frank, seated next to him; the Army veteran looked outright amused. Ellis's scowl got just a little deeper, while Miss Maggie—well, it was tough to get much out of Miss Maggie these days beyond a sort of bemused calm. Calm, sure, but with some edge behind it, too. Of all the Variants Cal worked with, he worried over her the most these days.

Mrs. Stevens dropped the duffel on the table in front of her as she referred again to her checklist. "So, I see you've been training with Mr. Mulholland—what a nice man he is! Mr. Stevens and I saw him in New York on our honeymoon. Just lovely. Anyhoo, you should all be trained up on how to deploy these fun little items."

"Wait a second," Frank interjected. "You're here for what, exactly?"

Mrs. Stevens opened her mouth to reply, but Danny beat her to it. "Mrs. Stevens is part of our engineering team, Frank. She invented this stuff."

Frank looked positively shocked. "No shit?"

"Language, Mr. Lodge!" Mrs. Stevens said, looking genuinely aghast.

Cal couldn't help but smile a bit as Frank stared at the woman with visible confusion, while Maggie reached over to punch him in the arm. Women gotta stand up for women, Cal figured. Now, Cal was all for women having a little more responsibility here and there—his mother worked hard her whole life to bring Cal and his brothers and sisters up right. But putting a woman in charge of the equipment for a spy mission? Especially one where he might be expected to kill somebody? He wanted to be OK with that, but that wasn't sitting right. And yet Commander Wallace seemed fine with it, so he figured he'd better get used to it. He supposed that if the government was going to trust a Negro man on a spy mission, trusting a woman was pretty much the same thing. And there was Maggie, after all.

The quartermaster, meanwhile, was rustling through her duffel bag and setting items out on the table. "So, first we have these packs of cigarettes, one for each of you. Lucky

Strikes, which is what Mr. Stevens smokes. I admit I sneak one from time to time," Mrs. Stevens said with a smile as she tossed four packs on the table and held up a fifth. "Now, you'll see that there's a black dot on the edge of the filters on six of these in each pack." She held up the pack; Cal had to lean in to see the specks, which looked like tiny little flecks of tobacco. "These aren't manufacturing defects. It indicates which cigarettes in the pack are loaded. Inside each of them is a small dart, with a knockout agent on the tip. All you have to do is light, point at the person you need to take a nap, and let our R&D handle the rest."

Mrs. Stevens produced a cigarette from her pack, lit it, and took a big draw—it looked to Cal like the lady liked a good cigarette more than occasionally. She held it idly in her hand, but Cal saw the tip was pointed at the surface of the table. A moment later, there was a small sound, like a quick exhale of breath, and the dart embedded itself into the table. It was no larger than the tip of an old fountain pen.

"Effective range up to fifteen feet, but in a pinch, you could probably get thirty feet out with a favorable breeze and a bit of luck," she said, folding up her pack and slipping it into the pocket of her dress. "Total incapacitation for around ten minutes."

Maggie raised her hand and looked to Danny. "Commander, we don't *need* that if I can just—"

Danny cleared his throat and cut her off, looking pointedly at Mrs. Stevens. "Security, Maggie. Not everyone here is cleared for everything. And you might not always be around, so these are a good backup."

Maggie nodded and looked back to Mrs. Stevens, who smiled sweetly at Maggie. "Well, then. If I may?" She looked to Danny, who gave her a small wave. "Good. Now then, you're also getting this lighter. If you just use it normally, you'll probably never run out of fuel. It contains a highly concentrated, highly flammable liquid, and the lighter itself has three uses. One, of course, is you can just light your cigarette. But when you depress the valve for more than two seconds, you'll see just how handy this little gadget can be. At that point, one quarter of the fuel supply is expended, creating a flame six feet long in front of you for five seconds. Remember to point it away from yourself. Safety first!"

Mrs. Stevens then turned away from her audience, put the lighter out in front of her, and produced a burst of fire that looked like it came from a flamethrower in the old war movies.

"I won't demonstrate the third option, as it's significantly more dangerous. But should you find yourself in dire straits, all you have to do is pop open the lid of the lighter and throw it as far as you can. The resulting grenade explosion will set fire to everything in, oh, let's say a twenty-foot radius. Again, it's powerful, so don't say I didn't warn you!"

Her demonstration concluded, Mrs. Stevens then handed over a lighter for each of them, along with a pack of her knockout Lucky Strikes. Cal picked his up and eyed it warily; he was never much of a smoker to begin with. But he could see how he might need one or two after all this was said and done. And besides, he could probably heal himself of any ill effects after. He would just need to remember not to pick one of the marked ones.

Mrs. Stevens, meanwhile, was still rummaging through her duffel bag. "One more thing for you here. For the men, a nice new billfold, and for the lady, a nice new compact, complete with mirror and powder."

The three leather wallets looked a little bulky but otherwise normal. The powder compact was smaller but had a hard case. Cal picked his wallet up off the table and weighed it in his hands. "It's a little stiff, ma'am."

Mrs. Stevens shook her head at the complaint. "With some use over time, it'll be a little more flexible. And I'd encourage you to keep it in your front pocket rather than the back. I don't think you'll be wanting to sit on your handie-talkie."

"A radio?" Frank asked, eyes wide. "This thing's a radio?"

"Yes, dear, it's a radio. Just open it up and hold the left side to your ear and let the right side fall to your chin. Short range, less than a mile, but I imagine it'll be handy," Mrs. Stevens said.

"So, what happens if someone tries to call while this thing's in my pocket?" Ellis drawled. "My pants gonna start talkin'?"

Mrs. Stevens's laugh was like something you'd hear at a cocktail party. "Oh, Mr. Longstreet! Give us a little more credit than that! The audio doesn't turn on until you flip open the wallet. If someone's trying to reach you over the channel—and it's a dedicated channel, by the way—your wallet will vibrate a little bit. Just a buzz. You'll feel it, and when you're in the clear, you can answer." Mrs. Stevens turned to Maggie. "Yours vibrates just a little bit more, so you'll feel it when you have it in your clutch."

Maggie frowned. "I don't really use makeup. And I don't have a clutch."

Mrs. Stevens looked positively shocked at this, but Danny intervened. "Your cover identities will include all the clothing and accessories you need. And we can get someone to help you with your makeup once you're there." He turned back to Mrs. Stevens. "One more thing, I believe?"

"Oh, yes. I have them right here," Mrs. Stevens said. She pulled a small case from the duffel bag and opened it, revealing four small automatic pistols. "These are Spanish make, Regina pocket pistols, .32 caliber. They weigh just twenty-one ounces, not even six inches long. We chose them because carrying around an American-made weapon, wherever it is you're going, might not be the brightest idea. These have been around a while. Six rounds in the magazine and another in the chamber. If you remember Mr. Mulholland's tricks, you should be able to get this into wherever you need to go, no problem."

She then pulled four small metal tubes from the case. "Now, I know the OSS folks liked the High Standard HDM pistols during the war. Those had an integrated suppressor and a bigger magazine. Impressive, but really big—not suitable at all for parties!" Mrs. Stevens giggled. "These suppressors screw on, which will take a few seconds, but you'll be far less likely to be spotted carrying a gun this way."

Danny cleared his throat again. "Again, I really want to stress that if we end up having to shoot, I'd consider that a pretty big failure all around."

Cal looked down at his gun, frowning. "I couldn't agree more, Commander."

"And that's that," Mrs. Stevens said, tossing her clipboard into the duffel. "Now, you folks be careful, all right? And please bring as much as you can back in good condition, will you? They may seem more like slightly dangerous toys, but your newly acquired equipment represents a significant percentage of my department's operating budget!"

With that, she strode back out the door, leaving the Variants in an amused silence for several long moments—until Maggie spoke.

"She's got to be one of us."

"Excuse me?" Danny asked.

Maggie tilted her head toward the door. "Mrs. Stevens—she's a Variant. No other explanation why you'd have that woman handling weapons and gear like that. She was proud of this stuff. I think she helped make it, and I think from the look of her, it's kind of new to her."

Danny smiled at Maggie, revealing nothing. "Mrs. Stevens has been a great addition to our technical services department. She's a genius with chemistry and engineering."

Frank narrowed his eyes a bit. "Why don't you put her on the big science project down at Area 51?"

At this, Danny grew serious. "She's not cleared for that, Frank, and neither are you."

"But if she's a genius, why not?" Ellis asked.

Danny sat down with the others and took a deep breath. "What you saw there—and I know Frank told you what he saw in Berlin—is one of the great scientific discoveries of the twentieth century. It's also still one of the most mysterious and dangerous. If Mrs. Stevens is a Variant—and I'm not saying officially whether she is or isn't—she could never be the one to figure out how it works. Not with folks like Jim Forrestal looking over her shoulder. Understand?"

The others look confused, but Cal caught his meaning fast. "If the Variants are the ones who figure it out, then the government's afraid it won't be able to control it—or us," he said. "It's got to be the normal folk. Otherwise, people gonna get real nervous."

"Exactly," Danny said.

Frank smiled a bit. "You basically confirmed just now that there are other Variants on the payroll, you know."

Danny fixed him with a hard look. "You're hearing what you want to hear, Frank. And you didn't hear it from me. Now . . . let's go over that ops plan one more time and see where these new toys will fit into some of the contingencies."

With a chorus of groans, the team opened up their file folders. Again.

April 22, 1948

The Topkapi Palace had been home to the Ottoman sultans for more than four centuries and looked every inch the palace of pashas and moguls to Frank's eyes.

"Sultans. Sultans ruled the Ottoman Empire until 1922, when Turkey became a republic under Ataturk. Pashas and moguls are from India," corrected the voice of Ibrahim Irkan, a Turkish historian and antiquarian who'd died two nights earlier, Frank at his bedside. Ibrahim knew much of the history of the Middle East, given the Ottomans' involvement in it, and it was determined that Frank knowing Turkish—and Arabic as well—might come in handy.

Ibrahim was also the twelfth person Frank watched over and took memories from. Mostly he felt fine, but every now and then, there was a feeling in his head—like the tiny, dull background headache you'd get from being a bit dehydrated—that told him it just might be getting crowded in there.

Retention wasn't the problem, he mused as he idly watched the assembled dignitaries in the gold-glittering, blue-tiled Imperial Hall of the palace's harem. Frank had gotten to the point where he could definitely retain what he wanted and, to put it bluntly, toss out the leftovers. Doing so felt almost sacrilegious, but he was starting to feel as though he had no choice. The memory games were running their course—he was increasingly feeling like he needed more space to file away new incoming information.

Oh, and he'd still have to deal with the voices anyway. They only chimed in when appropriate—as Frank needed their expertise—but occasionally he felt like they were . . . hoping . . . to be called upon. Lined up, waiting.

Frank took a sip of club soda and sighed. That champagne looked good. It was a '34 Dom Perignon, and there was an idle whisper in his head—Frank didn't even know who it was from at this point—which sounded excited about that. Waiters wearing turbans and other presumably Turkish dress rotated among the guests under the vaulted dome of the room. Along the sides, separated into alcoves and hallways by columns, small groups gathered to talk away from the string quartet playing. Opposite them, the heads of the US and Israeli delegations sat on a tufted bench once reserved for the sultan himself. The Soviet delegation was off to the right, chatting animatedly with robed diplomats from some Arab nation or another.

"*That one is Jordanian. The other is Palestinian,*" Ibrahim whispered.

"Fine," Frank muttered between sips.

In the middle of the room, General Vandenberg was talking and laughing with his opposite number from the Soviet Union, a fellow flyboy from the looks of his elaborate uniform. Two steps behind and to the right of Vandenberg was Cal, dressed as an Air Force NCO and scanning the room idly, a Handie-Talkie attached to his belt. Cal was probably more adept at subtlety than Ellis, but there was one thing about Cal that stuck out like a sore thumb—the color of his skin. And the Turks were barely more enlightened toward Negroes than Americans, so Cal had little choice but to accept the role of valet/guard.

Shame that, because Cal had the makings of a fine operative, at least to Frank, whereas Ellis . . .

* * *

"And that's when I told him the whiskey was in the cabinet!" Ellis finished, leaving the circle around him in stitches.

He took another healthy sip of champagne, orders be damned. If he was going to be the assigned distraction, he might as well have a little fun with it. Shit, one of Danny's backup plans was having Ellis make a drunken scene, so he might as well get a little into character, right?

"You are most charming!" exclaimed one of the Russians, a bald, fat man in an ill-fitting suit with a large tumbler of vodka in his hand. "You Americans, you can be so dull sometimes at these events!"

Ellis lifted his glass, and the two men toasted. "Well, the war's over, my friend. Figure if we don't loosen up now, we'll be back at it before long. Hell, I think we gotta get Stalin and Truman over to my house in Alabama and have some drinks on the porch. We'll get things ironed out in no time!" More laughter, more toasting, and Ellis could see a few otherwise bored delegates wander over curiously. "Maybe the Jews and Arabs can join us, too! Everybody come on down to my place and let's get things squared, all right?"

Ellis thrust his glass up to address the building crowd around him, only to realize he wasn't holding anything anymore except wet liquid, which immediately splashed to the floor. *Aw, hell. Not now!*

Surreptitiously—using a maneuver Mulholland had taught him—Ellis withdrew a small sherry glass from his pocket and let it fall. The loud shatter prompted those in his circle of partygoers to step back almost as one. Moreover, it hid the fact that his own drinking glass had spontaneously transmuted to water while he was holding it.

"Oh, no! Oh, I'm so sorry!" Ellis cried, looking around for help even as three turbaned waiters came rushing forward, one with a broom and dustpan at the ready. Another immediately replaced his disappeared champagne glass with a full one. "Oh, thank you! My, these boys here are thorough. So sorry, everyone. Perhaps that whiskey was so good, the memory of it got me a little tipsy."

That defused the tension quite nicely, and Ellis's large circle laughed once more. The more senior fellows—the ones in the uniforms or with nicer suits—were still talking with one another, but he could see more eyes his way. Sure, some of them looked annoyed at his American boorishness, but they were *looking*, which meant he was doing his job. It also meant they weren't looking at Maggie.

Which was a surprise, since that girl cleaned up mighty fine for the evening.

* * *

I hate this dress. I'm gonna burn it when this is over.

Maggie looked down at her outfit for the umpteenth time that evening and marveled how it could stay on or how she could even walk. It was a shiny green number, shoulderless and sleeveless, that hugged her breasts, stomach, and hips like a vise. At least it allowed a range of movement for her to walk, given that the slit up the side exposed her leg a quarter of the way up her thigh. She'd wondered, the first time she'd put it on, how she was ever going to strap a gun to her leg in that getup, but a careful application of Mulholland's misdirection, along with a quick emotional tug or two, got her past the bag search without incident—the pistol was safely sequestered in her clutch, tucked under her arm.

"Anything?" whispered Frank from behind her.

She turned and gave him a practiced, winning smile. "No, and it's pissing me off," she said quietly.

She could feel the waves of amusement off Frank, along with a sense of . . . was that pride? Camaraderie? It was positive, whatever it was. Why was it harder for her to identify the positive emotions? "Keep looking," he said out the corner of his mouth, wandering off to introduce himself to another circle of delegates.

Thankfully, the women dragged out to this party—and let's face it, they were only there for the men's amusement—either stuck close to whoever they came with or huddled in small groups by nationality. Maggie only had to bust out her cover story once—"I'm married to that charming gentleman over there, the Deputy Undersecretary of State for Planning"—and that was that. The other American women smiled politely and nodded at her but quickly resumed their conversation as though she wasn't there. She wasn't part of their circle, and they weren't chomping at the bit to make the new girl feel welcome. And the Russians, Zionists, Arabs, and Turks all left her alone. She did have to shoot down a drunk British envoy and a young Russian officer, the latter's painfully earnest attempt leaving her with a twinge of regret. But it was working out.

Except that Yushchenko hadn't bothered to show up.

I hate this dress. I'm gonna take a pair of scissors to this thing like nobody's business. She looked at Cal's uniform as he stood at Vandenberg's right hand, thinking how much more comfortable it looked. And, for that matter, how comfortable Cal was becoming in his new role.

* * *

"Master Sergeant, would you be so kind as to inquire if these fine people have some proper Scotch lying around? I developed a taste for it during the war. Scotland, you know."

Cal stood ramrod straight and nearly saluted—but he remembered that, no, the Air Force boys didn't salute at every little thing. "Yes, General," he replied, and turned on his heel to head for the bar, next to the violin players.

Except he never made it there—that was Vandenberg's cue releasing him from duty so he could actually get to work. It was just another of Mr. Mulholland's tricks, blending into the background until nobody even remembered you were there. Cal had stood there at Vandenberg's beck and call long enough for folks to think he was part of the furniture, an accessory to the fancy couch or the chandelier. He'd gotten a few looks when he first walked in, of course—not hatred, but certainly not acceptance. Curiosity, like he was a sideshow at the carnival. But it seemed most folks had accepted that he belonged in the room, or at least that there were more interesting things to keep occupied with, like an obnoxiously tipsy Ellis, and he'd quickly faded into the background again. Which was the point.

Cal took a meandering route through the room, sticking to the walls and, where possible, the hallways and alcoves. He made to look a little lost, which worked well when he stumbled onto one of the delegates—a Frenchman, if he remembered the introductions right—lingering a bit too long in a secluded corner with a very tall Russian girl. "Excuse me," the man muttered, bowing and turning quickly before anything more could be said.

So, he could find a couple making out like schoolkids, but he couldn't find the Russian soldier with a face matching the grainy photo they'd been given, nor the composite sketch the CIA folks had done up. Cal reached down and gave his Handie-Talkie key a couple taps. *Nothing yet.* The Variants had discovered that the vibrations caused by opening and closing a channel could be just as useful as actual conversation and much more discreet, and so had devised for themselves a little code system.

Having done a circuit of the room, Cal sighed and shrugged. He swung back by the bar and asked about the Scotch—the bartender just shrugged—so Cal grabbed another glass of champagne and headed back in Vandenberg's direction, waiting patiently until his presence was noticed.

"Apologies, General. No Scotch here."

Vandenberg took the champagne off Cal's hands. "Well, Sergeant, do me a favor and head on out to the cars. I think the Deputy Undersecretary over there might have a bottle or two of whiskey tucked away, and I do believe I outrank him sufficiently to warrant some."

The crowd around the handsome Air Force general tittered at this, but only Cal caught his true instructions: *expand the search.*

Cal took his leave and left the room. If he walked fast enough, like he was on an errand, he could not only get away with leaving the party without being stopped but also cover a lot of ground. And these days, Cal had young, strong legs.

* * *

Frank had a couple European ladies on the ropes with one of his few funny war stories—where exactly in Europe he couldn't remember and really didn't care—when he felt his wallet vibrate against his chest. *Twice . . . three times . . . four . . . five!*

Drawing himself back up, Frank managed to bring his story to a truncated but amusing conclusion in under a minute and then excused himself to attend to his boss. Once out of sight in an alcove, he pulled out his wallet and opened it, turning his back to the crowd. "Yeah?"

"Outer courtyard, the one with all them fountains. Just sitting there on a bench, looking all tired. Couple others with him," Cal replied. "You better get Maggie and get out here."

Frank folded up his wallet and turned just in time to see Maggie sauntering off down one of the other hallways. Either she'd listened in or she'd figured something else out on her own. Either way, Frank did what he could to follow her lead without attracting attention, until he got to the hallway and broke out into a jog to catch up.

"Stop looking at my ass," Maggie whispered when he fell in beside her.

"I wasn't!" Frank hissed.

"Look. I see Cal up ahead."

Cal nodded subtly as he walked toward them, then split off into a side corridor so he could circle around and emerge on the other side of the courtyard; his job was to keep watch and use the radio if he spotted trouble.

Maggie and Frank walked into the courtyard separately. There were a number of smokers who had congregated there, clusters of men and a handful of women scattered around the vast expanse, some alone, some in small groups sharing the international camaraderie of cigarettes. The setup made talking to a stranger plausible, and unlikely that they'd be overheard. Frank and Maggie split off—and after a few minutes of aimless wandering and smoking, Frank saw her sit down on a bench across from a man in a Russian uniform.

Yushchenko. INSIGHT.

Frank took out his wallet and tapped the channel key three times. *Contact.*

* * *

Maggie rifled through her clutch until she found her pack of Lucky Strikes. Looking carefully, she chose a real one and put it to her lips, then made as though she was looking through her clutch once more.

She looked up at the man across from her and smiled. It felt like she was acting out the lines from a movie. "I'm sorry. Do you have a light?"

Maggie started to make the now-universal gesture of flicking a lighter, though she wasn't quite sure why, but the Soviet simply nodded, reaching into his pocket. "Of course," he said in accented English.

She got up and walked the three steps over to his bench, because that seemed like the right thing to do, sitting down next to him. She drew in closer to light her cigarette and took a long drag, exhaling out the side of her mouth like she imagined Jane Greer might. "Thank you," she added, because he hadn't said anything else and she wasn't exactly sure what to do next. "I can't imagine where I misplaced mine."

The officer closed the lighter with a snap. "Of course, miss." He then turned back toward the courtyard, watching the other people smoke or mill about randomly.

The last thing he's expecting is a contact who's a woman, Maggie realized. To anyone else, he might have looked cool and calm, but this close, she could sense that he was nervous inside. Not intensely frightened, but definitely on edge. He was in his late forties, maybe early fifties, black hair graying at the temples, lean and strong. She knew Yushchenko had been at Stalingrad in '43, so there was no doubt he was a tough customer.

"You remind me of someone," Maggie said as firmly as she could manage. "Have we met?"

A flicker of annoyance pushed through the soft blanket of tension in his mind. "I would remember, I think," he said with a charming smile. "But I don't think so, miss."

Maggie fumbled for her next words, ashing her cigarette awkwardly.

"I think it might have been in Poland," she finally said. "I attended a diplomatic soiree there a few months ago. With Mr. Parrish."

There you go, Maggie thought as tension and fear suddenly gripped the man's heart. Parrish was one of the Warsaw station chief's cover names.

"I might, yes," the man replied slowly. "I was there as well, though I do not remember a, how you say, 'soiree' of any kind. But I seem to remember your Mr. Parrish."

"He sends his regards, Comrade Colonel," Maggie said quietly, reaching out ever so slightly with her Enhancement to smooth over any anxious nerves. "He recommended that you and I meet."

Maggie didn't need her ability to note the surprise on Yushchenko's face. "Well . . . that is very kind of him, and you are a beautiful woman," he said. "I am surprised he had the time to meet someone like you. He works very hard."

I'm your goddamn contact, Maggie thought. *What the hell are you talking about?*

Yushchenko nodded, as if he had just made up his mind, and stood up. "Please give him my regards, miss," he said as Maggie scrambled to her feet. "Now, if you'll excuse me. It has been a pleasure."

Maggie was about to protest when the Soviet officer turned around again, his hand outstretched. "Here. I have another. Don't lose this one."

Smiling, Maggie took his lighter, feeling the small piece of paper pressed up against the side of it. Not a bad bit of tradecraft, that. "Aren't you the sweetest thing?" she smiled. "Have a wonderful evening, Colonel."

She sat back down and opened her clutch, her cigarette dangling from her lips as she deposited the lighter and glimpsed at the note. It was in Russian. *Dammit*. She took a long drag, then placed it at the edge of the bench next to her, balancing it so it wouldn't fall. After that, she opened her compact, subtly keying the side of it as she grabbed the powder puff inside and gazed into the small mirror.

"Got a note. I need Frank to translate," she said quietly. "And somebody else should follow our guy."

A moment later, she heard a faint static pop as the line opened up; thankfully, she had the volume turned far down and there wasn't anyone in earshot. "I got him. On his tail," Cal replied. "I'll send Frank along."

Maggie snapped her case shut, just in time to see Yushchenko leave through a corridor at the far western side of the courtyard, Cal in his Air Force uniform following shortly after. So, that was taken care of. She picked up her cigarette again and took a long drag—she'd grown a little too attached to smoking over the past several months of living at military bases. Frank arrived a minute later.

"Got a light?" he said with a little gleam in his eye.

Maggie passed it over along with the note, just as Yushchenko had. "For you, darling, anything."

Frank lit his own cigarette and handed the lighter back, keeping the note. He unfolded it with one hand—it was about an inch around, all told—and began reading. His smile faded quickly.

"Key the talkie. Bail out."

Maggie immediately reached back into her purse and began keying a single long buzz, over and over. "What is it?"

Frank read from the note. "'One of Them here. Many eyes on us. Dangerous. Get out now. Prague, soon.'"

"Shit," Maggie said, dropping her cigarette to the ground and grinding it into the stones of the courtyard with her shoe. "One of them? Who?"

"The 'T' in 'Them' is capitalized," Frank said. "Intentionally. You don't suppose . . ."

Maggie's heart sank as she watched Ellis enter the courtyard and saunter toward them as they sat there. He *was* an excellent actor, and she knew this because underneath his laid-back exterior, he was a nervous wreck. If the Russians had their own Variants . . .

"Either of you got a cigarette?" Ellis asked quietly. "I'm plumb out. The general went and smoked all mine." *Vandenberg wants a report.*

Frank offered one of his. "Gonna have to chase down a new pack. Hate to be one short." *Cal followed the target. He's out of contact.*

Ellis grimaced as he lit up. "Just the one? Don't worry about it. I'll get you back later, friend." *Fuck Cal. Let's go.*

Frank smiled and stood. "You know, I think I'm gonna look for another pack. I think it's gonna be a long night. Lots of people smoking the place up here. And I hear our hosts may have a surprise or two later." *Fuck you, Ellis. We're looking for Cal. And we may have company. Variants.*

As Ellis's eyes widened, Maggie nodded toward where she'd seen Cal follow Yushchenko out of the courtyard. "I thought I saw them selling some by one of the coat checks over there," Maggie said sweetly. "I can show you."

Frank gestured toward the exit. "Lead the way, miss."

Maggie quickly walked off toward the corridor with Frank close behind. She could feel Ellis's anger as they left.

"Wait up," he finally called out, barely concealing his concern. "I might as well get a pack too."

Frank turned and smiled. "Why don't you go see if the general wants some?" *Report to Vandenberg.* "I'll get you some smokes, and you can pay me back later."

"Mighty kind of you. All right, then," Ellis said curtly, veering off back toward the party. Neither Frank nor Maggie needed code words or Enhancements to get that he was pissed and scared.

19.

April 22, 1948

Ellis was looking for General Vandenberg, scanning the room for that impressive-looking blue/black formal uniform. Ellis liked this party. He liked the people he was surrounded by. They were smart, witty, a good crowd. Not like the damn fools he used to sell Chevrolets to, or the folks down at the country club in Mobile . . . who were also the people he sold Cadillacs to. There were real things going down in this room. Important things. Sure, it was all about the Jews and whether they got their own country. Whatever. He didn't give a damn about that.

But there was power in the room, and he liked being a part of it, feeding off the energy. It felt like everyone else was discounting him, and Ellis knew he worked best when he was being underestimated. But this spy stuff was getting out of hand, especially with that fool Cal running off to God knows where. Ellis had a feeling that whatever was happening, the fun and games were gonna end fast.

"General, sir," Ellis said, finally locating Vandenberg and tapping him on the shoulder. "The Deputy Secretary wants a word, if he may?"

Vandenberg scowled briefly at Ellis, then turned and smiled at the other bigwigs in his circle, excusing himself. He then motioned toward one of the alcoves in the harem's audience hall. "What is it?" he finally asked when they were out of earshot, brusquely.

"Hooks ain't responding to the bail-out—he went and followed the Russki. Lodge and Dubinsky went after him,"

Ellis said. "We got company, too. May even be a Russian Variant around."

Vandenberg looked stunned for a moment, then gathered his reserve. "Contact Wallace. Find Hooks ASAP. Then track down the others and provide backup."

"That wasn't the plan, sir," Ellis objected quietly. "That damn . . . Hooks messed up. The MGB guys may be here. We gotta follow the ops plan. Time to go."

The general arched an eyebrow at Ellis. "The stars on this uniform aren't some kind of costume, Ellis. I just gave you orders. Your job is to follow them. Get cracking."

Vandenberg stepped out of the alcove and walked off back toward the party, leaving Ellis furious, conjuring up images of traditional Southern justice against Cal. But he nonetheless left the hall and went back toward the entrance, down one corridor and the next, past kitchens and security guards, until he came out where the cars were parked.

Danny Wallace was Vandenberg's driver, boasting the rank and insignia of an airman first class. Between the spectacles and the boyish looks, the Navy officer managed to pull it off.

"Sorry, sir!" Danny said, folding up the newspaper he'd been reading, and throwing it onto the seat next to him. "Is the general leaving?"

Ellis looked around—there was no one in earshot—then leaned in close. "Yushchenko called it off, we sent the bailout order, but Cal done wandered off. Frank and Maggie went after him. The general told me to tell you, then go back 'em up, but damn if I know where everyone went off to." He threw up his hands. "INSIGHT passed a note; maybe there's a Russian Variant around. It's a fuckin' mess."

"A Russian Variant? I didn't sense . . ." Danny's voice trailed off as he closed his eyes a moment, looking as though he were either deep in concentration or just completely asleep—then his eyes flew open and a look like none Ellis had seen before crossed the young officer's face. "We gotta go. It's worse than you think."

* * *

Cal kept tapping the key on his radio furiously—four quick bursts, *Somebody talk to me*—but wasn't getting a response. It was dark, he was now in some godforsaken basement in a five-hundred-year-old palace, and he was pretty sure the reception on the radio was shot anyway.

Worst part was that Yushchenko was nowhere to be found.

Cal remembered the exercises at Area 51, where he'd follow someone through their little encampment and do his best to stay hidden while keeping the target in view. Back at the base, it'd been easy as pie, but as he now stumbled clumsily over ancient stones in the cellar of this harem, he knew he succeeded in practice only because he'd known the layout of the camp like the back of his hand. Here, in the dim light, he'd spent too much time trying not to fall down on his backside and, in the process, had lost the man he'd been tailing and also realized he hadn't even been paying attention enough to find his way back out.

Turn, another turn, and another. Deeper, down some stairs. He felt like he was being herded through a maze but didn't know who was herding or what was at the end. The hallways were lit with dim electric bulbs too far apart to cast enough light to reveal where he actually was. He was grateful not to have seen anyone else, though, since he'd have a hard time explaining why he was down there to begin with. The stock reply was something about a security check, but he knew that wouldn't hold water for long.

But now, thoroughly lost, that excuse was looking better and better—so long as he could actually bump into someone else to use it on.

Finally, after what seemed like forever, Cal heard something that didn't sound a whole lot like Turkish or Arabic—the two languages he'd been listening to for days now. And then, clear as day, he heard:

"*Da. Da, tovarishch.*"

Cal didn't get much in the way of language training at Area 51, but he did remember a bit of basic Russian.

He stopped and thought about his uniform dress shoes—he would have to have a word with that Mrs. Stevens when he got back, because they might as well have been tap shoes on the stones of the basement. Cal moved slowly, and hopefully quietly, as he heard the two Russians—no, wait, three Russians—talking in a room up ahead.

"*Harasho. Dasvidanyia.*"

Good. Good-bye. That might've exhausted all Cal's Russian knowledge, but it was enough. He looked around and, heart racing now, realized that whoever was in there would have to walk right by him on the way out—and no excuses about security checks would save his bacon. He braced himself as best he could, hoping he could work his Enhancement so that he wouldn't permanently harm whomever might come out of the room.

No one did.

Sweating and gritting his teeth, Cal edged slowly closer to the room. Only when he ventured a peek around the corner did he see there was another exit on the other side—and a Russian still in there.

Cal quickly edged back out of sight and tried to process what he'd just seen. It looked like a storage room or pantry of some kind. Lots of canned goods there, a bunch of sacks—probably flour or sugar or something like that—and some kind of well. Could be where the palace got some of its water, being that it was pretty old.

But no Yushchenko. He thought for a moment that maybe that fellow inside could let him know one way or the other. He quickly dismissed the notion, knowing that the Soviets, if that was who they were, wouldn't take kindly to being interrupted for any reason. And if Yushchenko was trying to hand off information or even switch sides, well . . . it wouldn't do anybody any good to bring that kind of notice down on him, now, would it?

Maggie said she got a note from Yushchenko. Maybe that would have to do.

Cal was about ready to retreat and try to get back upstairs when he heard echoes of footsteps from somewhere else in basement, followed by a familiar voice from inside the room. "Say, friend, can you tell me where the washroom is?"

Without thinking, Cal's training kicked in. He whipped around the corner into the room and placed his hand on the Russian's neck, draining enough life force from the man to exhaust him and put him to sleep without hurting him, thank God. As the man collapsed, he turned to Frank, who was pointing a gun at him—and then quickly pointed it away again. "Christ, Cal! I almost shot you. Where've you been? We're in trouble here."

Cal eyed the gun nervously until it was back in Frank's pocket. "Got turned around. Yushchenko's not here. I lost him. What's going on?"

"Russians may have a Variant here," Frank said curtly.

"Oh, Lord, no."

Frank and Cal were quickly joined by Maggie, and the three of them looked around the room. "This is at the very edge of the complex," Frank said. "I didn't see Yushchenko circle back. Where'd he go?"

"There were three of 'em in here," Cal said. "Three voices, all speaking Russian. Couldn't make it out other than a few words. Then I heard someone say good-bye, and then nothing except this guy."

Maggie put her hands on her hips. "God damn it. How'd we lose two Russians like that?"

"I don't know, Miss Maggie . . ." Cal began.

He stopped when he felt something pulling at his belt.

Cal looked down and saw nothing—but felt it grow more intense, an invisible force that seemed to be wrapped around his waist now, like ghostly arms, pulling him physically away from the others.

He stumbled. "What the . . ."

And then in a blur, he was gone, receding into darkness.

* * *

"Cal!" Frank shouted as he ran toward the well in the cellar room. One moment, they were all standing there talking. The next, Cal was literally *sucked down the well* as if by a powerful magnet. Except he wasn't made of metal, and . . . there was a lot wrong with the analogy, which was the point.

"He's terrified," Maggie said quickly. "Something's got him, but I don't sense anyone else."

"No kidding," Frank said. He quickly took stock of the room and, finding folded linens, began tying tablecloths together. "Shine a light down there and see where it goes."

Maggie took a small flashlight from her clutch and pointed it into the well. "I see a bottom, I think. Maybe thirty feet down?"

Frank dashed over to the edge of the well and looked down. "Only about twenty-five feet. About four of these should do. Help me tie it off."

They managed to affix the end of their crude rope to a thick wooden shelf stocked with heavy sacks of grain and large cans of food, and could only hope they wouldn't knock it over. Time wasn't on their side; it would have to do.

"I'll go first," Maggie said. "If there's anybody down there, I can keep 'em in check until you join me."

Frank opened his mouth to argue—then closed it. She was right. She could do a number on anybody down there: make them scared enough to run, or have a heart attack, or calm them into utter tranquility. Frank's best defense would be to go in shooting. "All right. Go."

Maggie kicked off her heels and tried to clamber up the side of the well in her dress, then swore vociferously and tore the gown's slit all the way up to her hip. Frank tried to look away but didn't quite get there in time, and winced in anticipation of her rebuff.

"Eyes ahead, soldier," Maggie teased as she went over the edge and started rappelling down the well.

Frank waited at the top, gun drawn with suppressor attached, until Maggie tugged at the tablecloth-rope twice. *All clear.* Frank proceeded down after her, only to feel the tablecloth-rope suddenly give way about halfway down, followed by the sound of a crash above. Frank fell the last ten feet, remembering to roll with the impact—and nearly plowing into Maggie in the process.

"Careful!" she hissed.

Frank dragged himself to his feet—his legs would be sore in the morning, but otherwise he managed the fall pretty well. "Sorry. I weigh more than you."

The two looked around to get their bearings in the low light. There was a roughhewn tunnel leading off to the . . . west, maybe. West and slightly south, if Frank's memory of the palace's upstairs layout was correct.

The tunnel was barely five feet high, just wide enough for them to walk single file. It looked old—easily a hundred years. "*Ancient cistern,*" Ibrahim's memories whispered. "*This may lead to the Basilica Cistern underneath Aya Sofia and the rest of the city.*"

Frank checked his gun and held it in both hands, leaving Maggie with the torch. "These tunnels may get bigger. Might run all under the city," Frank told her. "Old water supply."

"Looks dry to me," Maggie said quietly. "We gonna end up in sewage or something?"

"Well, if the Russians came down here, chances are they've scouted it out pretty well," Frank whispered. "So, I don't think we'll drown. But sewage is possible. Let's go."

Frank led the way, using his lighter as a torch and pointing his gun ahead as much as possible while picking his way across the stone floor. Maggie followed, *tsk*ing silently from time to time; the stones were probably hell on her bare feet, but heels would've been worse. The tunnel remained straight but sloped ever so slightly upward as they went, which made sense to Frank if water had once flowed through there to Topkapi.

Then he felt a hand on his shoulder and nearly jumped out of his skin. He whipped around, but it was just Maggie, who had a finger to her lips. She pointed down the tunnel, then held up three fingers.

Frank cursed himself for being so jumpy—he ought to have known better—then mouthed, "Cal?"

She shrugged and made a so-so motion with her hand.

Motioning her to stay put, Frank flicked the lighter closed and allowed his eyes to adjust for several excruciating moments. Finally, a slightly less dark patch of something coalesced out of the blackness around him: another light source. And so, he carefully, slowly stepped forward, just as he was taught, sweeping each foot out in front of him to check for obstacles before setting it down on the floor again.

They hadn't really told him in training how goddamn tedious it was to walk like that.

Finally, he was able to make out an archway ahead. Murmuring sounds reached his ears. He quickened his pace slightly, the archway now in range. They needed to find Cal or, if necessary, ensure that the Reds didn't get their hands on him. Frank didn't like that second option one bit but worried that Vandenberg, with Ellis at his ear, might prefer to deny Cal to the Russians and just get out of Dodge. And it was pretty likely the Russians had a Variant who could suck people down wells, apparently. *Time to move fast.*

In his haste, he kicked a stone.

It skittered loudly down the tunnel and then stopped, as if it dropped off into space. The murmuring immediately stopped.

Fuck.

Frank raised his weapon ahead of him even as he heard Maggie's footsteps behind him, bare feet slapping against stone. Then he felt a strange tug at his midsection, then another . . .

. . . and then he shot forward as if being pulled by a goddamn rocket.

Frank shot through the tunnel so fast, his feet didn't even drag. All he could see was the mouth of the tunnel getting closer at a phenomenal clip. Seconds later, he was through—and flying through the air in the middle of what seemed to be a huge cavern. Below him he saw a small light and at least two people blur past. But then he looked up and there was a pillar ahead of him—a huge, thick column of stone racing to greet him—and all he could do was ball up and swing his feet around.

He felt his shins bow . . . and break, sending lances of pain up his body.

Then the tugging sensation left . . . and he started falling.

* * *

As she dashed down the tunnel after Frank, Maggie felt his terror acutely as she saw his body fly out of the tunnel, then sheer horror and immense pain—and thank God she couldn't actually feel the pain, just the emotions stemming from it—and finally felt everything wink out altogether as he lost consciousness. Hopefully it was just that, rather than something more permanent.

And for the first time in months, Maggie felt something powerful well up inside her. She worried for Frank and Cal. She actually cared—and cared a lot. It was actual, genuine, one hundred percent real emotion—a shit-ton of it cascading inside her. Worry and grief, fear . . . and anger.

Lots of anger.

She reached out and could sense three minds ahead of her, none of them Frank or Cal, all buzzing with new tensions and worries. So, before she even reached the mouth of the tunnel, her mind grasped the strings of these emotions and began twisting . . . hard.

The screams were beautiful.

Then the guns started going off. The outline of the end of the tunnel expanded as she raced closer, and she twisted again, even harder. *Fuck you. Be afraid. I'm coming and if you don't fucking flee right now, I'm going to make you die of pure fucking terror.*

She was so occupied that she charged through the mouth without realizing it—and suddenly started falling.

With a scream, she twisted her body just enough for her hands to catch the lip of the tunnel, saving her from falling into the cistern. Swearing enough to make a sailor turn red, she grasped at a rope that had been anchored there and quickly rappelled down into the darkness, even as bullets careened off the stone several feet away. She'd lost the emotional grip she had on the people here, unable to concentrate on them while at the same time keeping herself from falling. Thankfully, aiming in the dark was a bitch for anyone, and she managed to get to the bottom and take cover behind a pillar.

She reached out again, finding those threads of fear, and pulled as hard as she could, watching the threads in her mind's eye turn bright red as they became taut. The shooting stopped, and the screams of terrified men echoed in the chamber, along with their fleeing footsteps.

Peeking around the corner of the pillar, she saw Cal was there, lying on the ground at the very edge of the light, unconscious; that's why she couldn't sense him. She knelt down beside him and saw he was breathing. *Thank God.* She then scanned the rest of the room as best she could, trying to figure out what had happened to Frank. Was he shot? Knocked out and captured? She looked back at the tunnel, then across the cavern . . . to a massive pillar. And at the base of it was a dark, crumpled heap.

Maggie ran over to him and struggled to remember the cursory first aid training she'd received at Area 51. First, assess the situation. *Patient unconscious. Blood at his mouth and nose. Legs askew and, at second glance, at horrible angles.*

Pulse. She put two fingers to Frank's neck and felt a heartbeat. That was a start. She put her hand against his nose and mouth, and felt breath. *Good.* After that . . . well, she knew she shouldn't move him, and wasn't quite sure how she would, anyway. He seemed to have a head wound in addition to all the damage to his legs. Maybe his spine, too, for all she knew.

She looked around and went through her options. Cal would be their best bet. He would probably be able to stabilize Frank, maybe even get him walking again. She started scrambling toward him to figure out *his* condition . . . then felt two more minds entering her range. Had the goons in the chamber doubled back? Should she have followed them?

Didn't matter. They'd run again if they got closer—and if they didn't, she'd make their hearts burst. She started to reach out with her mind, waiting to grasp at the threads of their emotions as soon as they presented themselves.

Then her clutch started vibrating.

She reached in and pulled out her compact, flipping it open. "Where are you, dammit?" she hissed quietly.

"We're in a big old underground vault of some kind, with pillars," Ellis replied. "Where are you?"

Maggie ran over and grabbed the left-behind lantern, raising it high. "Over here!" she called out, her voice racing and bouncing around the chamber.

Two sets of footsteps echoed through the cistern as Ellis and Danny ran toward her. "Where's Frank and Cal?" Danny demanded. "There are at least two Variants down here that weren't around an hour ago."

She pointed. "Both down. Frank's hurt bad. Cal, I don't know. It was . . . I don't know what. They flew."

Ellis ran over to Frank while Danny knelt down next to Cal. "'They flew,'" Danny repeated, a statement of numb disbelief, as he checked Cal over. "Probably just the result of one of the Variants. Who knows what the other one might be able to do. We need to get out of here now. Right now."

"We need Cal awake. He's the only one who can get Frank moving. Between the two of them . . ." Maggie's voice trailed off as her ears pricked up. There was a new sound barely audible in the air, something she couldn't put her finger on, like a low background hum.

Danny heard it too, pausing and cocking his head for a moment. Then he stood up suddenly. "Oh, shit. Water."

Maggie paled as dust started falling from the ancient ceiling and bits of masonry began raining down the walls and pillars. "They're flooding the place?"

"Probably," Danny said, racing into action. "Give me a hand."

Together, Maggie and Danny carried and dragged Cal over to Ellis, who remained at Frank's side by the base of the pillar.

"What the hell's that noise, and what the hell are we supposed to do now?" he said. Maggie could sense Ellis was near breaking point.

Danny knelt down next to him, grabbed his shoulders, and got in front of his face. "Ellis, listen to me. I think they're going to flood the cistern. But you can save us. All of us."

Wide-eyed, Ellis gawked back at Danny. "How the hell am I supposed to—" He stopped midsentence as he suddenly understood.

"Change it. Change it into something else," Danny urged as he looked at his feet. A thin stream of water flowed across the floor of the cistern, a harbinger of the wave to come. "We don't have time. Make a stone wall. Make a dome. Keep us safe."

Looking from Danny to Maggie, the color gone from his skin, Ellis shook his head to clear his thoughts and began nodding. "Yeah . . . yeah. I think I can do that. I can do that. Yeah."

Clapping him on the shoulder, Danny stood up and motioned to Maggie. "Put Cal next to Frank. We need to gather around this pillar. Ellis can then form the wall around us. The water's flowing from that direction," he said, pointing. "Start building there, and form it up around and behind us as you go."

Ellis put his hands down in the water—it was about a half-inch deep and flowing faster now—and closed his eyes. The water around his hand immediately went dark and gray, as if muddied, and the color spread outward all around Ellis. Then the mud solidified in a second wave, becoming smooth rock that thinly coated the cistern floor. "I think I got it. But I can't build off it. Not working like that."

"Then think!" Danny urged. "You got a lot of water coming. We need to put something between it and us!"

Ellis looked up and saw white-capped water at the very edge of the light. "It's coming!" He screwed his eyes shut and shoved his hands back down into the now three-inch-deep water.

"Get behind the pillar!" Maggie shouted over the increasing roar of water. "Drag them over!"

As she dashed over to Cal's limp form and grabbed a leg, Maggie thought she heard shouting—but the din of the rushing water was growing too loud to hear what was said. She pulled for all she was worth, slowly dragging Cal toward the pillar.

But it was too late. A wall of water at least ten feet high rose toward them now out of the darkness, rushing and roaring. Ellis was still out in front of them, completely exposed to the oncoming wave, his hands moving across the water at his feet, quickly turning it to stone. He was as afraid as anyone whose head she'd ever been in.

"Ellis!" she cried out. "Move!"

He didn't. Instead, he stood up to face the oncoming water and reached out in front of him both hands. Just as it was about to hit, Maggie turned her head and braced for impact.

It never came.

Maggie looked back up to see Ellis standing there, his arms still outstretched, before a massive wall at least twenty feet long and ten feet high, made of stone, and yet still curved and looking like it would flow forward at any moment. There were tendrils and eddies in the wall, frozen in rock as if carved by the best goddamn sculptor in the world, arched as if poised to fall down on Ellis at any moment and crush him.

But it didn't. The rest of the water diverted around the new wall, well away from the Variants.

Ellis turned and smiled. "Well . . . how about that?" he said quietly.

Then he collapsed to the floor in a faint. Around where he lay, the stone turned to glass as his Enhancement's side effect took hold. The stone wall held, however—Ellis's Enhancement was permanent.

All Maggie could do was stare and come to grips with the fact they were still alive.

Then she noticed something at the top of the wall.

A leg.

Reaching for the nearby lantern, she held it aloft and saw a body at the top of the stone sculpture, hanging over one of the waves, with everything below his belt encased in stone. He must have been flushed through the tunnel with the water, then trapped inside it as it turned to stone.

He was wearing a Soviet military uniform.

FIELD REPORT—ADDENDUM

AGENCY: Department of Defense / Central Intelligence Agency
PROJECT: MAJESTIC-12
CLASSIFICATION: TOP SECRET—MAJIC EYES ONLY
TO: DCI ADM Roscoe Hillenkoetter USN, SECDEF James
Forrestal, GEN Hoyt Vandenberg USAF, Vannevar Bush,
Detlev Bronk
FROM: LCDR Daniel Wallace USN
SUBJECT: Istanbul operations
DATE: 30 Apr 48

This report is an addendum to the CIA case file #327,
which does not carry the TS-MAJIC designation. The case
file includes information about the Istanbul operations
of 22 Apr, but does not include any details that are
TS-MAJIC compartmentalized. The case file provides a
streamlined narrative of the operation timeline, and you
are urged to read it prior to this addendum.

The following provides details of the MAJESTIC-12 opera-
tives and related intelligence gleaned from the operation.

FOREIGN AGENT ENCOUNTERS

We must now assume, with a high degree of certainty, that
the Soviet Union has recruited as least one, if not more,
Variants who are currently working as agents.

Both Lodge and Hooks were physically moved through
open space without any visible means of propulsion. Both

002

described being "grabbed" or "tugged." Both described
the sensation of flying. Dubinsky corroborated this; she
saw both Lodge and Hooks being "lifted" or "pulled"
away, again without any visible means.

Given the proximity of individuals believed to be Soviets,
our assumption is that the Soviets possess some means of
affecting this kind of kinetic movement. Therefore, we
must assume for the sake of national security that this
kinetic effect was produced by a Variant.

There is also the matter of flooding within the Basilica
Cistern under Istanbul. The cisterns under the city have
been dry for decades, if not longer. Examination of the
site by the U.S. Army Corps of Engineers, on invitation by
the Turkish government, showed no single place where that
volume of water could have come from. The conclusion we
must logically reach is that either the cistern was opened
to the sea or other large body of water and subsequently
closed to it again in rapid succession, or that a massive
volume of water was spontaneously created within the cistern complex itself.

Either possibility, by definition, would have to include
the potential of Variant involvement.

Finally, Subject-1 has reported the presence of at least
two unidentified Variants within the cistern—both new to
Subject-1's experience.

* TOP SECRET *
****

CAPTURED FOREIGN AGENT

Subject—1 believes that the individual trapped within the effect of Longstreet's Enhancement—the stone wall—is one of the two Variants previously on site. This individual has been thoroughly sedated since discovered—initially through Mrs. Stevens' darts, then through medical means. This sedation continued through his transport out of the country and transfer to Area 51 for study and containment.

The individual involved—a Caucasian male, believed Russian, mid 30s—was wearing the uniform of a MGB major. He carried no other identification. Photos have been taken and are being cross-checked with military and CIA files. It is worth noting that his physical condition—somewhat portly and unkempt—does not indicate someone with the extensive military or intelligence experience his rank might imply.

Until a plan of assessment and interrogation can be determined, the subject—codenamed POSEIDON—will remain sedated and restrained at all times.

VARIANT INJURIES

Lodge suffered two broken shinbones, four cracked ribs, and a major head injury, the latter of which had the potential for permanent brain damage. Timely intervention by Hooks allowed Lodge to prevent lasting or irreparable injury, and he has since undergone subsequent treatments by Hooks. He has recently been cleared to resume duty.

Hooks sustained a concussion while inside the cistern, and could provide no further intelligence beyond the reports given by other agents. He was able to heal himself of the condition, as well as Lodge's injuries, over the course of several days. A total of fourteen goats were donated to Turkish charitable institutions. Hooks is now cleared to resume duty.

Longstreet required no medical assistance beyond rest, as the use of his Enhancement on such a large scale exhausted his body mentally and physically. He is now cleared to resume duty.

Dubinsky suffered no physical injury during the incident. She has, however, grown increasingly withdrawn. It is my supposition that continued manipulation of others' emotions may have a profound psychological effect on her. I cannot tell whether this is a side effect of her Enhancement, or simply because of the nature of her ability. More testing will be required, and we may need to provide TS-MAJIC clearance to a psychologist for further assistance. Despite this, she remains on active duty.

Overall, the MAJESTIC-12 operational team remains engaged, and all of them have expressed a desire to make further contact with INSIGHT and obtain more information about their potential adversary or adversaries in the cistern

••••••••••••••
• TOP SECRET •
••••••••••••••

below Istanbul; they are particularly curious as to the
nature and variety of Variants that may be in the employ
of the Soviet Union. I believe that they are individually
and collectively prepared to return to operations.

NEW OPERATIONAL PROPOSAL

INSIGHT's cryptic message regarding Prague indicates that
city may be a more appropriate place for him to make
contact with us. There is some concern that the elected
government there is near collapse, with Communist Klement
Gottwald preparing to seize power. Given Stalin's support of Gottwald, it is likely to be a rapid affair; our
analysts anticipate the installation of a new, Communist-
controlled government within weeks. It is highly likely
that the Soviets will send a large delegation to whatever
inaugural events or festivities may be planned as part
of that, and we can assume INSIGHT will be among them.

I propose that Station Chief—Prague be placed on alert.
If INSIGHT is located, Station Chief—Prague should establish full surveillance as soon as possible.

I further propose we place the MAJESTIC—12 team on 24—hour
notice and keep them on the East Coast, rather than returning them to Area 51, to expedite transfer to Prague. Agents
Dubinsky, Lodge, and Longstreet may retain their cover identities for insertion into Czechoslovakia; Agent Hooks may
require new cover if GEN Vandenberg is unavailable. He may
cover as Lodge's aide—de—camp if practicable.

Given the Soviet presence in Istanbul, I believe we may
need to extract INSIGHT from the Soviet sphere and
bring him to the West. Learning more about any potential
Soviet program regarding Variants is, I believe, critical
to national security. If he cannot or will not provide
such information while in Prague, I firmly believe he must
be brought over. (I respectfully suggest that Secretary
Forrestal's operational suggestion regarding INSIGHT be
considered a last resort.)

I further propose all efforts be made to begin extraction
plans for INSIGHT's family as soon as possible, as to encourage further defection from the Soviet sphere over time.

(SIGNED) LCDR Daniel Wallace

There is no way in hell we're going to create another
MJ-12 clearance for a goddamned shrink. Otherwise, I
think the kid's right. What are we doing with the prisoner? —Forrestal

We need to brief HST on this ASAP. I want clearance from the top before authorizing any further MJ-12
ops. National security won't be well served if our own
Variants are killed or, worse, captured by the Reds. As
for the prisoner, we're still trying to figure that out.
Containment first, then study. —Hillenkoetter

20

May 4, 1948

POSEIDON lay on a gurney in his cell, his arms and legs restrained, the IV next to him dripping a sedative into his veins. The drugs were designed to last five hours; the sixth hour was spent coming out of the stupor long enough to be fed mushed-up food, like a mother would give to her baby. Then a new IV went in, and the Russian went back to an amorphous, dreamless slumber with just the barest hint of awareness.

Probably enough to drive him crazy, Danny thought as he looked down at the man.

"I wonder, Commander Wallace, how it is that the Russians, they do not miss this man. Would they not have filed a complaint or an inquiry by now?"

Danny turned to regard Dr. Schreiber with barely hidden disdain. "The Russians probably know we have him, just like they know we have Variants of our own," Danny said tightly and quietly, as if he were afraid to wake the Variant before him. "But they want to keep their program as secret as we do ours. So, they're not exactly going to walk on over to the State Department to ask about him."

The two men stood in silence for several long moments before Danny turned and left, the German scientist on his heels. Danny could sense the barest hint of the Russian's Enhancement while in the room, and it faded once he left the man's presence. Sedating an actual Variant confirmed to Danny that he was most effective sensing Variants when they were conscious, and probably more so when they were actively using their Enhancements.

"Have you developed a plan for testing and containment yet?" he asked Schreiber. "I asked for one last week. You finally get to run experiments on a real-life Variant for yourself after all. I thought you'd be excited."

The German shrugged. "These things take time. We do not even know what his power could be, or the extent of it. We have not finished our analysis on his blood and tissue samples. We are looking for everything possible that may tell us what the difference is between Variants and the rest of humanity."

"But you at least have some preliminary research ideas."

"Yes, we do. I believe we must place POSEIDON in a locked chamber with nothing else inside it, and one that can be easily flooded with knockout gas should things get, how do you say, out of hand," Schreiber said. "Camera for observation. Let him wake up and lash out, then put him down. Repeat with test subjects nearby in case his Enhancement works on people rather than objects or his own person."

Danny frowned. It pissed him off that this was how Forrestal and, worse, his own boss Hillenkoetter wanted to treat the man. Danny wanted to go in and talk, try to see if the guy would listen to reason, maybe switch sides. Join the good guys. That kind of persuasion was a lot harder to do when the good guys were acting like jerks.

The two walked out of the main scientific hangar toward Danny's office. The heat was really kicking up a notch or two at Area 51, and Danny found himself coated with sweat by the time he made it to the relatively cooler shade of the administrative building. The trek was worth it, though, as no one at Area 51 was allowed to talk about classified materials outside, which meant he didn't have to listen to Schreiber.

When they arrived inside Danny's office, Schreiber dove in before Danny could even take a seat. "Now that we have a confirmed Variant as prisoner, I hope you will reconsider my testing proposal for the anomaly."

"Tossing a Variant, even if he's a Russki, into the vortex isn't gonna happen," Danny said with what he hoped was authoritative finality. "Period. POSEIDON goes nowhere near that vortex. Are we clear?"

"We are," Schreiber said, looking down at his hands. "But you and I both know that these anomalies—this one and the one in Berlin—they created the Variants. This relationship must be explored somehow."

"You're the one who anticipated the vortex event in Berlin. You knew it would do these things. You're supposed to have the answers, Doctor," Danny shot back. "You tell me how that relationship works."

The scientist leaned back in his chair. "What occurred in that bunker below the Reich Chancellery was as much a surprise to me as it was to your men."

"Yeah, those who survived," Danny said, rubbing his eyes. "Look. Nobody goes near it except to study it. Our guest and the other Variants don't get involved."

"What about the criminal? Can we not use him?"

Use him. What a way to talk about a human being, even if he was some Vegas mobster. "Use him for what?"

Schreiber shrugged and smiled. "We have, as you know, sent a dog into the vortex. The animal came out the other side as if the phenomenon weren't even there. Since the energies from the vortex make alterations to human consciousness and physicality, it is reasonable to hypothesize that introducing a conscious, physical person to the vortex may produce a more measurable reaction."

That prompted Danny to sit upright in his chair. "So, you want to shove that sorry son of a bitch through the vortex and see what it does to him? What happens if it fries him? Or if he undergoes Permutation?"

"If he begins showing signs of Permutation, we shall have your security people there with their knockout darts. And if he fries, as you say, well, is that any great loss?"

God damn this Nazi bastard. We're better than that. Aren't we? "We haven't determined the final disposition of Mr.

Timofeyev quite yet, Doctor. He's an American citizen. At some point, we're going to have to treat him like one."

That prompted a dismissive smirk and a wave of the hand from Schreiber. "Commander, we both know that this man will never be released from custody. Perhaps you will charge him with something, or perhaps you won't pretend that criminal charges will make a difference. Either way, his life is over. But he may yet be useful if we allow him to. He may even render a great service to our cause!"

"Since when have you given a damn about truth, justice, and the American way?"

"That is not my cause, this is true, but neither is it yours," Schreiber replied. "You and I, we have one goal: to discover the truth behind these Enhancements and, if possible, unlock the potential of this vortex to empower all peoples!"

And there goes another official protest off to Hilly, Danny thought. "That's your fantasy, Doctor, not mine. Anything else?"

"Yes, Commander. When might we have a look at the other Variants?"

"That's not your department, and you know it," Danny replied. That was Hillenkoetter's one sop to Danny when Schreiber was brought on board—he literally wasn't allowed within a football field of any Variant at Area 51. At least, any Variant Hillenkoetter knew of. "We have others studying the Variants, and you're getting the data. That's all you're cleared for."

Schreiber opened his mouth to protest, then seemed to think better of it. "Very well, Commander. Is there anything else?"

Danny shook his head and waved his hand, then picked up a folder from his desk and started flipping through the papers. Schreiber hesitated a moment, then got up and left without further comment. Danny hoped the dismissive approach would remind Schreiber of his place—and, sure, just how far he'd fallen from the days when he could buddy up with Adolf Hitler. Answering to a junior officer had to rankle a bit. Danny hoped it did, at any rate.

Besides, Schreiber didn't know that Danny himself, Subject-1, had already been in very close proximity to the vortex—had been regularly, in fact—with zero discernible effect for nearly three years. But Schreiber wasn't cleared for Subject-1, and Danny was quite intent on keeping it that way.

Pulling his chair closer to his desk, Danny grabbed a piece of paper and rolled it into his typewriter. While it would probably feel really damn good to fire off another protest about Schreiber, it would end up being useless. But maybe—just maybe—there was a shot at keeping the Russian Variant from becoming another scientific guinea pig for an amoral German.

He was about three lines in when he saw Detlev Bronk at his door. "How is it that you're always furiously typing up a new report every time you meet with Schreiber?" he asked mischievously.

Danny smiled and waved him in toward the chair recently occupied by the German. "Guess he motivates me to work harder. How's it going?"

Bronk settled into the chair. He had traded his typical business suit for a short-sleeved linen shirt and golf pants, and looked for all the world like a Florida retiree rather than one of the nation's foremost scientists. "Anderson is really whipping them into shape nicely. They might be ready to go in a couple months."

Danny frowned. Much as he wanted to have Anderson reassigned, the Marine remained at Area 51—probably under Forrestal's direct orders. So, all Danny could do was to shunt him off to the training areas as much as possible and keep him out of security matters altogether. "Side effects?"

Bronk just shrugged. "Still there. Aside from Lodge and that mythical Subject-1, who you're keeping hidden from everyone else here, everybody seems to have side effects. No getting around it."

"I didn't think there would be. Any other leads?"

"No. Seems to have quieted down. We finally have a network of detectors in place, in case the vortex decides to perk up again. We'll be able to track it anywhere in the US or Canada, and certain places in Central and South America, too." Bronk held up a hand as Danny was about to chime in. "And yes, you're first on the call list when we get one."

Danny smiled. Bronk was a good guy, probably the most forward and affable on the MAJESTIC-12 program. He so very much wanted to trust him with his reservations about Schreiber, or Forrestal for that matter. Or the real identity of Subject-1.

But he didn't. "Sounds good. Thanks."

21.

May 12, 1948

I think there's someone tailing us," Frank said as he walked along Pennsylvania Avenue between the White House and Capitol building. "Here we go again."

Next to him, dressed in a sharp navy skirt and jacket with a subdued, wide-brimmed hat, Maggie looked at her reflection in a store window—and used it to check behind her as well. "And here I thought we might get a day in town without a babysitter."

The two were at liberty in Washington with very little to do other than wander. Both Cal and Ellis had been granted time with their families; Danny had arranged for relatives to come up to the nation's capital for several days. He had offered to do the same for Frank, but Frank had just shrugged. He hadn't been in touch with his family since just after the war, so a reunion would be . . . difficult, at best. And he knew his girl was long gone by now, probably married with kids. Things could change a lot in three years.

So, they went into town together—but not alone. Never alone. MAJESTIC-12 wanted to keep an eye on them, just in case they were put in danger. Or put others in danger.

"I see him," Maggie said coolly. "Half a block back. Double-breasted suit, tie, kind of short and pudgy. Not really good at this, is he?"

Frank smirked. "Well, we're the pros now, right?"

"Don't know about you, but I did OK," she teased. "What do you want to do?"

"Prank 'em again?" he asked with a smile.

A week ago, he had convinced Maggie to have some fun with their escorts. They'd grabbed a cab in Foggy Bottom with no warning, then switched to a bus a mile later that took them to Anacostia, and then turned right around and headed to Dupont Circle in another cab, where they waited at a café as no fewer than six agents finally showed up to stake out the perimeter, glowering at them. Frank thought it was a hoot. Maggie was less impressed but went along with it anyway.

"Nah, not today," Maggie replied. "I want to go to a bar and get drunk, but it's only 11 a.m. Little early for that. Let's head over to the Capitol, have a seat on the steps, watch the world go by for a while . . . I'm getting a little tired of the games, frankly."

Frank gave the man another surreptitious glance. "He doesn't look like Secret Service. There's something about him that's different than the others. What if he's a Russian?"

Maggie, placid as ever, simply shrugged. The threat of danger never seemed as real to her, Frank thought. "Then I guess it'll get interesting," was all she said.

With that, Maggie took Frank's arm, and together, they strolled down the broad avenue without talking. That was one thing Frank liked about Maggie—she didn't feel the need to fill the silence with gabbing. He wasn't even sure if she enjoyed his company or not—and frankly, he could say the same of hers—but they could at least coexist in the same space well enough. There were worse things. That said, he wished she'd be a little more animated. She seemed to be getting more distant with each passing day.

By the time they reached the shadow of the Capitol dome, they'd picked up two more tails, both of which they immediately pegged for Secret Service—cheap suits, bags under the eyes, and, most evidently, shoulder-holstered revolvers bulging out from their jackets. It had gotten to the point where they were starting to see familiar faces among their chaperones. At this point, they didn't think Danny ordered the tails himself, but they also knew by now that he was pretty low on the MAJESTIC totem pole. The four Variants had batted around the idea of who was doing what and who was on their side, but all they really knew was that maybe some higher-ups liked them, and probably some really didn't.

"They're scared," Ellis had said one night over dinner in their new digs, a heavily guarded townhome in Foggy Bottom near the CIA's headquarters. "We got these abilities, these extraordinary powers. They're scared of that, even though they want to use us. Maybe they're right to be scared, especially now that we know there's more out there like us."

At first, Frank had dismissed that notion with a laugh and a swig of whiskey, but the more he thought about it, the more it made sense; maybe the fact that his Enhancement wasn't as in-your-face as the others' were colored his perceptions of it. And so, he kept his head up and eyes open. The first time he saw the Secret Service tails, he chided himself for being so naive. And now, with someone new watching, Frank's list of people to trust was getting pretty thin indeed.

Maybe it really was a Russian. That seemed a little paranoid at first, but after Istanbul, anything seemed possible.

Frank left Maggie on a bench by the east steps of the Capitol and got a bag of popcorn from a nearby cart. When he returned, she looked off to her right; the fancy-suit guy was sitting on the steps of the Capitol, munching on a sandwich. Frank took a seat next to Maggie and held out the popcorn. "What about the others?" Frank asked.

"One's up top of the stairs for the wide view," she replied. "Other's in the park across the way. Keeping their distance but looking hard. Not like this guy. Maybe he's better than I thought. Using his peripherals more."

Frank casually glanced over to the man. "*Caucasian, Eastern European descent. Mid forties. Spare tire around the waist, but shoulders and arms look built. Could be a tough customer.*" The voice was that of the gangster in the Las Vegas hotel room, and it nearly caused Frank to jump out of his skin. So much for pushing the memories away—something stuck. At least it was kinda useful, but what else was floating around in his head that he didn't know about?

"Frank?" Maggie asked. "What's wrong? You got really worried there."

He shook his head to clear it. "Jesus, Maggie. Stay out of my head."

She just shrugged. "Doesn't work that way. I can feel it coming off of you. I wasn't prying. You all right?"

"Yeah, sorry. Got a bead on that guy, he's—shit, where'd he go?"

Frank cast around as subtly as he could, but the guy in the nice suit was nowhere to be found. He hadn't even left any litter on the steps.

"Maybe he wasn't a tail," Maggie said. "Could've read him wrong."

"I doubt it. Maybe he saw the others and bailed."

Then a cluster of tourists directly in front of them parted, and the man was walking right through toward them. He was so close that Frank barely had time to react, and his heart started racing a mile a minute. Definitely not Secret Service. Question was: Who?

"Say, excuse me," the man said, a Chicago accent coming through. "Don't suppose you know which way the train station is?"

Maggie gave her best smile; she only did that, Frank knew, when she was acting. "Sure, it's right over there, mister. Just a block or two. Want some popcorn?" She held out the bag to him.

"Well, don't mind if I do. Thank you, miss!" The man reached in, grabbed a few kernels, and tipped his hat before walking off toward the station with purpose.

They sat in silence for a few more moments before Frank spoke up. "That was real dangerous, Maggie. Care to tell me what's going on?"

"I could feel his anxiousness as he got close. He was nervous, excited. Bet he knew exactly who we were. So, I gave him a chance to do something."

"Right, the popcorn. And?"

Maggie stood up, popcorn in hand. "And I need to use the ladies' so I can see what he left us." She made her way toward the building. "Be right back."

Frank half-smiled after her; she was so goddamn good at this spy stuff, it was scary. Frank began to wonder if there were any aging OSS officers he might sit with. Next to Maggie, he felt like a greenhorn. He watched as the agent at the top of the stairs casually followed Maggie inside, but he knew darn well that the man wouldn't dare follow her into the bathroom. And that would give her enough time to figure things out. The other agent still sat in the park with his eyes glued to Frank. Hadn't any of them noticed the man from Chicago?

For the next ten minutes, Frank sat and watched people mill about the Capitol grounds. There were young men with sharp haircuts and clean faces carrying stacks of files around—Washington's young politicos, probably. Someday, they'd go back to where they came from and probably get a seat on the city council or something, beginning the climb that would hopefully land them back here, with a bunch of young politicos fetching their own paperwork. Then there were the tourists with their guidebooks and their souvenir fans, waving them around to stave off the heat of the typically warm day. They all looked completely innocent, unaware of what was unraveling under their very noses. The thought made Frank's skin crawl. This spy shit was really getting to him. He was starting to feel like he couldn't trust anybody.

"Well, that was interesting."

Maggie sat back down next to him and offered him some popcorn, which he took. "Yeah?" he asked.

"Note. Flushed it. We need to get the team together. Danny, too."

Frank tried his best to look casual. *What the hell was going on?* "Anyone else?"

Maggie smiled, and this time it seemed genuine and, if Frank were being honest with himself, a little scary. "No. Just Variants."

* * *

Danny ran down the details of the operation that Hillenkoetter and Forrestal—who were sitting in the back of the room—had approved earlier that day. The only hitch was that Hillenkoetter had nixed the idea of letting Danny lead the effort himself—it'd been determined that Subject-1 was too important to lose should things go sour like they had in Istanbul.

But he felt the team was ready, and he knew Frank was a capable leader. They would be in Prague within two weeks, in time for the inauguration of the new government, unless Station Chief-Prague flagged them sooner that Yushchenko was in town.

"As for prep work, we're tracking down suitable candidates in the hospitals over there so that Frank can get some language and local information. Any thoughts, Frank?"

"Actually, yeah. The professor in Istanbul was helpful and all, especially since we were in an old palace," Frank said. "But this time, maybe get me someone who knows the whole city real well, like a cabbie or a cop. If we're pulling INSIGHT out, that kind of information could be handy."

Danny made a note on his clipboard. "Good idea. Anyone else?"

Ellis raised a hand. "Yeah. If you want me to work on that car, maybe have another one handy in case the side effects cause a larger issue or I need parts or something."

"You got it," Danny said, scribbling again. "Oh, and Cal, we're going to find and secure a farm on the outskirts of the city proper in case you need to grab some life energy from some livestock. We'll aim for somewhere between Prague and the West German border, just in case we have to grab him—could double as a safe house if needed. Anything else?"

Danny looked around. Frank, Cal, and Ellis seemed done, while Maggie . . . Danny had to do a double take. He knew that look.

A moment later, both Hillenkoetter and Forrestal stood. "Looks like you have things in hand, Wallace,"

Hillenkoetter said with a forced smile, while Forrestal just glared at the CIA director. "If you'll excuse us."

The two men walked out of the conference room and, a few seconds later, could be heard arguing out in the hallway. "Maggie, what the hell did you just do?" Danny snapped. "I worked for weeks to get them to approve this!"

She smiled slyly, probably knowing full well the effect it had on Danny. "They're not angry about the operation, Commander. Right now, they're just irritated with each other. Honestly, it wasn't that hard of a push. And by the way," she continued, cutting him off before he could interrupt, "that Forrestal guy is pretty scared, just being in the room with us. Your CIA boss, there, though, he's nice enough."

Danny slumped down into his chair. "Jesus, Maggie. Why would you go and do that?"

"We made contact with someone today. Someone new. He slipped us a little note," she replied, lowering her voice.

"While you were under surveillance?" Danny asked incredulously.

"And who was the one who did that?" Frank countered.

Danny sighed; it was going to be one of *those* conversations. "Not me. You can take your guesses. What did the note say?"

Maggie recited from memory: "'You are not alone. We are Empowered, like you. You can be free. We will help you.'"

The words hung in the air for long moments. "Dammit," Danny said finally. "They made us."

"The Russians?" Cal asked, sitting up straight. "They know who we are? Thought we got off clean in Turkey. If they've made us, what happens? What about my family?"

"Who else?" Danny replied. "It was like they were waiting for us in Istanbul. That's why we have to get our hands on INSIGHT. Hate saying it, but we're at an intel disadvantage here."

"How do we even know it's the Russians?" Maggie asked. "Maybe it's, I don't know, some kind of independent group."

"They did capitalize the *E* in *Empowered*," Frank added. "Kind of like the way you capitalize the name of a baseball team, isn't it?"

Danny looked at Frank and Maggie incredulously but thought better of an immediate retort. They'd obviously had time to hash this out before bringing it to the rest of the team. Cal and Ellis looked stricken—both of them had families, after all, and if the Russians found out who they were, those pressure points could be easily leveraged. Frank looked worried too. But Maggie almost seemed excited— but with the tiny cues she gave off, it was damned hard to tell. It made sense, though, that she'd perk up at the prospect of finding more Variants. That was one of the things that drove Danny, after all—finding others like him.

But an independent group?

"Look, we have to assume it's the Russians. Far as we know, they're the only game in town. Yes, there are ways Variants could track each other down," Danny ventured. "My Enhancement allowed me to find all of you, after all. But there's also good old-fashioned footwork. Newspaper reports of strange phenomena, for example—we have a team on that right now."

"Or y'all got a leak in your ship," Ellis said.

Cal nodded in agreement. "Mr. Longstreet here could be right. All them scientists out at Area 51. All them soldier boys. And you got people here in Washington who may know pieces of this. No such thing as a real secret nowadays."

In for a penny, Danny thought. "Look, I shouldn't be telling you this, so we're going to keep all this between us, all right? We still have the mobster in custody. He hasn't given us anything, and we've been working very hard to be . . . persuasive. In fact, we've considered flying Maggie back out to have a crack at him."

"Why haven't you?" she asked.

"Well . . ." Danny started, and then took a breath. *Screw it.* "Because we think the guy we picked up in Istanbul is a Variant, and it's been determined that we don't want you all around him right now. Anderson is keeping them in the same facility to maximize our security and keep the need-to-know down."

The silence around the table was expected. Danny was committing any number of court-martial offenses by revealing this information, but the obligation to his fellow Variants—the people he himself recruited—seemed more important. He'd become increasingly conflicted lately about the line he'd been straddling. Whose side was he on? There were times when he regretted being so forthright with his superiors about his Enhancement—usually after talking with Secretary Forrestal. His patriotic fervor didn't seem like such a high priority in the face of unreasonable fear and a closed mind.

"You know? Screw this," Ellis said. "I'm done. You can lock me up, whatever you want, but we got Russians tailing us, we got the Soviets with Variants now. You're keeping way too much from us, and I don't like it one bit. You're putting us in real danger, and that ain't what I signed up for."

"And what the hell, locking up Variants like that?" Maggie added. "That Russian is one of us. We can show him what we're doing. Get him to switch sides. He's one of *us*, Danny!"

"The only *us* I care about is this team!" Danny shot back. "I have bent over backward to shield you from the worst of this. There are people, important people, who still think we should be locked up. All of us. Put down a hole and buried. You're here because I'm trying to find a better way for us. And you know what? That Russian used his Enhancement *against* you. Now you want to be pals? If he's not interested, what then? He goes AWOL and that only gives people another reason to lock us up!"

There was an uncomfortable silence in the room for several moments while Danny calmed himself and gathered his thoughts. "We thought the Russians were clueless. They're not. They have Variants, and they probably have the other anomaly. It's not like the nukes, where they can't get theirs to work yet. They're on par with us here—they may even know more about Variants and what caused this than we do. And if you want to find out more about what happened to us and why we have these abilities, then you're going to want to go to Prague and get Yushchenko. We can find out what the Russians are up to, who your mysterious contact was today, what the hell is going on. And we'll do it without some paranoid son of a bitch trying to lock us away for not playing ball. Understood?"

Danny stood up and left the four members of his team behind. Outside, in the hallway of the Foggy Bottom office building, it seemed Forrestal and Hillenkoetter had mended fences—or at least walked away from each other, because they were nowhere to be found.

It never even occurred to Danny to tell either of his superiors that they had been under the influence of a Variant.

* * *

"I'm telling you, Hilly, she had us under her goddamn spell or something," Forrestal said, a mix of frustration and pleading in his voice. "I've never wanted to actually hit you until today."

Hillenkoetter sat behind his desk and smiled at his colleague and adversary. "Well, Jim, I've wanted to hit you pretty much every goddamn day I've known you, but I will say that today's the first day I came close to throwing the punch. And for no good reason."

"Exactly!" the defense secretary said, his hands spread. "That girl is dangerous. She assaulted us, basically. She needs to be locked up. Throw away the key."

"Jim, she's the most effective agent we got. Her Enhancement works at range, for one, and she can pretty much kill a man with her mind. And then there's the interrogation applications she brings to the table. You try to bring her in line, you either get her pissed enough to let loose, or you drug her up so she's useless. I don't want her useless."

"She's dangerous," Forrestal insisted.

"They all are. That's the risk we agreed to take."

Forrestal leaned back in his chair with a sigh. "What do you think they're doing in there?"

"Talking about us, probably. Or maybe about the other Variants out there in Soviet hands. It's healthy for them to be able to have the freedom to speak amongst themselves. Not too many others have the same kind of experiences."

"You're a soft touch," Forrestal said, throwing up his hands as he stood. "Maybe I should've hit you."

Hillenkoetter just smiled as he stood, and extended his hand. "That's how I got this pretty, getting punched in the face. Good to see you, Jim."

"You're coddling them. This isn't over," Forrestal said as he stormed off. Despite Forrestal's threat, Hillenkoetter couldn't help but feel good. He enjoyed having a one-up on someone, and on Forrestal in particular. He figured Truman would back him up, anyway—the President had a short temper when it came to Forrestal's antics. Besides, whatever the Variants were talking about, the reel-to-reel recorder in the conference room would tell him soon enough.

22.

June 14, 1948

That's contact," Frank muttered as he watched the dignitaries file onto the dais overlooking the long, narrow Wenceslas Square in the center of Prague. Tall old buildings lined the sides in baroque splendor, with flags—a blue triangle with two fat stripes of red and white—hanging from nearly every window. The crowd had a kind of muted excitement, as if they were sort of happy to be there, if only because they didn't have to be at work. Up on the stage, there were plenty of Czechs and Slovaks in suits and ties, a couple women as well, and a number of foreign dignitaries—many of whom looked very, very Russian. The Red Army uniforms were, of course, a dead giveaway.

One of them was Yushchenko.

Frank looked around the square, trying to gather intelligence from what he saw—or rather, what the woman inside his head was picking up. Last night, Frank had visited an elderly washerwoman on her deathbed, Mathilde Cizek, who'd pushed a cart around the Old Town of Prague for nearly a half century. She knew everything about everyone, it seemed, and her family assured Danny that she knew the city as well as her own children.

Frank later learned she'd had ten kids and, at last count, twenty-three grandchildren. A lot of children to know. And as he looked around, Mathilde . . . fed him information about the streets and boulevards, alleys and service doors, what the various buildings housed—all mixed in with anecdotes about her family. A lot of it seemed useless, but Frank did his best to remember it all, just in case.

Finally, Klement Gottwald took the stage, his freshly scrubbed and beaming family trailing behind him. There were more spirited cheers from the crowd, though Frank knew the armed security in the square had been "encouraging" people to get into the spirit of things. Orders to "Be happy. Cheer loudly," followed by a hard look and a tighter grip on their SKS carbines, and everybody seemed to take it pretty seriously. Of course, the Soviets had engineered Gottwald's ascendancy, which is why Yushchenko could reasonably deduce he'd be in Prague for the festivities.

Frank didn't need Maggie's Enhancement to tell Yushchenko was nervous and haggard. He wondered why. The event was pure theater, the Czechs and Slovaks weren't making noise about their new overlords, things seemed nice and pacified. But INSIGHT looked pretty bad. Maybe it was just a hard night of vodka and Czech girls. Maggie would be able to gather more information, as she was posted closer to the stage.

So, Frank turned to more pressing matters—like how to get close to Yushchenko while he was out in the open, so he could pass him a note.

"*You're not going to get to him here*," came Mathilde's voice, unbidden. "*They have the entrances blocked. Even the service ones I used. When they do things here, it is impossible to get anywhere without having your papers checked every ten feet.*"

Frank sighed and brought his Ansco Speedex camera up to his eye to squeeze off a roll of film. Every face on that stage needed a good sharp photo—a favor to the overworked Prague station chief. Least he could do, given he probably wouldn't get anywhere close to Yushchenko anyway.

* * *

"Well, it's sure nice to see you again, Mr. Kyranov. Next time, I'm gonna be sure to pack a bottle of Jack Daniels for you!" Ellis said, gripping the Russian's hand firmly in the middle of Vladislav Hall in Prague Castle, where the new president was celebrating a peaceful, if not entirely above-board, transition of power.

"And I you, Mr. Davis. I shall bring you Stolichnaya from Moscow. It is our finest vodka, and we shall compare which of our nations produces the better liquor!" Kyranov exclaimed, his broad face sweaty from the packed room and the large tumbler he'd just consumed. "And you must tell me more stories of your charming Alabama."

Ellis put a hand on the man's shoulder and smiled. "Oh, I got plenty of stories, *tovarishch*. Can't wait to share 'em!" And with that, Ellis nodded and extricated himself from the gregarious Russian so he could sidle up to Maggie over by the bar, a rickety-looking thing, given the vaulted arches and flowery stonework of the hall.

"Renewing old friendships?" Maggie asked with a slight grin. She had on a red number that, Ellis had to admit, worked pretty well for her. Gowns seemed hard—so many ways they could cut and fit. Tuxedos, in Ellis's estimation, were both easier and more elegant. Any man looked better automatically by putting on a tux—even Cal, who was wandering the party in full formal wear, play-acting as the deputy ambassador of some African country or another.

"Kyranov is a drunk and a talker. Shame is, he doesn't say anything worth listening to," Ellis said as he flagged the bartender for another glass of champagne—a taste he was quickly acquiring.

"Read the files next time," Maggie said quietly after sipping her own drink. "He's a deputy commissar in their agriculture department. His uncle helped whack dissidents when Stalin took over, after Lenin died. He's useless."

Ellis frowned. "You stick to your tactics, and I'll stick to mine. I see you haven't spotted our friend yet."

"No INSIGHT," she confirmed, looking out over the crowd. Ellis followed her gaze to where Cal was standing—of course, he stood out like a sore thumb in a tux. But he also seemed relaxed—Ellis had serious reservations about trying to put Cal in the middle of a fancy ball as anything other than a flunky, but so far, so good. Of course, Frank was with him, acting as his "translator," meaning that Cal didn't have to really say or do anything important. Ellis had to admit that Cal had been useful to the team, but still couldn't shake his feeling that it was just plain wrong to have him around. It's not like there were any other Negroes in attendance. Maybe that was the point, a bit of misdirection so the Czechs would be busy looking at Cal while the rest of the team did their jobs. But still . . . it was hard to stomach sometimes. Some things, Ellis believed, shouldn't be done. . . .

Maggie cleared her throat slightly. "Simmer down, Ellis. Cal's doing just fine."

"Stay out of my head, woman," Ellis hissed.

"I don't read minds. Your emotions come off you like a bad stink. So, rein it in." Maggie put her empty champagne glass firmly on the bar and strode into the large crowd, looking left and right as subtly as she could, on the prowl for Yushchenko.

Ellis sighed and took a big swig of bubbly. It was going to be a long trip.

* * *

June 15, 1948

"The ambassador sends his regards and humblest apologies, President Gottwald, and the deputy ambassador hopes our two nations may enjoy new prosperity together in socialist brotherhood," Frank said with a bright smile as Cal stood next to him stoically, hands clasped in front of him, feeling just uncomfortable enough to be believable . . . he hoped.

Gottwald took the proffered letter from Frank and scanned the credentials they had managed to grab—taken off the actual Botswanan ambassador two nights before. Cal knew he wasn't a smooth actor like Frank or Ellis, but they'd assured him that his natural discomfort with this whole con game would be fine, given he was playing the part of some minor flunky pressed into service to meet a president. Meanwhile, someone was translating Frank's English into Czech, or whatever they spoke around here.

Gottwald smiled and nodded at Cal, saying something in Czech that sounded friendly enough. The English translation came a moment later from the Czech interpreter. "The President accepts your credentials and hopes your ambassador has a speedy recovery. We hope he will accept our invitation to dinner soon, so that we may discuss the spread of socialist liberation throughout the African continent."

Cal was about to nod and smile, but Frank leaned in just in time to remind him that he was supposed to wait for his "translation." "The new president of Czechoslovakia hopes to never see you or me again, and will probably never have dinner with anyone, not even his own wife, unless Stalin gives the say-so," Frank whispered, causing Cal to smile broadly and nod—probably Frank's intent.

A moment later and the two were off to the side of the ornate reception hall, their diplomatic "duties" completed. "I don't know, Frank," Cal said with a straight face. "I think I make a damn fine ambassador, if I say so myself."

Frank nodded deferentially. "You're a natural world leader, Cal. Now let's circulate and see if we can find our man."

The two split up to cover more territory. All Cal would have to do was just smile and nod his way around the room. He'd originally been worried about running into someone who spoke anything African, but what became immediately obvious was that he was the only Negro in the room, and other than the fact that he felt a bit like a peacock at the zoo, no one really wanted to do anything other than stare at the colorful attraction. The ugly, colorful sash he wore over his suit didn't help matters much.

Cal did a couple circuits, then settled down next to the refreshments; somehow, the 11 a.m. diplomatic reception still called for wine. How did politicians get anything done with all this drinking going on?

Then he saw Yushchenko, and his heart stopped.

The Soviet officer was standing in a cluster with a couple of other Red Army men, drinks in hand, laughing and chatting amiably. Cal looked around for Frank, but he was nowhere in sight. *Well, I suppose this is what they trained me up for.*

Cal walked over to the group, fishing a lighter out of his pocket—the very same one Yushchenko had passed to Maggie in Istanbul. "Gentlemen!" he said broadly, his arms raised, speaking in what he hoped was a believable African accent. "Do you have cigarette for me to have?"

The group looked stunned a moment, and Cal wondered if he'd put on too much of a show. Finally, one of the officers made a smoking motion, putting two fingers to his lips. "Yes! *Da!*" Cal replied, beaming like that damned Al Jolson character that everybody assumed black folk were like.

The officer fished a pack out of his pocket and said something in Russian that caused the rest of the group to laugh—probably at Cal's expense. Didn't matter. "Thank you," Cal said as the officer handed him one, and lit the cigarette with Yushchenko's own lighter—while looking right at the man.

Cal watched INSIGHT's eyes widen for just a flash.

With a nod and a bow, Cal retreated out the glass doors and onto the balcony overlooking the hustle and bustle of Prague, all cleaned up and open after yesterday's inauguration. He decided to count to a hundred to keep himself from looking around too much.

He only made it to forty two. "It is your first time to Prague?" came a voice from beside him. Cal turned to find Yushchenko there next to him.

"Yes, it is," Cal said, still trying to keep his accent on. "It is very nice here."

Yushchenko held up a cigarette of his own. "Can I borrow your light?"

Bingo. "Yes, sir," Cal said, handing over his lighter—and the note palmed beneath it. To Yushchenko's credit, he barely flinched.

"Thank you, comrade," Yushchenko said, handing back the lighter.

"No, you keep," Cal said. "I have another."

The Soviet colonel nodded and gave a faint smile, then turned and sauntered off down the balcony, idly puffing away on his cigarette. Cal managed to get to seventy-four this time before his nerves got to him and he extinguished his cigarette, leaving to go find his "interpreter" and report success.

* * *

June 17, 1948

Frank sat in the tiny, cramped Volkswagen, wishing to hell that people in Europe would drive real goddamn cars. Frank wasn't even that tall, but he was beginning to feel like the tiny little vehicle, marked with a makeshift TAXI sign in Czech, was his own personal cocoon.

For the millionth time, Frank went over the plan in his head, wishing Danny had been along for this one. The note given to Yushchenko was very specific: *Let's meet, baby. Use chalk to mark the hydrant on Bělehradská Street between Rumunská and Koubkova Streets when you are ready. The following night, meet me at 25 Sokolovská Street. Come alone. Kisses.*

Baby and *Kisses* were a clever way to throw off the scent, and the note had been written in Maggie's hand. The hope was that if Yushchenko were burned, the note might look like he was having a little rendezvous with a lady—and Maggie was willing to play the part of an American lover, Ellis the role of angry husband. Things seemed pretty deniable, really. Even the chalk mark, an old standby from the OSS, could simply be a lover's code. Yushchenko would probably get in trouble . . . but not executed. Hopefully.

Frank's reverie was broken by a man walking down Bělehradská Street toward Danny's cab, in a hat and trench coat. Frank could see a normal suit underneath—not a military uniform. The dim lighting and fog from the river made it tough to make out his face. Was he holding something in his hand?

The man approached the hydrant with a slightly unsteady gait and brushed by it—either an expert bit of tradecraft, Frank thought, or a sign the man had been drinking. Maybe both. He then continued down the street, swaying ever so slightly.

Frank looked at his wristwatch—2:43 a.m. He waited until 3:06 a.m. to be absolutely sure that nobody else was around and that his potential contact—if that's who he was—had had a clean getaway. Finally, Frank got out of the cab, locked the door, and walked up the street, hands crammed into his pockets. He crossed Bělehradská Street and made for a small park nearby, resisting the urge to walk past the hydrant immediately. Instead, Frank took a leak in a bush just inside the park, then slowly walked back to his car, passing the hydrant as he went.

There was a bright white chalk line on the hydrant's dome.

It took every bit of discipline for Frank to keep the same slow pace as he made for his car.

* * *

June 18, 1948

"I hate all of you, you know," Maggie groused as she paced the front room of the unassuming townhouse on Sokolovská Street. "I'm not a goddamn dress-up doll."

Frank smiled at her from the dining room, where he was poring over a map of Czechoslovakia for what seemed like the hundredth time. "If he's burned, you're gonna need to play the part, Maggie. You're taking one for the team."

Maggie stopped and put her hands on her hips. "Why don't you just put me out in the red light district and rent me out?" she said. "Why couldn't I just wear something normal?"

"Because it's 1 a.m. and people don't wear normal clothes at 1 a.m. unless they're up to something no good," Frank said, his voice sounding both bemused and slightly impatient. "If our guy has a tail, seeing you at the door is going to buy us a lot of time. You know this—it was in the ops plan."

Maggie knew, of course, that Frank was right, but still really wanted to punch him in the face. She knew she was a better athlete, a better shot—a better *soldier*—than Ellis, probably better than Cal, too. Only Frank seemed to be much of a match for her, but Maggie also knew that having military experts whispering information in your head was quite an unfair advantage.

At least Cal had the decency to avert his eyes from her before heading upstairs to take his post; he was staking out the neighborhood from the roof of the building, a safe house purchased by the OSS in the wake of the German retreat and during the chaos of the initial Soviet occupation. Someone, Maggie knew, had been on the ball at OSS, because apparently there were safe houses like this from Sarajevo to Vilnius. She knew she'd probably visit a few more of them down the road. Maggie could feel Cal's discomfort with the job from the first floor and most definitely got the sense Cal, armed with a suppressed pistol, wouldn't use it, even if a whole army of Reds came down the street for them.

That was fine. She'd shoot enough for both of them. She'd be good at it, too, if they let her. She'd be better than Ellis, for sure, who was out back in the garage putting the final touches on the car.

A crackling sound from the radio interrupted her train of thought. "Somebody turning onto the street now," Cal reported. "Looks like INSIGHT."

Frank keyed his radio. "Thanks, Cal. Stay put and see if he has company. Ellis, come on in. He's here." He then nodded to Maggie as he stowed his map in his pocket and checked the sheathed knife he'd secured in his belt at the small of his back. "You're up. Give it a five count before you go for the door. Then dazzle him." He then wiggled his hand in a so-so motion. "If I do this at any point, take him down completely."

The knock interrupted whatever retort she had in mind, so she simply flipped Frank the bird and counted to five before pasting a really fake smile on her face and slowly walking to the door—slowly, of course, because the four-inch spike heels were just far too impractical for anything else.

She opened the door to see the man who gave her the lighter in Istanbul. "There you are, baby," she said, reaching out with her Enhancement to calm his surge of nerves even as she gave him a long hug and a very slow kiss on the cheek—with the door open, in case anyone was watching. "Come on in," she purred.

Looking surprised and all too nervous, Yushchenko walked through the door Maggie held open. She didn't get the sense that the Soviet would try anything funny with her, but the sooner she was able to drop the pretense, the better. "I have some champagne on the dining room table, if you want some," she said before closing the door, hoping that if there was someone out there, they'd hear her.

The lock secured, she took a confused and scared Yushchenko by the arm. "In here," she said brusquely. She led him to the dining room table—there was no champagne—and let Frank and Ellis step out into the open, giving the Soviet a bit of a start.

"Colonel Yushchenko," Ellis said, extending his hand but not introducing himself.

Maggie went to close the curtains in the front room—another potential sign of intimacy—before joining them in the dining room. "I expected someone older," Yushchenko said tentatively as he took a seat.

"I'm older than I look," Ellis said; Maggie could read his irritation at the slight like a headline. "Now, you have some information for us."

Yushchenko smiled. "I do. Have my conditions been met?"

Frank nodded. "We have a team on the outskirts of Leningrad, about a mile from your family's home, and a fishing vessel that can get them to Finland in less than a day. Were you able to give them any kind of notice?"

"No, I have been very busy. And the phones have ears listening."

"We figured as much. Are you ready to go now? Because we can get you out tonight," Frank said.

Yushchenko took a deep breath and nodded. "I am. Tonight, yes."

Here comes the hard part, Maggie thought as she settled down into a chair next to Ellis, reaching out to Yushchenko's emotions. "You know, Colonel, it's not easy doing all this for you. We're going to help you out, but we need to know if you have what we need, too."

Maggie layered sympathy and commiseration over her words, but for whatever reason, it didn't seem to be having much effect. "Of course. And you understand I cannot give everything away here and now, for why then would you help me?"

Ellis smiled. "We're Americans, Colonel. We don't leave people hanging out to dry like that. If I say you're getting out with your family, then that's what's going to happen." He slid a letter over to the Russian. "This is from my boss. He went to our President to get this approved. You'll see everything in writing. You can keep the paper, though frankly, I'd recommend you burn it when you're done with it."

Yushchenko read it over and nodded. "This program you wish me to help you with, this is what you call, what is the word, MAJESTIC?"

Maggie and Ellis traded a look before Ellis responded. "You'll learn more about that when we get where we're going. Right now, though, I need something from you that'll assure me you have solid information for us. I hope you understand."

Maggie, of course, made sure he understood.

"It is the Bekhterev Research Institute in Leningrad," Yushchenko replied. "This is a medical institute, yes, but it is run by MGB, for people who are . . . powered? Empowered. That is the word. Empowered."

Ellis nodded, his poker face well in place; Maggie could feel his emotions roiling, and even hers were getting a little bit of a workout—it was the same word used in the note they got in Washington. "All right, that's something. How many are there?"

Yushchenko smiled slightly and shrugged, leaving Maggie frustrated. The threads of his emotions were awfully hard to grasp, and she had no idea why. "Please, you must understand, all I have is what I know, and I cannot just give—"

The radio crackled to life with Cal's rapid-fire voice. "We got company. Two pairs of men, either side of the street, heading for our door. Suits, hats, and coats, walking fast. We gotta go."

Frank bolted to his feet and grabbed the radio. "Get down here, Cal. Now." He keyed off the radio and turned to a surprised Yushchenko. "Ellis, get the colonel to the car out back."

The Ukrainian scrambled to his feet. "How did they know?" he stammered. "I was careful, I assure you!"

Ellis shrugged. "Doesn't matter now, does it? Let's go."

"What about my family?" the Soviet demanded, his worry for them cutting through Maggie's control as he resisted Ellis's attempt to drag him away. "They will come for them!"

Frank nodded to Maggie. "Get the door, Maggie. Colonel, I'll send the signal to the extraction team in Leningrad before we leave town, I promise. Right now, it's time to go. Move it!"

Yushchenko growled, realizing that he was in no position to negotiate, and finally took off with Ellis toward the back exit. Cal came thundering down the stairs just as Maggie was adjusting her robe to look more disheveled and mussing her hair—like she'd been doing something quite different from an interrogation. "You need me?" Cal asked.

She graced him with a smile, for once. "You go help Ellis. I'll be fine. Go on."

Cal nodded and Maggie felt his relief settle onto him like a favorite blanket. Frank checked his weapon and positioned himself away from the windows, ready to fire cleanly at the open door. "Ready when you are, Mags. If you can't make 'em leave, make 'em useless," Frank said with a little smile.

The house got dead quiet, everyone in position. Thirty seconds later, a loud knock practically rattled the door on its hinges. Maggie took a deep breath and nodded at Frank, who nodded back.

She threw the door open and grimaced. "You have any idea what time it is?"

23.

June 18, 1948

Frank drove the little Volkswagen at high speed down the narrow alley, tearing onto the main road too quickly. Thankfully, it was the middle of the night and the streets were empty. If it had been daytime, someone would've pulled him over already. The two Russians in the trunk wouldn't have helped much either.

"You're over-adjusting, Frank. These little suckers pack a punch," Ellis remarked from the front passenger seat. "Doubt I could sell many, though. Barely any room in 'em."

Frank eased off on the gas and fell in behind Cal's car, which had Maggie and Yushchenko inside—and another two more bound and gagged Russians to boot. That left Frank with Ellis . . . and the usual advice in his head.

"*Hang back another ten feet or so. Give yourself room to react if things turn south,*" the Las Vegas gangster whispered in Frank's head. "*If you pass, do it fast and get in front quickly. Have someone else keep an eye on the prize. You watch the road.*"

"Just tell me if they make any sudden moves ahead," Frank told Ellis. "I need to watch the road."

Frank glanced in the rearview and saw nothing, but now, there, driving through Prague toward an inevitable police checkpoint, he started to worry. Maggie'd told him a hundred times she didn't think Cal would be able to pull the trigger, not even in self-defense. At the time, Frank had been dismissive; Maggie struck him as gung ho and itching for a fight, and clearly felt anyone who wasn't was soft. But remembering Cal's movements in the house a little while before, Frank could see the hesitation, the tentative moves of the overly cautious and uncertain. Cal had been a rock throughout everything else, but knocking out those goons . . . it was the first time Cal had been asked to deliberately harm someone, and Frank figured it didn't sit well with him.

So, it made sense to put Cal with Maggie—she was as much a soldier at this point as any of them, and Cal could make sure she wouldn't get too gung ho. Despite his best efforts to the contrary, Frank had grown attached to him and to Maggie—even to Ellis. They were his team. He wanted them all back in one piece, with Yushchenko in tow.

And maybe they'd get some answers out of the Russki— information that wasn't exactly forthcoming from the folks at CIA or Area 51.

". . . a whole program, just like ours . . ." Ellis remarked. "Gotta wonder what kinds of Enhancements their Variants got."

"Could be anything," Frank said quietly. "So many possibilities, it's probably not worth speculating."

"World's getting a little crowded with superpowered people, Frank," Ellis remarked. "Makes me think that there could be a whole lot of us out there. And wonder why we're doing this MAJESTIC business when there are surely more . . . lucrative opportunities."

Frank turned to see Ellis smiling slightly at him, his eyebrow cocked. Always the salesman. "Eyes on the other car," Frank ordered. "Finish the job first. If we get out of here in one piece, then I promise to sit through the entire pitch."

* * *

It was risky to use a telephone at 3 a.m., but Frank was running out of options. He needed to report in, get the team in Leningrad moving, and figure out what to do with four bodies before reaching a checkpoint. The fact that they hadn't stumbled blindly across one yet was a stroke of good luck they couldn't expect to last much longer.

Frank eased his car to the side of the street. There was an awning on a building there with a phone number on it. He figured if it had a phone number up front, it had a phone inside. Besides, there weren't any pay phones in this goddamn city.

The squat, two-story, cinder-block building was next to a fenced-in yard—a repair shop or junkyard of some kind. The awning was ragged, the glass on the windows streaked with filth. Not much chance there was anyone at work at that time of night. It was perfect, really. Well, as good as they were going to get.

Frank got out of the car with Ellis and headed toward the building, stopping first at Cal's car. "If anything happens, get Maggie and INSIGHT out of here."

Cal nodded and wisely kept the engine running. Frank turned to Ellis, who was eying the building's strong wooden door.

"Make it subtle," Frank said.

The Southerner smiled and reached for the doorknob, screwing his eyes shut for a moment. When he released it, it was soft clay. Ellis put a shoulder to the door, and it opened readily. "After you, Frank."

Frank walked in and looked around. The room was bare except for a single desk, a threadbare couch, and open boxes of what looked like used parts. No phone.

"There," Ellis said, pointing to a door labeled in Czech. "Looks like a side office."

Frank opened the door, and sure enough, it was a private office with a large, clunky telephone on the desk. A minute's worth of rapid-fire Czech later and he had an English operator. "Amalgamated Exports, Roger-65143," he said.

It took less than fifteen seconds for the line to connect. "Amalgamated Exports, to whom may I direct your call?" came a prim, female British voice.

"Mr. Hill, if you please," Frank replied. *I'm reporting in, all's well, but there's a complication.*

"One moment, please."

A few seconds later. "This is Mr. Hill. How can I help you?"

Frank smiled. Danny had deepened his voice to sound older. "Mr. Hill, this is Mr. Rush," Frank said pleasantly. "We have your order in hand, but I was wondering if you were interested in a few extra items that are on special." *We have Yushchenko. And a few others as well.*

"Interesting. Are they similar to the one I ordered? Good condition?" *More useful assets?*

"Sadly, they're off-the-shelf items that may be in need of repair. But they're quite ready to be shipped." *Goons. Unconscious. Under control.*

"Well, that's mighty kind of you, Mr. Rush. But I think I'm going to have to pass. I'm sure you can find a place for them." *No. They need to be taken care of.*

Frank grimaced. "I thought it was worth a try. Also, I wanted to be sure of the other shipment we discussed." *Roger on the goons. Get the Leningrad team moving.*

"That shipment is fine, Mr. Rush. It's being taken care of." *Leningrad team will move.*

"Thank you, Mr. Hill. Is your address still the same?" *Is the plan still intact?*

"You should have the alternate address we discussed. I'd prefer it if you used that." *Shit's hit the fan. Go to plan B.*

"I'll do that, sir. Anything else?" *Please tell me if we're about to get burned.*

"No, Mr. Rush. Looking forward to your shipment, thank you. Have a great day." *No, but you need to get moving. Now.*

"You too, Mr. Hill."

Frank hung up the phone and turned to Ellis, who was busy trying to wipe up an oil slick on the floor, likely from his Enhancement's side effect. "Leave it. We're going. Plan B is in effect."

"Shit. They made us?" Ellis said, dropping the cloth on the floor.

"No, but they may be on to something. Let's go. We need to dump the goons here. Let's make damn sure they're hidden well."

* * *

Prague's lights grew dimmer and dimmer as Cal drove the little Volkswagen down the darkened road away from the city. Homes were getting fewer and far between, and they'd stopped passing streetlamps about five minutes before. After stowing the four Czech agents—bound and gagged—in a variety of junked-out vehicles, they resumed their journey west, this time with Frank and Ellis's car taking the lead, leaving Cal to look out for tails—and to think about what he'd done back there in Prague.

Those men who had tried to catch Yushchenko weren't the good guys—of course, Cal knew that. They represented a Godless regime trying to keep a man with important knowledge away from America, where that man could live free for the first time in his life. But those four men were still men, and they probably had families too. Cal didn't hurt them too badly—he only drained just enough life out of them to render them unconscious. But he figured he'd scraped a few days off their lives. And that was something that he'd have to live with. He could only pray that those days would matter somehow—either by keeping them from doing more evil, or by keeping Cal alive longer to try to do some good in the middle of this spy game.

As they drove, Maggie tried to use her powers on Yushchenko, trying to get him to open up. But there was too much going on and Cal figured she just couldn't get her mind to focus. After about twenty minutes, she'd given up. Now, every time Cal looked in the rearview, he saw the colonel's eyes looking right at him.

"You all right back there, Colonel, sir?" Cal asked, trying to sound friendly.

"I have never seen an African man like you up close before," Yushchenko replied bluntly.

"Well, hope it don't disappoint you to learn I'm just the same as you. Two arms, two legs, whatever brains God gives us."

"They tell us in Moscow that the Africans in America, they are slaves to European people and treated poorly. Is this true?"

Cal cleared his throat and glanced at Maggie before answering. "Well, we ain't been slaves for more than eighty years now, sir. Are we treated bad? Depends on where you are. Lots of Negroes up North, out West, they're doing fine. Still got a lot of problems in the South. And yeah, many of us are poor. We're working at it. We got faith the Lord will see us through, make things better for us and our children."

Cal watched as Yushchenko took this in. "We also were slaves, not so long ago," he said finally. "Slaves to the tsars, the tyrants who ruled Russia until Lenin freed us. But yes, it took time to overcome this. Too many of us still want to be ruled, and too many of us wish to rule as the tsars did."

"Is that why you want out so badly?" Maggie asked, and Cal thought she was perhaps trying another tack to get the MGB man to open up.

"No, miss. They say there is no class, now, just the proletariat, but I am one of the people who rule in the Soviet Union, and it is not a bad thing to rule. I am leaving because of what I know, and what you are doing, and what must be done together. And that is all I will say."

Cal and Maggie traded a look but didn't press further, preferring to ride in silence for a while as the road ahead grew darker still, to the point where only the taillights of the other car were visible.

Then the handheld radio crackled to life. "Checkpoint ahead," Ellis reported.

Maggie lifted the bulky radio from the floor in front of her. "We'll pass you. I'll take care of it."

Frank's voice came back a moment later. "Negative. You have INSIGHT. We'll manage."

Ahead, Cal could make out a couple of bright lights along the side of the road and, a moment later, a wooden barrier hanging across it. There was also an army truck and maybe three . . . no, four guards. Soldiers, armed with rifles.

"How close do you need to be, Miss Maggie?"

She smiled that smile of hers that, to Cal's eyes, made her look like a hunter. "Get them up there, close as you can," she said.

Cal nodded. They'd been given orders not to talk about their Enhancements with Yushchenko present, but they could still be subtle. So, Cal shifted gears and sped up until he was right up behind the other Volkswagen. Meanwhile, Maggie clambered into the backseat with Yushchenko—no mean feat, given the size of the car.

"What are you doing?" the Ukrainian asked.

"You get up front," Maggie said. "There's a hatch there by your feet that'll get you into the trunk. Don't worry—if they open it, it'll look like there's a bunch of boxes and stuff in there. You'll hide in there until we pass the checkpoint."

Yushchenko looked pretty put out, but he did as he was told. Yet a minute later, he was safe inside the hideout Ellis had created with his Enhancement, and Maggie was back in the front seat.

"You know, this ain't gonna be easy," Cal said quietly as he pulled up right behind the others at the checkpoint. The guards had already approached the first car. "Ain't no Negroes out here, and they'll be curious."

Maggie gave him a sidelong look. "Don't think it'll be a problem, Cal. Even if—oh, shit!"

Startled by her sudden outburst—he never quite got used to a lady swearing like a man—Cal looked forward to see one of the guards dragging Ellis out of the back seat by the arm, and another aiming his rifle at Ellis's head. The two other guards were standing directly in front of their VW, weapons pointed at the front windshield.

"Miss Maggie . . ."

"I got 'em," she said, closing her eyes. "I . . . wait. Wait. What the hell?"

Cal gripped the steering wheel tightly. "What? What is it?"

Maggie opened her eyes and quickly pulled her gun out of her handbag. "It's not working. My Enhancement isn't working. At all."

"How do you know?" Cal asked, wide-eyed.

"I can't sense the people around me," she replied, her voice quick and tense. "I can't sense anything."

Cal threw the car into gear and jerked the wheel to the right. "Suppose that's why they trained us. Hang on."

Maggie cocked the pistol as Cal sped forward. Thankfully, Ellis had noticed the engine revving and threw himself out of the way just as Cal's VW surged ahead, sending the guards leaping away in the other direction—where a shot from Maggie caught one of them in the chest.

Cal wheeled around to the left, just as the other two guards were aiming their rifles at him. One went down immediately—probably a shot from Frank's car, but it was too chaotic to tell.

The other guard fired, and a searing pain tore through Cal's left shoulder before he even realized the windshield had shattered. With a cry of surprise and anger, he swerved into the guard at speed and watched as the man bounced off the hood and tumbled away before he finally hit the brakes.

Maggie was out of the car before it even finished coming to a halt, her gun out to cover the downed men from across the roof of the VW. "Cal's hit!" she shouted.

From the driver's seat, Cal could see Frank already out of the car, his gun trained on one of the guards moaning and groaning on the ground. Ellis, meanwhile, staggered to his feet; the Southerner seemed unharmed but spared Cal a withering look anyway. Cal couldn't help but smile a bit, but that quickly turned into a wince as he felt his shoulder throb. *The Lord's little reminders*, he thought.

Frank then dashed over to Cal. "How bad?"

"Hurts something fierce. I ain't never been shot before," Cal said, gritting his teeth. "Gonna need another goat or something."

"No time," Frank said, pulling Cal's door open. "Ellis! Anybody . . ."

Frank's voice slowly trailed off. Cal slowly got out of the car, trying—unsuccessfully—to minimize movement in his left arm. When he finally got to his feet, Frank was standing there, looking stunned. Paralyzed, even.

"What is it?" Ellis asked.

"I can't tell. I can't feel it, one way or the other," Frank said, turning ashen.

"My Enhancement's gone too," Maggie said. "I couldn't get ahold of those guys. Couldn't even feel them."

Cal looked at the four guards on the ground. Two were only now starting to get up—bruised but unharmed, and now covered by Frank and Maggie. The other two were bleeding out. Frank shook his head to clear it, then pointed to one. "Cal, you're gonna need to heal up. See if you got something left."

Cal shook his head. "I'll grab a little from each of the healthy ones. Won't condemn a man to death if we don't know he's already on the way there."

Frank opened his mouth as if to complain, then seemed to think better of it. "All right. Let's hurry it up."

Cal walked over to where the two guards were kneeling, their hands now raised. He placed a hand on each man's shoulder . . .

. . . and felt nothing. Nothing except the pain still throbbing through his arm and chest.

"I got a problem here," Cal said.

Then shots rang out from the trees around the checkpoint, and Cal knew his problems had just gotten a whole lot worse.

June 18, 1948

Ellis dove for cover behind one of the Volkswagens with a multitude of oaths and profanities in mind that he had no time to use. Gunfire erupted from the trees to their left and in front of them—thankfully not from behind, or they'd all be dead from the crossfire.

"What the hell happened to Plan B, Frank?" Ellis growled as the Army man clambered down next to him, gun drawn.

"This *was* Plan B," Frank groused. "Someone's on to us."

Ellis turned and fired a few shots blindly into the trees, then ducked back down as the other guns barked back and bullets whistled past overhead. "Good thing I reinforced that little hidey-hole we stuffed INSIGHT in. Now what?"

Frank popped up, fired, and flopped back down to the dirt in one smooth motion. A second later, the glass from the passenger window shattered all over both of them. "We've walked into a trap. I think someone's found a way to dampen our Enhancements."

"I hope you didn't just realize that."

"Grab INSIGHT. We've got to go backward, away from here, circle around."

Ellis looked over to the other car, where Maggie and Cal cowered. Yushchenko was in the modified trunk in the front of that car. "Now, how the hell we gonna do that?"

Frank jerked the car door open and, staying low, climbed back inside. "Use this car for more cover. I'm going to drive it over there. Keep up and stay low."

Before Ellis could give a highly negative assessment of that plan, Frank had revved up the car, and as he lay across the two front seats with one hand on the wheel and a foot on the gas, the vehicle slowly began to move. Despite his better judgment, Ellis popped up and emptied the rest of his clip at the trees ahead, and saw Cal and Maggie doing the same. *Guess the training really worked.*

Then Ellis realized he was exposed and raced after the car, a trail of bullets in his wake sending dirt streaking through the air around his feet.

"Shit shit shit shit!" he swore, diving down behind the other Variants. "Damn fool gonna get us killed."

"What's the plan?" Maggie asked after she hit the dirt.

"Get our boy out of the car. Then run like hell," Ellis said.

"Shitty plan," Maggie said.

Ellis grabbed another magazine from his belt and shoved it into the gun. "Don't I know it."

He popped up and started firing again as Frank kept low, scuttling to the passenger door of the other VW, wrenching it open, and fiddling with the hatch in the floor. A moment later, a pale, terrified Yushchenko crawled out and flopped down onto the dirt beside them.

Meanwhile, Ellis noticed Cal tinkering with his lighter— the one Mrs. Stevens had given him. "What the hell you doing, you jackass?"

Cal scowled up at Ellis. "Just get ready to run."

A moment later, all five of them were behind the second VW. "We need to go," Frank said. He then saw Cal hold up the lighter and nodded. "Good call."

Frank took the lighter from Cal, and fished his own out of his pocket. One was placed under the VW, the other he held onto. "Maggie, you and Ellis give us some cover fire. Cal, run directly away from the car, stay low. And . . . go."

Uttering another ferocious string of swears, Ellis popped up and started shooting madly toward the woods. He thought for a moment he heard a scream, which felt good. He then ducked back down as the return fire whizzed past, coming face to face with Frank.

"Now?" Ellis asked.

"Now."

The two got up and ran for their lives, heading toward Cal, who now stood at the edge of the other treeline. Frank paused, turned, wound up, and threw the lighter in his hand, which arced over Ellis's head.

"Aw, hell." Ellis didn't bother running anymore—he just hit the ground and began praying.

A moment later, the night lit up with a fiery explosion as the lighter erupted. Ellis could feel the heat on his backside as he scrambled up and started running again. A second flash produced even more heat. *That would be the second lighter. And then . . .*

Ellis reached the treeline as the first VW exploded. It was another five seconds before the second car blew, and by that time, they were well into the woods, down a ravine and running through the dark undergrowth at a desperate clip.

"You're scared," Maggie said as he caught up to her.

"Damn straight I'm scared, woman!" Ellis panted as she fell in beside him. "What else am I supposed to be?"

"No, you're *scared*! I can feel it!" She seemed almost excited.

Ellis reached out and touched a leaf as he went past, feeling it turn into water on his fingers. *About damn time.*

* * *

Frank led them deep into the woods, running for a solid fifteen minutes straight, weaving back and forth, up and down paths, through undergrowth. He hoped it would be enough to buy them a quick break, because Yushchenko was winded and Cal looked pale from blood loss. Finally, Frank raised his hand, signaling for everyone to stop, tucking them under a ridge out of sight so he could work on Cal's shoulder with a proficiency and dexterity born of years of experience—someone else's experience, sure, but what did that matter right now?

"Where to now, boss?" Maggie asked him when Frank was done. "Any idea where we are?"

Thankfully, there was enough light from the gibbous moon to let Frank pull out his map—a waterproof, silk-screened handkerchief, one of the neat tricks developed during the war. He pressed it to the ground where a patch of moonlight shone down through the trees, and traced his finger over the route it seemed most likely they'd taken.

"I think we're about . . . here," he said, pointing as Maggie looked over his shoulder. "About ten miles from the West German border."

"That's a long hike," Cal said, keeping his hand on the slipshod bandage Frank had improvised from his shirttails.

"Gonna be longer than you think," Frank said, stuffing the map back in his pocket. "We need to stay away from the roads, from villages, from rivers—all of it. The hard way, all the way."

Ellis peered at his watch. "About 5 a.m. Gonna be light soon."

Frank turned to Maggie. "Any luck getting through to him in the car?"

She grimaced. "Something's not right. I couldn't seem to grab him. I nudged him a bit, but he wouldn't open up. I feel like I could do it, but it would take a while. Hours. Don't know why, but he's a hard nut to crack."

"That's not good. All right, everybody on your feet. Let's move," Frank said. "I'll take point. Maggie, I need you with me. You're the only one who can sense other people at range. We lose that, and at least we know that whatever dampened our abilities is back and we'll have bought ourselves a little bit of time before trouble arrives."

The group formed up and headed northwest. Ellis pointedly left Cal to fend for himself, but Frank saw Yushchenko fall in beside the injured man and offer to help. *Ellis and I are gonna have a real long talk if—no, when—we get back,* Frank thought.

"What was that?" Maggie asked Frank quietly as they walked steadily through the forest.

"What was what?"

"Whatever stopped our powers."

Frank sighed. "No idea. The science guys at Area 51 have been studying the energy coming out of that white light.

I imagine the Reds' scientists have been doing the same. Maybe they invented some kind of . . . antidote."

"Really comforting to hear right now," Maggie said. Frank looked over and saw she was looking particularly grim. "I didn't like that feeling one bit."

"Why? Aside from the obvious reason?"

"I felt cut off. Trapped in my own head. Not to mention powerless."

Frank let it drop but eyed her carefully regardless. Frank had never really identified with his Enhancement in any way—it was just something he did. But Maggie had really embraced hers. It had become part of her personality. Or maybe it had taken it over.

As Frank trudged through the undergrowth, away from the dawn, he felt the strings of patriotism and practicality holding the group together growing thinner and thinner. Ellis was never in it for anyone but himself, and when his time was up, he'd be long gone—no matter how much time the MAJESTIC-12 folks added to his "deal." Maggie was an absolute cipher at this point. Cal seemed on board for now, but the more violence he saw, the more likely he'd bail out, Frank wagered. And as for Frank himself, how many voices could he manage before they proved to be too much?

"Idiots," Frank muttered.

"Who's an idiot?" Maggie asked quietly. "You're all worried all of a sudden."

Frank shook his head and smiled at her; he ought to have known better than to let his mind wander near her. "Us. MAJESTIC-12. We thought that we had the advantage, just like we have the bomb and they don't. We keep thinking that the Soviets just aren't as good as we are. But they took away our Enhancements. They obviously have their own Variants. We simply assumed that they couldn't possibly keep up. And yet here we are, with the one guy who can clue us in to what we're up against, and we're *this* close to having it all blown."

Maggie nodded. "We may have to go to Plan B here. Or Plan C. Whatever letter we're at now."

"What's Plan C?" Frank couldn't think of any more contingencies in the ops plan—they'd run through the big ones already.

Before she could answer, the muted *pop-pop* of distant gunfire sent them all crouching for cover. Frank looked at Maggie, who shook her head in confirmation. "Four of them. About a mile away. And they're gaining," she said, just loud enough for the rest of the team to hear. "They'll have figured out that we're racing to the border. We have to move. Double time."

Frank scrambled to his feet, pulling Maggie up, and turned to face Ellis and Cal, who looked worried. "We move that fast, we're gonna leave a trail for them to follow and they'll catch up quick. And then radio for help up at the border," Ellis said.

"No choice. Move out."

Frowning, Ellis took off at a light jog, while INSIGHT helped Cal move as best he could—Frank had managed to stop the bleeding, but Cal remained weak. Frank screwed the suppressor onto his pistol and made a note to take down whatever the hell wildlife existed in this godforsaken forest in the hopes that Cal could use it to heal himself before it died.

Maggie followed suit, holding back to keep from passing Cal and Yushchenko. Frank knew she would automatically feel new minds entering her range, but by that time, it would be too late, so he held back as well to walk with her.

"Any other ideas?" he asked her.

She gave him an incredulous look. "I got nothing. You're the military genius. Anywhere on the map we might go to catch a ride? Call in an airlift?"

"I don't think invading Czech airspace is a great idea," Frank said, panting. "Border. Only way. The guys in my head agree."

"Then we're screwed," Maggie said, stopping to pull her own kerchief-map from her pocket. "We go here . . . I think they're gonna wait for us . . . here." Maggie's finger pointed to a glen near the road from Prague to Munich, about a mile from the border. "If we go here, toward Austria, it's a longer hike and I bet Cal gets worse."

Frank nodded. "We head for the road."

"Showdown," Maggie said.

"Only way." Frank gazed at the map for several moments longer. "I think we have a shot. We'll be there in about three hours. I should have a better plan by then. But if they have a way of sensing us, just like we sense them, we're really screwed. Colonel Yushchenko, anything you can tell us about what we might be up against here?"

The Ukrainian looked pale and wide-eyed and could only shrug. "I am not cleared on many individuals in the Bekhterev program. Yes, there is one who may take your powers, but you know this. As for others, I cannot say."

Maggie stared hard at Yushchenko for a moment but seemed to think better of it and turned back to Frank. "They'll take away our Enhancements soon as they find us, one way or the other," Maggie said. "Put *that* into your plans, too."

"*Your situation is terrible but not impossible. Focus on the soldiers, stay away from any Variants,*" General Davis said in his head, bringing Frank a strong sense of relief he didn't know he needed. "*So long as it's a squad or less, you have a chance to take a vehicle and make a run for it. Look for other opportunities to fire at range—snipe your way through if you can.*"

Frank smiled sadly at Maggie. "We better hope they don't have more than a squad with them. Otherwise, we're done. Let's stop about a mile before, on this ridge here," he added, pointing to a spot on the map. "We'll have work to do."

"Already got a plan?"

"Mostly complaints," Frank said with a small chuckle. "I'm being chided for placing ourselves in such a poor tactical position."

Maggie forged ahead up the path. "They can blame Danny."

"I already do."

June 19, 1948

N *ext time, bring binoculars."*

Frank shunted aside the critique in his head—there were at least four voices now chiming in as he crouched atop the ridge, trying to get a read on the clearing below. The advice was becoming contradictory. General Davis wanted to get closer, while Sergeant Collins was far more interested in picking off folks one by one and using the high ground as an advantage.

Frank knew he, or rather Collins, was a fine shot, but sniping wasn't their best option, especially when all they had were pistols. Plus, the idea was to go forward or around—not stay put. They had to get to the border at any cost. Unfortunately, all the voices agreed on the last-ditch plan, and it wasn't pretty. Frank put it out of his mind as best he could. Focus on the objective first, which was getting everyone out in one piece.

He crouch-walked back to the rest of the group, who were resting on the hillside near a spring, a welcome sight after hours of marching through the wilderness. Thankfully, they had passed by a cattle farm on their way, and one dead steer later, Cal was near one hundred percent. That brought back memories of Area 51 barbecues.... They hadn't eaten since the night before, and it wasn't likely they'd eat again until well after the upcoming engagement.

"Two vehicles. I count at least eight uniforms, guessing probably close to twenty total, including a couple who were just sent out of the clearing," Frank whispered to the group, who were taking turns gulping water from the trickling spring. "At least two in civvies. What are you getting, Maggie?"

"Just one, passing by on the roads on either side of us," she replied glumly. "Someone angry, anxious—and looking for something, but at those speeds, I don't know how they would. And . . . wait." Maggie cocked her head a moment, then ducked down and whispered, "We have company."

Frank heard the snapping of twigs below the ridge. He held up his hand for quiet and pulled his gun. Crouching forward, he peered off the side of the ridge . . .

. . . and saw four soldiers heading up a deer trail toward them.

Looking back, Frank held up four fingers, then pointed at Maggie and Ellis—the two best shots after him. Waving them forward, he turned his attention back to the patrol below. They hadn't heard anything.

Frank carefully aimed his weapon. *They're wearing helmets and vests. Aim for the necks. At this angle, it'll go through the body.* Frank turned to the others and pointed to his own neck, then at the guards. Ellis and Maggie nodded. It would have to do.

Frank took a moment to lock eyes with Cal, who looked grim and saddened. He wanted to say something to him— he'd coached many a greenhorn just before their first firefight—but the soldiers were too close. Frank simply nodded at him and turned back to the task at hand.

Collins coached Frank through the prep—positioning his arms, breathing, aiming. And then he fired.

One of the men dropped immediately. He quickly shifted to another target, who conveniently looked up just in time for Frank to place a bullet between the eyes, at the same time that Maggie and Ellis squeezed off their shots. The two others went down—but one rolled down the hillside, shouting in Czech the entire way. *"Jsou zde! Jsou tady! Jsem zraněný!"*

They're over here! Man down!

"Move," Frank hissed. He took the time to take one more shot, silencing the shouting man permanently.

Everyone was on their feet, and Frank quickly made his way down off the ridge. They would circle around and try to come at them from the road. If possible, they'd commandeer a vehicle and race for the border. If not, well . . . it would get ugly fast. As planned, they kept Cal and Yushchenko in the middle—the Ukrainian because he remained the objective, and Cal because, frankly, Frank knew Cal wouldn't shoot anyone. However, he was a good last line of defense, because he could drop people with a touch without killing them. Best to play to people's strengths.

Frank rushed ahead as quietly as possible, planting his feet on rock and avoiding brush as best he could. He stopped suddenly as he heard another twig crack, whirling around with his gun before him. There—thirty yards off, looking away—was another soldier. A single shot felled him. There were no shouts. A straggler.

For now.

"*Get to the—*"

The voices went silent.

Frank whirled around, gun still raised, looking. There was nothing but tall trees and dappled sun. In the far distance, he could hear soldiers in combat gear trying to move quietly and failing—the Czechs and Russians would be after them. And if they had Variants, they'd be right there with 'em—if they weren't already on top of his position.

And he'd just lost his Enhancement. *Shit.*

* * *

Ellis raced down the hillside, one hand around Yushchenko's arm as the mud and rock threatened to send them both over the edge and into a dense copse of trees— trees probably teeming with Reds.

"You tell me right here, right now, what the hell else we could be up against, old man," Ellis growled quietly as they rushed down the trail. "You tell me right now before I shoot you in the goddamn head."

And the funny thing was, Ellis meant it. Screw orders, screw MAJESTIC-12, screw it all. His job here wasn't to find out what the Russkies knew about Variants, or get this goddamn Red over the border. His job was to make it home alive to see his wife and kids, and he'd be damned if some intelligence operation was gonna get in the way of all that.

Yushchenko, perhaps, sensed some of that. "If there are others, they will not be able to use their Enhancements while the negative field is active," the colonel said as he tried not to slip and fall, prompting Ellis to help him remain upright despite his better judgment. "It is when you feel your power returning that you should be worried."

"I'm already goddamn worried," Ellis retorted. "Who else could be out there? Your guys, your Variants."

Yushchenko wrenched his arm free from Ellis's grip but kept walking. "That was not part of the agreement."

Ellis stepped in front of the colonel and put his pistol to the man's forehead. "You're gonna tell me, *comrade*, or so help me, I'll kill you. And then what happens to your precious family, huh? Because I tell you what, I care a lot more about seeing *my* family than yours right about now."

Yushchenko looked wide-eyed, then looked off over Ellis's right shoulder. Ellis turned to find Cal, standing there, looking on, impassive. "Reason with him," Yushchenko said, half-pleading, half-ordering.

Cal looked from the Russian to Ellis and back again. "Colonel, we ain't gonna get out of this unless we know what we're up against. So, maybe Mr. Longstreet puts that gun down, and you tell us what they got down there."

Before Yushchenko could answer, Maggie interrupted from behind. "I'm back up. We're not being blocked."

And then Ellis's pistol disappeared from his hand.

He turned to see a young man, no more than seventeen, smiling right next to him, holding his gun right up against Ellis's chest. "We're already here," he said in Russian-accented English.

Then he fired, and Ellis looked down to see blood seeping from his abdomen. His body blossomed into exquisite, unrelenting, all-encompassing pain. It was the last thing he remembered.

* * *

Cal had never seen a man shot before. There was a flash of crimson from behind Ellis's back, blood spattering onto Maggie's face as she rushed forward. Cal saw the deep red spot expand across Ellis's white shirt as he sank to his knees, a grimace of agony and . . . something else . . . on Ellis's face. Fear.

The Russian teenager who'd literally come out of nowhere grabbed Yushchenko's arm just as Cal ran toward him. Cal leapt forward to tackle him, grabbing him in a bear hug, determined not to let him escape—and they both landed in a thicket of trees that sure as heck wasn't anywhere near where he'd been a second ago.

Cal heard the click of a gun and instinctively used his left arm in a sweep. The shot missed his ear by less than an inch. Cal grabbed the wrist and began to drain the boy.

"*Yob tvoyu mat!*" the Russian spat as he struggled. But the struggling grew weaker as the boy aged, rapidly crossing though middle age and into his dotage in three seconds, while Cal felt himself get younger and stronger once more.

The boy would live, just not as long as maybe he might've otherwise. Cal thought momentarily about giving some back to him, at least a few years.

But suddenly there was a new pain in his torso, a searing hit that cracked ribs, punctured his lung, and sent him flying fifteen feet in the air across the forest clearing, slamming him into a tree.

"Agh! Ow, sweet Jesus," Cal breathed, barely able to talk, his eyes squeezed shut in a vain attempt to somehow make the pain go away. It was like someone had taken a sledgehammer to his ribs.

When he opened his eyes again, he saw a girl crouched over the teenager he'd turned into an old man, no older than ten. She had dark hair and eyes, and a humorless pout on her face. And she was wearing a small, fitted Russian army uniform.

"You gotta be kidding me," Cal whispered.

The girl stood with a look of pure determination on her face, then strode purposefully toward Cal, pausing only to grab hold of a young tree no more than six inches in diameter.

Her fingertips sank into the bark as if it were a pillow, and she ripped it out of the ground as if she were just pulling a weed. It didn't even look like she was exerting herself.

Cal coughed, blood coming out of his mouth and dripping down his chin. It was bad. Felt like he was on half a lung. Every breath was an exercise in new agony, and there was already a small part of his soul just looking forward to not having to breathe anymore, Jesus forgive him.

The girl lifted the tree and broke it in half across her knee, producing a club about five feet long and several solid inches thick—with a jagged, pointed tip.

"*Eto moy brat!*" the girl screamed, gripping her weapon so tight that the wood splintered around her hand. "My brother!"

Cal thought about getting up for a second, but even thinking about moving his muscles resulted in new waves of pain. So, he just closed his eyes and waited, picturing God in his mind's eye and praying he'd not done enough bad things to be kept from Heaven for too long.

But . . . he knew otherwise. The realization hit him like yet another hammerblow, this one to his very soul. All this sneakin' about, all these spy games they had him doing, they distracted him from using God's gift for a greater, nobler purpose. And when Cal went to meet the Lord—any moment now—he knew deep in his heart that he would be found wanting, and that the pain he'd endured this day would be a walk in the park compared to what the Devil would conjure up for him in Hell.

Cal was scared. God, he was so scared. He started to cry, to bawl, even as he knew that crazy little girl was about to put a tree through his head. "I'm sorry," he sobbed quietly. "I'm so sorry."

Then he heard a crash and footsteps. Was that it? Was dying this painless?

Cal ventured to open his eyes, only to see Maggie standing above him, her hand extended. "Sorry about that," she said with a smirk. "Didn't have time to focus as much as I wanted to. Can you walk?"

The existential sorrow that had engulfed Cal sloughed off him like an unneeded blanket, and in that moment, Maggie was the second most beautiful woman in the world after his own wife. "Oh, Miss Maggie . . . I'm busted up bad," he croaked, coughing up more blood. "I need to heal up again . . . before I can get far."

"What about that teenage boy? He still has some . . . *shit*. He's gone," Maggie said. Cal peered behind her to see only bare grass and leaves where the recently made elderly man had lain just moments before.

"I'll be all right here," Cal said. "Get . . . INSIGHT. Ellis. Let's get out of here."

Maggie nodded and put a hand on Cal's forehead—a brave thing to do, considering. Cal surprised himself by actually feeling tempted for a moment. Then she dashed off into the woods, loping away like a predator and leaving Cal up against his tree, wondering just how much of what he'd just experienced was Maggie's Enhancement. . . .

* * *

There.

Twenty yards to her right. Two men. Young. One angry but focused, the other fearful and all over the place.

Too easy.

Maggie crouched down amongst the undergrowth, her suppressed pistol at the ready. She was trying to get back to Yushchenko and Ellis but didn't want to waste the opportunity. *Angry one first? He's the threat.* But scaredy-cat would probably shriek like a baby, she thought. Scaredy cat first, then angry one could get off a shot.

Maggie made a mental note to herself that if she made it out alive, it might be useful to start training on two pistols, one in each hand.

The shots came quickly—she'd made a split-second decision to go for the competent one first, hoping that scaredy-cat was more of a deer-in-the-headlights kind of guy. Her first shot entered the soldier's ear, angling upward due to her crouched position, and ricocheted around the inside of the steel helmet he wore. At least it was quick.

By the time he fell, Maggie's weapon was already trained on the second target—but he was more competent than she'd given him credit for. He hit the deck immediately, screaming in Czech and firing his rifle aimlessly—in the complete opposite direction from where Maggie was.

Time to go.

Maggie ran off at a ninety-degree angle from where those soldiers were, hoping she wasn't about to run right into anyone coming to help them. She knew Cal would need at least one or two of them alive and in decently good shape, and she nominated scaredy-cat as her top pick. She'd seen his face and felt his emotions—she'd remember him.

Maggie cast out her senses once more, trying to find more minds out there—minds attached to bodies, bodies that needed either rescue or elimination. There, at the very edge of her Enhancement, about twenty-five yards ahead, were four of them. . . .

And then they winked out of existence.

Not again.

Maggie ran forward, heedlessly, in the general direction that she'd last felt the other minds. Nothing. They were gone. Her Enhancement was gone. Everything was gone.

"*Tady! Tady! Myslím si, že člověk je tady!*" came a voice from up ahead.

She quickly knelt behind a tree, her gun raised, eyes wild. She didn't recognize whatever language that was. She couldn't assess her targets. She didn't know where they were. How the hell was she supposed to actually fight them?

She stayed as still as she could and was finally rewarded by the sound of footsteps on twigs and leaves—they were attempting to move quietly, but failing miserably. Then there was a brief whisper. And another returned.

Remember your training. Remember it.

Her heart racing, breath short and rapid, Maggie turned from behind her cover and tried to get her targets in sight. But she moved too fast, too urgently, firing at blurs while exposing herself too much, diminishing the element of surprise. She retreated back behind the tree, having missed completely, only to hear more shouts.

"*Vot! My nashli yeye! Derzhite podal'she Natal'ya! Privesti soldat!*"

Maggie tensed up and prepared to fire again, but before she could, a shot rang out from behind her, up and to the right, followed two seconds later by another round.

Her Enhancement suddenly returned.

Thank God.

She reached out with her mind, pushing hard against the people in front of her—there were four, in fact, not three—frightening them into unconsciousness. One was already injured, scared and fading anyway, and the other three folded quickly enough.

Up from where the shot came out, she felt worry and urgency. Frank.

She turned and took off toward him at a jog. She had a feeling her Enhancement wasn't going to get blocked out again anytime soon.

* * *

"Sloppy," Frank chided when Maggie reached the ridge.

She shrugged and gave him a winning smile. "Panicked. My power went bye-bye again and I freaked out. But I think you may have solved that."

"Oh?"

"When you made your shot, my power came back in a blink. I think you hit whoever was dampening us."

Frank frowned. "And that means everyone else's power is back too. Move out!"

It was Frank's turn to march double-time. Whoever was out there, it was more important to get back to Yushchenko and get him squared. And so, he ran. At one point, a bullet whizzed behind him, but he left that to Maggie, who continued to relish having her powers back a bit too much. One problem at a time, he reminded himself.

Frank burst into the clearing to find Yushchenko holding a soldier's coat to Ellis's abdomen. "He is losing blood. We need to help him."

Kneeling down, Frank peeked under the coat. "*Severe internal injuries. From the angle and what he's coughed up, looks like ruptured stomach, some colon, maybe a bit of the lung if he's really unlucky today,*" the doctor said. "*Do not move the patient. Field surgery needed.*"

"That's a lot of goddamn field surgery, Doc," Frank muttered.

"*Either that or he dies in minutes.*"

"I don't have minutes," Frank replied, a little louder than he cared to.

"Are you communicating with someone?" Yushchenko asked, surprised and now looking at him suspiciously.

Shaking his head, Frank shoved the Czech rifle he borrowed into Yushchenko's hands. "If it ain't one of us, shoot it," Frank said. "I gotta get him stable so we can move him."

Yushchenko took up a position behind a rock on the trail, while Frank ripped open Ellis's shirt, prompting a sharp intake of breath from the Southerner, followed by a few choice words.

"Didn't realize you were awake," Frank said, drawing a knife, also borrowed, from his belt.

"I wasn't," Ellis replied weakly. "Where's Cal? I need Cal."

"No Cal right now," Frank said. "Just me and my ghost-doctor."

"Need Cal," Ellis repeated. "Need to go home."

Frank started cleaning the skin around the entry wound. "What? Don't want to take one for the team?" he asked.

"God, no. Find Cal," Ellis croaked as his eyelids fluttered and his body tensed.

"*Going into shock. Get that bullet out and staunch that bleeding. You'll need to cauterize everything before he bleeds out.*"

Frank went to work, cutting away blood-soaked clothing, using the tip of the knife to try to dig in and find the bullet. It was horrible, horrible going, and Ellis's breath was becoming shallower.

Then Yushchenko swore and cocked his rifle, prompting Frank to tense up and reach for his pistol. A voice came from the woods. "It's me!" Maggie cried out. "I have Cal!"

Maggie came up onto the trail, half-carrying, half-dragging a nearly unconscious Cal behind her. Frank had hoped Cal would be up for a miracle, but he looked ashen, and his hand weakly clutched his side. Frank ran up and took him off Maggie's hands, laying the man gently down onto the ground next to the trail. "He needs donors. Now."

Maggie shook her head. "You can't stay. Their tracker will have them on you at any moment!"

As if he needed confirmation, Frank began to hear the voices of soldiers coming from below. "Can you send them all off?" he asked her.

Maggie closed her eyes a second. "No, they're learning. Coming in from different directions, staggering their approach. I hit one group, another one comes up behind."

Frank looked up at Yushchenko, who was still focused on the perimeter of the trail but had undoubtedly heard every word. Cal, meanwhile, was breathing shallowly but steadily, and Ellis was slipping fast.

"*You have only one option to get your team out,*" General Davis said. "*You just don't want to take it.*"

Frank stood up and went over to Cal. "You awake, Cal?"

He got a half-lidded, weak smile in return. "Kinda. You found someone I can borrow from?"

Shit. Shut up, General. "Yeah, Cal, I think I do. But you gotta promise me to take it."

"Not sure . . . I have a choice . . . now, do I?"

"Nope."

Get the team home.

Frank stood up and turned to Yushchenko. Like Anderson said, it was time to make the hard choice. "Sorry." Frank lifted his gun.

But the Ukrainian already had his rifle trained directly on Frank. "I think it is time for you to drop your weapon."

26.

June 19, 1948

Maggie pointed her gun at Yushchenko as Frank let his pistol fall to the ground. "Drop it or you'll never see your family again," she said, and by God, she meant it.

But Yushchenko merely smiled. "Why don't you stop me? Is it because you can't?"

She reached out again with her mind but once again found the threads of his emotions incredibly elusive—she could barely fuel his already-present nervousness.

She pulled the trigger—and the gun merely clicked.

"God damn it," she spat. *Out of ammo. Rookie mistake. We're fucked.*

Yushchenko turned his weapon on her. "If you use your ability, I will kill you. Do you understand?" He didn't bother waiting for an answer, instead turning his head and shouting loudly in Russian.

"You weren't defecting," she said quietly, her head spinning, her heart sinking. "You were drawing us out."

Yushchenko smiled. "Of course. It took great effort, too."

Maggie altered her stance somewhat, preparing to lash out in whatever direction she could—part of a plan that came to her in the moment. "So, what do we do now, comrade?"

"Now we wait for my *comrades* to join us," he said, smiling at the word.

She sighed at this, then theatrically relaxed and leaned against a tree. She could hear the voices of Yushchenko's backup off in the distance. Slowly, with her eyes locked on Yushchenko, she used one hand to rustle around in her pocket for her cigarettes. "Then I need a smoke to get through this. You mind?" The MGB man merely smirked at her, so she carefully picked one out of her pack and lit it, then waited.

The cigarette disintegrated as the dart flew out and into Yushchenko's neck. His eyes grew wide as he turned . . . and fell to the ground before he could get a shot off.

"That makes everything a lot easier," Frank muttered as he picked up his gun. "Nice play."

Maggie tossed the butt aside. "Now what?"

"This."

Frank fired two shots into Yushchenko's chest.

Maggie watched in shock as Frank quickly dragged Yushchenko's body away from the trail. "INSIGHT was our whole mission!" she said. She had to deliberately stop herself from raising her gun at him.

"Tough choices," Frank said as he put Yushchenko down next to Cal and placed the injured man's hand on the Russian's chest. "Cal, he's going fast. You gotta get everything you can outta him. Right now, you hear me?"

Cal managed a slight nod—he probably didn't even know who he was about to drain—as Frank put a hand on Yushchenko's forehead and started whispering.

"You know, I'm trying hard to feel bad about this, but I don't," Frank said quietly. "Our mission was to get what's in your head back to the States, one way or another. Turns out we don't really need you around for that."

Then Frank stiffened—Maggie figured Yushchenko was far enough along to start the transfer of information. Not knowing what else to do, she assumed Yushchenko's position overlooking the trail and kept an eye out with the scope of the Czech rifle she'd found there.

It didn't take Cal long enough to realize what was going on. "What the hell just happened here?" Cal asked, sitting a little more upright. He seemed older and grayer, maybe around fifty years old now—maybe he was using whatever Yushchenko had left to trade age for healing.

"Yushchenko . . . turned on us. Just get as much . . . as you can," Frank said, seemingly struggling with the transfer.

"You all right, Frank?" Maggie asked, a bit more loudly than she should have.

"Trying to . . . get it all," Frank said. "There's a lot."

Cal gingerly got to his feet. He looked like a hale, strong middle-aged man—she wondered if he had looked like that back when he was working at the Firestone plant. "What now?"

Maggie tossed the rifle down toward him, which he caught. "Check on Ellis. See what you can do. It's bad."

Cal immediately rushed over to Ellis's side and looked under the bloody coat across his stomach. He stretched a hand over that area and closed his eyes for a few seconds. "Gonna take a lot just to make sure he don't die," Cal said. Maggie could practically see the concern radiating off him—genuine concern about a man who always seemed to feel nothing but contempt for Cal.

Frank finally straightened up a bit, grabbing something from Yushchenko's pocket before standing up. "Can you just get him stable for a minute or two?" he asked.

"Maybe. Gonna take something out of me, though, for sure. Why?"

"Just do it. Maggie, hold fire."

"What do you mean, 'hold fire'?" she demanded, her shock receding, replaced with thoughts of revenge.

Frank looked up at her. "Don't fire the fucking rifle, and stand down on your Enhancement, too."

She put the rifle down, reluctantly, and reached out toward his feelings. "You have a plan. You're scared. But also . . . I don't know what."

"It's called hopeful," Frank said with a slight grin. "Try it sometime. Cal, go ahead and stabilize Ellis, but make sure you can still run a bit if we need to do that."

As Cal placed a hand on Ellis once more and began praying, Frank lifted his head and shouted in Russian. "*My sdayemsya! Prikhodite, brat'ya i sestry!*"

* * *

A minute later, they were surrounded by soldiers with
guns—and four others, two of whom Cal had already
met. One was the once-teenage Variant who could disappear and reappear; he seemed to be stable at a healthy
sixty or so—about where Cal was now, given that he had
managed to keep that damn fool Ellis from dying. The
boy-turned-old-man fixed Cal with a righteous glare of
anger.

Then there was the little Superman-girl. Whatever anger
she had about her brother seemed spent for now, and she
eyed the MAJESTIC-12 agents with a kind of detached
curiosity. Cal figured it was the kind of look she had when
she looked at ants under a magnifying glass—right before
the glass caught the sunlight and fried them.

Third one was a bulky fellow, kind of Asian-looking,
almost Eskimo, really. He had a bandage tied around his
arm and a gun in his hand. Cal couldn't really say much
more about him than that, other than that he kind of
looked like a big statue—emotionless. He wore a dark suit
that seemed to stretch across his body like a canvas on a
frame.

And finally, there was a middle-aged, severe-looking
woman, blond-haired and dressed in a jumpsuit—kind of
like the coveralls Cal had had to wear in some of his factory
jobs, but this lady's was formfitting to the point of being
almost indecent. Cal had to admit she wore it well, but
admonished himself for the thought. Then again, his list
of prayers was growing real long, and his time to pray was
running short.

Ellis groaned slightly, and Cal knelt down beside him
again. "Doing what I can, Mr. Longstreet. I think Frank's
gonna try to get me some livestock or something, and I'll
fix you up, all right?"

Ellis's eyelids fluttered open. "Why am I still laid up?" he
muttered, brow furrowed.

"Ain't got the gas in the tank to get you where you need to go yet," Cal replied. "You just rest there, and I promise we'll get you taken care of."

Ellis seemed like he wanted to say a little bit more, but fact was, he didn't have the strength, and he fell unconscious again within a few seconds. Cal sighed and looked over to Frank. Whatever he had planned, it had better work.

* * *

"This does not look like surrender," the woman said in English. "Your weapons are not on the ground."

She is Maria Ivanovna Savrova. Her ability is to track a single individual once she has touched him. Do not let her touch you! Yushchenko said in Frank's head. *She tracked me, forcing you to be constantly on the run, in a position where you could not gain intelligence from me easily.*

Frank nodded at Savrova. "We are brothers and sisters, are we not, Maria?" Frank replied in perfect Russian. "We are all Empowered."

Savrova and the kid traded a look. "How do you know her name?" the girl demanded.

"The same way I know yours, Ekaterina Giorgievna Illyanova," said Frank as he switched to English for the benefit of Maggie and Cal. "I know all your names, and why you're all here, and your plans for us. That's why you had Yushchenko here pretend to defect, teasing us with information about your Bekhterev program."

Mikhail Tsakhia, the Mongolian man—he was the negative-zone generator, but through Yushchenko, Frank knew he had to be completely healthy to pull it off—cocked his gun. "You already know too much, American. Why let you live?"

Honestly, I was really hoping you wouldn't ask that. "Because your numbers are too small. There's a lot of people in the Soviet Union. There's a lot of people in America, too. Not enough of us to do what needs to be done in either place—unless we concentrate our numbers more effectively. We are, after all, brothers and sisters, right?"

Now all four of the Russian Variants started looking at each other incredulously. "We were told you were all working for your government," Savrova said. "We approached you and yet heard nothing since."

"And we were told you were all working for *your* government," Frank bluffed. "And at the time, we were being watched. Couldn't really respond. But here we are. Variants—that's what we call ourselves. You call yourselves Empowered. I admit, I kinda like that more. So, what do we do now? Especially since we switched to English so these Czech boys don't understand us?"

Frank stood through the subsequent awkward whispering between the Russians, hoping Maggie was keeping a bead on his emotions. If this was gonna go south, he wanted her on the ball and ready to unleash the worst sort of fear on these guys.

"Frank."

He turned to see Cal kneeling next to Ellis and looking a whole lot older—almost as old as they day they had first met. "He's slipping. I'm too low to help out. Gonna need something real soon."

Frank nodded and turned toward Savrova. "Before anything else happens, I need to borrow a few of your men here," Frank said in English. "Our man here can heal our wounded, but he needs life force to do it with."

Savrova cocked her head at this request. "And how many do you need?"

"We can spread it out over most of them here so that they don't suffer any long-term effects. And if we can get enough, we can make Boris Giorgievich young again, too."

"If we help you? What then?" Savrova asked.

Frank cringed inside. "We're not going to play it that way," he replied. "Or do I need to start talking here and now and ruin your day?"

Savrova's eyes went wide for a moment, while the other Empowered clenched their weapons tight; the little girl looked ready to rip Frank's throat out with her teeth—and probably could. "You would condemn these men to death, then," Savrova finally replied. "And you would still be without your precious life force, whatever this is. Now, you are right about numbers. So, this is why you will come with us, rather than we let you go." At this, Savrova switched back to Czech. "*Zamířit!*" A moment later, there were at least ten barrels bearing on the Americans.

Frank frowned. There really wasn't a good way out of this. He knew—rather, Yushchenko knew—that this particular team of Empowered wouldn't drift from their particular brand of ideology. It was worth a shot, but no luck.

He looked at the ground, trying to go for a defeated look, and dropped his weapon even as he felt his heart rate start to increase. *That's right. It's go time. Tense up. Broadcast it to Maggie over there.* "Fine," Frank said. "Then can one of your boys give our man here a hand? He's in pretty bad shape, and our colored fella here could use some help too."

Frank turned to Cal, who had a quizzical look on his face. Frank nodded at him, then turned to Maggie and motioned for her to lower her weapon—but giving his hand enough of a wiggle that, he hoped, would get her ready to deploy her Enhancement. Maggie threw the rifle aside with disgust—a little too real to be feigned—but gave Frank just the slightest of nods.

"*Vezměte své zbraně. Nápověda stařec,*" Savrova barked. "*Získejte nosítka pro zraněného muže.*"

Mikhail suddenly straightened up and blinked several times, his gaze wandering for a moment. "*Maria Ivanovna, ya chuvstvuyu, chto vernetsya,*" he said in Russian.

"*Slava Bogu. Rezyume negativnoye pole.*" Savrova turned and smiled at Frank, whose heart dropped.

Here we go. "Now!" Frank yelled, pulling his knife again and sending it flying toward Mikhail in a smooth, expert motion. It buried itself in Mikhail's stomach—not enough to kill him, but enough, according to Yushchenko's memories, to continue to keep him from disabling all the Variant abilities in the area.

"*Zachyťte je!*" Savrova yelled, prompting several soldiers to rush toward the three remaining Variants. For a moment, Frank was surprised they weren't just shooting, but then he remembered Yushchenko again—that wasn't the plan. They were to be captured. Taken to Leningrad. And experimented on.

Frank dove for the mud on the trail, grasping his pistol with his right hand. He hit the deck and looked up to find two bodies lunging for him. There were two shots, and then Frank was covered in wounded men—but only for a moment. Just as the two soldiers fell on him, they were lifted back up—by that goddamn girl. Frank immediately rolled away just as the girl tried to hit him with the bodies of the men he'd just shot.

"Maggie!" Frank yelled. He ventured a look up the ridge, only to find her wrestling with the disappearing guy—the *teleporter*, as Yushchenko called him—and another couple guards. They would keep her distracted enough to prevent her focusing. *Shit.* Instinctively, Frank dodged just in time, avoiding another 185-pound soldier being used as a goddamn club.

Ekaterina tossed the two guards aside—very, *very* easily—and picked up a rock from the side of the trail that was easily fifty pounds, chucking it toward Frank as if it were a baseball. Frank ducked again, rolling into a crouch and getting his gun up. And then he paused.

That's a ten-year-old girl.

The girl smiled wickedly at Frank, a smile that reminded him of a wolf baring its teeth, and then threw another large rock, sending him diving toward his left. He landed at the feet of Savrova, who trained a pistol down at him. "Don't move a muscle," she warned.

Suddenly, there was a horrible shriek.

Frank looked to see Cal—now looking like a goddamn twenty-year-old football player—with his hand on Ekaterina's shoulder. "You need to put the gun down, ma'am," Cal warned in the clear, baritone voice of his youth. "This girl here don't need to get hurt now, does she?"

Frank couldn't see what effect Cal was having on the girl, but he somehow seemed to be getting stronger—like someone was inside his body with an air pump, blowing up his muscles all at once. It was the damnedest thing in a long line of damned things Frank had seen lately.

Savrova turned to train her weapon on Cal—or at least, that's what Frank thought she was doing.

Instead, she fired two rounds into Ellis's prone body.

"Make your choice," Savrova sneered. "Her life or his."

Cal began to rush over, but the girl—apparently free of whatever Cal had been doing to her—grabbed him and leaped upon his back, pulling herself up onto him and shrieking hysterically in rage. She must've had enough strength left to unbalance Cal—she should've been able to throw him clear down the trail—and both came tumbling down onto the mud and rock.

Frank ran over to Ellis, sliding down next to him as if he were sliding into second. Immediately, Frank checked his pulse, felt for breath, all the little things the doctor told him to do. Nothing.

"Frank?"

Oh, shit. "Ellis? That you, Ellis?" Frank whispered, grasping the man's hand as the Southerner's voice echoed in his head.

"This isn't good, Frank."

"I know, Ellis. Cal's on his way. Cal's gonna help you."

"Ain't nothing that nigger can do now, Frank. He's not a bad man. Tell him that for me, will you? It weren't personal."

"You tell him, Ellis."

"They got me, Frank. They got me here. And it don't look good. What they got planned."

"Who? The Russians? What plan?"

"Frank . . . it . . . not . . . the Russians. Not the Russians. The thing that's . . . it's . . . no. NO!"

"ELLIS!"

And then Ellis was gone. Just . . . gone. Like nobody Frank had ever watched over before. All Ellis's memories, his knowledge, literally torn away from the world, torn away from Frank's waiting mind—pulled away violently, Frank realized with a dawning dread that focused his eyes down onto Ellis's face. Ellis stared back, glassy-eyed, his mouth open, his brow furrowed, frozen in a death unlike any other Frank had experienced.

The dread spread through him, and Frank squeezed Ellis's hand so hard. "Ellis, God, Ellis, you gotta come back. You gotta fight through."

Nothing. And inside Frank, the fear and abject terror grew and grew, like a beast trying to claw its way out of his very soul. Such intense fear . . . whatever had happened, Frank knew as surely as he knew himself, was so very, very wrong.

"Frank."

He looked up to see Maggie standing over him, Cal beside her.

"Wh . . . what?"

She shrugged. "They took off. Retreated. Like they heard a dog whistle or something and went running. No idea why."

Frank let go of Ellis's hand, felt his skin slowly peel away from Ellis's cold, clammy fingers. "Good. That's . . . good, I guess." Frank staggered to his feet. "Cal, we're taking Ellis home. Can you carry him?"

Cal nodded. "Could probably carry a truck right now, Frank. I got him." He stooped down and scooped up Ellis's limp body with the ease of picking up a baby.

Frank looked to Cal, then Maggie. "Got it from the girl. He somehow acquired her power," Maggie said. "Something, isn't it?"

Looking down at Ellis's still-scared face, Frank reached over and closed the dead man's eyelids. "Something, all right. Let's go."

FIELD REPORT—ADDENDUM

AGENCY: Department of Defense—Central Intelligence
Agency
PROJECT: MAJESTIC-12
CLASSIFICATION: TOP SECRET—MAJIC EYES ONLY
TO: DCI ADM Roscoe Hillenkoetter USN, SECDEF James
Forrestal, GEN Hoyt Vandenberg USAF, Vannevar Bush,
Detlev Bronk
FROM: LCDR Daniel Wallace USN
SUBJECT: Czech operations
DATE: 25 June 48

As before, this is a MJ-12 MAJIC addendum to the
report filed 24 June 48 with CIA and DoD, regarding
the failed extraction of INSIGHT from Soviet-controlled
Czechoslovakia.

While the mission was indeed considered a failure in that
report, I respectfully submit, on behalf of Agents Lodge,
Dubinsky, and Hooks, that the mission was highly successful in many respects, including the operation's primary
goal—discovering the extent of the Soviets' knowledge and
use of Variants.

DISCOVERY PROCESS

Subject INSIGHT was largely uncooperative during his
extraction, withholding information crucial to the success of the mission and to the safety of our agents.

INSIGHT was, in fact, still working for MGB and was leading our agents into a trap designed to capture them.

Thanks to quick thinking and extensive training, Agent Lodge was able to kill INSIGHT, however, and then used his Enhancement to learn all he could from INSIGHT's memories. His full report, including reel-to-reel audio recording, can be made available upon request. The following is a summary of Lodge's report.

THE BEKHTEREV INSTITUTE

The Leningrad Bekhterev Psychoneurological Research Institute, named for the Russian scientist Vladimir Mikhailovich Bekhterev, is the center of Variant study in the U.S.S.R. It is situated in a newer part of Leningrad, and the building is well guarded, with several subbasements below street level. The Berlin phenomenon is located in one of those subbasements, though that is only a supposition based on INSIGHT's conversations with others rather than personal experience.

Agent Lodge also recovered a small device on INSIGHT's person that we believe may have kept Agent Dubinsky from using the full extent of her Enhancement on him. Unlike the null field generated by the Variant, this device seems to merely delay or reduce the efficacy of certain Enhancements. We continue to study this device, but believe the implications of it are troublesome, as it represents a scientific and technological leap we have yet to make.

We have no real sense of the Soviet research program
or its successes when it comes to the phenomenon. Given
that they have successfully moved the phenomenon, as we
have, we can safely assume they are, at most, less than
two years behind us—and we should, I believe, assume their
knowledge is at least on par with ours, if not greater,
given the device we obtained. (I would note here that Dr.
Schreiber has reported several of his staff missing—it's
possible they have been recruited, forcibly or otherwise,
by the Soviets.)

SOVIET VARIANTS

The Soviets have managed to locate and recruit more
than 15 Variants across their sphere of influence—not
just the U.S.S.R., but also from Poland, Romania, Bulgaria,
Czechoslovakia, and East Germany. Others have been found
in the Soviet Far East and as far south as the Afghan
border. INSIGHT did not have complete visibility into the
program, as will be explained below, so it is highly likely
the Soviets potentially have more assets than this.

As with the MAJESTIC-12 program, most Soviet Variants
were recruited by the Soviets' security apparatus, and
divided up into independent "fiefs" run by the MGB and
the Red Army, rather than using them as a single, flexible
resource to be drawn upon by multiple agencies, as we
have developed.

INSIGHT knew seven of the Soviet Variants well enough,
as well as their abilities. Their names and dossiers will
be sent separately. To summarize, the Variant abilities
at their disposal are:

- A 10-year-old girl from Georgia capable of super-hu-
  man feats of strength.

- A 17-year-old boy from Georgia, the aforementioned
  girl's brother, who can disappear from one place and
  appear up to 3 miles away instantly (this Variant is
  now aged to his 60s, though his Enhancement apparently remains intact).

- A Russian-Mongol man who can dampen the
  Enhancements of other Variants, provided he is
  healthy and uninjured.

- A woman from Moscow who can track anyone in the
  world she has come into physical contact with before.

- A Polish man who has the ability to send and receive
  radio messages of any type—including mimicry of
  voices and even music—solely through his mind.

- A Leningrad man who can swim great distances under-
  water, at high speed and without needing air (he has
  already been seconded to the Soviet Navy).

- An elderly Kazakh woman whose touch can produce temperatures several hundred degrees below zero at the point of contact.

INSIGHT was aware of several others, but these are the ones he worked with in his MGB capacity—he served as their coordinating officer, similar to my official capacity within MAJESTIC-12.

INSIGHT did not have full clearance for the rest of the Institute's Variant program, but it is worth noting that he was personally distressed by the introduction of new "political officers," or commissars, in 1947, who departed from Communist Party orthodoxy in troubling ways.

INSIGHT additionally knew of the existence of a third "fief" drawing Variants away from the Institute, spear-headed by the commissars in an attempt to covertly take control over the entire Bekhterev program.

INSIGHT was, in fact, a loyal member of the Communist Party and inquired further as to the commissars' agenda before he left for Prague. His latest discovery was the identity of the commissar leader: Lavrentiy Beria.

June 27, 1948

Truman threw the report on his desk. "Commander Wallace, you mean to tell me that the deputy prime minister of the Soviet Union—a man I've met on several occasions, mind you—is covertly gathering his own band of Variants together? What for?"

Danny cleared his throat. "He is, Mr. President. Yushchenko found out that Beria was starting to gather his own Variants, separate from the MGB or the Army. And he found out why."

Truman stared hard, so much so that Danny almost lost his train of thought. "Well?" the President demanded.

"He's planning a coup."

The words hung in the air for a long while, then inexplicably, Truman barked out a short laugh. "Well, hell, son, everybody in Stalin's circle wants to be the next guy in charge! Abakumov, Zhdanov, Bulganin—they all want in on it. The MGB and the Army all have their own self-contained Variant programs too, right?"

"Yes, Mr. President."

"So, why is it such a big deal that Beria has his own little group?"

"According to INSIGHT, Beria believes the Soviet Variants are destined to become the new leaders of the proletariat, the true leaders of the Revolution, the sons of the new age of socialism. INSIGHT saw his job as controlling the Variants for the good of the Party, not the other way around. If we'd known any of that, we might've been able to actually turn him. He didn't like the thought of Variants being in charge."

Truman leaned back in his chair, thinking, then slowly began to nod. "Been on my mind a bit too, son. We have a Variant of ours start getting ideas like that, it'll be a tough thing to deal with, you know."

"We've been developing contingency plans, Mr. President."

Truman smiled. "I know, son. And I know what you *are*. You, me, and Hilly are the only ones who do. Can you honestly tell me you're ready to arrest one of your own or, worse, *kill* one of your own if they start down that road?"

Danny looked the President hard in the eye. "My own, Mr. President . . . 'my own' are Americans. I swore an oath, sir, just like you did."

Truman fixed Danny with an appraising look, then nodded. "So, you got Beria jump-starting the whole master-race dogma again, just with a coat of Red paint."

"Seems like it. Just trying to figure out why."

Truman handed the folder back to Danny; the papers would be burned to ash before he left the room. "Theories?"

Danny shrugged. "Well, nothing official, but . . . think about it. We're not telling our Variants that they're the next level in human evolution or anything like that. Why?"

"Because you're Americans and you have a duty to the people of the United States to use your abilities for the good of all," Truman said, looking a little confused. "I wrote that line myself, you know, in their briefing books."

"Yes, sir. And that's because the government we serve is headed by an everyday person—you, sir. Nobody at the highest levels of government has turned out to be a Variant. The folks in charge are still normal, if you will."

"Where are you going with this, Wallace?"

"What if one of the folks in charge of the Soviet Union wasn't?"

It wasn't very often that Danny saw the President at a loss, and couldn't help but take pride in the look on Truman's face before he finally found a response. "Stalin's a Variant?"

"No, sir!" Danny quickly said. "No, no, no . . . latest we have on the power structure in Moscow is that Stalin doesn't one hundred percent trust Beria. I think it's Beria or someone close to him."

Truman considered this. "You know, that Beria's a real son of a bitch. Brutal fellow. Just brutal."

"Yes, he is, sir."

Finally, Truman rose and extended his hand. "Thank you, Commander. You trained a good team there. We got a lot of good information from that mission."

Danny took the President's hand and tried not to smile like an idiot. "Thank you, Mr. President."

"We'll need a replacement for Longstreet."

"We have several candidates, sir. The other Variants are starting to be cleared for operations. We'll be able to make substitutions as needed."

Truman nodded and let Danny's hand go. "Very well. Thank you. You're dismissed, son."

Danny saluted smartly and left the Oval Office, where Hillenkoetter was chatting amiably with the President's secretary. He looked up and smiled at the junior man. "Well?"

"I'm alive, sir," Danny said. "Went well, I think."

Hillenkoetter gave the secretary a friendly nod, then stood and walked outside onto the colonnade in front of the Rose Garden, his outstretched hand shepherding Danny with him. The door closed, and the two began a slow walk. "What's your take on him, Commander?"

"Sir?"

"The President. What's he thinking about Variants?"

Danny looked down at his shoes a moment as he walked. "He's worried. I think me being there helps, because I put a face to the idea. I look normal. My abilities aren't scary. But yes, I think there's some concern. Why?"

Hillenkoetter sighed and turned toward the younger man, putting a hand on his shoulder. "I admit, *I'm* worried. You got folks like Forrestal scared shitless of people like you, and now it's possible that Beria's building his own army of supermen. Men like Forrestal get too antsy about that and, well, you and yours are gonna find themselves in hot water."

"But the President, sir?"

Hillenkoetter resumed his stroll into the garden. "I think he's a good guy, Commander, but you've seen the polls. Dewey's gonna clean up in November, and honestly, I don't know where that fella's gonna come down on all this. We need to keep our record as pearly white as we can so that MAJESTIC can keep operating as it has been."

The two walked on in silence for a few moments until Danny piped up. "Sir, I gotta ask. Why are you standing up for us? Maybe Forrestal's right—just look at what Beria's commissars are telling the Variants over there. If some of our men start feeling that way, well . . ."

Hillenkoetter smiled. "I remember when I was the new XO on *West Virginia*, before Pearl Harbor, I chewed out a Marine lieutenant something fierce one day because of some slapdash something-or-other. And I saw such a look in that man's eyes—he really wanted nothing more than to kill me. And he could've, too—just drawn and fired and ended me right there. And he didn't. Instead, he went and drilled his men to the point where they were not only good—they were the best in the damn Pacific Fleet. I personally pinned a medal on that man's chest after Okinawa. He trusted me that I was doing right by him, and I trusted him that he'd do his job and not let his anger get the better of him."

"So . . . you're going to trust the Variants."

"No, Commander. I'm gonna trust *you*. I'm gonna do right by you, and you're gonna be like that Marine lieutenant and make sure that these folks are on board with the program." Hillenkoetter suddenly picked up his pace, prompting Danny to scramble to keep up. "Let's get to work. We're gonna need to find more of 'em."

June 30, 1948

Maggie looked around at her new place with an actual stirring of pride. It was a nice little apartment about three blocks from the "office"—CIA headquarters in Foggy Bottom—a second-floor flat with a separate bedroom and its own bathroom. A real nice one, as far as places went. Far better than the room she had rented with a family in Mill Valley. Nicer than the place she grew up, in fact. Heck, it even came with furniture and a brand-new radio.

The pride waned a bit as she thought about how she'd gotten there, though. It wasn't because she was good at anything she'd worked for. She'd had this *thing* thrown at her, completely at random, and because of that, she was being treated well. It wasn't really hers. And she was damn sure they'd take it away if she stopped playing ball. Or at least stop covering the rent.

Maggie'd only be there part of the time, anyway. Danny was talking about going back to Area 51 again for "integration training." There were other Variants, he'd said, and they needed to see how best to put together teams for various missions. So, it looked like everyone would be thrown in a pot and mixed around to see how well they complemented one another. Maggie couldn't help but wonder just how many there were and what they could do. Would their powers be better than hers? More effective?

She smirked to herself a little as she got up from her new sofa and grabbed her purse. She was, without a doubt, the most effective Variant on her little team. Cal could kill a

man, but he needed to touch him. Frank was becoming
an expert in pretty much everything, but he was still con-
strained by . . . well, *normalcy*. But Maggie, she could stop
a dozen men in their tracks and reduce them to trembling,
bawling balls of nothing. They *needed* her, and she'd make
damn sure they knew it.

With a spring in her step, she locked up her place—and
it *would* be hers, one way or another, for the foreseeable
future—and left her little brownstone. She'd noticed an
out-of-the-way bar a couple blocks away, and she figured
nobody would mind if she went for a drink.

Besides, as she walked, she kept watch on the man in the
bad suit who'd been tailing her for the past several days—
the same one who'd dropped the note at the Capital before
they shipped out to Prague. She hadn't reported him yet.
And maybe she wouldn't.

Maggie walked in and took a table in the corner, facing
the door. The man entered a few minutes later, looking
around casually. When his eyes met hers, she sent him a
little friendly nudge and smiled at him. To his credit, he
looked away and made for the bar. So, she nudged harder
. . . and harder . . . until he eventually approached the table
with two drinks in his hand.

"Hi, there," he said, his Chicago accent coming through
cleanly once more. "Thought you could use a drink."

She took the drink and smiled her best fake smile.

"How kind of you. Now . . . tell me everything."

* * *

Cal rode the bus in silence, his head against the window,
eyes closed. He was hale and healthy now, roughly the same
age as when this whole business had begun. The energy
he'd taken from that girl—so *much* energy, it was scary—
sloughed off quicker than normal, probably because she
was a Variant like him. Over the last couple weeks, he'd
reverted to normal, and despite Danny asking if he wanted
to take on some cattle or pigs and remain young, he'd
opted against it. His wife and his son had just moved into

a modest home in Washington's Adams Morgan neighborhood—he kept having to remind himself that he had a whole other life outside of the MAJESTIC-12 program, and he wanted to keep the two as separate as possible.

He considered, not for the first time, whether he would have to watch his wife pass on someday. If he wanted to, could he remain young for . . . well, how long? Forever? Would that be a blessing or just delaying the Lord's Judgment? And how many lives would it take? Sure, he could stick to cows and pigs and goats—he could see himself running a farm up North somewhere, really—but was that right?

Too many questions. Danny had provided Cal with head-shrinkers and reverends—there was one preacher who was a particularly good listener, though Cal had to be careful what he said, of course—but ultimately, it always came back around to doing what he felt was right. And there was nothing in the Good Book, or any book really, that laid a clear path for him under these unusual circumstances.

"Get up."

Cal opened his eyes and looked up to see a middle-aged white man in a bad suit, looking down at him with tired disdain, standing expectantly with a newspaper tucked under his arm, a briefcase in his hand.

"Excuse me?"

The man looked confused. "Get up. You're taking up a seat."

Cal made to move . . . then stopped. He worked hard—twice as hard—as anyone. He'd spent the day at Foggy Bottom in meetings and doing training and intelligence meetings—the reports were slow going, but his reading was getting better after all this time. He would continue to work twice as hard to be just as good.

But he was beginning to hate that phrase, handed down through generations of his family. He did a lot for his country. Put his life on the line out there. This arrogant white man in the bad suit had no idea.

Cal deserved to sit as much as anyone.

Cal looked up and gave the man a small smile. "Sorry, this seat's taken."

* * *

Dr. Kurt Schreiber was, for the first time ever, alone and unsupervised at Area 51. He had waited for this moment for months—years!—building up trust by working diligently and agreeing to everything his "superiors" requested and demanded.

Superiors . . . a laughable term. Politicians and soldiers, and that odd junior man who seemed utterly unfit to lead a project such as MAJESTIC-12. Schreiber had to admit that Commander Wallace was competent and unusually perceptive. But overmatched nonetheless.

Schreiber pulled a key from his pocket and left his office, walking down the hallway and out of the building toward the main laboratory—one of the most secure facilities in the world, and one to which he had nearly unfettered access. The key, in fact, represented the very last fetter, and now, late at night with naught but pimple-faced guards pulling the worst duty, he would put it to use.

Showing his ID to the bored guard, Schreiber entered the secure building, barely giving the anomaly he had studied for years any regard. Because the building was indeed so well guarded, the "superiors" at Area 51 had decided to keep all kinds of treasures in there, some of which he barely understood.

Schreiber opened a side door, walked down a set of stairs to the basement, and proceeded down a very long, dark hallway, opting to leave the lights off, just in case. When he came to a heavy, reinforced metal door, he worked the key and opened it.

Inside, POSEIDON lay unconscious. Schreiber felt an unusual pang of sympathy for the Russian. When he was not being tested, he was kept in a room far from anything he could use his Enhancement upon. All his furniture was bolted to the floor. Everything within two hundred yards, in fact, was bolted to the floor.

"Wake up," Schreiber said in Russian.

The man stirred. "It is too late for more experiments," he mumbled. "For God's sake, let me sleep."

"I am not here to experiment. I am here to talk about your future, should you choose to have one."

POSEIDON sat up and saw Schreiber smiling in the dim light. "What do you mean?"

"Soon, comrade, I believe it will be time for you to illustrate what you can really do. And I will help you."

The man looked confused. "Why should I even listen to you? You are a Nazi."

"The Nazis no longer exist, comrade," Schreiber said. "Hitler was wrong. The Aryans were not the master race after all."

* * *

July 10, 1948

Jim Forrestal tucked into his steak with relish. It'd been another long week, but a successful one. Success in politics was often measured in inches—a good conversation here, a couple tidbits of information there. Pushing the agenda forward, one tiny step at a time, and doing everything possible to make America safe once more.

"Are you sure about your source, Jim?" his dining companion said. "Are they trustworthy?"

Forrestal smiled. "They may be different than us. They may not even be human anymore. But some of them, at least, still see themselves as patriotic Americans. And most of them are scared."

The other man, a large, slightly pudgy fellow with a fine suit and piercing eyes, grimaced nonetheless. "Not human . . . what are they, then?"

"They *were* human, don't forget that," Forrestal said between bites. "I don't know what they are now. But the most important thing is that we contain them before we use them. We're not doing that. That goddamn Hilly has 'em set up in apartments and houses, for God's sake! Might as well leave your wallet in the middle of the National Mall for someone to take."

The other man shook his head. "They're not a wallet, Jim. From what you're telling me, they're dangerous. They're a time bomb. They're *more* than human now. And they'll be even more dangerous once they start realizing that."

"Exactly, Joe. They don't have oversight. They aren't contained. Technically, they're citizens, but both Hilly and Truman want to keep treating them like normal people. They aren't." Forrestal paused for a swig of wine, a fine Bordeaux from the cellars of Washington's storied Old Ebbitt Grill, where the two men sat ensconced in comfort and luxury. "I'm glad you're on the same page here."

Senator Joseph McCarthy, freshman Republican from Wisconsin, nodded. "These whaddyacallits, Variants . . . it sounds to me like they're the biggest threat to the United States other than the Reds. What do you need from me, Jim?"

Forrestal smiled. "It's not an overnight thing. MAJESTIC-12 is too entrenched right now. But when Truman loses to Dewey—and he *will*, I'll promise you that—then it's going to fall to Congress to start pushing hard. And I know you, Joe. You know how to push."

McCarthy offered up a grim smile as he finally unfolded his napkin and looked over his plate. "I know how to push. Don't worry about that."

* * *

July 13, 1948

The room was very much as Frank remembered it—and unfortunately, try as he might, he remembered it very well indeed.

Deep below the streets of East Berlin, the room was well preserved, despite the demolition of the old Reich Chancellery above. The access tunnels and secret doors were preserved, then apparently forgotten by the Soviet occupiers once they cleaned the place out.

And they had cleaned it out pretty damn well. The stone walls and dirt floor were all that remained, and even the floor looked somehow swept clean—Frank figured the

Russians would leave no stone unturned. They certainly took the table and all the machinery.

And, of course, they took the anomaly.

Frank turned to Danny and shrugged. "Told you. The Reds saved my bacon here. Figured they'd take it all."

Danny smiled back, while Captain Anderson kept his eyes on the exit. "They didn't count on us, now, did they? Zippy?"

Behind them, a small, thin young woman—no older than twenty, Frank guessed—nodded grimly. "There are things they couldn't take," she said, a light Boston accent creeping in. "Nobody can take the past."

Zipporah Silverman walked forward into the immensity of the room, stopping to crouch down almost exactly where Frank remembered that the anomaly appeared. She moved her long, dark hair from her face and placed her hands on the floor.

"What are you calling this again?" Frank asked.

"Psychokinesis," Danny replied quietly.

"Fancy."

"Better than the long explanation."

Frank had gotten that explanation on the flight over, the three agents tucked in a cargo plane full of food and fuel for West Berlin's trapped residents. The Reds put up a land blockade of West Berlin in order to—well, whatever they thought they could get away with, Frank supposed. But the Air Force and the Brits had put together a massive airlift, daily flights to West Berlin that would probably last until the Reds gave up—because Frank knew the Americans were more stubborn than the Russians would ever be.

It would likely take a long, long time, though. For now, another stalemate. This Cold War was turning out to be a corker.

From the airfield, Danny led them through West Berlin, and they used forged passports to enter the Soviet sector of the city. That part had been easy enough—getting back would be tougher, no doubt.

Zippy—the nickname belied the girl's too-serious demeanor—crouch-walked forward, her fingertips still brushing the ground. "They were here . . . for months. After the city fell, this was their new headquarters. They . . . they didn't think their experiments would work. I see one man, a thin man, widow's peak, angry . . . he's telling someone they would need . . . experimental subjects."

Frank's eyes widened. "Me and Mike Petersen," he breathed. "We were handy."

Danny put a hand on Frank's shoulder. "Sorry."

Zippy finally stood and turned toward them. "That's it. Everything else is a blur. There was too much activity here to get a better read on it. But I don't think there were any other Variants created here. Just Frank."

"All this just to hear that?" Anderson groused.

"Not entirely," Frank said. And with that, he raised a pistol at Anderson from just five feet away.

"What the hell, Lodge?" the Marine demanded before turning to Danny. "Commander, tell this man to stand down!"

"I can't do that, Andy," Danny said sadly. "And you know why."

"Commander?" Panic flashed briefly behind Anderson's eyes. He made to reach for his gun, only to find Zippy was already busy relieving him of it.

Frank cocked his pistol. "You see, Captain, I got in Yushchenko's head as he died, and he knew a lot of things. A *lot* of things. Like how Area 51 had been compromised. How someone was passing him intel from deep inside the base."

Anderson straightened up. "There's a leak? Is Silverman here even cleared for this?"

"Cut it out!" Danny shouted, drawing his own gun and leveling it at Anderson. "What happened, Andy? What made you turn on your country? Your friends?"

Looking from one face to another, Anderson finally caved. "Look, Danny. I'm sorry, but these Variants, these *things* you want to keep on a leash, they're dangerous! My contact knew that. They told me the Russians, they were keeping them locked down. I didn't know they were gonna use them just like us, I swear!"

"You betrayed us," Danny said coldly. "Not just the Variants. Your country. You've seen the reports—the Russian Variants want to take over. And your intel walked Frank and the rest of them into a trap. You helped kill Ellis Longstreet."

Tears started falling from Anderson's eyes. "Look, it wasn't supposed to happen that way! If I knew the Variants over there were making a play, I wouldn't have done it!"

Frank stepped forward so that the gun was inches from Anderson's chest. "Sure, you were saving the human race— and lining your pockets, too."

Anderson fell to his knees, his hands up. "Yeah, all right, I'm sorry. I got into debt after the war. Gambling, drinking . . . it was hard, doing the things I did for the OSS. So, I reached out to some Reds I worked with in Hungary during the war. They set it up."

"And when Longstreet escaped?" Frank prompted.

"Yeah, OK, OK. I did it. I let him go. I called my contact in Vegas," Anderson said, the words tumbling out rapid-fire. "They were gonna pick him up, smuggle him over to Russia. And yeah, when we captured one of them, I took charge of security, made sure he wasn't talking to anyone. Kept that damn woman away from him. The others, too. Those Variants, Danny, we have to keep everyone safe from them! These people, they're dangerous!"

At this, Danny smiled. "People like me, Andy?"

It took a moment for the words to register. "You . . . you're one of them too?"

"You're not really cleared for that," Danny replied, then turned to Frank. "Well?"

"Time to make the hard choice, I guess." Frank said.

Danny fired two rounds into Anderson's chest.

"Jesus, Danny," Frank breathed, lowering his weapon. "I thought . . ."

His hands trembling, Danny thumbed the safety back on his pistol and gingerly put it back in his pocket. "Needed to happen, Frank," Danny said quietly. "Get moving. We need whatever he knows."

Frank knelt down next to Anderson and started whispering to him while Zippy stood by, her hands over her mouth, her eyes wide. "Sir, what are we going to do with his body?" she asked after a moment.

Danny looked down at his hands and wished they'd stop shaking. "Leave him here. Let the Russians find him. It . . . sends a message."

"What message?" Zippy asked, incredulously.

Danny finally just jammed his hands in his pockets. "Whatever they want to believe. They've kept us guessing. Time to return the favor."

Acknowledgements

There are a lot of folks who helped me get to the point where I could launch a new series, and more still who helped with this particular book. But first, I want to talk about the first real "spook" I ever met.

In 1991, while at American University in Washington, DC, as part of a journalism internship program, I took a grad-level course called "The US Intelligence Community." Dr. John Macartney, Col. (Ret.) USAF, was the professor—and he was fantastic. Dr. Macartney taught at the National War College and was a former commandant of the Defense Intelligence Agency's Defense Intelligence College. His clear and simple teaching style, which nodded to the glamour of spycraft while underscoring the *real* work of intelligence, made the topic fun and accessible. My final report was on foreign intelligence in business and trade affairs; Dr. Macartney loved it and even asked if he could include the paper in the syllabus for future classes. That kind of recognition from a real "spook" made for a very proud moment. Sadly, Dr. Macartney died in 2001. I'll be forever grateful to him for that first introduction to intelligence studies.

There was a point in my life—two separate points, actually—where I considered actually working for the US intelligence community. I think Dr. Macartney's professionalism, humor, and enthusiasm played a large part in that. Ultimately, I decided that life wasn't for me, but my experience in the classroom, and in starting the employment process, left me with a profound appreciation for those who sacrifice so much and perform their duties with integrity in order to keep us safe. Yes, the intelligence community's track record is blemished—repeatedly—with scandal and unsavory activities. Yet there are 113 stars carved into a wall at CIA headquarters, each one representing an officer fallen in the line of duty, thirty-three of them remaining anonymous even in death. Those individuals deserve our thanks, and they have mine here.

MJ-12: Inception is the first book in the *MAJESTIC-12* series, and I wouldn't be sitting here with a new series without the folks who made the first possible—namely, all the folks who bought and enjoyed the books in the *Daedalus* trilogy. At this point, the number of fans and reviewers and bloggers is getting too numerous to mention, but each and every one of you has made a major difference in my life and has made this book possible. Thank you.

Sara Megibow remains one of the best literary agents— and one of the best people—I know, and she's done so much to ensure this new series gets off the ground properly. Jason Katzman and Cory Allyn at Night Shade Books continue to believe in my work, and are superb editors besides. They're a joy to work with. And let it be known that Richard Shealy is one of the finest copyeditors I've had the pleasure to work with.

Finally, and as always, none of this means a thing without my wife, Kate, and my daughter, Anna, to share it with me. Their love and support make it all worthwhile.

Michael J. Martinez

COMING FALL 2017 FROM
MICHAEL J. MARTINEZ AND NIGHT SHADE BOOKS

"*X-Men* meets *Mission: Impossible*. Martinez takes a concept as simple as 'Super spies that are actually super' and comes away with a hit. *MJ-12* is my new favorite spy series."
—Michael R. Underwood, author of *Geekomancy* and the Genrenauts series

MJ-12
SHADOWS

IN THE COLD WAR,
EVEN SUPERHUMANS CAN FALL

MICHAEL J. MARTINEZ
Author of *The Daedalus Incident*

IN THE COLD WAR, EVEN SUPERHUMANS
CAN FALL . . .

$7.99 mass market original – 978-1-59780-926-9

An Excerpt from MJ-12: Shadows

Damascus, March 9, 1949

Maggie, check in," came Frank's voice over the handy-walkie on the table. She could sense his annoyance from across the house.

She picked up the radio and keyed it. "Nothing yet. I told you, I'll know when they're in range." Indeed, that's why she and Cal were stationed in the courtyard, in the exact center of Copeland's house—so that she could sense new emotions from anybody approaching the building. She did another little sweep of the area, to the furthest extent of her senses, just to be sure.

"Roger. Out."

This was their third night of sentry duty, and it was getting to be pretty damn dull. Copeland was all nervous energy, to the point where Danny had threatened to tie him to a chair lest he be seen moving around the house. He ended up sitting in his study, in the dark, looking out the window. Danny, Frank, and Zippy were stationed near other windows and doors, quietly monitoring the empty streets around the house, which stood on a corner and abutted two other homes. In a few minutes, Cal would head up to replace Zippy for a spell, and she would come down for tea and more conversation.

Maggie was honestly running out of polite things to say. Maybe she'd start getting impolite and see what happened.

"Maybe there's a knitting circle or something you can join up with," Cal suggested helpfully. "You know, get to know some folks in the area."

Maggie grimaced and resisted the urge to make Cal weep like a little girl. "Not really my thing. I—" She suddenly caught the wave of amusement from Cal and couldn't help but smile. "Oh, you jerk!"

"Maybe there's a knife-skills circle instead," he chuckled. "Target practice circle? Ladies' boxing?"

Maggie was about to reply with something particularly colorful when something crept into the edge of her perception. She quickly grabbed the radio. "I got two nervous nellies on the street, approaching the intersection from different angles."

Zippy replied first. "Eyes on target. Male, early twenties. Wearing . . . a military uniform?"

Cal sat up straight. "That ain't no burglar."

"And he's got no good reason to be nervous walking down the street." Maggie said.

"Eyes on target two. Male, mid twenties, army fatigues," Danny said. "Just walking down the street and . . . shit, scoping out the house with binoculars."

Maggie and Cal got up and rushed toward the front of the house, where Danny was stationed in the ground floor parlor. "He's just standing there? Out in the open?"

Danny shook his head in amazement. "Like a walk in the park. No craft to it at all. What kind of nervous are they?"

Maggie reached out again with her mind, the puce-colored threads of anxiousness visible from afar. "Like . . . the kind of nervous you get before a race or a big game. Like when you're at the top of a diving board about to dive in. Nervous but . . . ready."

The radio crackled again. "Guys, I got three guys in the alley," Frank reported. "Repeat. Three targets in the alley. Fatigues and rifles, heading for the back door."

Danny swore. "Counter-op. Five bucks says they'll plant something incriminating on Copeland. Ten says the Russians are in on it."

Zippy's voice came next. "Three more on my side, total of four. Armed and advancing toward the side door."

Maggie ventured a look out the window and saw that the binoculars guy had been joined by three other soldiers, all similarly armed. "That makes eleven. Squad and leader," she said.

"Pincer move. No way out," Danny said before keying the radio. "Zippy, grab Miles and get him to the courtyard. Frank, meet us there. Move out!"

They quickly dashed through the empty, dark house to the courtyard. Frank had gotten there first and had already shut down the water to the fountain so they could hear better. "Mags, I think you're up. How many can you handle and how close do they need to be?" he asked.

"Maybe all but they'd have to be real close," she said. "Everybody would have to be in the courtyard. And one or two will probably freak out and try something dumb."

"What? What the hell are you talking about?" Copeland said. "They brought a goddamn army! We need to get out of here!"

Frank looked over to Cal, who gave a deep sigh before reaching over to put a hand on Copeland's shoulder. "It's gonna be OK, Mr. Copeland."

Copeland collapsed into Cal's arms, drained of just enough life energy to render him completely unconscious. "Now what?" Cal asked as he propped Copeland in the chair next to the fountain.

Frank and Danny traded a look, Danny acquiescing to Frank's expertise, backed up as it was by the memories of several highly decorated soldiers. "Maggie: you, Miles, and Zippy in the center. Cal and Dan: get over there behind the vines along those columns and stay out of sight. When Maggie switches on, you two need to neutralize any stragglers. Non-lethal. Mags, try not to affect our guys."

"And you?" Maggie asked.

Frank smiled. "I'll take care of whoever doesn't show up here."

With that, Frank jogged off back into the house, while Danny and Cal took their assigned positions. Zippy chambered a round into her pistol.

"Easy there, Calamity Jane," Maggie said, reaching out to assuage Zippy's nervousness. Unlike the rest of the team, Zippy hadn't been in combat before. "Remember your training and let me take care of these guys, OK?"

The younger woman nodded, but the grip on her pistol remained tight. "Right. Just so long as—"

Maggie felt the bullet enter her right calf almost before she heard the shot.

"Fuck!" she yelled as her leg gave out, sending her crashing to the cobblestones. Zippy immediately returned fire, and a soldier fell from the second floor balcony into the courtyard with a sickening thump.

"*La tatlaquu alnnara!*" came an angry voice from inside the house. Immediately, soldiers started swarming the courtyard, weapons at the ready.

SET SAIL AMONG THE STARS WITH THIS UNCANNY TALE, WHERE ADVENTURE AWAITS, AND DIMENSIONS COLLIDE!

THE DAEDALUS INCIDENT
Book One of the
Daedalus Series
Michael J. Martinez
978-1-59780-858-3
Mass Market / $7.99

"Genre bending often comes at great peril, but Martinez pulls it off with an assurance that makes all the pieces slot together perfectly."

—*Buzzfeed.com*, "The 14 Greatest Science Fiction Books of the Year" (2013)

Unexplainable earthquakes are disrupting Mars's trillion-dollar mining operations in 2132, and investigations by Lieutenant Shaila Jain and her team lead to the discovery of a mysterious blue radiation and a three-hundred-year-old journal that is writing itself.

Lieutenant Thomas Weatherby of His Majesty's Royal Navy is sailing aboard the HMS Daedalus in 1779, a frigate sailing both on the high seas between continents . . . and across the Solar System, chasing a powerful mystic toward mankind's faraway colonies and bizarre alien worlds.

What neither Jain nor Weatherby realizes is that their journeys have more in common than either might think, as powerful beings have embarked upon a sinister quest to upset the balance of the planets—the consequences of which may reach far beyond the Solar System, threatening the very fabric of space itself.

THE FATE OF TWO DIMENSIONS WILL BE DECIDED IN THE ALIEN JUNGLES OF VENUS!

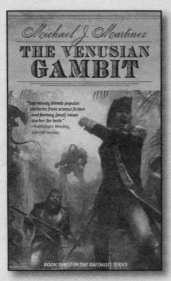

THE VENUSIAN GAMBIT
Book Three of the
Daedalus Series
Michael J. Martinez
978-1-59780-860-6
Mass Market / $7.99

"[Martinez] skillfully handles the intricacies of characterization and the many moving parts, building to the trilogy's utterly satisfying and quite epic finale."

—*Publishers Weekly*, starred review

In the year 2135, dangerous alien life-forms freed in the destruction of Saturn's moon Enceladus are making their way toward Earth. Lieutenant Commander Shaila Jain is scrambling to beat them there, but her crewmember, Stephane Durand, is possessed by an evil being intent on reopening a transdimensional rift and destroying the human race.

In 1809—a Napoleonic era far different from our own—the French have occupied England with their Corps Eternélle, undead soldiers risen through the darkest Alchemy. But there are rumors that an ancient weapon has been located in the jungles of Venus that could end the war once and for all.

Weatherby must follow the French to the green planet. Jain must decide if it's possible to save the man she loves, or if he must be sacrificed for the good of two dimensions. On Venus, everything points to all-out war on the alien planet—and past and present will join forces one final time to destroy an ancient terror.

© Anna Martinez

About the Author

Michael J. Martinez is a critically acclaimed author of historical fantasy and genre-blending fiction, including the Daedalus trilogy of Napoleonic-era space opera novels and the new MAJESTIC-12 series from Night Shade Books. He lives in New Jersey with his wife, daughter, two cats, and several chickens.